Emily's Home

Over the Bakery

~ a novel by Sharon Armstrong

**Living Springs
Publishers**

WWW.LivingSpringsPublishers.com

Praise for "Emily's Home Over the Bakery"

"Emily went from living in a house in the last book to living in a home, with all the love and support that the word implies. She is learning how to make a home for herself someday while encouraging her friends to acquire the skills to do the same."
~Kathy Anderson, Superintendent/Principal (retired)

"I absolutely loved the original 'Emily's House' and was really excited when I found out that a sequel was being released! 'Emily's Home Over the Bakery' was even more suspenseful than the first book. In this story, Emily faced betrayal from her own family, and she experienced some truly terrifying moments with the people she cared about. Reading this book taught me that the problems in the world are too big to tackle on your own, and it's good to rely on others for support during tough times. While the first book emphasized the importance of shaping your own destiny, this one focuses on actually making it a reality. It's a valuable lesson that every young person should learn more about."
~Augustus Armstrong, Middle School Student

"In the first book of the series by Sharon Armstrong, 'Emily's House', we are introduced to Emily. We learn how she was on a journey to find the family she always wanted, yet never had. Through her continued growth in her relationships, she begins to find the life she's always sought.

In Sharon Armstrong's latest work, "Emily's Home Over the Bakery," Emily makes a return. Through a very relatable character, Emily is on the path of growth shown metaphorically through gardening and farming, cultivating what she's been wanting. Emily helps to show those who are struggling with friends, family, and even boy dilemmas, that they are not alone.

This was a great read and I definitely recommend it!"

~Olivia Louis, High School Student

"Emily is a delightful heroine. Her story teaches us that a broken family origin does not sentence us to a broken future. Like Emily, it is our choices that define our future. Emily's home is filled with love and beauty, and I envision amazing scents coming from the bakery. After reading, everyone will want to be Emily's neighbor."

~Josie Ramirez, Women's Ministry Director

"Awesome light-hearted read!!

I thought 'Emily's House' was good! In 'Emily's Home Over the Bakery', following Emily on her journey through family turmoil and how she maneuvered through it was enlightening. She grows through adversity as she trusts in the Lord for her outcomes. There are so many twists and turns through Emily's life that you can't wait to read the next chapter. I found I couldn't put it down. I think anyone can relate to this life or know someone who has lived through it. I would recommend this series highly, and I can't wait for the next book in the series!!!"

~Carolyn McReynolds, Court Reporter

"'Emily's Home-over the Bakery' is truly a delightful read. You find yourself drawn into the lives of the familiar characters! You will experience heroism, to heartbreak, to the innocence of First Love, as this sweet, small-town community lives out the true meaning of Family! This book is a must read!"

~Tonya Smith , Grief Support Co-facilitator

Paperback ISBN: 978-1-953686-25-1
eBook ISBN: 978-1-953686-26-8

To My Father,
Augustus Jay Cooper,
Who taught me to see the world differently.

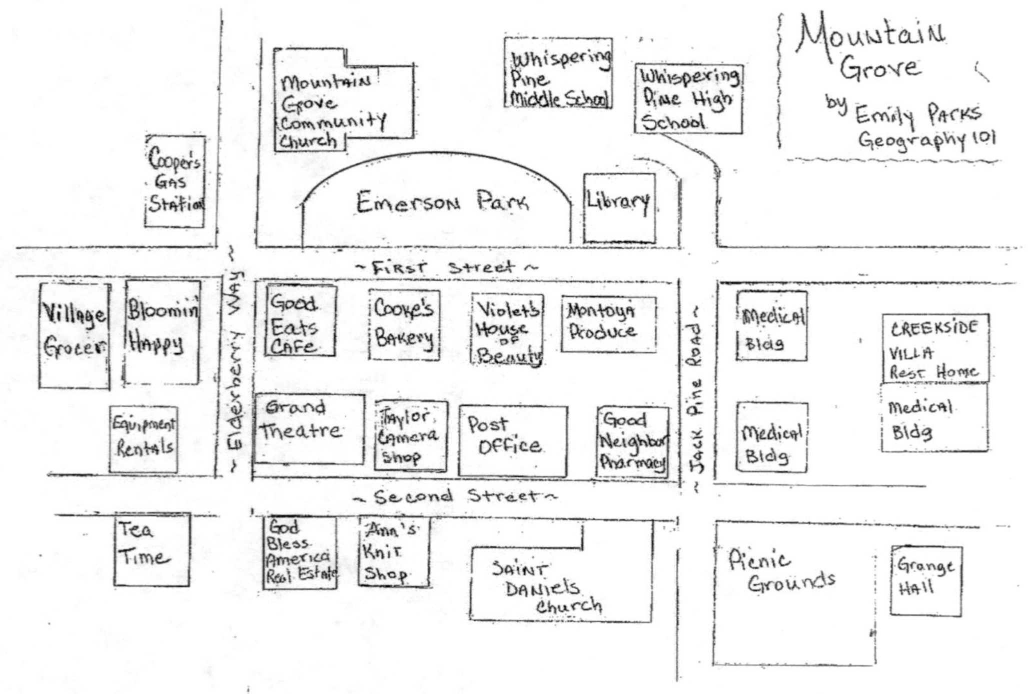

Mountain Grove
by Emily Parks
Geography 101
Cooper's Gas Station
Mountain Grove Community Church
Whispering Pine Middle School
Whispering Pine High School
Emerson Park
Library
~ First Street ~
Village Grocer
Bloomin Happy
~ Elderberry Way ~
Good Eats Cafe
Cooke's Bakery
Violet's House of Beauty
Montoya Produce
~ Jack Pine Road ~
Medical Bldg
CREEKSIDE VILLA Rest Home
Equipment Rentals
Grand Theatre
Taylor Camera Shop
Post Office
Good Neighbor Pharmacy
Medical Bldg
Medical Bldg
~ Second Street ~
Tea Time
God Bless America Real Estate
Ann's Knit Shop
Saint Daniels Church
Picnic Grounds
Grange Hall

Chapter - 1

Emily's eyes flew open, and for a moment she was confused. Looking around the bedroom nothing looked familiar - then she remembered. This was her new home. Her safe home over the bakery, a world away from her last home with her mom and dad and grandmother.

She stretched and sniffed the familiar sweet air. Her foster mama, Miss Mattie, must have just taken freshly baked pies out of the huge bakery oven downstairs. It made her mouth water. Feeling ravenous, she threw back the bed covers and hurried out to their small kitchen.

Emily noticed a note propped up on the kitchen table as she made her way to the warming oven, where breakfast would be waiting. Her mama always made a hearty breakfast before going downstairs to open the bakery, and the gesture touched Emily deeply. She couldn't recall anyone ever fixing breakfast in her old home and found herself humming as she took the plate of scrambled eggs, country potatoes, and warm biscuits to the table, grabbing the note as she sat down.

Good morning, Sugar! Have your breakfast and come on downstairs. I might need a little help in the bakery today. Blessy has to leave early for a vet's appointment for Tiger. Fleas, again!

"Who names their dog Tiger?" Emily laughed, spreading homemade jam on the biscuit, then, out of habit, reached for her phone to check for messages. She knew the checking had become borderline obsessive, looking at her phone four or five times a day, hoping her parents would call or message her. Hoping, yet dreading it if they did.

"Life sure can be weird," she said out loud, while scrolling. Nope, no calls or messages! Not today, or the day before, or even the month before!

What kind of parents move to another state, and just leave their daughter behind without making sure she's okay? Emily wondered, pushing the phone away a little too hard, and knocking over the saltshaker.

Some days when Emily woke up, it slammed into her like a wrecking ball, and her mind would conjure up mean thoughts about herself: *worthless, throw-away, insignificant.*

She'd fight against it. Or go talk to her mama. That always helped. Bad thoughts can be a very tricky thing to maneuver on your own.

The phone beeped, bringing her out of her daydream, and she reached for it, quickly scrolling through. From all the way across the Atlantic, a picture of Jonathan appeared standing beside a hot dog vendor in some London Park, holding up two hotdogs smothered in mustard and relish.

Emily laughed out loud. This was his code message for, *I wish you were here eating with me!* She wished she were there having lunch with him, too! Or was it dinner time there? She'd never gotten used to the time difference. Whichever it was, it filled her heart with happiness, and she pressed the phone to her face.

Jonathan Charles had been a college exchange student in England for the last five months, and sent pictures from all over London, usually with the *I'm missing you!* message. Emily sighed and finished her breakfast. Having Jonathan away was a lot harder than she thought it was going to be.

"He'll be back in the summer," she said out loud, comforting herself. Then, remembering that her mama needed help downstairs, quickly finished breakfast, and ran for the shower.

Walking into the bakery, Emily sang out, "Good morning, Mama!" Miss Mattie, who was behind the tall pastry case, gave her a smile that rivaled a harvest moon as she finished up an order for Mrs. Kingery, the grocer's wife.

Emily greeted Mrs. Kingery, then went over to kiss her mama's beautiful brown cheek. "New apron, Mama?" she asked, trying not to laugh at the outlandish apron covered with peacocks and toucans.

"You know I can't resist a pretty apron, Sugar!" her mama said, hugging her. "Now go put one on, and then please come back and help Miz' Kingery with these boxes of donuts. Her backs hurtin' her today."

Emily hurried back to the kitchen where a pegged wall held her mama's vast array of aprons, all in eye-popping, primary colors. Emily grabbed the jade green apron with red roosters and yellow hummingbirds, and hurried back out, tying the apron strings as she went.

"You must be having another grocery special," Emily said to Mrs. Kingery, picking up four of the boxes.

"Mr. Kingery 'bout drives me nuts with his specials, along with given' out free donuts," Mrs. Kingery sniffed. She picked up the remaining box, hobbled to the door, and out to her Buick parked at the curb. "My back's 'bout give out on me," she said, opening the car trunk.

"Do you need any help later?" Emily asked, setting the donuts in the trunk. "I work here until noon, but then I can come over to the market!"

"Thanks, honey," Mrs. Kingery replied, as Emily slammed the trunk closed. "Pop on over, and I'll put you to work if the crowds are still comin' in!" She put her hands on the small of her back and bent back as far as she could go; Emily heard popping sounds and stood amazed as Mrs. Kingery swooped down and touched the sidewalk with her fingertips.

"Are you okay?" Emily asked, stifling a laugh.

"Almost!" the grocer's wife grunted, ending the exercise with both arms spinning wildly, as though she were skipping rope.

Emily clamped a hand over her mouth, hoping Mrs. Kingery didn't notice her belly jiggling.

"Well, that oughta' keep me goin' for a while!" Mrs. Kingery snorted, climbing into the Buick and gunning it down First Street.

At noon, the customer traffic at the bakery had dwindled down to a manageable few, so Emily said, "I'm going to run over to the *Village Grocer* and see if the Kingery's need help."

"Don't forget to take your apron off, Sugar!" Miss Mattie reminded.

"I won't, don't worry," she chuckled quietly, untying the strings. Her mama's colorful aprons were not something she wanted to run around the village in. Grabbing her backpack off a nearby hook, she stuffed in a couple of cookies and a water bottle, then headed out.

As Emily hurried up First street, she saw that all the parking spaces in front of the *Village Grocer*, and those across the street, were full. When she walked through the door it was like a circus in progress; Mrs. Kingery was sitting on a high stool handing out coffee and donuts; Mr. Kingery was checking out a line of customers, bagging their groceries as he went. Her friend, Gilbert, was at the next register, doing the same.

She walked up to Mr. Kingery. "How can I help?"

"Grab an apron, and start baggin' for me and Gilbert," he said, running canned goods over the glass scanner. "And thanks for showin' up!" he added, raising his voice over the noise of the registers and customers talking to one another.

Emily hurried over to the wall where tan aprons were hanging, grabbed one, and went to the end of the check-out counter to bag for an older woman with dread locks and earth sandals.

"Plastic or paper?" she asked politely.

"Paper!" snorted the woman, glaring at her. "I'm surprised this grocer here even offers plastic bags anymore!"

As the woman snatched her brown bag of vegetables off the counter, Emily glanced up at Mr. Kingery, who was muttering something under his breath that she couldn't exactly hear. She quickly stepped over to the next counter to bag for Gilbert.

Emily went back and forth between the two registers for the next two hours, until the customers started dwindling. She glanced over at the donut table and saw that the pastries had also dwindled. "Should I run to the bakery and get more?"

"Naw," the grocer replied, "they like their donuts early in the day. The late afternoon crowd just wants their supper."

"Is there anything else I can help with?" she asked, taking her apron off.

"Well, if yer' not busy, you could deliver some groceries up to Gus at the service station. He's allergic to shopping for hisself. Also, don't forget to fill out a timecard. Payday is on Friday."

"You don't need to pay me, I volunteered!"

"That ain't gonna' happen around here," Mr. Kingery snorted. "You work, you get paid. It's in the Good Book!"

"What's the Good Book?" Emily whispered to Gilbert as the grocer went to go get Gus's order together."

"The Bible," Gilbert whispered back. "It's what he tells people to settle arguments."

"Is paying people even in the Good Book?" she laughed.

"Beats me," he laughed along with her, "but probably if Mr. Kingery says so!"

As Emily put on her backpack, Gilbert whispered, "You heard *from Kelly Ann?*"

Dread filled her. "Yep!" she answered brightly, wishing Mr. Kingery would hurry up with Ike's order.

"When she comin' back here?"

Emily sighed, wishing she could just tell him that Kelly Ann was pregnant by a guy she didn't even like anymore. It was going to break Gilbert's heart, and she just wanted it over with. "Kelly Ann will be here in a week or so. I don't know exactly when," she finally replied.

"I can't quit thinkin' about her," he sighed. "I really, really like her."

"I know," Emily whispered, grabbing a timecard and filling in her hours.

"I think I may even love her."

"Wow, Gilbert," Emily sighed, feeling her stomach wrench.

"You didn't tell her how I feel about her, did you?"

"I told you I wouldn't…" She saw Mr. Kingery coming down the aisle with two grocery bags, and hurried towards him, relieved to get away from Gilbert's questioning.

She handed the grocer her timecard, took the bags, and walked over to where Gilbert was waiting on a customer. "See you later," she whispered, feeling bad for him.

"Let me know when Kelly Ann gets here," he whispered back.

Emily trudged up Elderberry Way towards the service station, shifting the heavy grocery bags twice, and saw Gus sitting on a stack of oil cans engrossed in *The Mountain Grove Gazette*, the local newspaper.

"Hey, Gus!" she called, toting the bags across the gas island.

"Hey, Em'ly!" he said, with a grin that showed an even row of choppers.

She was relieved to see that his teeth were in his mouth this time, and not laying on the station desk grinning at her. She'd actually screamed in surprise last time it happened!

Gus turned to his old gray Schnauzer lying nearby, and said, "Yip Yap, looky who's deliverin' our groceries today!" The dog raised his head up off the pile of clean oil rags that Gus had provided for his afternoon nap, bared his teeth in a grin, then lay back down.

"Come sit down and visit with us fer' awhile, Em'ly!" he said, taking the groceries. "Look how happy Yip Yap is to see you!"

"He just looks sleepy to me, Gus!" she chuckled, unfolding one of the chairs Gus kept handy for anyone who stopped by for a chin wag, as he called it.

"Naw, he's excited!" Gus insisted, beaming at the sleepy dog.

"How're you doing, Yip Yap?" she said, scratching behind his ear.

"Where's yer' manners, Yip Yap," Gus said, nudged his dog. "Say hi to Em'ly, fer' goodness sake!"

The dog looked up with droopy eyes. "Rye" he yipped and put his head back down.

Emily burst out laughing. "I still can't believe it!" she said, patting the dog's head.

"Yep, he nearly talks me ta' death when no one's aroun'," Gus said, heading towards the station office. "Let me put these groceries in the fridge, and git' you a Orange Crush, Em'ly! Be right back!" He stuck his head out the door a second later. "I have some leftover enchiladas that Carlotta made me if you're hungry!"

"No thanks," Emily replied, grabbing Yip Yap's wire brush off a nearby newspaper rack, and giving the dog a thorough brushing while she waited, willing herself to quit thinking about Gilbert and Kelly Ann.

"Yer' gonna' be that dog's favorite person if you keep that brushin' up," Gus said, handing her the cold drink.

She smiled and popped the lid on her Crush. "How's Carlotta doing these days?"

Gus stared at her for a second. "That's for me to know, and you to find out, Miss Nosy!"

Emily laughed.

"Anyway, what's on yer' mind today, Em'ly? You came here lookin' like you got the weight of the world hangin' on you."

Emily sighed, not knowing what to say since she'd promised not to tell anyone about her friend's pregnancy. "Oh, just thinking about Kelly Ann coming soon!"

Gus looked at her; she looked at him.

"You know Kelly Ann's havin' a baby, right?" he finally asked.

"What?" she yelped, surprised he'd found out. "Did Ike tell you?"

He nodded. "Me an' Kelly Ann's grandpa been friends over fifty years; you think he's gonna' keep a secret like that from me?"

Emily was actually relieved he knew.

"We're both wonderin' how she'll do at bein' a mama, since her own mama neglected her, and devoted all her time to alcohol and drugs," Gus said, shaking his head.

Emily started to answer, but a green Oldsmobile turned into the station, the horn beeping like a parade was in progress. Gus stood up and gawked. "Heaven he'p me, it's Cousin Alice!" he said in a low moan.

"Yoohoo! Augustus!" Cousin Alice hooted from the car window, waving like crazy.

Gus muttered something that Emily couldn't exactly hear and set his Crush down on an oil drum.

The large woman threw open the Oldsmobile door, as she slid out, a broom and dustpan came clattering out with her. When she opened the rear car door to toss them in the back seat, Emily could see that it was filled to the brim with cleaning supplies!

They both watched in stunned silence as Cousin Alice shoved the rear door shut with her left foot, then turned to them, all smiles, with arms extended. "Augustus! Come hug my neck!" she cried, hurrying over. The woman was larger than Gus and nearly knocked him over with the hug.

Gus retreated from her quickly. "What're you doin' in town, this time a' year, Alice?" he asked, rubbing his neck.

"Well, I come to see my favorite cousin!" she laughed, poking him playfully in the ribs with her elbow.

"Ow!" Gus said, stepping back before she could hug or poke him again. "This is Em'ly," he said, standing a good distance from her.

"Em'ly!" Alice squealed, throwing her arms around her, rocking back and forth.

"Hello," Emily said, her voice muffled by Cousin Alice's broad shoulder.

"Well," Cousin Alice said, looking very pleased, "I brought my broom and cleanin' supplies, Augustus, and I aim to tidy this station up and give it a woman's touch!"

"Since when does a service station need a woman's touch?" Gus asked, folding his arms.

"Oh honey, you're gonna' love it!" she gushed. "Then we'll work on that house of yers'. I got all kinds a' plans!"

Emily thought it might be a good time to leave. "I'll let you visit with your cousin, Gus, and come by another time. Nice meeting you, Cousin Alice!" she said, hurrying away before the woman could hug her good-bye.

Walking down the hill away from the service station, Emily's thoughts were still on Kelly Ann, trying to think of different ways to help her. Gus was right to be concerned; Kelly Ann had no idea what a stable home life looked like.

Emily's own family had been neglectful like Kelly Ann's, but she had been surrounded by a whole village that cared deeply for her, and she had learned from them. Kelly Ann had the same opportunity, often coming to live with Ike, her grandpa, but going back to her mom if she didn't like the way things were going. She bolted if there was any kind of pressure, always running with the wrong crowd, always looking for a fun time. And now she was having a baby.

Emily was deep in thought when an idea came to her. Books! A person could learn anything from books! Taking care of a newborn, being a good parent...it would all be there! She hurried towards the library.

Pushing open the huge double doors of the library, she heard a blast of laughter and headed in that direction, knowing well the laughter of Mrs. Green, the librarian. Emily found her talking to one of the high school students, looking much like a student herself in a mini skirt with black leggings; the cowlicks in her short red hair sticking straight up, as though she had purposely spiked it. Emily wandered over to the fiction section and waited for her to finish. When Mrs. Green finally noticed her, she hurried over.

"Looking for adventure books, Emily?" Mrs. Green teased, giving her a hug.

Emily opened her mouth to speak then clamped it shut, realizing her mistake. How was she going to explain to Mrs. Green that she wanted books on pregnancy and raising a child without ratting out Kelly Ann?

With a sigh, she jumped in. "This is confidential, but I have a friend who is going to have a baby...."

Her mouth had gone dry. *What should she say now? What if Mrs. Green thought it was really her?*

Mrs. Green nodded for her to go on.

Emily gulped and cleared her throat. "I need a book on having a baby and raising a baby." "For my friend," she added, feeling her face grow red. "Parenting books on parenting." "Not for me. For my friend..." She didn't know how to stop talking.

Mrs. Green stood there blinking waiting for her to finish, and finally put a hand up for her to stop. "I've got it, Emily, and you've come to the right place," she said brightly. "Follow me!"

Emily trailed behind over to the check-out desk, where Mrs. Green handed her a flyer.

"What's this?"

"Parenting classes," the librarian fairly crowed. "They're starting in three weeks right here in the library conference room. Bring Kell...I mean bring your friend!"

Emily stared at her. "How did you know who I was talking about?"

"I heard a couple of rumors, plus her grandpa looked worried last time I ate at *Good Eats*."

Emily sighed. "You're right, it's for Kelly Ann."

"I won't tell anyone," Mrs. Green said, "although she'll probably be showing by now."

"You're right again. Gilbert loves her and he doesn't know," Emily blurted out, deciding to tell it all. "I wish Mrs. Apple was in town."

"Why do you wish that?"

"She'd tell me I'm assuming too much responsibility."

Mrs. Green grinned. "I would've told you that if I thought it were true. I think you're just being a good friend."

"That's a relief," she sighed, and they both laughed.

Mrs. Green helped Emily pick out a couple of books on pregnancy. "I think Kelly Ann will learn everything she needs to know with these," she said, sounding pleased.

"I'll probably take notes and talk to her about it," Emily said, thumbing through the books. "I forgot; she doesn't like reading much." She thought for a moment. "Are there any videos? Kelly Ann loves watching those."

"Yes! Come right this way." On the way to the video section, Mrs. Green said, "Did I ever tell you that you're an exceptionally good friend?"

"Or an exceptionally crazy one," Emily murmured under her breath.

Later, at the check-out desk, as Emily put the books and videos in her backpack, she asked, "Do you have any books for Gilbert on what to do when the girl you love comes to town pregnant?"

"Nope, fresh out of those," Mrs. Green laughed, "but Gilbert will be alright eventually."

"I think so too...eventually," she replied, turning to leave.

"Oh Emily!"

Emily turned and looked at her.

"Mr. Green is still working on finding your sister, it's just hard with so few leads, but I didn't want you to think he'd given up."

Emily nodded that she understood. "I wish I had more information to give him, but my mom and dad never talked about family, and my grandmother knew very little." Just saying it out loud depressed her. Her family was so weird.

That evening Emily opened her journal to write, and the photos fell out. One was of her as an infant, the only picture she had of herself as a child; the other was of her sister, Eva, taken as a toddler. The photo of her sister was the only link she had to her. Emily squeezed her eyes shut. "Please help Mr. Green find her," she murmured, in the form of a prayer, while pressing the picture to her heart.

Dear Journal,

How do I make it happen? I need a link to my family. The villagers are my family and I love them, but it feels like there is a missing piece, and I need to find it.

Where are you, Eva?

E.

Emily stopped in at *Good Eats Café* Sunday afternoon to check the work schedule. She only worked there part-time, and the schedule changed often. Pushing the café door open, she heard loud laughter coming from the men sitting at the counter. Ike Peavler, the owner of the café, Glen Kingery, and Montana Chan, who ran the local newspaper, were howling. She caught part of the conversation..."and Cousin Alice cleared all of that junk outta' the service station office and put up fancy window curtains and blue throw rugs," Glen Kingery snorted.

"An don't forget the potted ferns, and framed pictures," howled Ike, who had begun to wheeze from laughing so hard.

Millie, Ike's full-time waitress, was serving two meat loaf specials to an elderly couple in the back booth but came over when she saw Emily.

"Let me guess," Emily said, "Aunt Alice redecorated Gus' station!"

"You got it, Honey," Millie said. "I never heard so much hee-hawing! They're all stoppin' by Gus' station, then high tailing it back here to add to the story."

"Guess I better go see it for myself."

Millie laughed and hurried off to wait on another customer. Emily greeted the men, then went back into the kitchen where the schedule hung on a clipboard near the swinging doors.

Copying down her work schedule, Emily chuckled as she listened to the men at the counter laugh and wheeze.

"I gotta' quit laughin', my sides hurt," Glen Kingery gasped as she was leaving. Their laughter could be heard all the way out on the sidewalk, and part way up the hill as she headed for Gus's station.

Opening the door to the service station office, she couldn't believe it.

There sat Gus reading a newspaper at a tidy desk with a new ink blotter, a pen holder, and a telephone. Nothing else. The clutter was all gone. He glanced up at her but didn't say a word as he watched her look around.

The windows had been decorated with blue curtains that were speckled with tiny filling station pumps, oil cans, and minuscule hydraulic jacks. There were braided rugs on the floor that already had oily footprints, since no one in their right mind would take off greasy shoes just to come into a service station office. She counted three pictures on the wall: one of an elephant performing in a circus; one of a snow skier doing a somersault; and one of Cousin Alice sitting on a wharf with a basket of fish and chips. The huge potted plants created a jungle ambiance.

"Where's Cousin Alice?" she whispered, before going through the door.

"Oh, thee's ruint my thathion, now thee's over ruinin' my houth!"

"Gus! Where's your choppers?" Emily laughed as she went in. "I can't understand a word you said!

"Oh!" he said, reaching into a desk drawer. "Scuth me!" He ducked his head below the desk and came back up all smiles with his even row of choppers in place.

Emily laughed. "Now tell me again what you said!"

"I said, that woman ruined my station. Now she's over ruinin' my house!" The smile had disappeared.

"You don't like window curtains and throw rugs?" she asked, feeling a belly laugh coming on.

"No, I do not like window curtains and throw rugs," he said, punctuating every word. "That woman is drivin' me nuts!"

"Can't you tell her to stop?"

"I haven't been able to tell her to stop nothin' since we was kids and she painted my dern toenails pink!"

Emily clamped a hand over her mouth, but it didn't do any good. She snorted with laughter. She cleared her throat once and tried to talk but cackled instead. "That's the funniest thing I ever heard, Gus!" she wailed, holding her sides with laughter.

Gus shook his head. "I know. I know. I'd be laughin' too, if I was you!"

Gus got up and went to the old fashion soda dispenser, pulled two orange crushes out of the chilled water, and handed one to Emily.

"My treat if you'll quit yer' dern' laughin' he said," trying to keep a straight face.

"Deal" she said, twisting the cap off, and willing herself to quit thinking about Gus with pink toenails.

Chapter - 2

There was one thing that Emily really missed from her old house. Her garden. While scrubbing the large mixing bowls in the bakery's kitchen sink, she wondered if there was any kind of a yard behind the bakery where another garden could be planted. She rinsed off her hands and was just unbolting the back door when her mama walked in.

"What're you doin' Sugar?" she asked, checking the timer over the huge oven where five of her world class apple pies were baking.

"I want to see if there's anywhere out back to plant another flower garden. I miss mine!" She gave the door a tug, but it was warped and weather worn.

"Now that's just a fine idea," her mama said, hurrying over to help with the stubborn door.

They both tugged and pulled, and the door scraped half-way open, allowing them to squeeze through the narrow opening, and out onto a wooden porch. Emily was delighted to see a small, fenced plot of ground. "Yay," she said, hurrying down the wooden steps.

"It's just right for a garden!" her mama said happily, surveying the small yard from the top of the stairs. "We'll need to get you some garden tools!"

"I have a few I brought from my old garden," she replied, looking around, and already loving this sheltered spot. She had stashed a couple of her boxes in the utility room when she moved in, and knew just where her trowel, gardening gloves, and small shovel were.

"I'll need to buy a large shovel to turn the dirt over," she said, planning it all out. "I'll water the ground to soften it up, then run over to *Bloomin' Happy*."

She turned in a complete circle looking for a garden hose, but there wasn't one. "Guess I'll buy a hose, too," she said, searching the length of the building until she found a water spigot.

"You have enough money for all of that, Sugar?"

"I think so," she said, dusting her hands off as she came back up the stairs. "I'll run over to the nursery and Jonathan's dad can help me pick out what I need."

"Hey, Mr. C!" Emily called out as she went through the gate of *Bloomin' Happy Nursery*.

Mr. Charles spun around with a big grin on his face. "Emily! Good to see you!"

"I'm planting another garden!" she said, happily. "Miss Mattie said I could dig up her tiny back yard!"

"Wonderful! Grab a hand trolley and start loading up. I was just going into the *Village Grocer*, and I'll grab us a snack."

He headed into the side door of the store, as Emily found a hand cart and started searching for her favorite flowers.

She had loaded the wagon with red and blue pansies, Jupiter's Beard, and blue hydrangeas by the time Mr. Charles returned, carrying two small cartons of chocolate milk and two snickerdoodle cookies.

"Come and join me, and let's catch up," he said, holding the refreshments up. "We haven't had a chance to visit in a while!"

Emily was touched and pushed the hand cart up against a picket fence, then took a seat in the folding chair he'd set out for her. "Thanks," she said, accepting the cookie with one hand, and the chocolate milk with the other.

"How are things going, living with Miss Mattie?" he asked, opening up his small carton of milk.

"I love living with her," she said happily, biting into the cookie. She had worked past lunchtime and didn't realize how hungry she was.

"Do you hear from Jonathan much?"

"He sends me pictures almost every day! Want to see the one he sent today?"

"Absolutely," he said, setting down his milk and cookie.

She scrolled through her phone, then handed him a picture of Jonathan holding out two tacos.

"What in the world?" Mr. Charles laughed.

"He bought me a taco and wishes I were there having lunch with him," she laughed.

Mr. Charles looked up at her and smiled, "I think my son cares very much for you!"

Emily gulped and her heart began to hammer. "I like him, too. He's a good friend." She stuffed the phone back in her pocket.

"Jonathan likes you more than a friend, Emily," he said, looking puzzled.

She stared at him, not knowing what to say.

"You seem to have feelings for him..." Mr. Charles wasn't one for pretense.

"I'm afraid to have feelings for him."

"Trust issues?"

She nodded.

"It's okay, we don't have to talk about it if it makes you uncomfortable," he said, taking a swig out of his milk carton.

"Well, I probably should talk about it," she sighed. "It's not Jonathan, you know. He's the best."

Mr. Charles nodded and waited for her to go on.

"I'm afraid of commitment, and of marriage. I saw pictures of my parents' when they first got married, and they looked so happy!" She looked up at Mr. Charles. "They wound up despising each other."

"You're not like them, Emily," he assured her.

"That's what Miss Mattie says, but how can I be sure?"

"We get to make our own choices in life," he said, smiling at her, "and you've made different choices than the ones you were raised with. Good choices."

"Thank you," she said, meaning it.

"Anyway, you're only sixteen! There's a long road ahead for both of you. We'll see what the future holds, and who it holds for both of you!

She just stared at him. *Or who it holds?* She didn't like that answer one bit.

"Sorry everyone!" Emily apologized to the customers, as she rolled the rickety, flower-filled hand cart through the bakery. "We don't have a gate in our fence yet and I'm planting a new flower garden!"

Everyone seated at the small parlor tables chuckled as the cart rolled past towards the kitchen. One elderly man warbled, "You go, girl!" pumping a shaky fist in the air.

Miss Mattie just stood there with her mouth open. "I'll clean it up!" Emily whispered, as she rolled past, the cart shaking small bits of dirt onto the clean floor.

After the floor was swept, Emily went out and hooked the new hose to the faucet, realizing she also needed a sprayer. She soaked the small yard the best she could with her thumb over the end of the hose, and when the ground was thoroughly saturated, began to turn over the dirt with her new shovel. The sun was high by then, and warmed her quickly, but she shoveled on, enjoying the smell of rich soil, the sound of the shovel biting into the earth, and the feeling of being in touch with nature again. The chore calmed something deep inside of her.

After an hour of turning soil, she went back up the wooden steps and began unloading flowers, keeping them in their containers until she could decide the best layout for the garden. She kept arranging and rearranging them in the places her heart wanted them to be. A corner spot for the blue hydrangeas; a center spot for low grasses: baby tears and mondo grass; in another corner, an arched row of yellow pansies, followed by an arched row of blue ones. Two rows of lavender against the bakery wall.

She looked around at the order of everything and tried to think of what was needed. Pots! She needed flower filled pots to add dimension, and seed posters to brighten the fence. She wrote it all down for when she returned the cart to *Bloomin' Happy*.

Emily planted the flowers in the newly turned soil, making sure to keep an open spot for her red chair, and the beautiful pot of purple pansies Jonathan had brought the first night she'd spent in the church basement after her parents abandoned her. The red chair had come from the garden she'd been forced to leave behind. Jonathan had brought both pieces those many months ago, as she sat all alone in the church basement, so devastated and lost, stricken that her parents had just driven off in the middle of the night and left her. She remembered it well. There had been a knock on the basement door and when she opened it, there stood Jonathan with the red chair, and a beautiful earthenware bowl of purple pansies, her favorite flower. She smiled when she thought of it. He'd hugged her and said that the flowers were for her *next* garden.

Emily would never forget that time and selected two special spots in her garden for the chair and earthen bowl, ringed it with pebbles, then hurried back up the stairs to get the wagon back before *Bloomin' Happy* closed.

The bakery was empty when she pulled the cart back through, more dirt coming off the wheels. Her mama just shook her head. "I won't wheel it through when customers are here anymore," she said, looking back over her shoulder. But her mama wasn't there. She'd already gone for the broom.

As she pulled the handcart through the gate at *Bloomin' Happy*, Mr. Charles came over with a fifty-pound bag of fertilizer. "Emily," he said, "we forgot about this; you'll need to work it into your soil for healthier flowers."

"How much?" she asked, knowing that her small savings were dwindling quickly.

"Hmmm…" he said, noticing her concern," how about an hour's worth of work on Saturday?"

"How about I work all day," she laughed. "I need a couple of your pretty pots, and potting soil, too!"

"Perfect!" he said, smiling as they fist-bumped.

Emily was working the afternoon shift at *Good Eats* when Gilbert came in and took a seat at the counter.

"Hey Gilbert, what's new?" she asked, puzzled to see him.

"I came to ask Kelly Ann's grandpa when she'll be here," he said, almost whispering. "He oughta' know since no one else does."

"I asked Ike earlier and he doesn't know either," she said, hoping to stop Gilbert. She didn't know if Ike would blurt out Kelly Ann's pregnancy.

"I can't sleep at night, thinkin' about her."

Feeling sorry for him, Emily gave him a quick hug. "I'll let you know if I hear anything," she handed him a menu. "How about something to eat?"

"Naw," he said, handing the menu back. "I'm good."

"Stay put, it's my treat," she said, pushing the menu back toward him. She knew his life was hard, living with an alcoholic father in the Sawmill area, often staying in the church basement when his dad became violent, and working two or three jobs to get by.

"You sure?"

"Of course!" It would take a bite out of her tips, but she didn't care.

She saw Ike watching as she put Gilbert's order up on the chrome spinner. "Don't give him a bill," he whispered.

"I can pay for it," she whispered back.

"This one's on me," he insisted. "He can be a member of my *Pass It Along Club*."

Emily smiled. She had joined Ike's *Pass It Along Club* when her parents had left her. Ike had filled her belly more than once and told her to pass the favor along to the next person who needed it.

The café stayed fairly busy all afternoon. Just after five o'clock, Miss Violet, the owner of Violet's House of Beauty, sashayed through the door with a gentleman that Emily didn't recognize. The man looked like a character she'd seen in a 50's movies, with an overcoat and fedora hat, which he carefully placed on the rack by the door. Miss Violet had outdone herself, attired in a silver satin dress with sequined boots, a glittering headband, and her jeweled cigarette holder—minus the cigarette—which she held aloft to emphasize her many flamboyant hand movements. They stood just inside the door, waiting to be seated.

Emily looked at Ike, who rolled his eyes.

"You better go escort them to a table, Em'ly," he whispered. "I think she's pretendin' this is New York City and waitin' for the maitre d'!"

Emily stifled a laugh, grabbed two menus, and hurried over to the couple. "This way, please," she said, deciding to play the maitre d' role, with a slight bow and a swoop of her hand.

The gentleman presented his arm, Miss Violet laid a jeweled hand on his cuff, and the procession started for the back table. The fumes of Miss Violet's *Evening in Paris* perfume caused Emily's eyes to water, and she discreetly fanned them with the menus.

Heads turned in the café as the couple marched by, and Ike wondered if he should dig out a white tablecloth and candelabra since royalty was here.

Emily seated them, opened their menus and gave one to each, then hurried back over to Ike. "They want to know if you have any Pierre Water!"

"What the dicken's is that?"

Iris Head, seated at a nearby table, going over her real estate listings, whispered, "I think they mean Perrier!"

"Pierre or Perrier, I don't have it," Ike snorted, heading back to his kitchen. "Give 'em tap water like everyone else."

Emily served the two iced waters with a lemon slice. It was as fancy as they got at *Good Eats*. She left them to look over the menu and walked back over to see if Iris needed anything.

"Where did Miss Violet meet him?" Iris whispered.

"She's been on a dating site," Emily whispered back. "Last week she was here with a cowboy!"

"Miss Violet with a cowboy?" Edith snorted. She tried to control her laughter and snorted again.

"Shhh! Don't make me start laughing!" Emily said, already laughing.

From the back of the café they heard a bell jingle. They both looked up as Miss Violet's gentleman friend raised a gloved hand with a small bell and gave it another jingle.

Emily clamped a hand over her mouth. "I can't do this," she said, choking with laughter. "Where'd he get that bell..."

The bell jingled again.

Ike came out of the kitchen, looking around. "Is Santy Claus here? I hear bells!"

Iris pointed discreetly to the rear booth, where the bell was about to be rung again.

Ike said something that they couldn't exactly hear and stomped back to his kitchen.

Iris' shoulders shook with laughter as Emily walked over to take the couple's order.

On Monday morning, bright and early, Emily received a text from Kelly Ann: *I'm back in Mountain Grove now. Can I walk to school with you today?*

She's going to school pregnant? Emily wondered, but sent back a text saying, *Glad you're here! Come by the bakery and get me.*

About twenty minutes to eight, Kelly Ann walked through the bakery door, greeted the customers sitting at the small parlor tables, and waved to Miss Mattie, who was busy behind the cash register.

Emily glanced at her friend's stomach and saw that she was just beginning to show. "I'm happy to see you!" she said, giving her a hug. "You ready?"

"Ready as I'll ever be," she replied, in a strong Mississippi drawl.

"Your accent sure thickened!" Emily teased.

"Thick as chowder?"

"Thicker!" Emily laughed.

Before leaving, both girls went over and hugged Miss Mattie, who whispered to Kelly Ann, "I like brave girls!"

"Thank you, ma'am," she replied, her face lighting up briefly.

As they walked to school, Kelly Ann said, "This is the only day I'll be walkin' with you. I'm just signin' up for home schooling today."

"They'll let you do that?" Emily asked, surprised at the information.

"Of course! I could do it even if I wasn't pregnant."

"Hmmm…I'd like to do that, too!"

"I thought you liked school," Kelly Ann said, eyeing her.

"I like learning, but I don't like school. I don't have much in common with the kids there."

"I know what you mean," Kelly Ann replied. "When I'd go to school, the girls were wonderin' what to wear to the prom, and I'm wonderin' if my mom's gonna' be sober when I get home."

"Exactly! At least that's the way it used to be for me. I have a good home now, but they still remember where I came from and say stuff sometimes."

"That's awful! You should bust 'em in the mouth."

Emily laughed, "I'm not much into mouth-busting. Anyway, it's just a few of the girls that are mean."

"A few girls like Bitsy Callahan?"

"That would be one, yes," she replied. "But that's not the main reason. School just takes up a lot of time, and I'd rather be working, or doing other things."

"Well, why doncha' homeschool then? It would be fun to study to-gether."

The question struck something in Emily. *Yes, why didn't she?*

"You ever find out any more about that sister yer' lookin' for?" Kelly Ann asked.

"No, but Mr. Green is still working on it."

"Well, I hope you find her," Kelly Ann said, giving her a quick hug.

"Me, too!"

When they got to school, Emily asked, "Do you want me to come to the office with you?"

"Are you scared somebody will say somethin' mean?" Kelly Ann asked, as though reading her thoughts.

"Maybe!"

"Thanks, but I'm just gettin' my books and schedule. I already talked to them about the baby, and they were nice."

They hugged, and Emily went to her first period class.

That afternoon, as soon as Emily got home from school, she brought the homeschooling subject up with Miss Mattie.

"Why would you want to homeschool, Sugar?" she asked while loading the pastry case with freshly baked chocolate chip cookies.

"I don't have much in common with the other kids, and I'd rather work or do other things."

"Well, you only have two more months of school," her mama said, walking towards the kitchen with empty trays that needed washing. "Stick it out for now and try joinin' in more. Maybe it would even be fun for you!"

"Endless chatter about music, cute boys, and what color nail polish to wear isn't fun to me," Emily said, following her back to the kitchen. "And that's about all the girls at school talk about."

"Jus' make an effort to join in for the rest of the school year, Sugar," her mama said, turning and looking at her. "Really put your heart into it. Make friends, invite them over, go places with them. You're around adults way more than you are kids your own age!"

"That's because adults are more interesting to me. My life is different, and I don't have much in common with girls my age." She didn't add the part about mean girls making fun of her. She knew it would stress her mama out.

"Just make more effort," was the only answer she got, and Emily knew to just leave the subject alone for now.

"Mama, will you be able to handle the bakery this afternoon if I go with Kelly Ann to her first doctor's appointment?" Emily asked a few days later.

"Absolutely, Sugar, things are really slow in the afternoon these days."

"I wonder why?" she said, thinking she needed to pay more attention to the bakery business.

Her mama shrugged. "I'm not sure, but anyway, I'm glad Kelly Ann is finally goin' to the doctor. Did you talk her into it?"

"No, but I gave her a video that talked her into it."

"That's my girl," her mama said, hugging her. "What doctor is she goin' to?"

'Dr. Blackstone, the one who took care of you."

"He's a fine doctor, but shouldn't she be goin' to an obstetrician?"

"There's not one in Mountain Grove, and Kelly Ann won't go out of town."

Her mama shrugged. 'Well, as long as he agrees to it, he's certainly capable."

Dr. Blackstone's nurse took Kelly Ann's vitals and wrote down her medical history as she and Emily sat in the examining room at the medical clinic. As they waited for Dr. Blackstone to come in, Emily noticed that her friend looked really pale, and asked, "Are you okay?"

But Kelly Ann didn't have time to answer because Dr. Blackstone came hurrying in.

"Emily!" he said, looking happy to see her. "We meet again!"

"I didn't know if you'd remember me."

"I remember you well," he said, patting her shoulder. "How is life going with your foster mom?"

"I love it, and I love her!"

"Excellent!" he replied, then turned to Kelly Ann and stuck out his hand. "I'm Dr. Blackstone; you must be Kelly Ann."

Kelly Ann nodded, growing paler.

"Let's take your blood pressure again, Kelly Ann," he said, after she climbed up on the examining table. "It's high, and you look very pale. Are you nervous?"

"I'm scared out'a my mind bein' here," she replied honestly.

Dr. Blackstone actually smiled. "No need to be. We're all here to help."

The doctor took Kelly Ann's blood pressure twice. "It's still a little high," he informed her. "Are you walking, or getting any kind of exercise?"

"Em'ly drags me aroun' town most every day!"

"How far?"

Kelly Ann shrugged, and Emily spoke up. "We walk a mile every day. I figured it out, from one end of town to the other and back."

"Very good," he said. "And you walk with her?"

"Yes, I need exercise, too!"

He looked at her and nodded, understanding what she was trying to do.

"Why don't we increase the walk to two miles and see if that doesn't bring your blood pressure down a little lower. Try it for a week, then come back in and we'll take it again."

They both nodded, agreeing.

He checked Kelly Ann's ankles for swelling and took out a stethoscope to listen to her heart.

"I think you're doing fine, Kelly Ann," he said after checking her over. He went to a large cabinet and took out a bottle of prenatal vitamins.

"Take two of these a day," he said, handing her the small brown jar. "Do you have any questions?"

She nodded, swallowing hard, unable to speak.

"What do you have questions about?"

"Everything…" she wailed, bursting into tears.

Emily went over and put an arm around her, not quite knowing what else to do. Dr. Blackstone handed her a tissue, pulled up a chair and sat with his arms folded like he had all the time in the world. "What's making you cry, Kelly Ann?" he asked.

"How am I gonna' support a baby?" she sobbed. "And how can I teach a kid what I don't know?" She blotted her eyes with the tissue. "I don't even know how to change a diaper, and I just want my baby to have a good life." She buried her face in the tissue. "And now I have high blood pressure!" she wailed.

Emily spoke, "You're just a little overwhelmed, Kelly Ann. "You'll have plenty of help for all those things."

Dr. Blackstone gave her a few seconds, then said, "A lot of the information you're needing can be found online, and in books, Kelly Ann."

"Em'ly already brought me books an' videos from the library," she said, tears continuing to course down her cheeks.

"Good," he replied, nodding at Emily. "Do you have a stable place to live?"

"My grandpa."

"Are you continuing your education?"

"Homeschool right now," she sniffed.

"Great! Never quit, no matter how hard it gets. That's how you'll support your baby."

"Ok," she said, and took a deep breath.

"I was in foster care when I was a kid, Kelly Ann," he said, handing her more tissues.

"You were?"

He nodded. "I decided back then that I wanted to be a doctor, so I used laser focus to get there. It didn't matter what was going on around me, or the problems that arose. Laser focus. Those are your key words. Use the same laser focus to become a good mom. Read everything you can, watch what good moms do, and do it yourself. And don't be afraid to ask those good moms for help."

"Okay, thank you," Kelly Ann replied, blotting more tears, as she sat on the edge of the examining table with her feet dangling, looking very much like a scared three-year-old.

"Anything else that you're worried about?" he asked.

"Yes, what hospital am I gonna' have this baby in? I don't want to go all the way to Clayton."

"Well, I have some good news then. We're completing a birthing center right here in Mountain Grove, and it will be open before your baby is due."

Letting out her breath, "That's a relief," she whispered, her shoulders relaxing.

"Also, an obstetrician is coming to town and will be available if we need her."

"Okay, but I feel better stickin' with you," she said, sliding down off the examining table. "Ya'll got a bathroom aroun' here? I have to go like ten times a day now."

"That's normal. Pregnancy causes your body to produce more fluids," he said, standing up and opening the door. "The bathroom is second door on the left, and I'll see you next week."

"Well, I liked him, and I like that he didn't make a big deal outta' me bein' pregnant," Kelly Ann said as they walked out the door of the doctor's office. "Know what I mean?"

Emily nodded. "It helped me after my parents left when he talked about being in foster care."

"I know! It's sorta' like, if he can make it...I can make it!" Kelly Ann said, yawning.

"Do you want to come to my place and rest?' Emily asked, as they walked towards town.

"Naw, I'm just gonna' go get me a big pillow at grandpa's and lay on the couch an' watch old movies."

"You want me to have Miss Violet come over and show you which old movies are her favorites?" Emily teased.

Kelly Ann gave her a side glance. "Yeah right! When I git' within two feet of the woman's perfume, I lose my lunch!"

Emily laughed and hugged her goodbye.

"Thanks for comin' with me today!" Kelly Ann whispered, hugging her tightly.

Chapter - 3

S aturday, while Emily was working the morning shift at *Good Eats*, Mr. and Mrs. Green came in for breakfast. They were holding hands walking in the door; Mr. Green let go of his wife's hand long enough to shut the door behind them, then grabbed it again as they made their way to a back booth.

Emily watched them as she took platters of food to a couple in the front booth. After setting the couples food down, she went to get them more coffee, all the time watching Mr. and Mrs. Green chatting and laughing. *How could a marriage be so perfect?* she wondered.

The thought came that maybe she could just ask them.

Should I? she wondered, grabbing two menus and heading back to their table. The café wasn't very busy, and it was now or never!

They were holding hands across the table and laughing like school children when she walked back and handed each a menu, asking, "Is it okay if I ask you both something?"

They looked up expectantly. "Go for it!" Mr. Green said.

"'I'm being nosy, but how do you two have such a perfect marriage?"

Mrs. Green looked at her husband for a moment, then back at Emily. "We don't have a perfect marriage!"

"You don't?"

"No!" They both chorused.

"It looks perfect," Emily insisted. "What's really going on then?"

They both laughed.

"Tell her what works for us," Mr. Green said to his wife.

"Ummmm," Mrs. Green said, tapping her cheek as she thought about it. "We get over stuff!"

"You get over stuff? What?" Emily was totally confused.

"I think Emily needs an example," Mr. Green said.

His wife went back to thinking. "Gargling!" she said brightly.

"Gargling?" Emily was beginning to be sorry that she'd asked.

"Yes! Mr. Green gargles every night for two minutes, and the sound drives me nuts!" she laughed, then turned and looked at her husband, "...but I get over it."

"Now you give her an example," she urged Mr. Green, who was laughing along with her.

"Cabinet doors left open; loose lids on the mayonnaise jar; mud on the floor of the car!" he said, and they both howled.

Emily just stared at them.

The laughter subsided and Mr. Green said, "But I close the cabinet door, tighten the lids, and sweep up the mud, and I get over it!"

There was a pause as Mrs. Green gave her husband a quick peck on the cheek.

"Okay!" Mrs. Green said, warming up to the subject, "you told three things! Now I get another one."

"Go for it," her husband urged, already laughing.

She stared off in the distance for a moment, then looked up at him and said, "Mumbling!"

"Mumbling?" he asked, appearing confused.

"Yes! You mumble!"

"I do *not* mumble!" he mumbled, and they both howled with laughter.

Emily just stood there watching them, thinking they must have forgotten she was even there. "I'll be back in a minute to take your order," she murmured, and walked away to the kitchen.

"What's all the laughin' about?" Ike asked, as he got hamburger patties out of the freezer.

"They were telling me what makes their marriage work," she answered with a shrug.

"Well, the secret ingredient musta' been laughin'!" he said, as more laughter erupted from the Green's table.

"No, they said it was, *getting over it!*" Emily shook her head. "They're laughing about the different things they "get over" with each other."

"There must be a pile of things," he chuckled. "Maybe you oughta' go listen in some more!"

Emily gave it a couple of minutes, then went back over to see if they were ready to order.

When she got to their table, Mr. Green was wiping his eyes with a napkin, and Mrs. Green had her hand over her mouth, trying to muffle any more laughter. She composed herself as Emily stood ready to take their order.

"Oh, Emily," she said, "thank you for that question. I haven't laughed this hard in ages!'

She looked as though she were going to start laughing again, so Emily said, "Thanks for your advice!"

"I don't know if we explained it very well," Mr. Green confessed, causing his wife to snort, and clamp a hand over her mouth.

"You explained it with your laughter," Emily replied. "I understand."

"We talk things over to solve problems, too," Mrs. Green said, once more composing herself, then looked up at Emily, "But mostly, we just get over it."

Emily and Kelly Ann turned left on Second Street, where they would walk up to Good Neighbor Pharmacy and hang another left. Emily had charted out a two-mile course for them after Dr. Blackstone's advice. Kelly Ann was still prone to just sitting and watching TV after she got her schoolwork done, so Emily made time to go with her nearly every day.

Does everyone know that you're pregnant now?" Emily asked as she and Kelly Ann walked, thinking more of Gilbert than anyone else.

"Nope, I've only told three people here: you, Miss Mattie, an' Grandpa... unless you've told people," Kelly Ann said, her walk slowing. "It's not like I go hangin' an advertisement around my neck ya' know!"

"It's your job to tell people, not mine," Emily said, deciding not to mention that Gus and Mrs. Green knew. "And you don't need to be so touchy!"

"It's just another pressure. Wanna' help me make up flyers tellin' people I'm pregnant and post them everywhere?"

"No," laughed Emily," but you really should start mentioning it to people!"

"I think I'm gonna' just let my belly mention it to them!" she said.

Emily looked at her. "That might not be the best way to do it," she said, once again thinking of Gilbert. This was going to break his heart, and he needed to know sooner rather than later.

She had no more than had the thought, when they saw Gilbert coming down the steps of the library.

Kelly Ann laughed, "Let's go tell Gilbert about the baby! I'll practice on him!"

Emily's mind scrambled, trying to think of a way to stop her. This was a terrible way to tell him!

But there was no stopping Kelly Ann once she'd made up her mind, so Emily just tagged along, not knowing what else to do.

"Hey Gilbert!" Kelly Ann's voice rang out.

Emily's stomach knotted as Gilbert's face lit up with a huge grin. "Hey, Kelly Ann!" he said, hurrying up and giving her a big hug. He didn't let go, but stood there with his arm around her shoulder, and a big goofy grin on his face. "You in town for good?"

"Yep, and I brought a lil' package with me," Kelly Ann said, patting her slightly protruding belly.

But Gilbert was staring at Kelly Ann's face and didn't notice what she was trying to show him.

Kelly Ann patted her belly again, and Emily felt herself groan.

"What's wrong Em'ly?" Gilbert asked.

Emily just shook her head, cringing at the way Kelly Ann was breaking the news to him. She felt physically ill.

"She's scared of me tellin' you somethin'," Kelly Ann laughed.

"What?" he asked, laughing along with her.

"Well...I'm gonna' have a baby," she said cheerfully.

Gilbert's mouth dropped open, and his eyes bulged as he stared at her. "What?"

"I know it's a shock," Kelly Ann rambled on, unaware that she'd just broken his heart. "It was to me, too, but I wanted to let you know cuz' you been a good friend and all."

They just stood there staring at each other, Gilbert looking very pale.

"Ok, Gilbert, say somethin'!" Kelly Ann yelped. "Yer makin' me feel really creepy..."

Gilbert rubbed the back of his neck, and just stared at her.

"Gilbert!" she yelled, "quit bein' weird!"

But Gilbert just shook his head, spun around, and took off walking towards the park.

"What in th' world..." Kelly Ann said, staring as he hurried away.

She turned to Emily with tears in her eyes. "That's it! I'm not tellin' anyone else! You tell 'em!" And with that she spun in the opposite direction and headed for home.

Emily stood on the sidewalk watching her walk away, wondering what to do. But she knew what to do and headed for the park to find Gilbert.

She found him under the willow tree.

"You ok?" she asked, sitting down beside him.

""Course I'm not okay!" he said angrily.

She nodded. "Want to talk about it?'

"Like that would do any good!" he exploded. "I hate this life!"

She listened to him rant for the next few minutes and said nothing. He fell silent for a moment, then quietly asked, "You still keepin' that promise not to tell her I like her?"

"I told you I wouldn't tell, and I won't," Emily said, softly. "That's for you to say to her, not me."

"Oh right! Like I'm gonna' confess my love now, jus' like in the movies..." He was angry again.

"You shouldn't do anything right now, Gilbert. Kelly Ann gave you shocking news. Just sit with it awhile. You don't need to do *anything*."

Gilbert just groaned and put his head back against the trunk of the tree. Emily put her hand on his arm, and said nothing, just leaned back on the tree and sat with him.

Emily kept an eye out for Gilbert, but when she didn't see him for a couple of days, grew concerned and decided to go looking for him.

Her concern grew after checking the park, and the library and he wasn't in either place. She knew he lived in an old trailer in the Sawmill area but wasn't comfortable going there and asking for him. His dad was too unpredictable, and maybe even dangerous when drinking. Besides, Gilbert stayed away from there as much as possible.

She remembered that Pastor Alex often took Gilbert under his wing, and decided on a visit to the church parsonage to see if they knew his whereabouts.

Penelope, the pastor's wife, answered the door. "Emily, come in!" Her beautiful almond shaped eyes actually lit up when she saw her.

Emily explained her mission, not sure if she should tell Penelope about Kelly Ann.

Pastor Alex came walking through the front door as they were talking. "Emily, good to see you," he said, going over and hugging her, as Penelope went off to the kitchen to get refreshments.

They sat and chit-chatted for a few minutes, catching up on Emily's life with Miss Mattie before Penelope came back in with mugs of spiced tea. Emily accepted a mug and said, "I'm actually here looking for Gilbert."

"I was just with him," the pastor said, sipping his tea. "He's staying in the basement for a few days."

Emily nodded, knowing that the only reason Gilbert would be staying in the church basement was because his dad was drinking again. That meant it was a double whammy for him: the girl he loved was pregnant, and his dad was on a drunken rampage.

"Did he mention Kelly Ann to you?"

"He's talked of little else," the pastor replied. "He's pretty upset."

"I know it was a really big blow to him," she said, setting her tea mug down on a side table. "Do you mind if I go see him?"

"I'm not sure he wants to talk about it."

"I won't bring anything up if he doesn't," Emily assured him. "I think I'll run across to the bakery and bring him back a box of donuts. If he wants to talk, fine. If he doesn't, that's fine too!"

"Perfect," said Pastor Alex, "and I understand that he loves chocolate, if that helps you with your pastry choices!"

"Chocolate it is!" Emily said, walking over and hugging both of them before she left.

"Oh, and ask him to play you a game of checkers!" the pastor laughed.

"Why?"

"Just play a game with him. You'll see!"

Emily knocked on the door of the church basement a little later, reminded of the time she had stayed there when her parents left her. Gilbert peeked out the window and she held up the box of pastries so he could see it. The lock on the door clicked, and Gilbert ushered her in.

"Wow! Thanks! I've been hungry for somethin' sweet," he said, taking the offered box.

He set it on a small table, opened it, and looked hungrily at the variety she had brought him.

"Man! Where do I start?" he said, his voice tinged with happiness.

Chocolate donuts, eclairs, brownies, fudge!" Emily said. "I brought you a sample of every chocolate thing we have at the bakery!"

"Well, thanks!" he said, reaching over and hugging her. "Wanna' have a seat?"

"Sure!" she said, pulling out a chair. "I think there's games in that storage closet. Want to play?"

"Okay," he shrugged.

She went into the closet and brought out a checkers game and Uno, hoping he'd choose Uno. "Which one?" she asked, holding them both up.

"Checkers!" he said, his face lighting up. "I've been beatin' that ole' pastor when we play!"

"Well, you won't beat me!" Emily laughed as she set the board up.

But he did beat her. Five games later she mumbled, "I really do hate this game!"

Gilbert snickered. "You just need a better strategy, Em'ly!"

"No, I just need to throw this checkerboard out the window!"

She was rewarded with a cackling laugh, and it made her happy to see him happy.

"Hi, Ike!" Emily sang out, walking through the door of *Good Eats Café*, where she was working the afternoon shift.

"Well, hello, darlin'," Ike said, downing the last of his coffee.

She went over and gave him a quick hug, surprised he wasn't wearing his customary chef's hat. Reaching into the drawer under the counter, Emily saw it was stacked with new green aprons. She shook one out, noticing the bib had been embroidered in large cursive lettering, *Good Eats Café*, and down a little lower, *Ike Peavler, Owner and Chef*.

"New aprons?" she asked, slipping the bib over her head.

"Yep," Ike replied. "Latest thing in New York City; chef's name in big lettering, alongside the establishment's name."

"Wow, Ike! You're getting fancy!" she grinned, tying the strings.

"Yep! Gotta' keep up with the competition, ya' know."

"New York City is competition?"

"Well, of course!" he said, staring at her in disbelief.

She didn't know what to say, and was relieved that the café door opened and Glen Kingery, Miss Violet, and her sister, Miss Rose, came in.

While Emily got a couple of menus for the ladies, Mr. Kingery grabbed his personal coffee mug from the rack, went behind the counter and poured himself a cup of coffee, then grabbed a spoon and menu, and sat at his usual spot at the end of the counter.

"This way, ladies," Emily said, noticing that Miss Violet had on new fuchsia colored parachute pants, and a small vest, looking as though she might break into a belly dance at any moment. Her five-inch heels clattered as they walked, and Emily slowed down, concerned that Miss Violet might slip on a french fry or something.

When they were safely seated, Emily handed them both menus, noticing for the first time Miss Violet's outrageous earrings that resembled little jeweled pizzas, with sparkling red rubies for the pepperoni. She watched, mesmerized as they fanned with every move, flickering when the overhead light struck them.

"Emily!" trilled Miss Violet, startling her out of her daydream. "We have an advanced session of the Young Ladies Academy starting in five days! May we expect to see you there?"

"I won't be able to come this time, Miss Violet!" she replied, meaning it. "Too busy!"

"Well, that's a shame," she murmured, drumming long, manicured fingernails on the table. Emily could tell she was trying to think of another angle, so she turned to Miss Rose.

"What will you be having today?"

"Does this say *squid* on the menu?" Miss Rose asked, pointing to an item, as she drew back in disgust.

"Squid?" Emily asked, puzzled as she picked up the menu and stared closely. She flicked off a dried crumb that was partially covering the word and handed the menu back. "It says, "squab", Miss Rose. One of Ike's friends went pigeon hunting at the old barn on Colfax Road, and Ike thought he'd stuff and bake them."

"Pigeon!" Miss Rose gasped.

"You know, like the fancy restaurants in New York City," Emily shrugged. "Ike's in competition with them."

Miss Violet stepped in. "Let's just share a tuna fish sandwich, Rose dear."

Miss Rose looked as though she'd lost her appetite, and just nodded.

"Bring us each a cup of vegetable soup to go with it, if you please Emily," trilled Miss Violet, bringing out her empty sequined cigarette holder to flap around as she spoke. Miss Violet had many ways of drawing attention to herself.

Emily wrote it down on the order pad and hurried away as the café door opened and Iris Head, owner of *God Bless America Real Estate*, walked in with her real estate folder tucked under one arm, and a huge purse beaded in red, white and blue on the other arm. Emily chuckled; she couldn't remember a time that Iris was without a patriotic color displayed somewhere.

"Hi, Emily," she said, walking over to her. "I'm expecting a new client and need a bit of privacy. Could I have the rear booth?"

As Emily led her to the back of the cafe, the front door opened and in walked a lovely, elegantly dressed woman, who Emily had never seen before.

Iris motioned and the woman smiled and walked gracefully back to the table, heads turning as she walked by.

"Emily, this is Gabriella Brookfield," Iris said, by way of introduction.

Emily held out her hand, and said, "Nice to meet you Mrs. Brookfield" and was rewarded with a beautiful smile, and a warm handshake.

"Please, call me Gabriella," she said, her voice low and silky.

"Gabriella is opening a tea shop on Second Street," Iris told her.

"Wow! Great!" Emily said, and for no reason whatsoever, the thought of Dr. Blackstone entered her mind. Handing them both a menu she peeked at Gabriella's left hand to see if there was a wedding ring. There wasn't.

"Is *Mr.* Brookfield going to help with your new tea shop?" Emily asked, just to make sure.

"I lost Mr. Brookfield two years ago," she replied softly, then ordered coffee and a small salad.

"I'll take the same," Iris said.

Emily walked back to the kitchen with their order, humming. "Dr. Blackstone is just going to love her!" she whispered to herself.

She went over to refill Mr. Kingery's cup, just as Ike brought out a double cheeseburger for him.

"Where's yer chef's hat, Ike?" Mr. Kingery asked, squirting ketchup on his fries.

"Not wearin' it," snapped Ike. "Given me a derned bald spot!" He bent his head towards the light to show where his hair was thinning.

"Hmmm," observed Mr. Kingery, "I think nature's given' you that bald spot, buddy boy, not yer' hat!"

Ike glared at him.

Mr. Kingery bit into his burger. "Don't worry about it, just do a comb-over like the rest of us!" he shrugged, trying to be helpful.

"Whatever!" Ike snapped and stomped back to his kitchen.

Emily kept watching Iris and Gabriella as they talked over lunch. The café had lots of customers, which kept her running, so it was hard to get back over and engage in any sort of conversation. She saw Gabriella look at her a number of times, and smile. She always smiled back.

"You're a really hard worker, Emily," Gabriella said, when she went back over to refill the ladies' cups. "Would you be interested in part-time work in my tea shop when it opens?"

Bingo! "Yes, I would," Emily said, nearly breaking into a cheer. She'd need to ask her mama but was sure it would be okay. Then she'd invite Dr. Blackstone over to see where she worked! And just like magic, no more loneliness for Dr. Blackstone.

But her mama was not okay with it. "Sugar, you already work for me, Mr. Charles, and Ike! When are you ever gonna' have any time for your schoolwork?"

"It would only be part time," she insisted, seeing her plan for Gabriella and Dr. Blackstone tumbling over a cliff. "And I don't work for Ike and Mr. Charles that often anyway."

Her Mama just looked at her.

Emily decided it was time to level with her. "I'm going to invite Dr. Blackstone to come to tea and see where I work."

"And why would you do that?"

"He's lonely, and Gabriella is lonely."

"She told you that?" she asked, her eyes bugging slightly.

"No, I just know. My keen sixth sense, you know," she said, hoping it would make her mama laugh.

But it didn't make her laugh, so she tried another angle.

"How about on weekdays, I will only work a total of fifteen hours, either with you or Gabriella. Mr. Charles only needs me on weekends occasionally, and Ike usually just needs me when Millie goes to help with her grandbabies."

Her Mama looked at her, and finally shrugged. "Okay, we can give it a try, but your schoolwork has to come...."

But she didn't get the last word out because Emily threw her arms around her. "Thanks Mama," she said, giving her a bear hug.

"I don't know 'bout you, Em'ly," she said, trying to sound stern, but Emily could feel her chuckling.

About then, the bakery door opened and J.T. Callahan and Bitsy came bouncing in.

"Good afternoon, Mr. Callahan, Bitsy!" Miss Mattie greeted them.

"Afternoon, Ma'am," J. T. said, shifting an unlit cigar to the other side of his mouth. "Hey, Em'ly!"

"Hey!" Emily replied, as she put a tray of brownies into the pastry case. "How's the used car business these days?"

"We gotta' big shipment of motorbikes comin' in today, and a coupla' Harleys!" he said proudly, hooking his thumbs in his red suspenders. "Me an' Bitsy's gotta' inventory 'em and' get them out on the lot, ain't that right, Bitsy?"

"That's right, Big Daddy," Bitsy giggled.

"Three motorbikes are goin' over to Saint Daniels, along with one Harley."

"The convent wants motorcycles?" Miss Mattie asked, looking surprised.

"Yep," he shrugged. "Don't ask me why. I just sell em', I don't ask questions."

"Are you going to be riding a motorcycle now, Bitsy?" Emily asked, trying to keep a straight face.

"Little ole' me?" Bitsy yelped. "I'd die of fright." She clasped her hands over her heart for added emphasis.

"We got some pink cycles comin' in if yer' interested, Em'ly," J.T. laughed.

She actually was interested but didn't say so.

"Ya'all heard from that cute Jonathan Charles?" Bitsy asked Emily, batting her eyelashes.

"A little," Emily replied, batting her eyelashes back at Bitsy.

"I heard he's comin' in June!" she squealed.

"Oh, how'd you hear that?"

"A coupla' the girls told me," Bitsy giggled. "I'm not the only one with a big crush on him, ya know!"

"Oh, really?' Emily said, resisting an urge to dump the brownies on Bitsy's head.

"Yes, really," she continued to giggle, "Were all gonna' try for him. You know, sorta' like a competition."

Emily wondered what Big Daddy would do if she popped Bitsy in her pretty little mouth.

"Well, we gotta' get back to the lot before the shipment comes in," J.T. said, grinning at them with teeth the size of piano keys, then doing a slight bow, he left with Bitsy.

"You better get that scowl off your face, Sugar," Miss Mattie said.

"It's automatic when I'm around Bitsy," she replied, turning to go out to her garden.

"And I noticed that it's especially automatic when she mentions Jonathan's name," Miss Mattie intoned, giving her a side glance.

Emily didn't say a word, just kept heading for the back door.

"You ready to watch a movie, Sugar?" Miss Mattie asked, after the supper dishes had been washed.

"I'm going to journal for a few minutes, then we can," Emily replied, heading for her room. "How about you make the popcorn, and I'll be out in a few minutes."

Emily sat on her bed, still fuming over Bitsy's remarks about Jonathan earlier that day and pulled out her journal to pour out her feelings, in hopes of getting rid of them.

Dear Journal,

Bitsy came into the bakery today and asked about Jonathan. She said there are other girls that like him too! I wanted to punch....

She stopped writing. Did she really want to put in writing what she wanted to do to Bitsy? And why had she even let that dopey girl take up space in her mind all day? It took way too much energy to stay angry, and Jonathan could barely stand the girl. She put her pen away and closed the journal, thinking about what Mr. and Mrs. Green had said at the café earlier. "Okay," she said out loud, "I'm just going to get over it!"

She smelled the popcorn popping in the kitchen, tossed her journal on the bed, and hurried out to the living room to watch a movie with her mama.

Chapter - 4

E mily texted Kelly Ann, *I want to come with you tomorrow when you get your blood pressure checked at Dr. Blackstone's.*

Why? Came the return text.

Tell you tomorrow.

"Okay, so what's up?" Kelly Ann asked the next day as they walked towards the doctor's office.

"I'm playing matchmaker, but don't tell on me," Emily laughed.

"With who?"

"Dr. Blackstone, and Gabriella, the owner of the new tearoom."

"Are you crazy or somethin'?" she asked, staring at Emily.

"Probably!" Emily shrugged, laughing.

A harried, unsmiling, Dr. Blackstone greeted them once they were settled into a room. He got right down to business fastening the blood pressure cuff around Kelly Ann's arm, saying very little as he watched her numbers appear. "You're doing great," he finally said, unfastening the cuff.

Emily waited a moment, then blurted out, "I'm going to be working at the new tearoom on Second Street, and I'd like to invite you to be my guest on opening day."

"I'm not much of a tea drinker," he replied, folding the blood pressure cuff and setting it on the rack.

"Well, would you come anyway?" she asked, not knowing what else to say.

He turned and looked at her. "Is it important to you?"

"Yes, it is," she said, holding her breath.

He hesitated, running his fingers through graying hair, then said, "Okay, let me know where and when."

"Well, that worked out well, you goofy matchmaker," Kelly Ann laughed as they left the doctor's office.

"I know!" she replied happily.

Kelly Ann turned to head toward town.

"Hey!" Emily said, turning in the opposite direction, "Would you like to come with me to visit Mrs. Tupper?"

"Who?" Kelly Ann asked, yawning.

"You remember, I told you about her. She was my grandma's roommate at the rest home."

"No thanks," she yawned again. "I need a nap."

"You always need a nap," Emily teased, hugging her.

At Creekside Villa, she found Mrs. Tupper enjoying an afternoon snack of orange slices and buttered popcorn.

"How are you?" Emily asked, going over and hugging the frail woman.

"I'm so happy to see you," she warbled, offering her an orange slice. "Have a seat next to me on the bed. I've been thinking of you and that young man of yours. Do you have any pictures to show me?"

As she took the orange slice, Emily knew it was useless to tell Mrs. Tupper that Jonathan wasn't her young man. She popped the orange in her mouth as she thought about it. Maybe, just maybe he actually *was* her young man. The young man she felt safe with. The young man she wanted to care about her only. *How had this all happened?* she wondered, scrolling through her pictures, finding one of Jonathan at a park in London holding a flower out to her. She showed it to Mrs. Tupper.

"Ahhh, he thinks of you constantly," the elderly woman murmured quietly.

She opened her mouth to deny the possibility, but the truth of it washed over her, and she said nothing.

"I would like to see your young man again when he comes back home," Mrs. Tupper said softly, leaning back against her pillow.

"I'll have him come with me when he gets here in June."

She started to look for more pictures but heard Mrs. Tupper softly snoring. Excitement always wore her out. Emily kissed her forehead and quietly tiptoed away.

"Sugar," Miss Mattie said the next morning, "would you run over to the pharmacy and pick up my heart medicine?"

"Sure!" Emily replied, untying her apron, and hurrying over to Second Street.

At Good Neighbor Pharmacy, Mr. Carver, the pharmacist, put three small bottles of medication into a bag, saying, "This is some serious heart medication that Miss Mattie is taking, Emily, so make sure she reads the instructions and takes it properly."

"Okay," Emily said, alarmed at his tone.

"Just call me if she has any questions."

"I will, thank you," she said, thinking she needed to pay more attention to her mama's health.

Emily heard laughter coming from across the street as she left the pharmacy and looked up to see the nuns from St. Daniels picking blackberries from the vines that grew up the west wall of the parish, putting them into small pails that hung from their arms.

"Hello, Sisters!" she greeted, walking across the street.

Sister Susan, Sister Caroline, and Sister Mary Katherine—also known as Sister Merry Kate—all greeted her, smiling with berry-stained teeth.

Emily laughed and started to hug each one, but Sister Merry Kate shouted, "Group hug!" and Emily found herself swathed in the folds of the three sisters' veils, as they all hugged her tightly, murmuring their greetings.

"I hear you're all riding motor scooters now!" Emily said, getting right to the point.

"Yes, for visitation purposes," Sister Merry Kate said, appearing to be quite excited about it.

"Tell her about Father Patrick's Harley!" Sister Susan said.

"A priest is riding a Harley?" Emily asked, delighted with the idea.

"He's always wanted one," confided Sister Caroline, blinking behind large glasses. "He also got a winged helmet and hob nailed boots, but the bishop recommended he not get leathers...whatever those are."

"We are going out for visitations soon; would you like to ride with us?" Sister Merry Kate asked, her eyes twinkling.

"Absolutely!" Emily said.

The Sisters picked up their pails and walked single file back to the church with Emily following, thinking they looked like cute penguins ambling across the Arctic, like on a nature show she'd watched. She laughed, loving these women.

"This way to the garage," Sister Caroline said, as they walked onto the grounds, then whispered, "It's actually our shed, but Father Patrick started calling it a garage when he parked his Harley in it."

In the distance, Emily could hear the blub...blub...blub of a motorcycle engine. "Father Patrick?" she asked.

"Oh yes," Sister Merry Kate said, picking up her pace. "He's warming up the engine while he waits for us. He's quite faithful about keeping the engine warmed; sometimes I hear it five or six times a day," she said with a side glance at Emily, and they both laughed.

When they turned the corner, there was Father Patrick sitting on a chromed motorcycle with his hands on high handlebars, sporting a gold-winged helmet. He turned and looked at her, and Emily saw her reflection in his mirrored visor. He shut the engine off.

"Father Patrick! I love your new wheels," she laughed.

"Thanks! I've always wanted a Harley," he said, his voice echoing inside the helmet. "I used to ride motorcycles when I was younger."

"Well, yay for you then," she said, walking all around the bike. "It's beautiful!"

The priest gave her a thumbs up and restarted his engine.

"We're all set," Sister Susan called from a corner of the garage where she sat on a pink scooter, fastening her helmet, which was also pink.

"Here's an extra one for you, Emily!" Sister Merrie Kate said, handing her a pink helmet.

Emily was excited as she climbed on the small seat behind Sister Susan and hung on.

Miss Mattie was sweeping the entry way to the bakery when she heard, the blub...blub...blub of a powerful motorcycle. She looked down the street and saw it coming her way, the sun glinting off the rider's winged helmet. The Harley was followed by three nuns on pink motor scooters.

The priest waved, and Miss Mattie did a double take seeing his clerical collar, then shouted, "Good morning, Father Patrick!" The nuns zipped by waving, one of them having a passenger with strands of red hair sticking out from under a pink helmet, who was waving like crazy.

"Emily?" Miss Mattie whispered, as the motorcycle parade passed, then waved her broom and yelled, "Hang on tight, Sugar!"

"Here's your medicine, Mama," Emily said, returning to the bakery from her motor scooter ride.

"Thank you," Miss Mattie said, "but we need to talk."

"What about?"

"Sugar, you need to let me know before you do things like ride on a motorcycle!"

"I do? Why?"

Miss Mattie appeared to be at a loss for words, then said, "Well, how would you feel if I was supposed to be goin' to the pharmacy, but while you were out sweepin', I come ridin' by on a pink motorcycle holdin' onto a nun?"

She looked at Emily waiting for an answer, but all she got was a snort as her girl clamped a hand over her mouth.

"No, I mean it, Sugar..." she started to say, but was interrupted by Emily howling with laughter, holding onto a parlor chair to keep from falling over.

"Lord, have mercy..." she uttered, heading back to her kitchen as Emily cackled in the background.

Workers were coming in and out of the tearoom when Emily arrived early Saturday morning. She found Gabriella in the midst of unpacking linens; a smile of relief lighting up her face when she saw Emily. "Just in time," she said, motioning her over. "I could use an opinion."

Emily walked over and looked into a box the shop owner was unpacking, seeing brightly colored napkins and tablecloths in buttery yellows, sky blues, and light corals. "They're beautiful," she exclaimed. "They look happy!"

"Okay," Gabriella said, opening the box next to it, "What about these colors?"

Emily peered into the next box which held napkins and tablecloths in deeper tones: pine greens; deep turquoise, and burgundy.

"Which box would you choose for the table settings in my tearoom?" Gabriella asked, worry lines creasing her forehead. "I've been going back and forth all morning."

Emily glanced into each box again, and said, "Both!"

"Both?"

"Yes! Switching them out from day to day would make your tearoom more interesting. Or if someone is having a party, they could choose which they wanted, the bright ones or the darker ones."

"Good point," Gabriella said, her worry lines softening. "I'll keep them both!"

They began pulling the tablecloths and napkins out of the box, folding as they went.

"Let me show you where I'll be keeping these," Gabriella said. "I'll have you work on this project while I get busy on something else."

Emily was a little disappointed that they wouldn't work together. She had questions for her match-making venture that needed answering, and hurried through the chore so she could rejoin Gabriella.

At the end of the day, the lace curtains had been hung, the tables set, and everything was in picture perfect order.

"I'm nervous about my grand opening," Gabriella confessed, as she and Emily looked everything over to make sure it was as perfect as they could get it.

"What makes you the most nervous?"

"I guess I'm concerned that people won't come. A tearoom in Mountain Grove is a big gamble."

"Well, I've invited someone already, and I'll do a lot more in the next five days," Emily promised. "How about if we make up some flyers to let everyone know?"

"That's a lovely idea," Gabriella said. "Could I hire you to do that, also?"

"Sure!"

"And I want you to keep track of your time. I insist on paying for all of this work."

Yay, thought Emily. It would go a long way in buying a lens she wanted for her camera. Which reminded her. "Do you want me to bring my camera and take pictures of opening day?"

"Oh, lovely idea!" the tearoom proprietress said.

Emily smiled, knowing just the picture she was going to get of two special people. She hoped Dr. Blackstone wore a tie when he came, and maybe he wouldn't run his fingers through his hair before she got the picture. He'd done it at his office, and she left thinking he looked a bit comical, with strands of hair sticking up.

Emily was sitting next to Miss Mattie in church, when she happened to look up and see Gilbert and Kelly Ann walk in. Actually, Kelly Ann was waddling in, with an obvious big belly. She watched amazed as Gilbert led her down the aisle, a protective hand on her arm. Miss Rose looked up and saw them, then gathered up her Bible and scooted down the pew to make room for the two. Gilbert thanked her and motioned for Kelly Ann to go first.

Emily looked around to see how the rest of the congregation was reacting, but all she saw were smiles. She realized she'd been holding her breath and let it out slowly as Pastor Alex nodded to the two and smiled, then told everyone to open their hymnals to page seventy-two.

Monday afternoon, Miss Beasley came into the bakery with the usual frown on her face. "I'll have a half dozen blueberry muffins, please," she sniffed in Miss Mattie's general direction.

"How are you doin' today?" Miss Mattie asked, in an attempt to be friendly.

"I'm very disturbed by church attendance yesterday," Miss Beasley said, standing ramrod straight. "Imagine! An unmarried pregnant girl coming into church, as pretty as you please, and the pastor actually smiling at her!"

Uh-oh! Emily thought, looking up at Miss Mattie's face where a storm had begun to brew.

"Well, it's a shame you felt that way," Miss Mattie said, controlling her voice. "I imagine that God was very pleased to see her there though."

"Don't tell me you *approve* of that young girl's predicament!" Miss Beasley snapped.

"I approve of a young girl's courage," Miss Mattie said, "and doin' the best she can for her baby. And I approve of her comin' to church, and trusting us to love her, and not judge her."

"Well, I think you and I see things much differently!" Miss Beasley huffed. "It's simply outrageous!"

"And I think you should ask God how to see it, because you're remindin' me of one of those self-righteous, straight-outta'-the-New-Testament-Pharisees!" Miss Mattie said tersely.

Miss Beasley's eyes grew big, looking as though they might pop right out of her head. "Well, I never!"

"Yes ma'am, you got the Pharisees pegged!" Miss Mattie said, standing her ground. "You need to go home and talk to Jesus!"

Miss Beasley wheeled around and headed for the door. "I will never set foot in this place again," she called over her shoulder.

"Well, don't let the door hit you in the butt on the way out," Miss Mattie said, as the bakery door slammed. After a moment she turned and looked at Emily. "I'm not sure I handled that very well."

"I think you handled it perfectly," Emily said, meaning it.

Emily couldn't help herself, she had to see what had changed Gilbert's mind about Kelly Ann. She found him sitting alone in the school cafeteria the next day and set her food tray near him.

"Ok, what gives?" she asked.

"What do you mean?"

"You were mad about Kelly Ann being pregnant a couple of weeks ago, then yesterday you're escorting her down the church aisle!"

"Oh that..."

She just stared at him.

"Ok, so I've been hangin' out with Pastor Alex, and he's been teaching me about God and stuff."

"And?"

"I've been sort of practicin' seeing things from God's perspective and reacting differently."

She nodded for him to go on.

"I'm a mess and have done things I'm not proud of. Pastor Alex said Jesus took the hit for my mess when He was on the cross. I accepted that, and I accepted Him, and now I want to love the way Jesus does." He looked at Emily. "I'm practicin' on Kelly Ann, with no strings attached. For now, I'm just her friend."

Emily felt a ripple of delight. "Yay," she said softly. "What about the baby?"

"Kids need to be loved. You an' I know that better than most people. I will love that kid, no matter what happens between me an' Kelly Ann."

"How does Kelly Ann feel about all of that?"

He shrugged. "I can tell she sort of likes me, and I know she likes the way I look after her. So, I'll just take it slow. I have feelings that I have to sort out too; I was pretty shocked about the baby."

"Who wouldn't be?" Emily said, nodding that she understood. An idea came to her. "I'm going to go to parenting classes with Kelly Ann next week. Do you want to come too?"

"Why are you goin'?"

"Well, she'd probably be too shy to go alone, and the other reason is that I'm going to be the baby's aunt, and I need to make sure I know about babies, and parenting skills, or in my case, 'auntie skills'."

"And you'll probably be a mama one day too," he added.

She stared at him. "That overwhelms me to think about. For now, I'll focus on auntie skills."

"Good idea," he said, "and I'll go with you and Kelly Ann."

"Really?"

"Well, I haven't exactly been raised in a palace, you know, and I've got a lot to learn."

She smiled. "It'll be fun if we all go."

"Just let me know where and when."

"I'll text you just as soon as I have it figured out," she said, relief flooding through her.

"Does Gilbert seem to be actin' weird to you?" Kelly Ann asked as they went on their daily afternoon walk.

"What do you mean?"

"Well, now he says he wants to come to parenting classes with me an' you, and before that he asked me to church, and escorted me like I was the Queen of Sheba."

"Well, I think the three of us could use help in the parenting area, since we came from crazy homes, don't you?"

"I guess, but it seems weird."

"What's weird?"

"What I just said about him treatin' me like I'm fragile. It's like he's being protective or somethin'."

"Well, friends do protect each other, you know," she replied, side-stepping Kelly's Ann's line of questioning.

"Yes, I know. And I'm not complainin'." She turned and smiled, "He's really a nice guy."

"Yes, he is!" Emily replied, feeling very happy about the way things were going.

The three friends walked into the parenting class, which was being held in the library conference room. Emily noticed that a few people smiled at her, and she could tell they thought that Gilbert was the baby's father, and she was a tag-along friend.

The leader smiled as they walked in and handed them each a small book on parenting. "I'm Miss Vickie," the instructor said. "This will be our guideline for the class, but we can talk about any area of parenting you would like."

There were about twenty people there, and after everyone was settled, Miss Vickie said, "At the beginning of each class I always like to ask, "How many of you came from normal, well-adjusted homes?"

One person raised their hand. "I think I did!" she replied sheepishly, and the whole class laughed.

Miss Vickie laughed along with them. "How many of you really don't know if your home was dysfunctional, because it seemed normal to you?"

Half the class raised their hands on that one.

"And how many know you came from truly dysfunctional homes?"

Hands shot up, including Emily, Kelly Ann, and Gilbert.

"How wonderful you've all come," she said, meaning it. "And how wonderful that you've all said, *The dysfunction stops here!* I'm so proud of you. Now let's open our books to the first chapter."

"Mama, you don't happen to have a business directory, or a map of Mountain Grove, do you?" Emily asked, walking into the bakery kitchen one Saturday.

"No, I don't, Sugar. What do you need them for?"

Emily sighed. "A map project for my geography class at school."

Miss Mattie shrugged. "So draw! You know every buildin' there is on First and Second Street, and probably every store owner in them."

Emily thought for a moment. "I do know them all!" she replied, wondering at the happiness that filled her, just saying those words.

"There's rulers and pencils under the cash drawer, you can start right now."

"I'm going to walk the two streets and take notes. I don't want to leave anyone out." She was suddenly excited about the project.

As she walked up and down First and Second Street, penciling in every business, she realized that she wanted to include more places. Her places. Gus's service station, the church, and church parsonage on Elderberry Way, Mr. and Mrs. Apple's home, and her old house on Sycamore Lane, the Charles' home and Kelly Ann's home on Sugar Pine Road. She would draw it all, because it wasn't a true picture of her home if she left any of her village family out.

She returned and sat at a small parlor table in the bakery where there was ample light coming in from the large plate glass window. She labored over the map for hours, getting the streets just right, getting the homes of the people she loved just right. She wanted to leave out the school because it wasn't a happy place to her. "Too many mean kids," she murmured, but her teacher would expect it to be included, so she penciled it in.

As she sat drawing, she looked out the front window, across to Emerson Park. She would include all the details of the park, especially the willow tree, which she had sat under for many hours when life got too hard, and she would include the statue of General Emerson. How many times had she sat in the General's granite lap, her legs draped over his arms and her head against his stone chest. It had been her favorite place to read her library books or escape to when her home life got too hard to handle. She smiled as she remembered that the General was the first male she had ever trusted.

She felt her mama come up behind her. "What do you think?" Emily asked, holding the map up so she could see it.

"I think you love this village," her mama said, peering at the paper. "Jus' look at all the detail you put in! Your teacher will give you an A for sure!"

"I do love this village," she replied, then pointed to one of the little squares that read, *Cooke's Bakery*. "This place is my favorite. I'll never forget when I lived with my parents and my world was going crazy, I could always come here, and you would sit and listen to me, and help me!"

"Well," her mama said, taking her hand, "I loved that sweet red-haired girl, who had too much sadness in her eyes, an' I'm glad I was a help to you then."

"You were the world to me, Mama," she said, squeezing her hand. "You are still the world to me."

"And I always prayed for a daughter," her mama said, taking a handkerchief out of her apron pocket, and dabbing tears that flowed. "And jus' look how God answered my prayers!"

"He answered both our prayers," she replied, as the bell over the bakery door jingled and a customer walked in.

"You dry your eyes, while I go wait on him," Emily whispered, giving her mama a quick hug.

After the customer left with his lemon meringue pie, Emily went back over to the parlor table to put things away, glancing at the directions for the map assignment one more time, then cried, "Oh no!"

"What's wrong, Sugar?" her mama asked.

"My teacher doesn't want houses or landscaping on the map, just businesses! I should have read the directions more carefully."

"Oh, Sugar...and after all your hard work!" she said, hurrying over.

"Looks like I get to start over," Emily said, taking out a fresh sheet of paper. "I might as well throw this other one away..."

"Stop!" Miss Mattie said. "I want that one."

"Why?"

"Because," she replied, picking the map up, "my girl put her whole heart into it, drawin' the places she loves. I'm going to frame it and hang it up in my room."

"You are something else, mama," Emily laughed.

"True art speaks to your heart, and this speaks to my heart," her mama said, whisking the paper away.

Chapter - 5

Emily was sitting in her room doing homework when a strange text came in:

eM ily we ar e home no w .

It wasn't a number she recognized, and her heart leaped, wondering if it was her dad. She quickly texted back: *Who is this?*

mRss apple, came the reply.

Mrs. Apple? Are you home now? she quickly texted back, her heart doing a happy dance.

Yesssss an d Im text ing wi th my ne w phone. Wou ld you comeee 4 suppppper tomorrow nite?.

Emily laughed. *I'd love to*, she replied.

A skeleton emoji appeared, then the word *whooops*. Finally a heart emoji appeared along with a text, *seeeee you at 6;;00. Chiken pot pie onnn the menu.*

Yum! She texted back, as her mouth began to water.

The next evening walking up the hill toward the Apple's home, she thought about how, when one of the townspeople in her life was missing, it seemed like a part of her family was missing. She was so glad the Apples were back home where they belonged. She thought of the picture of the town sign she'd hung up in her room that read, "We aren't just a town; We're a family". It was the first thing she saw when she woke in the morning. It was also one of the things in her life that she was the most thankful for: that her dad had moved her here those many months ago. Thankfulness righted her world when it wanted to go over the cliff into despair or self-pity.

The next hard part was walking by her old house next door to the Apple's home. She tried to do it pretty often, hoping that the next time it wouldn't pierce her heart as she remembered the horror of being abandoned there, and all the unhappiness that house represented. It helped that a new family had moved in, as evidenced by the many toys scattered on the lawn. She could sort of feel happiness flowing out of the house now. It was a good thing.

She knocked on the Apple's door, and heard footsteps hurrying to let her in. Then she heard Mrs. Apple saying, "Scoot! Scoot!" just on the other side of the door.

The door opened with Mrs. Apple's wedged shoe blocking something. Emily saw a gray paw attempt to climb over the shoe, and Mrs. Apple reach down and grab it.

As the door swung open, Emily was greeted by Mrs. Apple, who was still as round as an apple, and holding a small grey kitten that boxed at her nose.

"Emily! Come in!" Mrs. Apple exclaimed happily, as the kitten gave her another gentle one-two punch.

Emily threw her arms around her. "I'm so glad you're home," she exclaimed, feeling the kitten pawing at her head.

As she pulled back from the hug, something was stuck in her hair.

"Mr. Whiskers," Mrs. Apple, admonished, "let go of her!"

Emily stood patiently as the cat's paw was untwined from her hair and looked up to see Mr. Apple hurrying from the kitchen, a big grin on his face. He stopped short when he saw the situation.

"That blasted cat, Helena!" he exclaimed, hurrying over to see if he could help.

His wife ignored him, as she gently freed the last of Emily's hair.

Emily kept her distance from the cat as she stepped over to Mr. Apple, who hugged her, thumping her heartily on the back. "So good to see you, dear," he said with a gentle squeeze.

"I'm so happy to be here," she replied, noticing that Mr. Apple was looking very thin, and had lost his own round, apple-look. "How are you feeling now?"

"Perfect!" he said, with a quick pound on his chest. "I plan to last another fifty years!"

"Yay!" Emily laughed, still not liking it that he was so skinny. "And I see you have a new family member!"

"Mrs. Apple has a new family member," he said gruffly. "I'm not exactly on board with the cat situation."

"Soup's on!" said Mrs. Apple cheerfully, again ignoring her husband. "Let's all sit down, and we can visit while we're eating!" She tucked the kitten into a small crate as they went into the kitchen.

On the way in, she whispered to Emily, "He actually loves Mr. Whiskers!"

Emily glanced at her doubtfully.

"So, how is life over the bakery?" Mr. Apple asked, as his wife served steaming bowls of chicken pot pie.

"I love it!" Emily said, her mouth already watering. "And I've started a new garden in the back yard. I'll show it to you the next time you come to the bakery."

Mrs. Apple pushed a basket of warm bread towards her. "And that young man of yours? What do you hear from him?"

Without skipping a beat, she said, "He misses me, but likes it in England. He'll be home in June." She wondered at the feeling she got when she said that. For today, he was her young man. Would that change? She didn't know. All she knew was today she wanted him to be her young man.

"Tell me about Mr. Whiskers," she said, changing the subject. "Where did you get him?"

"You tell her while I check on dessert," Mrs. Apple said to her husband, giving Emily a quick wink, as she rose from the table.

"Oh, that blasted cat!" Mr. Apple groused. "It's your story Helena, you should be telling it."

"You tell it, Herbert dear," she urged, opening the freezer door, "I'm busy."

"Alright," he grumbled. "Our young neighbor boy in Whitefield had a cat that had kittens. When they were old enough, his mother told him to find homes for them. He came to our door with a little sign, saying five dollars a kitten. I don't think his mother knew he'd be charging," Mr. Apple laughed. "I felt sorry for him, and knew Mrs. Apple loved kittens, so I bought her one."

"And gave the boy a twenty-dollar bill and told him to keep the change," Mrs. Apple added, her voice echoing from inside the freezer.

"Yes, I thought it was a good investment in a young entrepreneur," he agreed.

"And you wanted a cat," she heard Mrs. Apple murmur.

Mr. Apple scooped out the last bite of his pot pie, then rose from his seat, "Better go check on that blasted cat, he's been crated up a long time."

"Yes, a full twenty minutes!" Mrs. Apple mused, setting home-made ice cream on the counter, and grinning at Emily.

"We'll let the ice cream thaw a little, then I'll cut up some berries after I finish my meal," Mrs. Apple said, returning to the table and digging back into her pot pie.

"You spoil me!" Emily said, reaching for another piece of the warm bread.

"Nothing I love doing better, dear," she smiled, peering over large glasses.

Mr. Apple came back in carrying Mr. Whiskers. "I'll keep him on my lap so you can finish your lunch, Helena," he said, nuzzling the kitten against his cheek.

"I appreciate that," his wife responded, with a quick glance at Emily.

"How is school going, Emily?" Mr. Apple asked, as Mr. Whiskers climbed to his shoulder and pawed his left ear.

"I don't like it, and wish I could homeschool," she replied frankly, scooping the last bite of her pot pie from the bowl. It got very quiet, and when she looked up, she saw that Mr. and Mrs. Apple were both waiting for an explanation.

Another can of worms that she wished she hadn't opened, but knew she had to explain.

"I've tried making friends, like you told me to do last year, but it just doesn't work. I'm from a different planet than the other girls, and we don't speak the same language." She looked up at Mrs. Apple, "I can't breathe after a few minutes of their small talk. They don't know how lucky they are to have good homes, and small, fixable problems."

"I see," Mrs. Apple said.

"But I have two close friends in Kelly Ann and Gilbert."

"Sometimes having a couple of close friends is all we need," she agreed, as she stood and went over to the counter, taking out a knife and cutting board for the berries.

"And I've got a whole village of people I love," Emily reminded her, then added, "Did you hear that Kelly Ann is pregnant?"

Mrs. Apple dropped the knife on the counter and whirled around. "No!" she gasped.

Emily sat blinking, then found her voice. "I didn't mean to upset you!"

"It's alright, dear." Emily could hear the stress in her voice. "Is she still living with her mother?"

"No, she's moved here, and will have the baby here."

"I see," Mrs. Apple's voice broke slightly, as she resumed cutting up the berries. "Does she have any plans with the baby's father?"

"Are you crying?"

"I'm just a mite upset," she replied, bringing a flowered hanky out of her apron pocket and dabbing her eyes. "My heart goes out to young girls in that situation."

Emily stood up and walked over to the counter next to her. "No, she doesn't have any plans with the baby's dad; he's a creep and she doesn't want him involved. But he doesn't want to be involved anyway."

"How difficult that must be," she said, wiping her eyes again.

"But, guess what?" Emily said, trying to cheer her up, "We're all going to parenting classes with her!"

"We? Who is *we*?"

"Me, Gilbert and Kelly Ann."

"That's odd!" she mused, sprinkling sugar on the berries. "Does Gilbert have feelings for Kelly Ann?"

Emily didn't know what to say, and just stared at her.

"And you've promised not to say anything, isn't that right?" Mrs. Apple asked.

"How'd you know?"

"Because it all adds up, and it must mean that Kelly Ann doesn't know Gilbert has feelings for her either."

"Ugh," sighed Emily, "you're too good at this!"

Mrs. Apple chuckled and said, "Tell me what I can do to help her."

Emily thought for a moment. "I'm not sure. I gave her a journal, just like you gave me."

"You did?"

"Yes! I even told her the same thing you told me: one day she'd have her own home and to start planning now who she wanted in that home, and the things she wanted in a husband."

"And the traits in a husband that she *doesn't* want." Mrs. Apple reminded her.

"Yep, I went through it all," Emily shrugged. "I guess she forgot to follow the instructions."

They both laughed. "Well, we do have choices!" her neighbor chuckled. "Maybe give her another one for this new stage of her life. Tell her to also put in it what she wants for her little one and keep adding to it. Even the daddy she wants for her baby one day."

"I think a future daddy has already shown up," she confided. "Gilbert loves her."

"And he's okay with her having a child?"

"All I know is that since Gilbert started following God, he sees everything differently, and acts differently."

"I see," the older woman mused.

"He was raised in a crummy home," Emily continued, "and said kids need a good dad, as much as a good mom."

"How about Gilbert's mother, what is she like?"

"I don't think he even knows his mom; she left when he was a baby, and his dad drinks all the time."

"Oh dear!" Mrs. Apple said. "I've met him once or twice, but I think I would like to know him better. He sounds like an incredible young man!"

"He is pretty incredible now, but when I met him, he was a mess." She thought a moment, then whispered, "And he smelled awful too."

"Well, that sometimes goes with neglect."

"Pastor Alex helps him, and lets Gilbert stay in the church basement when his dad gets mean."

"Well, that's wonderful!" Mrs. Apple said, her eyes lighting up. "Everyone needs a good friend like Pastor Alex when things are difficult."

Emily looked at her. "You were a good friend when I lived next door with my parents. You helped me out so much, and you were a safe place for me to come to. I'll never forget it!"

Mrs. Apple resumed dabbing at her eyes with the hanky. "I don't know what to say, dear!"

"You don't need to say anything," she said, giving her a hug. "I just wanted you to know. You and Miss Mattie made a huge difference in my life."

"And we wouldn't have it any other way," she sniffed.

"And you both cried when I told you," Emily laughed, hugging her again.

Chapter - 6

Emily was bursting with ideas for giving Kelly Ann a baby shower, as she headed over to see Penelope about using the church fellowship hall to hold it in.

She knocked on the parsonage door and thought she heard some kind of scurrying inside the house, so she knocked again. The parsonage door opened slowly, and a forlorn looking Penelope peeked out from behind the door, a towel wrapped tightly around her head.

"Oh Emily, I almost didn't answer the door! I'm so glad it's you," she cried, pulling her into the living room. "Sit!" she ordered, pointing to the ottoman.

Emily did as she was told, and said, "What's wrong?"

"This!" cried Penelope, whipping the large towel off her head.

Emily stared in amazement as orange strands of hair fell down around Penelope's lovely face. "Oh!" she murmured. "What happened?"

"I dyed it myself," she wailed. "I was trying to save money!"

"Oh," Emily murmured again, making a quick mental note never to try dying her own hair. "Did you color it orange on purpose?"

"No," she sniffed, "It was supposed to come out blonde!"

Emily tried to think how to help. "Would you like me to run to Good Neighbor Pharmacy and see if they have black hair dye? Maybe we could fix it back to your natural color."

"I already tried that," Penelope said, drying her eyes with a corner of the orange-stained towel.

Emily thought for a moment. "How about if I called *Violet's House of Beauty* and see if they can help?"

"No! I don't want to go to a public place," she wailed, the tears starting up again, "they'll laugh!"

Emily thought they might laugh too, especially Charmagne, the bubble-gum-popping main hairdresser. But what choice was there? "Let me call ahead, I'll get them to laugh over the phone, so they don't laugh when you come in."

The plan actually made the pastor's wife chuckle. "That's so crazy, it might work!" she said, cheering up.

Emily phoned the House of Beauty and gave Charmagne a quick explanation of Penelope's predicament.

Charmagne murmured an expletive, popped her bubble gum twice, and said, "Send her over at 3:00, honey! Happens all the time!"

"You're all set for 3:00 today!" Emily said after hanging up the phone.

"Did she laugh?" Penelope asked mournfully.

"No, she swore!"

"Wonderful! I'm so glad," said the pastor's wife, then stopped and looked at Emily. "That probably wasn't a proper response."

"It was an honest one," Emily shrugged, and they both laughed. "And you'll have your shiny black hair back in no time."

"Thank you," she said, heaving a sigh of relief. "Sorry for being a crybaby, I should've just had them color it to begin with. Now it's going to cost a small fortune." She looked like she might cry again.

"It'll be fine," Emily assured her. "Just eat beans for a week to make up for the cost."

Penelope just stared at her. "And wouldn't my husband be thrilled about that!"

"Probably not!" Emily said, trying to control the belly laugh that bubbled up each time she looked at Penelope's orange hair. She changed the subject. "I came over to talk to you about a baby shower for Kelly Ann."

"What a lovely idea," Penelope replied, running her fingers absentmindedly through orange locks. "That new tearoom would be a perfect place to have it!""

"Actually, I was thinking the church fellowship hall would be the best place."

"Oh!" Penelope frowned, "it's not very festive."

Emily thought for a moment on how to word it. "Kelly Ann doesn't need festive, she needs acceptance."

Penelope nodded for her to go on.

"She feels really stupid and bad about being pregnant, especially since the baby's dad is a real jerk." She glanced up at Penelope. "Her words, not mine."

The pastor's wife grinned and nodded that she understood.

"She's uncomfortable coming to church, wondering what everyone is thinking because she's pregnant, but church is exactly where she needs to be."

"I see," Penelope mused, "and I couldn't agree more. How about if we decorate the fellowship hall and the church pays to have a lunch catered?"

Emily hesitated for a moment. "That's really nice, but it would be better if each of the church ladies cooked their best dish and brought it to her shower."

"Why is that?"

"Homemade food talks!"

Penelope laughed. "What does homemade food say?"

"It says, 'I went to a lot of trouble for you because you're worth it. I planned it out; I went all the way to the grocery store, and I cooked for hours—for you!'" Emily shrugged. "That's what homemade food says, and it's what Kelly Ann needs to hear right now."

"I think you're exactly right," Penelope said, a lovely smile appearing under her orange hair. "Let's get it on the calendar!"

Emily's next stop was at *Tea Time*.

"Welcome, Emily!" Gabriella greeted her, as she walked through the lace-curtained door.

Emily hugged her, then explained the mission. "I was wondering if I could rent your gloves, hats, and boas for Kelly Ann's upcoming baby shower?"

"Rent them?"

She explained her reasons for wanting it at the church, then added, "I feel weird not having Kelly Ann's shower here, but I want to support you and just rent what I need."

Gabriella assured her, "I am honored to have a way to support Kelly Ann. You must let me lend them to you, free of charge. I'll load up an old-fashioned trunk with all you've asked for, and have it delivered to the church."

"Perfect! Thank you!" Emily said, mentally crossing one more thing off her list. The cake for the shower was the final thing she needed to tend to, but her mama would gladly take care of that. She just hoped that she could pull off a surprise shower for Kelly Ann.

"Tell me what kinda' cake you have in mind, Sugar!" Miss Mattie said, when Emily explained the surprise shower.

"I know she loves chocolate, but we need a white icing to decorate it in blue and pink, since we don't know if she's having a boy or girl yet."

"Or yellow. They're even doin' cakes in neutral colors now," she said, shaking her head as though she wondered what the world was coming to. "How many women will it need to serve?"

"I hope around sixty," Emily replied, then frowned. "I just thought of something..."

"What, Sugar?"

"What if the church ladies aren't nice to her, or say something about her being single, and so young and having a baby?"

"They wouldn't say that!"

"They might go all churchy on her and quote scripture," she murmured, growing worried. *Why hadn't she thought of this before?*

"The only scripture anyone would quote would be, "the greatest of these is love" and love her and that sweet baby she's carryin'."

Emily looked at her doubtfully.

"Sugar, no one is goin' to come to a baby shower to insult the mama! No one!"

"What if they did?"

"We'd have us a fanny-kicking contest!" Miss Mattie said, folding her arms and meaning it.

"Perfect," said Emily, and they both laughed.

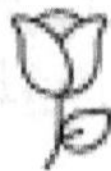

A week later, Emily headed up the hill to Ike's house, texting Kelly Ann on the way, "I'm on my way over! Let's walk!"

When Kelly Ann opened the door a few minutes later, looking sleepy and unkept, Emily said, "Come on lazy bones, put on a pretty top and let's go for a walk. It's beautiful outside!"

Kelly Ann frowned, and groaned, "I'm tired!"

"A walk will give you energy," Emily insisted, hoping her friend didn't get suspicious.

Kelly Ann groaned again but went in the other room and came back out in a cute pink maternity top and her hair combed. "Why are we goin' for a walk durin' the hottest part of the day?" she complained as they walked out the door. "You know my feet swell up!"

"I have something I want you to see!" was Emily's only explanation. "First, we have to stop by the church though. I need to return this to Penelope," she said, holding up a small bottle of *Chili Pepper* colored nail polish.

"She loaned you some derned nail polish?" Kelly Ann asked, appearing skeptical.

"Come on goofy!" Emily laughed, pulling her out the door. She wished she was returning something more substantial; Kelly Ann was suspicious now.

As they approached the church, Emily hoped Kelly Ann wouldn't notice all the cars in the parking lot.

"They aren't havin' a Bible study, are they," Kelly Ann asked, looking at all the cars.

"Nope, no Bible study," she replied, leading her to the back of the church. "Penelope told me she'd be back here doing something." She pulled open the door to the Fellowship Hall and motioned for her friend to go in first. Kelly Ann hesitated, but finally went through the door.

An arched entryway of pink and blue balloons was the first thing they saw. Emily motioned her on, as Kelly Ann gave a puzzled look. "Keep going," Emily said, gently pushing her through the arch.

"Surprise!" yelled forty-five women all at once, causing Kelly Ann to leap with fright.

"What in..." she cried, stopping short of a swear word. She stared at Emily, not knowing what to do.

"Come on, goofy!" Emily laughed, pushing her forward.

They walked past the smiling women, sitting at beautifully decorated round tables, attired in large fashionable hats, waving gloved hands, with colorful boas around their necks. Emily looked out over the tables. At one table were Mrs. Apple, Mrs. Kingery, and even Millie had come. Mrs. Green, Mrs. Montoya, Miss Rose and Miss Violet, Mrs. Charles, Gabriella, and many other women she didn't even know, all waving, all giving their best for her friend. At a table to the left Emily spotted the nuns from St. Daniels: Sister Mary Katheryn—or as some called her, Sister Merry Kate—Sister Susan, and Sister Caroline who were also known as *The Blues Sisters*. They all waved, grinning under white veiled habits, with musical instruments sitting at their feet, ready to perform. Sister Susan gave two thumbs up when Kelly Ann glanced her way.

"This is all for me?" Kelly Ann squeaked.

"Absolutely!" Emily said, ushering her to a table where Penelope and Miss Mattie stood with fashionable hats, gloves, and boas for them both. Laughing they swung brightly colored feather boas around their necks, pulled on long white gloves, and placed stylish hats on their heads. When they were properly attired, they turned towards the tables where the seated women gave them a hearty round of applause. Kelly Ann curtsied, not knowing what else to do, and quickly sat down in her seat, blushing profusely. Emily laughed and sat down next to her, with Miss Mattie on the other side.

Penelope remained standing near Kelly Ann. "Welcome Kelly Ann! These women are here to support you and your baby in any way they can. Each who are here want you to know that they are available anytime you need them, from delivery to help you might need with three a.m. feedings."

"Babies eat at three in the mornin'?" Kelly Ann yelped.

The women laughed and Penelope continued, "These women want you to know that they are praying for you and your little one. Here is a list of mothers who would welcome you to call them with any question you might have." She handed the paper to Kelly Ann, who glanced at it, then looked out at the women. "Thank you," she whispered, her lips trembling slightly.

"You're welcome," the women chorused.

"Each of the women has written you a card with their very best advice for motherhood," Penelope continued, and we'll give them all to you, but one of the mothers, Mrs. Charles, who has four children, would like to read hers out loud."

Mrs. Charles stood up and faced Kelly Ann, smiling, "Blessings on you and your baby, Kelly Ann. I have little ones, and here is what I've learned." She coughed nervously, then began. "Babies are a gift from God. That used to make me anxious, realizing I'd been trusted with a human life, but here's what I learned to do: Pray for God's wisdom, for what I call, "the knowing". When it comes, teach your child, unafraid.

Love your child lavishly and remind them often that God also loves them lavishly."

There was a hush as Mrs. Charles took her seat. The deacon's wife took out a hanky and dabbed her eyes, and someone blew their nose loudly.

Penelope stood back up, and said, "Before we eat, our older sister, Miss Gertrude, would like to say a prayer for Kelly Ann and her baby."

Miss Gertrude, a woman of eighty-five, rose to her feet, pulled a cane off the back of her chair, and thumped her way slowly to the front of the table and stood by Kelly Ann.

Emily felt her stomach tighten into a knot, "Let her be kind," she whispered in the form of a prayer.

"Greetings to you and your baby," Miss Gertrude warbled, her head shaking with a mild palsy, as she set a veined hand on Kelly Ann's shoulder.

Kelly Ann looked up at her and smiled, as everyone bowed their heads in prayer.

"Our great and good Father," Miss Gertrude began, and a Presence could be felt by every woman.

Miss Gertrude waited a moment, in no hurry.

"Bless this young woman," she prayed, her voice shaky, but strong. "You, who know all things, teach her. Give her great wisdom for this child You are sending to her."

Emily looked up, thinking the prayer was over, but Miss Gertrude continued, "As you have chosen this mother for this child, we pray also that the child be given just the right father. A daddy chosen by You."

Emily heard a slight gasp among the women, but everyone sat very still as Miss Gertrude told God exactly what she wanted for Kelly Ann. Emily peeked under her eyelashes to see if Kelly Ann was upset by the prayer, but her friend's eyes were closed and there was a smile on her lips.

Miss Gertrude thanked God for the food, for the women present, for Kelly Ann, and her baby, then said "Amen", and thumped back to her chair.

Penelope rose to her feet and spoke directly to Kelly Ann. "Each of these women has prepared their best dish for you, an offering to let you know that they are behind you all the way. We have some marvelous cooks here, and I think you're going to love the language they speak in."

The women laughed, and Kelly Ann led the food line, making sure to scoop out a little of each dish. Emily followed, looking over the small feast that the good women had prepared, her mouthwatering, and her heart overflowing.

Everyone laughed and talked as they ate. Kelly Ann got up twice to refill her plate and made occasional comments on how delicious everything was.

After the meal, a dessert cart was wheeled in with a beautifully decorated, three-layer cake. Sparkling baby toys made of colored sugar adorned the cake, and the women broke into spontaneous applause when they saw it. Miss Mattie's smile was as bright as the new moon as the women oohed and aahed over her masterpiece that had taken all day for her to bake and decorate.

As the cake was being cut and served, The Blues Sisters came to the front of the room with their instruments, and softly played two lullabies. The women applauded, and someone yelled, "Encore!" Delighted, Sister Merry Kate picked up her saxophone and played a solo of *Hey Jude*, one of her very favorites.

Later, when it was time to open the gifts, the generosity of the women overwhelmed Kelly Ann. At one-point tears streamed down her face as she tore open the pastel wrappings of gift after gift of every article of clothing an infant would need, thanks to the combined planning of Mrs. Charles and the president of the Woman's Auxiliary. Some of the women had combined their money to make sure the baby had a crib, a highchair, and a car seat for traveling. The very gifts spoke to Kelly Ann about how much these women cared about her, and best of all, how much they cared about her baby.

At the end of the day, Mr. Charles came with his pick-up, loaded up all the gifts, and took them to Kelly Ann's house. The leftover food was divided up and put onto paper plates covered with aluminum foil for husbands and kids, so the ladies didn't need to fix dinner when they got home.

Kelly Ann stood at the door of the Fellowship Hall and said goodbye to each woman, and thanked them for coming, thanked them for the food, and for the wonderful gifts for her baby.

Emily helped with the clean up as she waited.

Later, as they walked home, Emily had to ask, "Were you upset by Miss Gertrude's prayer for you and a daddy for the baby?"

"Nope," Kelly Ann replied, "it was exactly what I prayed for, too. Except I thought God was mad at me for bein' pregnant and all. She said my exact words that I'd said to God, even asked for a "daddy" like I said. But then I didn't ask anymore, just kept wonderin' if He was mad at me. He gave that woman word for word what I said to Him. Nothing coulda' made me happier."

"And you're praying for a daddy for the baby?"

"Course I am. I don't want her raised like me!"

"Her?"

"Oh, it's just a feelin'. I don't know for sure it's a girl."

Emily nodded and they walked on in silence.

When Mrs. Kingery got home late that afternoon from the baby shower, Mr. Kingery was lying back in his Lazy Boy recliner, with his stocking feet up and his hound dog, Blue, lying nearby.

"Here's yer' supper," his wife said, handing him the paper plate of food from the baby shower.

"What's this?" he asked, rising to a sitting position.

"We all ate 'til we was ready to bust, and still had enough food left over to feed a regiment," she said, taking her coat off and tossing it on the couch.

"Lotsa' wimmen' showed up, huh?" he asked, removing the aluminum foil, and taking out a fried chicken leg.

"Only the whole town," she replied, kicking off her shoes.

Mr. Kingery wasn't sure why that made him so happy. As his wife went off to the kitchen, he patted his dog, and said, "We got us a real nice group of wimmen' in this town, Blue."

Blue agreed, blinking his eyes twice.

Dear Journal,

I can breathe again. All the women loved Kelly Ann and they loved her baby. The gifts were important, but the food said it all. I could tell that Kelly Ann feels like she belongs here now. Yay!

E.

Chapter - 7

Emily's phone vibrated as she walked down First Street on her way home to the bakery, and she answered it.

"Emily, hurry over to the library!" Mrs. Green all but shouted. "We've found her!"

"What?" Emily asked, confused.

"Your sister! Mr. Green found your sister. Hurry over, I have to go! Hurry!"

Emily was about a block from the library and took off running, her heart thundering.

She flew up library steps and burst through the doors. Mrs. Green was behind the checkout desk helping a long line of people check out their books.

"Tell me, quick!" Emily panted, as she ran up to the desk.

Mrs. Green handed her a piece of paper. "Sit down over there and read it," she whispered, as the people in line leaned forward, straining to hear. "I'll be over after I've helped these people."

Emily hurried over, sliding into her favorite easy chair, her hand trembling as she stared at the paper. She read it over and over again, letting the meaning of the discovery sink in: Eva Miller, age 23, Seal Beach, California, and a phone number. She couldn't believe it! Less than ten words, but she knew her life had just pivoted once again.

She sobbed in Miss Mattie's arms.

"What's wrong, Sugar" Miss Mattie crooned, as she held Emily, and looked at the paper again. "Does it scare you to meet your sister?"

"It's too confusing," Emily cried. "She probably doesn't even know I exist, and I don't know what to do now!"

"Well, Sugar, we do what we've always done and take this one step at a time. It won't be too confusin' then," Miss Mattie assured her, rocking her like a child. "Do you want to call her?"

"I don't know," she wept.

"Well, why don't you see if you can find a picture of her on Facebook. Maybe seein' a picture would help."

"Okay, I'll try that," she sniffed, and hurried to her bedroom.

A half hour later she sat on her bed staring at a picture of her sister, hardly believing it. She looked like Emily; an older Emily. Their hair and eyes were the same color, and the face structure was the same. It was exciting and scary all at the same time, and she hurried out to show her mama.

"Well, would you look at that!" Miss Mattie crooned, staring at the picture. "I'd know that sweet face anywhere!" She turned to Emily, "Does that make you feel better about callin' her, Sugar?"

It actually did make her feel better. The next question was, how should she do it? There was no answer except to just pick up the phone and call the number.

Emily sat cross-legged on her bed as she listened to the phone ring. She hoped her sister answered, and she hoped she didn't. This was nerve wracking.

"Hello!" said the voice, over 2,000 miles away.

"Hello," said Emily, her voice shaking. "Is this Eva Miller?"

"Yes, it is," the voice replied cheerfully.

"My name is Emily," she said, uncertain of what to say next. "I'm your sister."

There was silence on the other end of the phone.

"Hello?"

"I'm here, Emily," the subdued voice responded. "I'd heard about you. I'm just shocked to hear your voice, but Emily...I'm so glad you called."

Emily let out her breath, as relief swept over her. "I'm glad I called, too!"

"Well, what did she say, Sugar?"

"She wants me to fly out and meet her," Emily replied, still feeling stunned.

"Oh! Is that what you want to do?"

"Do you mind?"

"Why, of course not, Sugar! Why would I mind? It's summer, and a perfect time to go before your school year starts here. I would just like to speak to her myself first though."

"She said she wants me to move there..."

"Move there!" Miss Mattie gasped, her eyes bugging slightly. She couldn't say anything more, and just gulped a couple of times.

Emily reached over and hugged her tightly. "I just want to meet her, Mama, then I'll come right back."

"Well, a California beach town would be a big temptation..." Miss Mattie said but couldn't finish.

"I'll be back," Emily said, planting a kiss on her beautiful brown cheek.

Miss Mattie nodded, but wondered if that would be true.

A week later Miss Mattie was at the wheel driving Emily down the mountain to Roanoke Regional Airport. "Now Sugar, even though I spoke to your sister, and she seemed really nice, you call me if things don't work out in California, and I'll bring you right home," her mama was saying as she swooped around a Chevy pick-up.

Emily gripped the armrest. "It'll all be just fine, Mama...look out for that biker!"

"I see him, Sugar!" she replied, as her tires threw up gravel on the soft shoulder. "Your sister said she would be at the airport early to pick you up, but you phone me if you don't see her..."

"It'll be fine, Mama," Emily repeated, keeping her eyes glued to the road as they passed another biker.

They arrived at the airport forty-five minutes later, and Miss Mattie pulled over to the unloading zone. Emily hopped out and went around to the trunk for her suitcase and backpack. Her Mama got out and came around to hug her. "Now don't forget to text me," she said, putting on a brave front.

"I will," Emily said, hugging her, thinking she looked really tired. "Why don't you just rest today, let Blessy handle the bakery."

"That's a good idea, I'll ask her," she whispered, without objection.

Emily hugged her tighter, surprised she'd agreed so easily. "Get a good rest, Mama."

Miss Mattie got back into the car and rolled down her window. "I'll be prayin' for you, Sugar," she said, and with a final wave, pulled away.

"And I'll be praying for you, Mama," she whispered, mad at herself for not noticing before how tired she looked.

At the ticket counter, Emily pulled out her ID and reservation for the trip to Long Beach, California. The map had shown it as the airport nearest to Seal Beach. She had told Eva to make her return trip for eight days later because Jonathan would be home for the summer soon after, trying not to let it bother her that he only got to stay for a month before returning to England. But it did bother her...a lot.

The plane flew out on schedule. Emily settled into her seat and put on headphones for the flight's movie. Her mind began to wander, and she had trouble concentrating, so she took the headphones off. This trip made her think of her parents, especially her mom. She tried reading a magazine, but that didn't work either. *What kind of person leaves two daughters*, she wondered over and over again, and what would her mom think about those two daughters meeting? Her excitement faded, replaced with a sadness she couldn't explain. Did her mom think she and her sister were just throw-away items?

Realizing that her emotional ship was sinking, she reined her thoughts in. "Stop thinking like that," she said out loud. The woman to her left turned and stared. "Sorry," Emily said, with a grin, "I was giving myself a lecture." They both laughed, and Emily was okay again.

Five hours later the big jet landed in Long Beach, and Emily unfastened her seat belt. She felt nervous, and her stomach began to do flip-fops as she stood up and retrieved her backpack from the overhead bin. She tried to calm herself as she stood in the aisle, but her stomach churned as she waited for her turn to exit, and she found herself gulping for breath as she walked down a long corridor towards the escalator. She stopped for a moment to calm herself. *This is crazy*, she reasoned, *your sister is just a person. Relax.*

The self-talk didn't work, so she gave up and got on the escalator. A crowd was waiting for passengers at the bottom, and she searched their faces looking for Eva. When she didn't see her, her heart dropped. *What now?* She scanned the crowd one more time just before she reached the bottom.

Suddenly, she felt arms thrown around her, and saw a flash of red hair.

"Emily!" her sister cried, giving her a bear hug, rocking her back and forth.

Emily stepped back and looked into the greenest eyes she'd ever seen. "Your eyes look just like our grandmother's!" was the first thing she said to her sister, giving her own bear hug this time.

"They look like yours, too!" Eva said, both laughing as they walked towards the luggage carousal. They chatted like old friends, interrupting each other as they watched the carousal turn. They hesitated, then both said, "You talk first!" and interrupted each other again.

Emily sighed. She didn't know how to describe this feeling, but it was somewhat akin to a "coming home" feeling. She loved this sister already.

They loaded the suitcase and backpack into the back of Eva's older Subaru. Emily noticed that one of the fenders was painted a different color than the rest of the car, and the passenger door was dented.

"It's not a Cadillac," Eva said, as they got into the car, "but it's all I could afford!"

"No problem," said Emily, pulling on her seat belt and noticing the smell of stale fast food. "How far are we from where you live?"

"About twenty minutes, unless there's lots of traffic," her sister replied, pulling on her own seat belt. As they drove off, Emily sent a quick text to her mama saying she'd arrived and was with her sister.

They talked and laughed all the way down the Pacific Coast Highway to Seal Beach, where Eva turned onto Main Street. "I'll give you a quick tour of our little village," Eva said, and began pointing out various shops and restaurants.

"It's so cute!" Emily said, thoroughly charmed with the quaint downtown area. At the very end of Main Street, she couldn't help but gasp, as she stared out at the sparkling water of the vast Pacific Ocean. "Beautiful!" she murmured.

"We'll walk out on that pier and spend time there soon," Eva said, as she turned left and began driving up and down small streets. "I thought you'd enjoy seeing the cute neighborhoods."

"What a great place to live!" Emily murmured, delighted with the rows of charming beach cottages. "I love it here!"

Up and down the streets they drove, as Eva gave her a tour of the tiny beach community. "It really is the best place ever," Eva said. "Expensive, too! Just to let you know, my place is really small, I couldn't afford more."

They turned onto Tenth Street and pulled into the driveway of a tiny cottage set back off the street. "Home Sweet Home!" Eva laughed, opening her car door.

As they went up the walk, Emily saw pots of bright flowers decorating the porch. "Pansies!" she said, turning to Eva. "I love pansies!"

"They're my favorite!" Eva replied, unlocking the front door, and motioning for Emily to go in first.

They walked into a tiny living room that was only large enough to hold a small couch, an easy chair and a TV.

"Let's put your things in the guest room," her sister said, motioning to the left.

There was a short hall, with an entrance into a small bedroom. Emily looked around the room, liking the simple furnishings: a twin bed, a nightstand with a small lamp decorated with seashells, and a knotty pine dresser. *Simple but nice,* Emily thought, setting her suitcase on the blue throw rug.

"Make yourself at home," her sister smiled, as she left the room. "I'll get us some dinner started."

Emily opened a door and found it to be a small bathroom. Another door opened to a tiny closet, and she set her suitcase inside. Not knowing what else to do, she went in search of Eva.

The kitchen was a galley-type, where Eva stood chopping vegetables on a narrow counter. "What do you think of my little house?" she asked, smiling.

"Really, really cute!" Emily said, "It looks like a little doll house!"

"It's all I could afford!" her sister remarked, pouring oil into a large skillet. "Living by the beach is expensive!"

This was the third time her sister had mentioned the cost of things, causing Emily to ask, "So where do you work?"

"At a small gift shop," her sister replied, putting pieces of cut up chicken into the hot oil. "I'll take you by there tomorrow." She turned the chicken once, then put in the vegetables and put a lid on the skillet. "Help yourself to cold drinks," she said, motioning to a small refrigerator, "but all I have is Orange Crush. It's the only soft drink I really like."

Emily smiled as she opened the refrigerator door. Later, she'd tell her sister that it was the only soft drink she really liked, also.

The next day, there was a balmy breeze as she and her sister walked down Electric Avenue, a tree-lined street that ran through the heart of the quaint neighborhood. "There's a little place I like to eat at the end of Main Street," Eva said. "On the way there, we can stop off at the shop where I work!"

Emily nodded, deciding that Seal Beach must be one of the cutest towns she'd ever seen! It was beautiful and simple all at the same time, and she couldn't get over how much it just felt like home to her. They crossed Main Street and walked into *The Glittering Starfish*, Eva's workplace. Her sister introduced her to a couple of co-workers, but the shop was very busy, and no one had time to chat. Emily sensed that they felt a little indifferent to her sister anyway. *Some people are just odd*, she reasoned as they walked out and headed down the street for lunch.

At lunch they sat side-by-side on stools facing the window and stared out at a magnificent view of the Pacific Ocean and the long pier that jutted out far beyond the breaking waves. It began as a light-hearted time of laughing and talking as they ate their cheeseburgers. "My schedule is pretty busy, but I want to hang out with you whenever I'm free," Eva was saying. "I'm dating a guy named Stanley, who said he'd be happy to hang out with you when I'm not around."

Emily hesitated, not really wanting that arrangement. "Thanks, but I'll be fine alone!" she said, dipping a french fry into Ranch dressing.

"Oh, you'll like Stan!" her sister said.

"I'm sure I will, but I really prefer exploring the town on my own."

"You'll like Stan," her sister repeated firmly, as though she hadn't heard her.

Emily was somewhat alarmed at Eva's insistence and disliked this kind of tug-of-war. She started to say more, but hesitated; sometimes she overreacted, and wondered if she was doing it this time.

The rest of their lunch was uneventful, and they decided to walk out on the pier afterward.

"Stan had some things to take care of, but he'll meet up with us later," Eva said, sitting down on a bench at the pier.

"Okay," Emily replied, curious to meet him. "Does Stan live in Seal Beach, too?"

Eva nodded but didn't offer any more information.

"Where does he work?"

"He's between jobs right now," she replied, an edge to her voice.

"It must be hard for him to pay rent," Emily said, wondering if the guy was rich.

Eva looked at her. "He's living with his grandmother temporarily."

Emily nodded as warning signs popped into her head like so many whack-a-moles but didn't say anything.

They met up with Stan at six o'clock in front of an Irish restaurant. Eva introduced them, and Stan gave her a huge smile and said, "Nice to meet you!" Emily tried to remember who he reminded her of but couldn't think of it.

They placed their dinner orders, and Stan was very attentive. He made sure their water glasses were always full, included Emily in the conversation, and tried telling a funny story or two. He was polite, talkative, and very charming, making Emily wonder why she didn't like him—not one bit.

The conversations were going along nicely when, out of nowhere, Stan said, "Heard you came into a lot of cash recently!"

Eva glared at him, and Emily thought she kicked him under the table.

"Where did you hear that?" Emily asked, with no intention of answering.

He shrugged. "Don't remember. Someone in Eva's family told her. You two want to get some ice cream down at the corner?" he asked, quickly changing the subject. "There's a band playing in the park by the pier in a few minutes, and we can take our ice cream and go listen to them."

They both agreed, and when the bill came, she saw Eva reach for it.

"I can get mine," Emily said, pulling some cash out of her pocket and laying it on the small tray. She watched to see if Stan offered money, but he didn't.

They walked to the end of Main Street and bought ice cream cones, then crossed the street to the park where there was a magnificent view of the ocean. The band started up, and the evening felt just right, with a warm breeze and the smell of the sea. Emily relaxed and enjoyed it immensely, wondering if she was judging Stan too harshly.

A text message from England came while she was sitting on the lawn listening to the music and relishing it all. No picture this time, just a message from Jonathan, saying, *How's everything going?*

She took a picture of the band, the ocean, a profile of her sister listening to the music, and sent it to him, along with the message, *We look just alike!*

Send a picture of both of you together, came the reply.

She tapped Stan on the shoulder and asked him to take the picture, then scooted over next to her sister.

"Say cheese!" he said, clicking off five pictures of the girls with their arms around each other, and their grins telling the story of how happy they were to be together. Emily's very favorite was the profile picture of the two of them looking at each other. The resemblance was uncanny.

She sent all the pictures to Jonathan, and five minutes later received a one-word reply: *Amazing!* And a few seconds later a second message saying that he hoped she had fun, followed by a screen full of red hearts.

She started to send the pictures to Miss Mattie, but remembered the three-hour time difference, and put her phone away. It tugged at her heart; she was already missing her mama.

"Good morning!" Eva said, when Emily came out of the bedroom the next morning. "There's coffee or tea in the kitchen."

"Good Morning!" Emily said, giving her a hug. "I left my bedroom window open all night so I could hear the ocean!"

"Don't you just love it?" her sister said, hugging her back.

"Yes ma'am, I sure do!" she replied, on her way to the kitchen. Reaching for a mug in the cabinet Emily noticed a glass with about an inch of amber liquid in it. Alarmed, she picked it up and sniffed, then drew back. "Whiskey," she whispered, and set the glass back down with a sinking feeling. She had smelled that odor on her parent's breath her whole life. "Please don't let this be a problem with Eva," she murmured, dumping the remaining liquid down the sink.

"Hey," her sister said, when she walked back into the living room with her tea, "I have to work today, but Stan said he'd come and keep you company, maybe go to the beach or something."

Emily tried to think of how to word it without offending. "I really prefer being on my own. Nothing against Stan."

"Well, you two talk it over," Eva replied, sipping her coffee. "I won't be here."

Emily nodded, deciding she wasn't talking anything over with Stan, and quickly made a plan to leave before he got there.

"I love having you here," her sister said, breaking into her thoughts. "I wish you'd think about living with me. It would be lots of fun! Two sisters together!"

"That's really nice of you, but I love living in Mountain Grove with my foster mother."

"We already checked into schools for you," her sister continued, as though she hadn't heard her. "The high school is only like four blocks away."

"*We* checked into it?" Emily asked, feeling uneasy. "Who is *we*?"

"Me and Stan! I also found out that I could be your foster parent!"

Okay, this is weird, Emily thought, alarmed that her sister already had a plan in place. All she could think to say was, "What time does your work start?"

Her sister looked up at the wall clock and jumped to her feet. "Yikes! In twenty minutes!" She set her cup down and hurried towards the bedroom. "Just think about how much fun it would be to live with me, Emily," she called over her shoulder.

Emily went into her room to get ready for the day, planning to leave right after Eva. She skipped her shower, threw on cut-offs and a t-shirt, and stuffed her journal and a few other things into her backpack.

When her sister came out with car keys in hand, Emily was sitting on the couch, with no intention of telling Eva her plans. She didn't know why she was doing this, but she didn't like Stan, and wasn't about to spend the day with him.

"See you around five," her sister said, heading for the door. "Help yourself to any of the food!"

"Thank you!" Emily said, and when she heard Eva's car start up, went into the kitchen and made a sandwich, then put a few chips in a baggie, and grabbed an Orange Crush.

She thought Stan probably slept late but wasn't taking chances on getting stuck with him all day. She borrowed one of Eva's beach towels and headed out the door.

At the beach, she found a secluded spot behind a sand dune, spread out the towel, and lay there with her eyes closed, listening to the rhythm of the waves crashing. The flight and the time difference had left her tired, but she couldn't stop thinking about the nailed-down plans Eva and Stan had made for her. She heard wings flapping and opened her eyes to see a large sea gull had landed two feet away, staring at her with eyes that appeared to be wise, its white feathered chest puffed out, as though to give her counsel.

Delighted, she sat up. "Mr. Seagull, I need your advice," she began, "Isn't it weird that Eva and Stan looked into foster care before they even met me?" The gull tilted its head from side to side, then gave a little nod for her to continue. "Did they think I'd be some dingy girl who would agree to anything they had planned, for Pete's sake?" The sea gull, who appeared to be as puzzled as she was, squawked twice, flapped its great wings and flew away.

"Wait!" she called after it. "I need to tell you about the booze on the kitchen counter!"

Laughing and feeling better after her feathered visitor, she took out her journal to put her thoughts on paper.

Dear Journal,

Here's something I can't stop thinking about it....there was left-over booze on my sister's counter this morning. I know that I automatically assume someone is a raging drunk if I see one drop of alcohol, because I've NEVER seen anyone drink and not be otherwise. So, there's that, and I need to be fair. I'll just have to wait and see.

The other thing is that Eva wants me to come and live with her. It's like she has it all planned out, and I'm just supposed to just say ok, and leave my other life behind. It's weird. It's like she doesn't even listen to me, and she has no idea what my Mama and the townspeople mean to me. Also, what Jonathan means to me.

E.

Jonathan, she thought, putting her journal back into her backpack. *What does he mean to me?* She didn't know if she ever wanted to get married. What if it turned out like her parents? As she grew up, she believed they actually hated each other most of the time. She had seen their wedding picture from years before, when they had eloped to Reno. In the picture they looked very happy. Then they weren't. Mrs. Apple told her that their "habits" had probably ruined their marriage. But what if she had "habits"? Anyway, she was hungry and tired of thinking about it.

As she took the sandwich out of her backpack, her seagull friend swooped back in, bringing five more gulls with him, and stood in a semi-circle around her. The gulls turned their tiny heads towards the ocean, as though they were staring out at sea, but she could see a single eye looking sideways at her food. "Want some lunch?" she asked, breaking off small pieces of bread and throwing it to them. They grew braver and took a step or two in as she threw more bread. She laid her sandwich down so she could open the bag of chips, and had no sooner done so, when huge wings were flapping her in the face. She swung her arms wildly, then looked up to see a large seagull fly off with her sandwich.

"What in the world..." she said out loud, as the bird flapped out of view. She found herself laughing and checked to see if her chips had been stolen, too. They were safe, and she kept them out of sight as the rest of the marauders focused an eye on her.

After lunch she read for a while, but soon grew bored and decided to walk around the village. She gathered all of her things and pushed them down into her backpack, shook sand off of the towel, and stuffed that on top.

Starting towards town, she suddenly halted, and ducked behind a palm tree. She peeked around, watching as Stan hurried down Main Street stopping at each store, where he would dash inside for a moment, then back out and on to the next store. He was looking for her, she was sure of it. When he went inside the hardware store, she turned and went in the other direction, walking behind a tall hedge, then making her way down side streets back to Eva's cottage, hoping Stan wouldn't think to come back there and look for her.

She was watching TV when Eva came in a little after five o'clock.

"Hey!" Emily said, looking up from the TV screen.

"Hey," Eva said, somewhat coldly. "How come you went off without Stan today? He stopped by the shop and said he couldn't find you!"

"I left early to go to the beach," she replied, standing her ground. "I told you I was fine by myself."

Eva didn't say anymore, just headed off for the kitchen. Emily listened, trying to hear if she poured herself some booze, but couldn't hear over the TV.

Eva came out of the kitchen a few minutes later and said, "Stan and I are having dinner tonight, we have some things to talk over. There's leftovers in the refrigerator if you'd like those."

"Thanks!" Emily said, kind of surprised that she wasn't included in the dinner invitation.

"I have the day off tomorrow and thought we could go to Huntington Beach and look around," her sister said, as she put her jacket on.

"Sounds good," Emily said, turning back to the TV, and thinking that Eva must be really mad at her, not to invite her to dinner, too.

Chapter - 8

—◁O▷—

"The plan for today," her sister said, the next morning as they sat having mugs of tea, "is a drive down the coast to Huntington Beach. We're thinking of leaving around ten."

"We?"

"Yes! I'll call Stan in a while and wake him up. Make sure he's ready by then," she said, taking a sip of her tea.

"It would be nice if it could just be you and me!"

Eva glared at her. "Stan gets really bored with nothing to do but hang around his grandma's all day."

"If Stan is bored, why doesn't he go look for a job?" The words flew out of her mouth before she even thought about what she was saying, and it didn't go over well.

The look on her sister's face was very close to hatred. "Don't be jealous just because you don't have a boyfriend," she snapped, then hurried into the bedroom to call Stan.

"Where did that come from?" Emily said to an empty room.

An hour later they were on their way down the Pacific Coast Highway toward Huntington Beach, Eva and Emily in the front seat, Stan in the back. Emily worked at being friendly towards the guy, even though irritation rippled through her every time she saw his smug face. *What does Eva see in him?* she wondered.

In Sunset Beach, they stopped for a red light behind a Chevy Tahoe full of teenagers. When the light turned green the driver in the Tahoe gunned it, pulling far ahead of Eva and pelting her windshield with gravel as he sped off. A tiny crack line formed on the passenger side, and when Eva saw it, she became livid.

"Hey!" Eva screamed, as she accelerated and took off after them. The Tahoe was way ahead of them, but Eva sped up, gaining on them. The Tahoe switched into the fast lane, but as Eva gained on them, switched back to their lane, cutting Eva off, and she slammed on her brakes to avoid plowing into them.

She screamed obscenities out the window as the Tahoe sped ahead, then jammed the accelerator to the floor, honking the horn like a crazy woman.

"Eva! Stop it!" Emily yelled.

"No one cuts me off!" she shrieked. "And they're gonna' pay for that crack in my windshield."

She sped up to within inches of the Tahoe's bumper, and lay down on her horn, motioning for them to pull over.

Emily could see the kids' scared faces in the Tahoe as those in the back seat turned and stared out the rear window. They looked terrified.

The Tahoe sped up and switched lanes; Eva switched lanes too, speeding up again to within inches of their bumper, as she continued to honk and scream out the window.

Emily looked at the speedometer; 75 miles an hour and climbing. "Eva! Stop!" she yelled again.

"No way!" she yelled back.

Emily clutched the seat, as she watched the speedometer climb to 75, then 80, then 85, still only inches away from the Tahoe's bumper. The kids in the Tahoe were screaming.

The car crept up to 90 miles an hour, and Emily had no doubt that Eva would accelerate up to 100 miles an hour, risking everyone's life, including a carload of teenagers. Her sister was shrieking and out of control. Taking a huge risk, Emily reached over and switched off the ignition, pulling the keys out, praying that Eva could steer with the engine off.

"What are you doing!" Eva screamed, as the car immediately slowed down. "Give me those keys!"

"Just put the brake on, and pull off the road," Emily yelled, so angry that she was shaking.

Eva swore at her as the car slowed, then guided it, powerless, off onto the shoulder of the road.

"I'm out of here," Emily said, when the car came to a halt. She reached for the door handle.

"You can't get out here," her sister yelled.

"Watch me," Emily said, shoving the car door open.

"Okay, okay, I won't drive fast," Eva said, realizing that Emily meant it. "Just get back in the car."

Emily hesitated. "I'm done. Take me back to Seal Beach," she said, climbing into the car, and throwing the car keys into Eva's lap.

"I won't drive fast, let's just go and have lunch," Eva begged.

"No way! I just want to go back!" Emily folded her arms, trying to stop trembling.

Eva tried a different tactic. "Wouldn't you have gotten mad if those kids had chipped your window?"

"Mad? You went berserk and put our lives, and those kids lives in danger!"

"Why are you shaking?" Eva asked, her voice lower this time.

"Why do you think? That was NUTS!"

"Okay, okay, I'll drive slower," Eva said calmly. "Let's just go get something to eat!"

"C'mon Em'ly," Stan whined from the back seat. "We're three miles away. Let's get lunch, then we'll go back to Seal Beach."

Emily shook her head, "I'm not going."

They turned around and headed back. Eva tried to start a conversation, but Emily only gave her one-word answers, until she finally gave up and rode the rest of the way in silence.

When they got back to Seal Beach, and were sitting at a red light, Emily grabbed her backpack and got out of the car. "You two can have lunch, I need some time alone."

"Emily, come on!" Eva whined, but Emily slammed the door and walked away.

The next morning, when Emily got up, Eva was already leaving for work. Emily spoke to her briefly, then headed for the shower, with plans to leave the house in case Stan showed up.

She was just picking up her backpack to leave when there was a knock at the door. Startled, she peered out the peep hole to see who it was. There was Stanley. She groaned, trying to think of what to do. Before she could decide, she heard the sound of a key in the lock and stepped back. Stanley swung the door open. "Hey, Emily, Eva thought you might like some company."

"I was just on my way out," she replied curtly. "I already have plans."

"Mind if I sit down for a minute and chat?" He sat down without waiting for an answer.

She turned towards him but kept her hand on the doorknob.

"How do you like it here?" he asked.

"What do you want?" she replied impatiently, ignoring his question.

He patted the couch and gave her that creepy grin. "Why don't you sit down for a sec?"

In that moment, she remembered who Stan reminded her of—Kelly Ann's old boyfriend, Logger!

"I'm leaving. What do you want?" she repeated, not bothering to conceal her dislike for him.

"I think your sister would like you to come and live with her."

"I know, she already mentioned it to me, but I'm happy living in Mountain Grove."

"Well, it's better to be with family, know what I mean?"

"Miss Mattie is just like a mother to me," she said, meaning to end all discussion of her ever moving here. What business was it of his anyway? She bent down and picked up her backpack. "I have plans. See you later," she said, turning towards the door.

"Whoa," he said, standing up. "Wouldn't you like to be with your sister?"

"I already told you, I'm happy living where I'm at. And really Stan, this isn't your business."

Stan ignored the comment, and continued, "Don't you think your sister should be entitled to some of that money your grandmother left you? It's Eva's grandmother too, ya' know."

"I have no intention of talking to you about any of this," Emily said, reaching for the doorknob again.

"Your sister is getting evicted from this place."

Emily stopped, "Evicted! Why is she being evicted?"

He shrugged. "She doesn't make enough money to pay the rent they charge around here!"

Emily stared at him in disbelief. "Well, the solution to that is to move somewhere cheaper!"

"She likes it here, bein' near me and all," he grinned foolishly.

"So what's she going to do?" Emily asked, her dislike for this guy growing by the minute.

"Why don't you move in and help her out? You're the one who's gettin' all that inheritance when you turn eighteen next year!"

She just stared at him. *So that's what this was all about.*

"Plus, the state would pay her *now* for bein' your guardian," he grinned, as though he expected her to see the cleverness of the plan.

"Why don't you get a job and help her out?"

He stared at her a second. "Ummm...I'm not much into commitment."

Emily nodded. "So let me get this straight. My sister is living in a place she can't afford because she wants to live near you. You don't work, and the plan is that you both expect me to live here so that Eva can get money from the foster care agency, and my grandmother's money when I turn eighteen!"

"That's pretty much it," he replied, the foolish grin returning. "You said you liked it here, and Eva likes you, too. And Eva's not one to lay down the rules, if you know what I mean. You could do pretty much as you please!"

"Because she would have what she wants--the state's money now, and my grandmother's money when I'm eighteen--and I would have all the freedom I want. Is that it?"

"You got it!" he said, giving her two thumbs up.

"Does she know that you're telling me all this?"

"She knew I was going to tell you about the eviction, we talked about it the other night."

"I see," Emily said, thinking Stan wasn't very bright to reveal the overall plan to her. "Is this the first time she's been evicted?"

"Naw!" he grinned. "She knows how to play the game."

"Oh! What game is that?"

"There's tons of ways of gettin' out of payin' rent,"

"I know, I learned a lot of them from my parents," she said.

"See!" he said, nodding his approval. "You two are cut from the same cloth!

No Stan, we're not! she thought, but something told her to just be quiet for now. These were not nice people.

She opened the door to leave.

"Want me to come with you?" Stan asked.

"No thanks, I have plans," she replied, just wanting to get away from him, and from this house.

He shrugged, laid down on the couch, and turned on the television.

Closing the door, she could hear a game show booming.

Emily stayed at the beach most of the day. She couldn't quit thinking about her sister, trying to understand how she could live the way she did: a boyfriend who was a big moocher, living in a place she couldn't afford, and hoping to get money that didn't belong to her. Should she just go home, or stick it out in Seal Beach for a few more days? Her heart wanted to stay, but that's because her heart hoped Eva would be the person she saw the first day she came. She thought about it until she couldn't think anymore, and still wasn't sure what to do.

She walked back to the cottage in the late afternoon and was surprised to see Eva's car in the driveway, two hours early.

Emily went in, and not seeing her sister, went into the kitchen, where she froze. Eva was just pouring a drink from a large bottle of Jim Beam.

"Hey!" her sister said, pouring a tumbler full.

"Hey! You're home early!"

"Yep!"

"Is everything all right?"

"Nope. I got into a fight with a customer."

"Wow," was all that Emily could think to say. "Do you still have a job?"

"Probably! They're too short-handed to let me go. Manager told me to take the afternoon off." Eva walked past her, drink in hand. "C'mon, let's sit in the living room." She swayed and bumped into a wall, and Emily realized this wasn't her first drink.

"Have you thought any more about living here with me?" Eva asked, settling into the easy chair.

"Not really," Emily replied. "Are you going into work tomorrow?"

"I'll try!" she shrugged, swirling the ice in her drink.

Emily thought she should change the subject. "Did you say that you were raised by a distant aunt?"

Eva sipped her drink. "It was some relative of my bio-dad."

"Did you know your dad?"

"Never met him," she said, taking another large swallow. "What was our mom like?"

This struck Emily as a very odd conversation, but she answered, "Very distant, and depressed most of the time."

"I always wondered how she could just leave me!" Eva said, tearing up.

"She left me, too," Emily said calmly. "The problem isn't us—it's her."

Eva finished off her drink, then after a few minutes, turned to her, and said, "Soooo, are you gonna' come live with me?" Her speech was slurred.

"Thanks, but not sure that would work." Emily decided not to give a definite answer when her sister was drunk like this. She stood up. "And right now, I'm going to walk to town and get something to eat."

"You don't wanna' talk?

"We'll talk when you're sober," she said, grabbing her backpack and heading out. She hated this. *How many times have I left home to escape a drunk person?* she wondered, as she headed for town.

There was no mention of the drinking the next morning, and Emily left the subject alone. Eva was going to work, and Emily needed to figure things out. She spent the day at the beach again.

Dinner was awkward that night, her sister seemed agitated. They made it through the meal of Chinese take-out that Eva had brought home and were just clearing plates when Eva stumbled over the throw rug, sending one of her square dinner plates crashing to the floor. There came out of her mouth swearing that Emily had not heard since her parents had left her. In her fury, Eva kicked at the broken plate, cutting her toe, and swore even more.

Emily went into the kitchen and wet a paper towel for Eva's toe. She handed it to her, and asked, "Are you okay?"

"No, I'm not okay!" Eva screamed, wrapping the paper towel around her bleeding toe. "While you traipse around the beach and text those hillbilly friends of yours, I'm over here trying to figure out how to pay for food and gas, and my credit cards are almost maxed out!" She stood up and glared at Emily, coming unhinged. "You're getting money that I should have too," she shrieked, dots of spit forming at the corners of her mouth. "Why would our grandmother leave it all to you?" Her chest heaved in fury, and she shrieked, "I NEED MONEY!"

Emily knew not to say anything; she'd been through this way too many times with her mom and dad. Her sister was out of control, and she needed to leave.

Eva stood there glaring waiting for a response.

"I think I need to leave," Emily said, quietly.

"Oh sure, leave! Don't help your sister," she shrieked. "Go back to that hick town of yours!"

Emily went to her room and shut the door, but her sister kept yelling. It was time to leave, to just go back home. She'd probably stayed too long already.

Her hands were shaking as she opened the small drawer where she'd put her airline ticket for the return flight home, but the drawer was empty. Shocked, she pulled the drawer out to see if the ticket had fallen down behind the drawer. No ticket.

She checked under the bed and emptied her backpack out in case she had forgotten and stuck it in there. No ticket. Would her sister have taken it? Surely not. And yet...

The screaming had stopped in the next room, and she went out to question Eva.

"Did you take my plane ticket to get home?" she asked.

A now subdued Eva said, "You told me you'd stay eight days."

"That's before you lost your temper."

"Well, wouldn't you be mad if I was getting all the inheritance?"

"No," she replied, "And I don't want to talk about that anymore, I'd like my plane ticket."

"Just stay," her sister said softly. "I won't get mad anymore. Just think about helping me out. I'm in a terrible mess."

"Is that why you asked me to come? To talk me into staying so you'd get money from the foster care people?"

"No," she said, not looking at her. "I'd like to have a family."

Emily didn't believe her, but she didn't know what to do. She stood there staring at Eva.

"I'll give you your plane ticket the day you leave, I promise," Eva said. "But I want you to think about living here with me. We'd have so much fun!"

Is she crazy? Emily thought but didn't argue. She needed to think. "We'll talk about it later," she said, and without waiting for a reply, headed for her room. She locked her door, putting the chair underneath the doorknob.

Later, after she was in bed, there was a soft knock on her door. "Just think about living with me, Emmy," her sister said softly. "Love you. Goodnight."

Well, that's creepy, Emily thought, pulling the covers up over her head.

Eva acted like nothing had happened the next morning as she got ready for work. They didn't talk much, and Eva said, "See you tonight!" and headed off to work.

Emily didn't know if Stanley would show up, so she got dressed quickly, not wanting to be in this house anymore. It was weird how a few days ago she loved it here, and now only wanted to go home.

Should she call Miss Mattie? She thought of how tired and pale she looked at the airport when dropping Emily off...and with her heart condition? "No way," she murmured out loud. She couldn't think of anyone else in the village who could be much help in this situation either. If she knew where Eva had put her plane ticket, she would leave now. She didn't have enough money to buy another ticket home.

Jonathan! Should she call him? He wasn't leaving England for a few days, but he could help her think of what to do, and he wouldn't panic. She would figure out where to go to call him on the way to town. *It's 10:00 am now, so it would only be 6:00 pm in England,* she thought, hoping she was calculating it right.

She walked toward the pier. It was always busy, and she could see in most directions and be on the lookout for Stan. It amazed her how quickly a situation could nose-dive. But, as she had found out, life was sometimes just that way.

Her life, anyway.

Emily realized a dark cloud of depression was looming overhead, and a touch of self-pity. *Stop it!* she lectured herself, remembering the goodness that was in her life now. Lots of people who loved her; a safe home; and her mama.

"The best mama ever," she whispered, hurrying on.

At the pier, she found a secluded bench, and with her heart thundering, dialed Jonathan's cell number.

"Hello!" came Jonathan's voice from across the ocean.

All her courage and resolve melted, and she burst into tears at the sound of his voice.

"Emily?"

"I don't know what to do!" she sobbed, turning sideways so people walking on the pier couldn't see her crying.

"What's wrong?" he asked, the concern in his voice carrying thousands of miles to her.

She tried to stop crying, but only hiccupped into the phone.

"Just take your time and tell me," he said.

Emily took a deep breath, "I think my sister just invited me here for money."

"What money?" he asked, sounding perplexed.

"She wants me to stay and live with her, so it would be money from foster care, and my grandmother's money when I turn eighteen. She has it all planned out."

"Wow!" he murmured.

"Stan told me Eva is being evicted from her cottage, then Eva lost her temper and told me, too."

"Who's Stan?"

"Her creepy boyfriend, who looks like Logger," she sniffed.

"Is he threatening you in any way, or dangerous?"

"I'm not in danger," she said, "I'm just hurt that it's not me Eva is interested in; it's money."

"Have you told them you won't stay?"

"I have a few more days here, and I don't think it's wise to give them a definite *no* yet. Anyway, she hid my plane ticket home!"

"Your sister *hid* your plane ticket?" he asked in disbelief.

"I don't think she's very stable."

"What else has she done to make you think that?"

"She yells and screams like a crazy person, one minute, then sweet the next. I think she has a drinking problem, too."

"Ok," he said. "Don't tell them anything. Just sit tight. I'm coming to get you."

"But your school..." she started to say.

"It's fine. I'll take care of it."

"And it's out of your way," she protested.

"Emily!"

"What?"

"I'm coming to get you."

"You are?"

"I am. I'm going to work out the details, and I'll call you back."

She didn't know what to say.

"Do you know where the police station is?" he asked.

"No."

"Where are you now?"

"On the pier."

"Ok, just go find the police station in case the situation goes over a cliff, then you'll know right where to go. I'm going to call you back in just a while."

"You're the best," she whispered, hanging up.

A man strolled by, walking his Dalmatian. "Excuse me!" she said, standing up.

The man stopped.

"Can you tell me where the nearest police station is?"

"Right over there," he said, pointing to the end of the pier.

"A police station by the pier?"

"Yes, it's a substation."

"Oh," she said, not really knowing what a substation was. "Thank you!" she said, turning and walking in that direction.

"Well, that was easy," she said, looking at the lettering on the glass door that read *Seal Beach Police Department, Pier Substation.* She stepped closer and looked through the door. A policeman sitting at the front desk looked up and waved at her. She waved back, deciding to go in.

"May I help you?" he asked.

"Are you open twenty-four hours a day?"

He laughed. "We are! Need some help?"

"Not right now. I just needed to know where to come in case I do."

He quit smiling. "Want to talk about it?"

"I have a sister who is pretty unstable, but I think I have it all worked out."

"Has she threatened you in anyway?"

"No, just acts crazy."

"Okay, well don't hesitate to come in if you find that it isn't worked out," he said. "What's your name?"

"Emily. Emily Parks. I'm from Mountain Grove, Virginia. This is the first time I've met my sister."

"Not going well, huh?" he said, as he wrote her name down.

"No, not really. I have a friend coming who is going to help me get home, and he said I should run here if things go over a cliff before he gets here."

"Sounds like a good friend," the officer remarked, opening his desk drawer and taking out a business card. "Don't hesitate to call if things do go over a cliff," he said, handing her the card.

"Thank you, Officer Hennessey!" Emily said, reading the name on the card before sliding it into a jean pocket, and deciding to keep it with her no matter where she went.

Jonathan texted her twice to make sure everything was going alright.

She texted him back that she was sitting in the town library reading, and Stan wouldn't think to look for her there—he wasn't the reading kind.

She had sought refuge in a library more than once, finding them to be warm and cozy and safe, and reading books helped her thoughts sail away when things around her were crazy.

It was another three hours before Jonathan actually called her. "I'm flying out tonight," he said, "and I'll be in Long Beach around 4:00 tomorrow afternoon. You won't be able to reach me for all that time, but I'll check in when I change planes.

Emily let out her breath slowly. "Should I try and get my airline ticket back from Eva?"

"No!" he said, meaning it. "That's not important right now. The airline can find your reservation when we get to the airport and can help us change your ticket. Let's talk about your plan for leaving Eva's house."

"I don't have one. I was waiting to hear from you."

"Okay, just be ready at the house and I'll come and get you. That's the only plan you need."

It sounded simple, but she felt her stomach tighten into a huge knot. When they said goodbye, Emily returned to her book, but found that she couldn't concentrate or breathe just right.

While sitting in the library she received three texts from Eva, but answered none of them. At closing time, she packed up her things and headed to a nearby McDonald's for a hamburger. Her plan was to stall going back to Eva's until late, then just go in and go to bed.

She sat in the corner of the fast-food restaurant eating, and a call came in. She nervously checked it and saw that it was Jonathan.

"What's the address?" he asked, "I forgot to ask you!"

They both laughed, and she gave it to him. "What time do you think you'll be here?"

"I'm guessing that it'll be close to six o'clock in the evening."

"Okay, I'll have everything packed when you come. I'm going to tell Eva that a friend is coming, and she'll probably assume you're from Seal Beach. That'll make her happy and maybe, just maybe, she won't blow her top."

"If she blows her top, she blows her top, Emily. Stop being so concerned about people and their temper."

"I try, but it throws me back to earlier days and my stomach goes into a knot," she said, feeling like she might burst into tears.

"It's okay," he said, his voice softening. "I'll be right there with you when she realizes you're leaving,"

"All right," she whispered, not trusting her voice to say more.

"I'll text you when my plane lands in Long Beach, and I'll text again when I'm almost to the house."

"How will you get here from the airport?"

"Uber, so quit worrying your little red head so much."

"Okay," she whispered, and they hung up.

Chapter - 9

Eva was asleep on the couch when Emily walked into the house later that night. She tried to tiptoe past her, but Eva woke up.

"Where you been?" she asked, sleepily.

"Talking with a friend," she said, making a beeline for her room.

"Who?" Eva asked. But Emily had already closed the bedroom door.

Emily woke up overwhelmed with dread the next morning. *Please let Eva be going to work today,* she said, as a silent prayer. This was going to be a long day.

"Good morning," Eva greeted cheerfully, as Emily walked into the living room.

"Good morning," Emily replied, noticing that Eva was still in pajamas. Her heart sank.

"Want to have a beach day today?" Eva asked, all smiles, "Just you and me, and I can pack us a lunch!"

Emily didn't want to, but also didn't want to stay in the house with her sister for the next ten hours either. She finally said, "We can go for a couple of hours, but a guy is coming by for me around 6:00."

Eva's eyes actually lit up. "So that's where you've been keeping yourself! Met a guy, huh?"

Emily nodded, and said, "I'll get my things for the beach, and be ready in just a while."

"And I'll pack us some food!" Eva replied happily.

Later, as they walked to the beach, she hoped Eva wouldn't ask any more questions, but of course, she did.

"Where did you meet this guy?" she asked.

"In a nursery, I was looking at flowers," she replied, not mentioning that the nursery was in Virginia.

"Ah-ha, you two have something in common then," she said, grinning at her.

Emily wondered if Eva might break into a dance, she looked so happy thinking there was a chance Emily might stay, and her money problems would be over.

The whole time at the beach Emily felt miserable and awkward. Eva peppered her with questions about Jonathan, and Emily kept changing the subject. The one thing good about it was that Eva was in a great mood.

"What's this guy's name, anyway? Eva asked.

"Jon, but you don't know him," she quickly added. It occurred to her that if Eva had snooped and found her airline ticket, she might have snooped and looked in her journal, also. Jonathan's name was all over that book!

They went back home after a couple of excruciating hours, and Emily quickly suggested they watch movies.

They had just settled in with popcorn and a movie when there was a knock at the door.

Startled, Emily jumped up and answered it.

It was Stan.

"Forgot my key," he said, walking past her into the living room.

"Hey," Eva said, waving her hand. "Thought you were coming over later!"

"Figured I'd come and check out Em'ly's date!" he said, giving one of his creepy smiles. "Got any good stuff to drink?"

"Pour me one, too!" Eva said, as he headed into the kitchen.

Emily heard the liquor bottle clink against the glass as Stan poured them both drinks.

Oh! Great! she thought, *let's just add liquor to this explosive situation!*

"Here you go," Stan said, handing her sister a drink.

He turned to Emily. "Tell us about this guy!" he said, twirling the ice in his drink.

She just shrugged and said, "There's not much to tell," and turned back to the movie.

Stan refilled their glasses two more times before Emily's phone finally buzzed with a text message, startling her.

Eva looked up expectantly when she heard it, and the creepy grin returned to Stan's face.

Emily quickly read the message. *Just landed, be there in about an hour.*

She stood up. "I'm going to go get ready, he'll be here in around an hour."

"Can't wait to meet him!" Eva said, raising her glass, and giving a lop-sided grin.

Emily groaned inwardly, forcing herself to walk calmly out of the room. She heard Stan whisper something to Eva, and they both laughed hysterically. The liquor was doing its job.

Emily locked the bedroom door feeling like she couldn't breathe, and went to the closet for her suitcase. She hated this. "Just let it go smoothly," she prayed, quickly pulling her clothes out of the dresser and shoving them into the suitcase.

An idea suddenly came to her, and she dug into her jeans pocket for the business card. In the bathroom out of hearing range, she held her breath and dialed the number.

"Seal Beach Police Department, Officer Hennessey."

"It's Emily," she said in a low voice.

Ten minutes later a text came in from Jonathan. *I'm in Seal Beach.*

Emily almost threw up.

She walked into the living room, where Stan and Eva sat all bleary-eyed. The room reeked of alcohol. "I'll be leaving soon," she said.

"Can't wait to meet 'im!" Eva slurred, raising her glass.

They all heard the car pull up and Emily went over and peeked out the window. There was Jonathan getting out of an Uber.

She turned and went into the bedroom and put her backpack on. When she heard Jonathan knock, she wheeled out her suitcase.

"What's that for?" Eva slurred, pointing at the suitcase.

"I'll get the door and tell you," Emily replied calmly.

Eva stood up.

Emily opened the door, and Jonathan said, "You ready, Emily?"

"Wha's going on?" Eva demanded, looking very angry.

Emily said nothing, just stepped out on the porch, and Jonathan picked up her suitcase.

"Emily is going home now," Jonathan said to Eva.

"Who are you?" Eva snarled.

"A friend of hers," he replied, turning to go.

"Stan, she's going home, do something!" Eva yelled, as Emily and Jonathan headed down the walk towards the Uber.

Stan came stumbling out the door, and down the walk where he grabbed Emily's arm. "You aren't leavin', we gotta' deal," he snarled.

Stan was suddenly yanked backward and thrown on his rear. "Don't you *ever* touch her again," Jonathan hissed, along with a few other words. It was the only time Emily had heard him swear. Stan just sat on the grass blinking at him.

Eva yelled an obscenity from the porch, grabbed one of her flowerpots and threw it. She was so drunk that her aim was off, and it rolled harmlessly out into the street near the Uber driver.

The frightened driver gaped at them all. In a flash he reached into the back seat of his car, pulled out Jonathan's luggage, tossed it to the ground, and sped off, tires squealing.

Emily looked at Jonathan. "What now?" she asked, as the car disappeared from view.

We'll walk somewhere and call another ride," he said, picking up his suitcase.

"Come on back in and let's talk things over," Eva said, stumbling toward them.

About then a police cruiser came rolling down the street and stopped in front of the house.

"Anyone need a ride to the airport?" Officer Hennessey asked, getting out of the car.

"We do," Emily said, looking up at Jonathan, who appeared to be quite puzzled.

"You called the police?" he asked.

"Yes, a while ago when I realized Eva and Stan were getting drunk."

"Good thinking," he chuckled.

In a last-ditch effort, Eva screamed at the policeman, "I'm her sister, Eva, and she's a minor, and I don't give her permission to leave!"

Officer Hennessey ignored her, reached over and grabbed Emily's suitcase and put it into the patrol car's trunk. Jonathan did the same with his, then they both got into the back seat of the car.

Eva came down the steps after them, still swearing.

When she reached the sidewalk, Officer Hennessey blocked her way and said, "I'll tell you what, Miss Eva, if you don't get back up on that porch, I will arrest you for public drunkenness."

She glared at him but hurried back up the steps.

"Stan, do something!" she resumed screaming from the porch.

Stan just looked at her like she was crazy. "Let it go Eva," he said, shaking his head, as he sat there on the lawn.

Emily glanced out the back window of the patrol car as they drove away, and saw that Eva was still back there shrieking. She watched her sister until the patrol car turned the corner.

Emily settled back in her seat as the plane took off out of Long Beach, then turned and looked up at Jonathan. "Did I already say, 'thank you?'"

"Yes, you did, about fifty-two times!" he smiled, looking at her with eyes the color of blueberries, that always made her heart flutter. "How are you doing?"

She thought a moment. "My biggest disappointment was that Officer Hennessey wouldn't turn on his siren on the way to the airport!" she yawned, sounding sleepy.

Jonathan laughed. "Yes, a true disappointment..."

"I'm so glad to be gone from there!" she said, putting her head on his shoulder, and closing her eyes.

"Just rest," he said, squeezing her hand, "we'll talk later."

But she didn't hear him because she was already asleep.

She woke somewhere over Colorado when the flight attendant came by and asked if they would like a snack. Emily asked for two bags of pretzels. She had been too upset to eat much for the last couple of days, and felt ravenous now.

"I'll pay you back for what you paid to change my airline ticket," she told Jonathan, crunching her pretzels.

"I'm not worried about it," he replied, watching her down the pack.

The contents of two bags disappeared quickly, and she peered into the last bag as if she expected more pretzels to appear, even turning it upside down.

"Take mine," Jonathan said, handing over the small bag.

"Are you sure?" she asked, ripping the bag open with her teeth.

"I'm sure, and I see you still eat like a lumberjack!"

Emily laughed and held the bag out offering to share, but he shook his head.

"So how are you feeling?"

She thought a moment. "Relieved and free," she said, popping a pretzel in her mouth.

"I understand *relieved,* but how do you feel free?"

"I'm not like them."

"What do you mean?"

"I somehow thought it was just a temporary fluke that I didn't drink and saw things differently than my family does, and I was always afraid that one day I would turn into them." She looked at him. "Crazy, huh?"

"No, not so crazy. So what did you find out?"

"It's choices. Making good choices. Your family doesn't doom you. Before, I sort of thought it did."

"Wow! How did meeting your sister do all that?"

"Well, it sounds silly, but she looks like me. And it was like looking at myself making bad choices, and all of a sudden, I knew that I wouldn't do that. Eva got to choose too, but she chose all wrong. Wrong guy, wrong attitude, wrong stealing the rent..."

"What?"

"I know it's weird, but that was a big thing to me. She didn't pay the rent on purpose and didn't care if it made the landlord lose the property! She only cared about herself."

"Her drinking didn't bother you?"

"Sure! I hated it!"

"But her not paying rent got to you the most, huh?"

"Yep! Stan told me that she hadn't paid it in a long time and knew how to con and make people trust her. It was a way of life with her." She wadded up the pretzel bag. "Being a bank robber would've been better. More honest. *Put your hands in the air and give me your money!* Say what you're doing and don't con people."

"You're a funny girl, Emily," he yawned, settling in for a nap as their plane flew over Texas.

When the Uber pulled in front of the bakery, Emily hopped out, and ran in as Jonathan paid the fare and collected their luggage.

"Mama, I'm home!" Emily called out, hurrying through the bakery door.

"What on earth...." Miss Mattie said, coming out from the kitchen wearing a cobalt blue apron with bright yellow moons.

"I missed you!" Emily cried, flying into her arms.

"How did you get here?" Miss Mattie asked, hugging her tight. "I didn't expect you until next week!"

About then, Jonathan came in with her luggage.

"Jonathan!" Miss Mattie said, looking from Emily to Jonathan, then back again.

"Have I got a story to tell you, Mama," Emily said, taking her arm. "But first, is there any food around here? We're starving!"

Miss Mattie bustled around, making sandwiches before they all settled in at a parlor table. A customer came in, and Miss Mattie got up to wait on them.

Emily turned, and for the first time noticed that her mama's recliner was sitting in a corner of the bakery. "That's odd," she said, pointing at the recliner.

Jonathan shrugged. "Ask her about it," he said, biting into his sand-wich.

Miss Mattie came back over with two desserts for them. "Now tell me about your trip, and why you're home early!" she said, settling into a parlor chair across from them.

"First tell me why your recliner is down here!"

"Oh!" Miss Mattie said, glancing at it. "I meant to have that out of here before you got back."

"Why is it down here?"

"Oh Sugar, I jus' got a little tired and the doctor said to keep my feet up, so Ike and Gus brought it down for me. I try and sit in it between customers, and I've been having Blessy help out a little more."

"You went to the doctor?"

"Yes, but I want to hear about your trip first!"

"No, tell me about the doctor!"

"Oh, I jus' had a little faintin' spell, and the doctor said I needed to rest more. Now tell me your story!"

"No! What's going on with you, Mama?"

Miss Mattie sighed. "My heart again."

Emily's jaw dropped. "I should never have left you!" she cried, scooting her chair over and putting her arms around her.

"It's okay, Sugar. Blessy and Clara have come in every day."

"Then why did you have the chair brought down?"

"Well, because I still need to remind the children of their manners, and because Clara will use chewin' tobacco when the customers are here if I don't keep an eye on her."

"That all could have waited, Mama! You should have just rested!"

"I'm not real good at that, Sugar," she replied sheepishly.

"Well, starting now, you will be. I'm taking over."

Miss Mattie opened her mouth to protest, but Emily shook her head. "No, I mean it, Mama!"

The bell over the door jangled and a woman and her young son came in.

"I'll take care of them," Emily said. "You sit tight!"

"Hello, Mrs. Steele, Hello Robert!" Miss Mattie greeted from the parlor table.

Mrs. Steele said hello, but Robert ignored the greeting and just pulled his mother's hand towards the pastry case.

Miss Mattie looked up at Emily.

Emily walked over to Robert and knelt down eye level with him. "Miss Mattie greeted you Robert, please say hello to her."

A shocked Robert looked in Miss Mattie's direction and murmured, "Hello."

Emily went behind the pastry case, and said, "What can I get for you two today?"

"Robert, what would you like?" Mrs. Steele asked her son.

He looked up at Emily and pointed to a chocolate donut, "Give me that one."

"May I have that one, *please,*" Emily corrected him.

But Robert just stared at her and folded his arms.

Emily glanced up at his mother, who turned to Robert and said, "Say *please*, Robert! Miss Mattie only lets polite boys have her donuts!"

Robert re-crossed his arms, put his chin on his chest, and murmured, "No."

Emily looked from the mother to her son and said, "Well, since Robert doesn't want to use his manners today. I guess we can't sell him that delicious chocolate donut!"

Robert uncrossed his arms, stuck his face out and glared at her. She stuck her face out and glared back.

All of a sudden, Robert lifted his arms, threw back his head, and in his best operatic voice sang, "May I have a choc-o-late donut pleeeeease?"

Not to be outdone, Emily threw back her head, and sang, "Yes you may! Yes you may! YES YOU MAY!"

Robert collapsed on the floor laughing as Emily got his donut.

"Now don't forget to hold the door open for your mother when you leave," Emily said, handing him the small white bag that contained one chocolate donut, and a surprise of two donut holes.

Robert not only held the door open for his mother but gave her a sweeping bow as she walked out.

"How'd I do?" Emily asked, walking back over to her mama and Jonathan.

"You're hired part time!" her mama said, laughing. "But I want to keep my chair down here so I can come and visit my customers when I get bored!"

"It's a deal!" Emily said, planting a kiss on her mama's forehead. "I'll keep an eye on Clara for you, too,".

"Alright! You work here four days a week, and Blessy can work the other three," the bakery owner said, planning it all out. "But jus' until school starts, then I should be fine, Sugar!"

Emily didn't reply, just kissed her again, and thought to herself: *No Mama, I'm not going back to school; You're going to rest and I'm taking over the bakery for you.*

Jonathan stood up. "I need to go surprise my folks now," he said, walking over to Emily. "I'll call you later. He gave her a hug, then went over to Miss Mattie, thanked her for lunch, and hugged her, too.

"I really like that young man," her mama said, as he left. "Now hurry up and tell me what happened on your trip."

Emily sat down and began the long story.

"That sounds like a story out of a bad movie," Miss Mattie murmured after Emily had told her about Eva and Stan, and her crazy visit. "I'm so sorry, Sugar," she said, shaking her head. "I talked to her and she seemed so nice. I wasn't the least bit worried."

"It's not your fault, Mama. My sister is very likable. She just happens to be an alcoholic, and a con artist. There's no way you could have known that."

Miss Mattie just shook her head, a look of immense guilt clouding her eyes.

"Didn't you pray for me when I left?" Emily asked, taking her hand.

Her Mama nodded. "And every day while you were gone, too!"

"Well, looks like God heard you just fine, and here I am all safe, and happy to be home!"

"Then we'll leave it at that, Sugar," she replied, thumping the table for emphasis. "Want to help me close up the bakery?"

"No, I want you to go upstairs and rest while I close it up," Emily replied, pulling her to her feet.

"Now tomorrow, don't forget to put on one of my nice aprons," her mama reminded her.

"I'll put on the brightest one I can find," she laughed, walking her to the door.

Chapter - 10

On her days off from the bakery, Emily worked the afternoon shift at *Good Eats Café*. Montana Chan came sauntering in one afternoon, and everyone greeted him as he hung his cowboy hat on the rack, sauntered over to the counter, boots clomping loudly, and sat down on the stool next to Gus.

"Howdy partner," he said, picking up a menu.

"What's goin' on in the newspaper world?" Gus asked, biting into his ham and cheese sandwich.

"Well, my honorable friend, we got the Mountain Grove Apple Festival coming up soon," Montana replied, getting up and grabbing his personalized mug off the wall rack. He went behind the counter and poured himself some coffee from the urn. "I'll take a bacon and tomato sandwich," he told Emily, walking back to his seat.

"Gotta' get someone to cover the festival though. Me and the missus are going on that cruise to Hawaii I've been promising her since before our son was born."

"How old is your son now?" Gus asked.

"He's twenty-two," Montana said, carefully measuring a quarter teaspoon of sugar into his coffee.

"Well, no one can accuse you of bein' impulsive!" Gus remarked, shaking his head.

When Emily was within hearing range, Montana said loudly, "Know anyone around here who'd like to earn a little extra money taking pictures at the town's Apple Festival for the special edition?"

"I'm your girl!" Emily said, walking by with two pork chop specials for the customers at the table near the window.

She served the platters and came back over. "What do you want me to take pictures of?"

"Anything that looks interesting," he replied, as Ike set his sandwich down on the counter. "If you haven't been to one yet, it's just like a county fair, but we just dress it up a little and call it a festival. Get me about twenty pictures, and I'll have Rusty stick them in the newspaper over the captions."

"Who is Rusty, may I ask?" Ike said, running a white towel over the counter.

"My new help!"

"Does he know anything about runnin' a newspaper press?"

Montana shrugged, "Says he does!"

"Do you need me to write the captions, too?" Emily asked.

"Naw! I'll write them before I go," he replied, taking a sip of coffee.

"How are you gonna' write about somethin' that hasn't happened yet?" Gus asked, turning and staring at him like he'd lost his mind.

"It's simple, my honorable friend," Montana said, applying a generous amount of salt to the tomatoes on his sandwich. "All fairs are alike! For example, I'll write about the ladies' baking contest—rave about the winning pie—and just leave out what kind of pie, and the name of the Blue-Ribbon winner. Same with the sewing entry, the crochet entry, pig and sheep entry, etcetera, etcetera!"

"I think yer' off yer' rocker, if you wanna' know what I think!" Gus said, popping the last of his sandwich into his mouth. "Ever hear of Murphy's Law?"

"It'll be fine!" Montana assured him. "I've already written a glowing review of the ladies' jams and jellies, the quilting category and needle-work, and ditto with the farm animals: the fattest pig, the best-looking sheep. You name it, and it's always the same, year in, and year out." He bit into his sandwich. "Emily can take pictures and Rusty will stick them over the caption, and Bingo! I'll be on my cruise ship sipping those little drinks with the paper umbrellas." He blew on his coffee, took a sip, and shrugged, "What could go wrong?"

"I can think of about fifty things that could go wrong with that little deal!" Gus said, standing up. "And you need more than just facts to make your article interestin'. Remember last year durin' the greased pig contest, the pig got away and run straight for the parkin' lot and got hit by that Dodge pick-up?"

Montana rolled his eyes.

"Pork chops for everyone on that deal," Gus said, heading for the cash register. "Year before that some kid threw up all over Miz King's prize-winnin' cake." He got his wallet out of his back pocket and handed Ike a twenty. "You need to write about stuff like that, not just who won which Blue Ribbon. You'll put your readin' audience to sleep with just facts, they want personal stories too!"

"It'll work out!" Montana growled, taking another bite of his bacon sandwich.

"And you might wanta' make sure ole' Rusty knows how to run a printin' press before you go galivantin' off to Hi-wi-ya on a cruise," Gus said, as Ike handed him his change. Putting a two-dollar tip under his coffee mug, Gus turned to leave, and thumped Montana on the shoulder. "That's what I would do anyway, partner."

Montana just shook his head as Gus left, and the screen door banged shut behind him.

"What's Murphy's Law, Montana?" Emily asked.

"Something about, *If anything can go wrong, it will...*"

She looked at him.

"It'll be fine," he growled.

A week later, Emily texted Jonathan on her break: *Want to come to the Mountain Grove Apple Festival with me tomorrow? I'm taking pictures for the Gazette.*

The reply came back with a winking emoji: *You're the first girl to ask me out on a picture-taking date..*

Emily texted back an emoji with its tongue sticking out and thought about what he'd just written. "I hope I'm the only girl that's ever asks you out on a date," she said softly, feeling her stomach cinch as she thought about what kind of commitment that really meant.

At the fairgrounds, Sheriff Mobley stood by the side gate checking the festival workers' passes as they came in. Emily didn't have a pass, and just held her camera up, saying, "I'm taking pictures for the Gazette!"

"Have to get you a *press pass* now that you're an official reporter, Emily," he smiled, opening the side gate for her and Jonathan.

She didn't know why that made her feel so good, but it did.

They headed over to the livestock area, and Emily wrinkled her nose as they got closer. "What is that smell?"

Jonathan looked at her like she was kidding. "Um...livestock!"

"Wow, poor farmers," she said, her eyes watering.

"You've never been up close to a cow or pig?"

"No," she said, getting tissues out of her backpack and stuffing them up each nostril. "I've only been around animals that get bathed."

Jonathan laughed. "Are you going to go around all afternoon with tissue stuck up your nose?"

She looked up at him as a breeze fluttered the nose tissue. "It's either that or throw up!" she said, sounding very nasally.

He bit his lower lip to keep from laughing as they walked towards the sheep pen.

Emily took two pictures, then leaned over the railing to get a close-up of the sheep's face. The sheep bleated and bolted, running over to the other side of the pen. It huddled as far away from her as possible. She heard a snorting sound from Jonathan and looked at him.

"I think the Kleenex fluttering out your nose may be scaring it," he howled, laughing so hard he had to hold onto a fence post to keep from falling over.

Pulling the tissues out of her nose, Emily tried to appear indignant. "Well, I see that you're on the sheep's side in the matter," she said, stuffing the tissues into her pocket.

The sheep bleated at her again.

"Give me one of your tissues," Jonathan howled, wiping tears from his eyes with the back of his hand.

"I only have the ones stuffed up my nose," she replied, haughtily.

"Oh my gosh, I've never seen anything so funny!" he gasped, wiping his eyes with a sleeve.

She glared at him, pinched her nose and strode over to the pig pens, gagging twice.

Emily's breath exploded as they left the huge barn area, and she gulped in the fresh air. "I would *not* make a good farmer!"

"Really?" he teased.

"I would need a HazMat suit!"

"Well, that's too bad," he grinned, pulling a piece of straw from her hair. "I was thinking we would have a farm someday."

Emily's heart skipped a beat, and she didn't know what to say, so she said, "I smell something good!"

"I think the baking contest is this way," he said, grabbing her hand.

On the way over, they saw that the high school had a fund-raising booth manned by Bitsy and four other cheerleaders. Emily wanted to skirt around the whole thing, but before she could manage it, Bitsy called out to Jonathan.

"Yoo Hoo! Jonathan!" she giggled, shaking purple and red pom poms at him, and totally ignoring Emily.

Jonathan put his arm around Emily and walked over.

"What are you doin' here," Bitsy cooed, batting her eyelashes at him.

"Just came with Emily to take pictures for the newspaper," he replied, pulling Emily closer.

"Take our picture for the newspaper," Bitsy squealed, acknowledging Emily for the first time. The other cheerleaders also squealed, grabbing their pom poms, and posing quickly.

Emily didn't say a word, just positioned the camera as they held the pom poms high.

"Take one with this pose!" Bitsy said, and the girls turned sideways with their hands on their hips, and their heads thrown back.

"Jonathan," Bitsy squealed, with an extra flutter of her eyelashes, "you come and stand with me in a picture!"

"No," he said, taking the camera out of Emily's hands. "We're going to the kissing booth to take a picture."

"Kissin' booth?" Bitsy asked, her eyes wide. "Where's the kissin' booth?"

"It's right here!" Jonathan said, holding the camera up at an angle as he pulled Emily close to him and kissed her, clicking off three pictures.

"Oh! Very funny!" Bitsy snorted, glaring at them.

Emily just smiled up at him, and he kissed her again as they walked away.

The next day, Emily went to *Bloomin' Happy* to use their computer to download the festival pictures and send them to Rusty. Jonathan looked over her shoulder as the pictures came into view, watching as she scanned through them. He did a double take when the pictures of Bitsy and the other cheerleaders came up on the screen. "What happened to their heads?" he asked, staring at the headless cheerleaders.

"Opps!" Emily replied innocently, as she scrolled through the pictures. "I guess I accidently cut their heads off."

"Are you going to submit them to the newspaper that way?" he asked, trying not to laugh.

"Hmmmm! No, that wouldn't be good. I think I'll cut and paste donkey heads on them."

Jonathan nodded. "Think Rusty will use their picture with donkey heads?"

She looked up at him and they both laughed.

"Hey you two, what's so funny?" Mr. Charles asked, walking up behind them and reaching for his receipt book.

"Oh nothing," Jonathan replied, "Emily's just searching the internet for donkey heads."

Mr. Charles looked at them both, shook his head, and walked off.

Emily loaded all the pictures into a folder, deleting the ones of headless cheerleaders. She typed in the newspaper's email address and hit send. The pictures had been promised by 10:00 am, and it was 9:50 now. She stood up and put on her backpack.

Jonathan came up behind and rested his chin on her head. "Want to go get something to eat?"

"I can't today," she replied, leaning back against him. "I need to help at the bakery, Blessy leaves in a while."

"How's your mama doing now?"

"Better. The doctor just told her she has to rest more. In fact, I need to run back now."

"Know anyone who might want to go fishing tomorrow?" he asked, as she put on her backpack.

"I'm your girl," she replied, smiling up at him.

"Yes, you are," he said, kissing her goodbye.

Emily stopped in at *Good Eats* the next morning to check the schedule. When she walked through the door, all the patrons started hooting!

She looked at Ike, then Gus, and asked, "What's going on?"

"Oh nothin' much," replied Gus, "just readin' the morning paper!" He turned it towards her, and there on the front page was a full-page picture of Jonathan kissing her!

"What?" she cried, hurrying over.

She looked at the headline: *Romance at the Mountain Grove Apple Festival*, it read.

Emily groaned. "I forgot to delete those pictures."

"Obviously," Ike hooted, and everyone in the café laughed. It seemed that they had all grabbed their own copies of the newspaper.

Thumbing through the rest of the paper she cried, "Oh no!".

The pictures were all mixed up with the wrong captions. Under the picture of the pigs, was the caption, *Ruby West looks mighty proud after winning the Blue Ribbon for her apple strudel!*

The names of embroidery winners were under pictures of the cows, and the caption read that the Blue-Ribbon winners were "udderly pleased" with their prize!

Emily read each caption out loud, laughing so hard, she could barely speak. The café patrons followed along, and the hooting and howling could be heard up and down the block. Across the street in Emerson Park, children on the playground stopped their chatter and listened.

Emily was still chuckling later as she pushed open the bakery door. She stopped laughing abruptly when she saw her mama sitting in the recliner staring intently at the front page of the Gazette newspaper.

"What in the world, Sugar?' her mama asked, frowning as she held up the picture of Jonathan kissing her.

"There's a story behind it, Mama," Emily assured her, walking over.

"Well, I'm listenin'," her mama said, meaning business.

Emily gulped. "You need to know who is just out of camera range in that picture."

"Okay..."

"It's Bitsy and her friends. First, she snubbed me, then she wanted me to take pictures of her posing with the other cheerleaders for the newspaper, so I did. Then she wanted Jonathan to come and stand with her while I took her picture."

"She wanted *you* to take a picture of her and Jonathan?" Miss Mattie asked, her eyes bugging slightly. "What did you say?"

"I didn't say anything. Jonathan told her no, that we were going to take our picture at the kissing booth."

"The festival had a kissin' booth?" Miss Mattie asked incredulously.

"It did when Jonathan kissed me in front of Bitsy and snapped our picture! I meant to delete it, but I forgot to, then that crazy Rusty put the picture on the front page of the Gazette for everyone to see!"

"And for Bitsy to see!" her mama said, a smile tugging at her lips. "Well, well. The Lord does work in mysterious ways, doesn't He?"

"I'm not sure the Lord was in on this one, Mama. I cut off all the cheerleaders heads on purpose when I took their picture. I told Jonathan I was going to paste donkey heads on all of them."

Emily was relieved to see her mama's stomach jiggling with laughter as she got up from the recliner and came over to her. "Emily, Emily! What am I gonna' do with you," she said, her voice breaking with laughter.

"I wouldn't have done it, but they aren't nice to me at school."

"What do they do, Sugar?"

Emily sighed. "They make remarks a lot, call me Little Orphan Emmy, poor lil' Em'ly. Junk like that."

"Hmmm. Mean girls, huh?"

Emily nodded.

"Check that camera of yours and see if there's any pictures of those cheerleaders left."

"Are you going to look for donkey heads?" Emily laughed.

"No," her mama replied, "donkey butts."

Emily and Jonathan stood on a flat rock at the river's edge as Jonathan cast his line out for the fifth time. "I think I waited too late in the day to fish," he remarked, reeling the line back in. He looked at her, "I really just wanted to be here with you anyway," and leaned over and kissed her.

He put his fishing gear away and they sat, holding hands, looking out over the water as it splashed and swirled around rocks and boulders. Sun rays sparkled and danced on the river, making it look as though jewels had been strewn across its surface. "What's on your mind, Emily?"

"How did you know I was thinking about stuff?" she asked, putting her head on his shoulder.

"Because I know you, and you're being way too quiet."

"Okay," she began, "I'm trying to think of how to tell my Mama I'm not going back to school in the fall, that I'm worried about her health, and I want to take over running the bakery. Then I've promised Kelly Ann I'll walk with her every day, and when the baby comes, I want to help her with that. I also want to work at *Good Eat's* for extra money. I don't want Mama paying for everything for me."

He turned to say something, and was surprised to see tears running down her cheeks. "Why are you crying?" he asked, pulling her close.

"It's gotten too big!" she sobbed.

"What has?"

"Life!"

"Ok, let's take one thing at a time. What do you think Miss Mattie will say about you homeschooling?"

"She puts education ahead of everything; but I can study at home and still go to college."

"Then tell her that."

"I did, but she thinks I need to be around kids my own age."

"Do you?"

"No! You saw how Bitsy and her awful friends treat me. But she wants me to keep trying, and I really don't even want a bunch of friends. I just want to manage my life the way I want to. I'm not used to having a parent!"

For some odd reason, they both burst out laughing at that.

"Miss Mattie knows you've got good sense," he said, getting a paper towel out of his tackle box and handing it to her. "It's all going to work out."

"When are you leaving?" she sniffed behind the paper towel.

"In four days. Is that also why you're crying?"

"I can't tell you; it would put pressure on you." She hiccupped behind the paper towel, and they both laughed again.

"You don't need to protect me," he said, pulling the paper towel away from her face.

"Ok, then yes, I'm sad about that. I like to tell you everything, and I like it that you don't get upset, you just figure it out." She looked up at him. "Like you're doing right now."

He smiled, "Want to walk through the woods?"

"I would, but I need to get back and close up the bakery." Emily stood up. "Blessy is working extra hours, and it's getting too expensive to have her keep doing that."

They gathered up all the fishing equipment and headed for town. As they turned onto First Street, Jonathan was the first one to notice the ambulance. "Emily…" he started to say, but Emily saw it too.

"No, no, no, no, no!" she gasped, and took off running.

The ambulance raced away before she could get there. Ike, Gus, and Mr. Kingery were standing on the sidewalk in front of the bakery, as she ran up to them.

"Is it my Mama?" Emily sobbed.

They nodded.

"Is she…"

"No," Ike said, "but she's pretty bad off."

"I'll go get the pick-up and drive you to the hospital," Jonathan said, hurrying off.

Emily ran into the bakery where Blessy stood looking pale and frightened.

"What happened, Blessy?" Emily cried.

"She jus' collapsed," Blessy said, reaching for a chair. She sat down heavily. "She jus' fell to the floor and I called 911."

Emily felt lightheaded and couldn't think of what to do.

Gus came in. "Jonathan's here, Em'ly. Let Blessy close the bakery, I'll give her a hand. You go on to the hospital."

She got in the pick-up with Jonathan but didn't remember the ride. She just clutched the arm rest, praying softly, "Please don't let her die; please don't let her die." Mouthing it over and over again."

When they got to the hospital, the nurse told them to wait in the waiting room. "Is she okay?" Emily implored, silently pleading with the nurse to say yes.

"No," the nurse answered, "but there's an excellent team of doctors working on her."

Emily buried her face in her hands.

Jonathan put his arm around her and led her to a chair. They sat for a moment, but Emily felt like she was suffocating. "I can't breathe in here," she said, standing up as panic swept over her. She looked this way and that but couldn't think of what to do.

"Look at me," Jonathan said, standing up and taking her hand.

She looked up at him.

"I'm going to give the nurse your phone number, then we'll walk around outside. You're just overwhelmed."

Emily nodded, not wanting to leave, but wanting to breathe.

Jonathan came back over and led her to the elevator. Outside, they turned left and headed to a nearby park. She felt her chest ease up, and breathing became more natural. "I don't know how to do this," she whispered.

"You don't need to do anything," he assured her. "We'll wait for the doctor together."

The wind in the trees, and children playing on the park equipment calmed something deep inside her. Normal. She needed things to be normal.

They sat for about twenty minutes, and Jonathan said, "Are you ready to go back to the hospital?"

"I'm afraid of what's there," she whispered.

He nodded. "Well, whatever is there, I'm going to be right by your side."

She stood, and they walked back.

Mr. Charles and Gus were sitting in the waiting room. Emily stared at their faces trying to read them. When Mr. Charles smiled at her, she stopped holding her breath.

"Any news?" Jonathan asked.

Before they could answer, a nurse came over to them. "Are you Emily?"

She nodded.

"Mrs. Cooke won't relax until I come out with her message. She said to tell you she'll be okay, and to please go back and take care of the bakery. I hope that makes sense to you, because it seemed very important to her. She's had a heart attack and is a very sick woman."

"Will she be okay?"

"I can't say for certain, but I believe so. I think it's important to listen to her though. If she wants you at a bakery, I'd like to tell her that's where you're going."

She looked up at Jonathan, not knowing what to do.

"Tell Mrs. Cooke that Emily is headed back to the bakery, and she'll be back first thing in the morning," Jonathan told the nurse.

Emily went over to Mr. Charles. "Are you staying?"

"I'll stay. Give Gus a ride back to town though, he needs to get back to his station."

The three of them rode back to Mountain Grove in silence. Nobody knew what to say. Emily was numb, feeling like she shouldn't have left, but wanting her mama not to worry about the bakery.

When she got back to town, Blessy was just clearing the pastry case, getting ready to close.

"I'll wash things up," Emily told her, tying on an apron. "I'm not sure what to do about tomorrow. Will you be able to come in?"

"I need to tell you somethin'," Blessy said quietly.

Emily nodded for her to go on.

"This bakery is too much for your Mama. It ain't the first time she felt pain in her chest. She jus' can't afford more help."

"I've been working most afternoons," Emily said, "and I thought you worked mornings."

"I work a couple of hours, and she's been doin' the rest."

Guilt slammed into Emily. "I should have been paying more attention!"

"That's why I'm tellin' you. She can't do this no more." Blessy looked at Emily. "She's goin' to be mad at me, tellin' you all this. But I had to."

"Of course you did, Blessy! And thank you." She gave her a reassuring hug. "I'll figure out what to do now."

Blessy started to gather up her things, then turned and said, "I also saw her fussin' over the bills. She's been worrin' too much."

The weight of this took Emily's breath away, but she said, "Thanks for telling me all this, Blessy. Is there anything else I should know?"

"Taxes went up on this place, nearly double," she said, looking guilty again.

"Do you know where she keeps that information and all the bills?" Emily asked, realizing she had no idea what was going on around here.

Blessy went over behind the counter, knelt down, and opened a small cabinet. She lifted out a large tin box and placed it on the counter. "Everything is in here." She shook her head and murmured, "Miss Mattie gonna' be real mad at me, showin' all this to you."

"You did the right thing, Blessy. No one is going to be mad."

After Blessy left, Emily took the box over to a small parlor table, emptied out the contents, and went through the information, paper by paper.

They were in trouble.

She spent the next half hour writing all the information down on a slip of paper, tucked the box under her arm, and feeling weary to the bone, went slowly up the stairs to her home over the bakery.

Chapter - 11

When her alarm went off at 5:00 am, Emily threw the covers back, and called the hospital, where she received a depressing report on her mama's condition.

She called Clara, their other part-time worker, to come in and help Blessy. They couldn't afford it, but she couldn't stay away from the hospital.

Should she call Jonathan and wake him up? There was no other way to get to the hospital in Monett, so she dialed his number. He sounded sleepy, but said he'd be there in half an hour. She hurried down the steps to make sure Blessy had started the day's baking. Clara came in, and she ran back up the stairs and got ready for the ride to the hospital.

When they arrived an hour later, Emily was surprised they let Jonathan come into the room with her. Her Mama was awake, and ready to give orders.

"Who is doin' the bakin' this mornin'?" her mama asked weakly.

"I've got everything under control, and I don't want you to think about it," Emily replied, taking her hand. "I just want you to get well and come home to me. I can handle everything else." Her Mama's hand was icy cold, and Emily drew the blanket up and tucked it around her.

"Do you need another blanket?" Emily asked.

Miss Mattie's eyes were closed, and she shook her head. "I'm goin' to jus' rest today, Sugar, and it would set my mind at ease if you went and took care of the bakery."

"Okay," she replied, realizing there was little choice in the matter. "Mr. Charles and Gus are coming up later."

"They are?" her mama asked weakly.

Yes, when I call and ask them to, Emily thought, but said, "Yes, ma'am." She knew she had to get back to the bakery and take over. This situation wasn't going away, and life would be changing. Right now the most she could do was to make sure that someone was always here with her mama during the day, and she would come and see her in the evening.

On the third morning of the hospital stay, her mama called. "They're releasin' me today," she said, sounding tired but happy. "Would you see if Joe Charles can give me a ride home?"

She would be so glad when she got her driver's license, but said, "Yes, I'll call him now. I'm coming with him to talk to your heart doctor."

"It's all right, Sugar, you stay with the bakery."

Blessy and Clara can handle it until I come back," Emily said, meaning it.

"That's too much money going out in salaries," her mama started to say, but Emily interrupted her.

"Remember, you're letting me handle things until you're better. I want to hear exactly what the doctor says, not second-hand information."

Miss Mattie sighed but didn't argue.

Mr. Charles was busy so he sent Jonathan. "I thought you'd be packing for London," Emily said as she climbed into the pick-up thirty minutes later.

He glanced at her. "I dropped my summer classes. I'm not leaving until Miss Mattie is home and you're okay."

Emily was stunned. "You didn't have to do that," she whispered, touched beyond measure.

"I don't want to leave you in the middle of a crisis like I did last year. I'll go back in late August. That should give you enough time to get your bearings."

"I don't know if the crisis will go away that soon," she said, deciding to tell him everything.

"What do you mean?"

"The bakery is in trouble financially. I think that was part of my mama's stress."

He let out his breath slowly. "Okay," he finally said, "how I can help?"

"Do you want to take the train down the mountain into Clayton and hand out flyers, the way you helped me last time?" she teased, suddenly feeling extremely happy that he was staying longer.

"It helped your dad, but not you," he said, as they wheeled into the hospital parking lot. He turned and looked at her. "But *yes*, if that would help, I'd do it."

"Thank you," she said, meaning it. "And if you come up with any money making ideas, I'd love to hear it."

Emily managed to catch the cardiologist just as he was leaving her mama's room. He was in a hurry, curt and to the point: "Mrs. Cooke's heart is damaged. She's to have complete rest until her appointment with Dr. Blackstone in seven days. I understand that she owns a bakery. Running that is completely out of the question now. Too stressful, it will kill her."

Emily, astonished at his abruptness, said, "That's it?"

"Just do common sense things," he replied gruffly, turning to leave. "Healthy foods, no stress," he called over his shoulder while walking down the hallway, then turned, "And don't start an exercise plan until Dr. Blackstone advises. The nurse will give you paperwork with everything you need to know."

She looked at Jonathan and shrugged. "Well, so much for bedside manners. I'll have to wait and ask Dr. Blackstone now."

She started to go into Miss Mattie's room, but Jonathan put out a hand and stopped her. "Emily, Dr. Blackstone isn't going to have anything magic you can do to make Miss Mattie's heart better. Listen to what this doctor said. He's a specialist. No, he doesn't have a great bedside manner, but you can't pretend that another doctor will make it all better."

Emily looked away. "I hate this," she murmured, biting her lip.

"I know," he replied, brushing her hair back. "Let's talk about it later though. You look like you're going to cry."

She nodded, and gulped a couple of times, bringing her emotions under control. They went into the room where Miss Mattie sat looking tired and pale in a wheelchair. Emily's heart literally squeezed at how frail she looked.

"Ready to go, Mama?" Emily whispered, hugging her.

A nurse hurried in with a sheaf of papers and began to go over them. It was all depressing, and Emily couldn't wait to leave.

The nurse wheeled her mama out to the pickup and Jonathan helped her into the back seat. Emily tucked a warm blanket over her legs.

"Quit spoilin' me, Sugar," her mama said.

"I love doing it," she replied, wishing they could stop at the Foster Freeze down the street and get her mama one of the ice creams she loved. But no more ice cream for a while, and Emily wondered how she could ever keep her from eating her beloved pastries.

When they pulled in front of the bakery back in Mountain Grove, Miss Mattie said, "I'll come and sit in my easy chair in the bakery."

"No ma'am, you won't," Emily said, "your easy chair is back upstairs where it belongs, and where you belong. I've got the bakery under control. You get to rest."

Miss Mattie opened her mouth to protest, but one look at Emily and she knew not to argue. "Looks like you mean business!" she said quietly.

"Yes, ma'am, I do," Emily replied, leading her towards the stairs.

Jonathan helped get Miss Mattie settled, hugged them both and turned to leave for the nursery. On his way out, Emily whispered, "I'm coming over to talk to your dad about some things after I close up the bakery. Would you tell him?"

He looked at her puzzled, but she put a finger to her lips, and nodded towards her mama who was starting to doze off in her easy chair.

After she was sure Miss Mattie had everything she needed to be comfortable, including her cell phone and the remote to the TV, Emily hurried downstairs to tell Blessy and Claire that she could handle the bakery now. She silently calculated how much it had cost to have both of them working all those hours and cringed. *No more of that,* she whispered to herself as they left.

Emily made a small sign to put on the counter telling customers she would be back in ten minutes. Every forty-five minutes, she ran back up the steps to check on her mama. Once when she came back, Gus was behind the counter, putting donuts in a bag for a customer, and then handed them their change. "You doin' this all alone, Miss Em'ly?" Gus asked, as the customer left.

She nodded. "Hired help is expensive."

"Tell you what, you go on back upstairs and get a load off yer' feet for awhile. I can handle sellin' donuts for an hour."

"What about your service station?"

"People know how ta' fill their own tank," he replied, with a tug on his ball cap. "if they need somethin' else, they'll come back. We're fam'ly here."

Touched and relieved, Emily hurried back upstairs.

Emily came back to the bakery an hour later, feeling refreshed. "Thanks, Gus!" she said, hugging him.

"Anytime," he said, awkwardly thumping her on the back.

She went behind the bakery case and put something in a small paper bag.

"What's this?" he asked, when she handed it to him.

"It's an apple fritter, your favorite...and it's me saying thank you!"

He grinned, thumped her on the back again, and left.

From three o'clock until the four o'clock closing time, there were only three customers, and Emily made a mental note of that. When it was time to close, she left the bakery clean-up for later, wanting to get to *Bloomin' Happy* before it closed. She gathered up the business records, went up to check on her mama, then headed over to the nursery.

Mr. Charles was nowhere in sight when she got there. "Where's your dad?" she asked Jonathan.

He's in the grocers getting you some hot chocolate," he grinned. "When I told him you were coming, he said that he knew you loved it."

"I sure do," she smiled, touched by the gesture.

Mr. Charles came through the side door of *Village Grocer* carrying a holder with three cups of hot chocolate topped high with whipped cream and set it on a potting table. He gave Emily a hug and said, "Let's sit over here."

After they had settled in, Mr. Charles said, "Jonathan mentioned you're needing some advice."

She took a sip of her hot chocolate and set it down next to her, and said, "Yes, financial advice."

"What's going on?"

"The bakery is going broke," she replied bluntly, "and I wanted to see if you have any ideas on how to save it."

Mr. Charles jaw actually dropped, and it was the first time she ever saw him speechless. "You're joking," he finally said.

"I wish I were," Emily replied, opening the small box she had brought with her, and handing the papers to Mr. Charles.

He studied them silently for a few minutes; a customer came in and Jonathan went to wait on her.

After looking them over, Mr. Charles said, "This isn't good news."

"I know," Emily replied. "Do you have any ideas of what I can do?"

"What *you* can do?"

"Yes, my Mama can't be involved; the doctor said *no stress*."

He nodded. "The only thing I can think of right now is upselling."

"What is that?" she asked, reaching for her hot chocolate.

"Well, you already have a building, and you already have customers, so bring other things into the bakery that your customers would be interested in," he began. "For instance, I sell flowers and bushes, but I have a rack of gardening books...that's upselling. The gloves, gardening tools, and pottery are all upselling. It's actually where I make most of my money, but the flowers bring the customers in. See what I mean?"

"Yes I do!" Emily was growing excited. "We sell pastries, but bring in other things, so when they come in for the donuts, I sell them something else too!"

"Bingo! Do you have any ideas of what would work?"

Emily thought a moment. "It seems like I should keep with the theme, so maybe baking supplies? Fancy rolling pins, and baking dishes? Bright aprons, for sure!" she laughed. "Am I on the right track?"

"That's exactly right, and a lot of those items can be bought on consignment."

"What's that?"

"You don't pay for the merchandise when it comes, you pay when it sells. You send the dealer their share of the money, and you keep the profit."

"Consignment would definitely be good!" she replied, thinking of the bakery's low bank balance.

"How about fancy coffee," Jonathan offered, "I've heard there's a big profit in that!"

"I think Ike tried it at his café, but no one was that interested."

"People usually just want regular coffee with a meal," Mr. Charles said, "but they would expect specialty coffee—I call it *foo-foo* coffee—in a bakery!"

"That's true!" Emily's mind began to swirl with ideas.

"Ike took that fancy coffee machine out of the café, and has it stored somewhere," Mr. Charles said. "Why don't you ask him if he wants to sell it?"

"I'll go over right after I leave here." Emily felt happier than she had in days.

"It would certainly help pay for Blessy and Claire's wages," Mr. Charles offered.

"I'm going to homeschool and cut their work time back to just baking."

There was silence.

She saw the concern on Mr. Charles' face and went on to explain. "I've been wanting to homeschool for a long time, so don't think I'm making some big sacrifice." She shrugged. "I'm not."

"You don't like school?"

"I don't like going to a place where everyone knows your parents left you, and a lot of them aren't nice about it."

Mr. Charles nodded that he understood, and she was glad he didn't make a fuss about it.

"Hi Ike," Emily said, walking into the kitchen of *Good Eats*.

"Well hello darlin'," he said, grinning as he flipped over three hamburger patties. "How's that Mama of yours doin'?"

"She's really tired and rests a lot, but I think she's doing okay."

"Glad to hear it," he replied, reaching for the hamburger buns on the prep table. "What brings you to my neck of the woods?"

"Do you still have your fancy latte machine?"

"I do! It's in my storage closet collectin' dust. Why'd you ask?"

She decided to give him an honest answer. "The bakery is going broke, and I need to start upselling. I'm going to try selling fancy coffee, and some kitchen stuff."

"I see," he said thoughtfully, as he put cheese slices on the burger patties. "Go check at the back of my pantry, I think that's where I stuck the blamed thing."

Emily went and checked and came back just as he was handing the burger platters to Millie.

"Is it back there?"

"Yes, will you sell it to me?"

"No, but I'll give it to you."

"Ike, no! I didn't come here and ask so you'd give it to me. They cost a lot of money."

"As I recall," he began, gesturing with his spatula, "you've been spendin' a lot of time with Kelly Ann, helpin' her exercise and get ready for that new great-gran'baby of mine."

"That's two different things, Ike."

"Naw, it isn't. You're helpin' my granddaughter, and now I want to help you. Remember our Pass It Along Club?"

Emily nodded.

"Well, you gotta' double load now, with your Mama taken' ill and the bakery needin' a little help."

She stood there staring at him, not knowing what to say.

"The latte machine is yours," he said, meaning it.

She threw her arms around him. "Thank you, Ike."

"You're welcome, darlin', and don't think another thing about it. Just pass it on to the next person!"

On the way home, she texted Jonathan, asking him to pick up the coffee machine for her and deliver it to the bakery.

That night Emily went online to see what she could find to sell at the bakery. There was one store that had everything she needed, but in order to get it at a discount for resell, she needed a merchant number. Digging through the tin box to see if the bakery had one, found nothing, plus she really didn't know exactly what she was looking for. "I need help," she said out loud, and Gabriella came to mind. She would ask her how she got all the beautiful items for her tearoom, and how to get a merchant number.

The tearoom was busy when she went in the next day, so she waved at Gabriella, who was pouring tea for a group of ladies, and went quietly into the kitchen where Gabriella's hired help was busy making scones.

"I'm Emily," she said, introducing herself. "Is it okay to wait here for Gabriella?"

"Of course," replied the small woman. "How is your mother doing?"

"She's home now," Emily replied, puzzled over who this woman might be. "Do you know my Mama?"

"No," she replied, smiling brightly. "I'm Gabriella's sister, Genevieve, here to help while she gets her business going; but my sister told me about you, and thinks you're very brave!"

Emily nodded, not knowing what to say.

"Should I come back another time? I just wanted some advice from Gabriella."

"I'll take over waiting on people so she can come and talk to you," she said, turning to a small sink and washing her hands before going into the dining area.

Gabriella came hurrying in moments later, looking lovely even in her haste. "Is everything all right, Emily?" she asked, giving her a brief hug.

"Ummm, not really," she replied frankly. "I'm here for advice."

"Let me get you some tea, and we can sit over in the corner and chat."

Emily started to say she didn't want any, but tea did sound good. "Thank you, and I'd like to buy one of your scones. I forgot to eat today."

"You must have a lot on your mind then," she said, rising from her seat and pouring Emily some tea. "Would you like a blueberry or an apple scone?"

"Blueberry sounds yummy!" Emily responded, her mouth already watering. She dug in her pocket for money to pay for it.

Gabriella noticed as she set the scone in front of her, and said, "You're not to pay me one cent. You're my guest."

"Thank you," Emily replied, biting hungrily into the scone.

Gabriella smiled and refilled her tea.

"I'm here to find out where you get your supplies," Emily said, adding a sugar cube to her tea.

Puzzled, Gabriella tilted her head, and Emily realized that a full explanation was needed. She took a deep breath and announced, "The bakery is going broke, and I need to upsell merchandise to bring in more money."

"Oh dear," Gabriella murmured, her violet eyes reflecting concern.

"Would you be able to show me how to get a merchant number? My Mama may have one, but I don't want to ask her anything about business right now. She's supposed to just rest until we see Dr. Blackstone."

At the mention of his name, Gabriella's eyes brightened. "I will gather up all the information you need," she replied. "Are you free to come back here at closing time? I'll be able to sit and chat longer then. I can't do it right now."

Emily breathed a sigh of relief. "I'll be here! Can I bring you anything from the bakery? A pie, or cake, or something?" It was all she could think of to show her thanks.

Gabriella laughed softly. "No, but thank you. I have enough trouble resisting our sweets here at the tearoom."

Chapter - 12

The next morning, on her way downstairs to the bakery, Emily texted Gilbert. *Would you stop by the bakery for a few minutes?* He texted back that he would be there at nine o'clock.

Blessy was waiting on a customer when Emily walked into the shop. She greeted them both and walked on back to the kitchen where Clara was busy washing mixer bowls. As she took an apron from the pegged wall, she saw that Clara had a wad of snuff—as Clara called it—stuck in her cheek.

"Clara," she said softly.

When Clara looked over, she tapped her cheek.

"Sorry, Em'ly. I forgot I was usin' it."

Emily didn't believe her, but said, "It's just not good business using chewing tobacco around the customers, Clara."

Sighing she went back out front. *Why do these small things wear me out so much?* she wondered, tying the apron strings in a bow. She went over to relieve Blessy from behind the cash register.

"Your mama will be pleased with you wearin' that apron," Blessy said, touching the ruby red apron with cobalt blue and green elephants. "How's she feelin' today?"

"She's just tired, Blessy, and she likes to make sure everything is just right in the bakery. I think it's hard for her to stay upstairs and let us handle it."

"Well, if she peeks in, I'm not gonna' let her do a thing."

Emily thought it would be a while before her mama could come downstairs and do any peeking in, but said, "Thank you for watching out for her."

"I love that woman," Blessy drawled, her eyes filling with tears, "and I'm gonna' make sure she's around a long time. She's been real good to me."

Emily smiled. "And she's been real good to me too, Blessy."

Clara came out from the kitchen putting her coat on, and Blessy got her sweater from under the counter.

"Thank you, ladies," Emily said.

"See you tomorrow," they both chorused.

Early morning customers kept her busy until nine, when Gilbert walked in the door. She finished up Mrs. Montoya's order, took a phone order for a blueberry pie, then walked over to talk to him.

"What's up?" he asked.

"Hungry?"

"Always," he grinned.

Emily took out a small doily-lined china plate, and put two chocolate donuts on it, knowing that was Gilbert's favorite.

They sat down at one of the parlor tables, and Emily got right to the point." I need your help."

"What do you need?" he asked, biting off a generous portion of donut.

"Would you be able to walk with Kelly Ann four or five days a week?"

"Sure, but why?"

"She won't walk alone, and I need to spend more time here at the bakery. I have to cut back on the help; the bakery isn't doing well financially."

"Wow! More problems, huh?"

Emily nodded and told him her plans.

"Here's what I'll do," he said after listening to her, "I'll walk with Kelly Ann five days a week. I don't know what times; it has to be around my school schedule, but Kelly Ann and I will work that out. Then one day a week, I'll work in the bakery, and take a load off you."

"You'd be able to do that?"

"Of course!" he said, biting into the second donut. "And I'll round up some more help for you."

She looked at him doubtfully. "What kind of help?"

"Beats me," he shrugged. "I don't have it all worked out yet, but you're gettin' help."

She smiled, and said, "Could you make sure they don't use snuff?"

He laughed. "That'll be the first qualification...no snuff."

Emily watched him laugh, thinking back to the first time she had met him, dirty and freezing, hiding in an alleyway from his dad.

"You've come a long way, Gilbert," she blurted out.

Gilbert looked puzzled for a moment, then said, "Well, you can give God all the credit for that."

She nodded, believing him as he sat there, clean-cut and capable. Gilbert was *thriving*. It was still her favorite word.

The bakery stayed fairly busy for the next couple of hours. Emily called her mama twice, and both times she told Emily that she was fine and didn't need a thing.

Jonathan came through the door just after noon.

"I'm here to help," he said, hugging her. "What do you need done?"

She leaned her head against his chest, wishing she could just stay there.

"My garden!" she said, popping her head up. "I've been neglecting it. Would you water it for me?"

"At you service, and here's a list of dinners coming your way." He took a paper out of his back pocket and handed it to her.

"What's this?"

"I've been setting things up for when I leave; these ladies have all signed up to bring you and Miss Mattie dinner on different nights. Tonight, it's my mom's turn, and I hear lasagna is on the menu."

"Thank you!" she whispered, giving him another hug. "But how can I give back to all these people?"

"Now's not the time to worry about that. You're going in five different directions already."

She just stared at the list, not knowing what to say. Gratitude filled her heart for these people.

She led Jonathan through the kitchen, and out the back door to her garden, leaving the back door open so she could hear the bell over the bakery door jingle if a customer came in. She was stricken seeing that her flowers had started to droop and felt guilty for being so neglectful.

Jonathan went down the steps, found the hose, and began watering. She watched a moment, and a thought occurred when she noticed some bare spaces in the garden.

"*Bloomin' Happy* carries vegetable plants, right?" she asked, as he watered her shasta daisies.

"Yes, what are you thinking?"

"I'm thinking that fresh vegetables would be good for my Mama, and I'd save money by growing them myself."

"What's your Mama's favorite vegetables?" he asked, reaching down and pulling out a couple of weeds.

She thought a moment. "Well, she's always talking about the fresh tomatoes her Herman used to plant for her."

"Who's Herman?"

"Her husband from many years back. I thought you knew."

"No, I didn't know," he replied, dragging the hose over to the pansy bed. "All right, she likes tomatoes. What else?"

"Zucchini, squash, corn, green beans...actually, I think the only vegetable she doesn't like is eggplant."

"Okay, I'll see what my dad has at the nursery."

"I need to go upstairs and check on her, I'll be back in a while." Emily put up the sign telling customers that she would be back in ten minutes. She didn't know if it was good business practice, but it was the best she could do for now—and she knew the villagers would come inside and wait for her. They were just that kind of people.

Jonathan sent a text while she was setting out her mama's afternoon medications. *I'll be back in a half hour*, it read. A few minutes later there was a knock at the door and when she opened it there stood Mrs. Charles wearing over-sized oven mitts, and holding a colorful casserole dish, the contents of which smelled absolutely amazing!

"Dinner is served!" she sang out, coming through the door. "Would you grab that bag, Emily? It's garlic bread and salad to go with your lasagna!" The wonderful aroma wafted through the whole apartment as Mrs. Charles walked into the kitchen, and set everything on the counter, then reached into her jacket pocket and brought out a mason jar of homemade salad dressing. After arranging everything, she turned and smiled at Emily, whose mouth had begun to water.

"Thank you so much!" Emily said, hugging her, and thinking she'd send a pie home with Jonathan, as a way of saying thanks.

"You are most welcome," Mrs. Charles said warmly, then hurried over and planted a kiss on Miss Mattie's forehead.

"How are you feeling, dear friend?"

"I have to admit...very tired," she murmured. "But I want to thank you for bringin' us supper. I know how busy you are with your little ones!"

"I'm not the only one bringing meals," Mrs. Charles replied cheerfully. "A whole brigade of the town's best cooks are pitching in!"

"And we surely do appreciate that," Miss Mattie replied, looking pale. Just the short interaction had caused her to become somewhat breathless. "I'll be on my feet soon and back down in my bakery."

Mrs. Charles gave Emily a glance. They both knew that overseeing the bakery again was out of the question for her.

"We're all happy to help," she responded warmly, giving Miss Mattie a hug before she left.

As the front door closed, Miss Mattie yawned. "Sugar, you run and do somethin' fun now. I'll take a little nap, and when you come back, we'll eat that fine supper Miz' Charles made for us."

Has she forgotten that I'm running the bakery now? Emily wondered, but said, "I'm going to make you a snack, then I'll go back down to the bakery; Jonathan and I are making surprise for you!"

"Surprise? What kinda' surprise?"

"Fresh vegetables! He's planting a garden for us!"

"Well now, isn't that jus' fine," she said, making an effort to sound enthusiastic as she folded her hands, and put her head back on the sofa. "I really like that boy…"

And she began to snore softly.

Emily made a quick snack and set it on the side table where her mama would see it when she woke up. Tiptoeing out, and closing the door quietly, she hurried down the steps.

When she opened the bakery door, she saw a note on the counter, along with two ten-dollar bills and a five. The note was from Gus:

A couple customers came in while you was out. Sold them some donuts and sugar cookies. Here's the $$. I bought me a custard pie. --Gus

Emily chuckled as she put the money in the cash drawer, and for the first time noticed the dirt tracks leading to the back and knew Jonathan had brought the plants over on a wagon. She hurried out back where he was just patting down the dirt around a tomato plant.

"Farmer Jonathan!"

"I like the sound of that," he laughed, standing up.

She walked over and he put an arm around her as she scanned the garden. "What are those plants?" she asked, pointing to rows in the corner.

"One is cucumber, one is zucchini. My dad said to just plant one of everything, and it would produce as much as you need for the two of you. We're planting late in the season, so he sent the most mature plants he had."

"Wow," she said, staring at all the plants on the wagon. "What are those?"

"All the vegetables you asked for. I'll mark them as I plant them."

"I love it!" Emily smiled happily. "How much do I owe your dad?"

"It's taken care of," he said, returning to his digging.

She didn't know what to say, so she said, "No!"

Jonathan looked at her.

"I can pay..."

"Sometimes," he said, shoveling a mound of dirt, "people who have always taken care of themselves and others, have a hard time receiving gifts..."

She just stared at him. "Am I one of those people you're referring to?"

"You might be," he acknowledged, reaching for a cucumber plant.

Emily still didn't know what to say. *Hadn't Ike said almost the same thing, and told her to just Pass It Along?*

"Can I work at his nursery to pay him back?"

"He doesn't want to be paid back; he wants to give," he replied, standing his ground.

She sighed. This was hard. "Can I give him some Snickerdoodles?"

"Yes, I'm sure he'd love them."

Emily stared at him, wanting to say more. He stared back.

"I'll go box some up," she finally murmured, and turned to go into the bakery.

"Emily..."

She turned around.

"It just takes practice. You give a lot; let people give back to you. It's just as important."

She nodded, wondering if that were true.

Her phone rang.

"Your supplies are in!" a silky voice said.

Emily's heart leaped. "Thank you, Gabriella, I'll be right over!" she replied, thrilled at the thought of her first business venture.

She left the bakery in the hands of Blessy and hurried down the street. As she approached, she saw Dr. Blackstone's car parked at the curb outside the tearoom, and almost did a cartwheel. "Yes!" she murmured happily.

Walking in, Emily nodded to a couple of patrons, then headed back to the tearoom's kitchen where Dr. Blackstone was standing in a dark blue apron, sleeves rolled up, managing a huge mixer.

"Hi Dr. Blackstone," she said, feeling the tiniest bit giddy at the sight of him in Gabriella's kitchen. "Have you gone into the scone making business?"

"Emily, good to see you," he replied, small crinkles showing around his eyes as he actually smiled at her. "Gabriella's sister wasn't feeling well today, so I dropped in to give her a hand."

"Do you bake?"

"No, but I'm a fast learner," he grinned.

Gabriella came in carrying a silver tea pot, and said, "Indeed, he *is* a fast learner!"

Emily watched to see if she would go over and hug him, but it didn't happen. *Just a little more time,* she thought.

Gabriella patted a box in the corner of the kitchen. "Here's the items for your new business, Emily!"

"Yay!" she replied, hurrying over and ripping the box open. The first thing she pulled out was a beautiful steel blue tea kettle.

"Lovely!" cried Gabriella.

Digging a little deeper, Emily came up with nesting measuring cups, shaped like colorful cooking pots. "I love these!" she exclaimed, and started to dig for more, then stopped. "I really should just unpack these at the bakery."

"Would you like me to help you set up a display for them?" Gabriella offered.

"I would love that," she replied, repacking the items. "When would be a good time for you to come over?"

"I can't come until tomorrow. How about 4:00 tomorrow after-noon?"

"Sounds great!" Emily replied, closing the box. She wanted to linger and watch the interaction between the two but knew it would be too obvious. Instead, she said, "I'm going to run up to Mr. Charles' nursery and borrow a wagon to carry the box; I'll be right back."

Emily took one last glance and saw Gabriella smile up at Dr. Black-stone, as she held up a flowered tea pot, offering him tea. He smiled back, and raised a cup for her to fill, not taking his eyes off of her.

Emily hummed all the way to *Bloomin' Happy*! The magic was begin-ning to happen!

Opening the nursery gate, she didn't see anyone, but heard giggles from the potted plant area. She walked over and saw Jonathan surround-ed by Bitsy and three other cheerleaders in their uniforms, all batting their eyes at him, giggling, and turning this way and that, to show off pretty legs.

She stood for a moment watching. Jonathan was asking questions, and the girls would answer and giggle some more. She wondered if he was enjoying the attention.

Finally noticing her, he hurried over, leaving one of the cheerleaders talking mid-sentence. All the girls turned and glared as he went to her.

"Hey Emily, what brings you here?"

"Could I borrow a wagon for about an hour? I need to pick up some things at *Tea Time*."

"Sure! Wait a few minutes until my dad gets back; I'll come and help you."

"It looks like you've got company..."

He rolled his eyes. "The girls are looking for a plant to give their cheerleading coach."

"How thoughtful," she murmured sarcastically, but stopped herself. She didn't want to become like them; snooty, sarcastic, unkind. "I'll wait over there," she said more pleasantly, and headed for the umbrella area.

As she sat waiting, Mr. Charles came through the gate.

"Emily!" he said, a huge grin appearing as he hurried over, skirting around the cheerleaders.

She smiled up at him, realizing he knew exactly what was going on. "Hey, Mr. C!"

"Out buying more vegetables for your garden?"

"No, borrowing a wagon. Jonathan said he would help me after he finishes with those girls."

"I'll take over, and he can go right now." He turned and headed towards the group.

As Jonathan walked through the gate with her, Emily wondered if there were any girls in England who had a crush on him. She felt herself grow frightened, then stopped. This line of thinking led to being committed to Jonathan, and she wasn't ready for that. Jonathan was free to talk to and date any girl he pleased. But she hoped he didn't.

"What're you doing with all the stuff in the box?" Jonathan asked later as they left *Tea Time* and he pulled the heavy load up the hill to the bakery.

"It's my new venture," she said happily. "Upselling!"

"Ahh, you've taken my dad's advice!"

"Yes! Your dad gives good advice!"

"He's a smart guy!"

"And he's got a smart son," she replied, looking up at him, batting her eyelashes.

Jonathan laughed. "I'll take the compliment, but not the eyeball stuff!"

"I thought you liked it!" she mused.

"I don't like eyelash batting, phony giggles, or phony girls," he replied, looking at her. "Understand?"

"Understood!" Emily replied, savoring the happy feeling that went from the top of her head to her toes.

At the bakery, Jonathan unloaded the box for her, and pushed it to a corner, then asked, "Do you need help with anything else?"

"No, I think I'm actually finished for the day," she replied.

Jonathan reached into his back pocket. "I forgot to give this to you the other day," he said, handing her a thick booklet.

"What's this?" she asked, thumbing through it.

"It's what I used to study for my driving test. It would make your life easier if you could drive places."

Emily felt overwhelmed. "I don't really even know how to drive yet! I was thinking I'd just get a pink scooter from Bitsy's dad!"

Jonathan stared at her a moment, then looked like he was trying not to laugh. "A car would be better," he began, his voice breaking. "You'd look really cute on that scooter, but.." He couldn't finish the sentence, and Emily saw that his belly jiggled with laughter.

She just stared at him. "I can learn to drive a scooter," she replied indignantly.

His shoulders were shaking with laughter, and he couldn't answer her.

"I'd wear a helmet," she started to explain, but saw it was useless.

"Emily, Emily..." he said, trying to get his voice under control. "I know you're capable of handling a scooter. A car would just be more practical, especially in the winter, and when you needed to take Miss Mattie places."

He looked like he was going to start laughing again, and she glared at him, and said, "I don't know how to drive, remember?"

"I've asked Gus to help you with that!"

"Gus?"

Jonathan nodded. "He wanted to help, so I figured he was as good as anybody for driving lessons."

"In his old pick-up?"

"You two work that out. In the meantime, you can study this, and get your learner's permit."

Emily was sort of excited. "I'll do it. Thank you!"

He hugged her, and she thought she felt his stomach jiggling again.

Dr. Blackstone's Mercedes pulled up in front of the bakery promptly at four o'clock Monday afternoon. He and Gabriella got out, and Dr. Blackstone went around to the trunk.

Gabriella came in and said, "I hope it's alright that I brought a couple of furniture pieces with me!"

"Absolutely!" Emily replied, giving her a hug.

Dr. Blackstone came in carting an antique table, went back out to his car and came in with a shelf that fit on the back of the table.

This will make a lovely display piece," Gabriella murmured, her violet eyes lighting up.

"Of course! They're beautiful, thank you!"

"Where do you want me to set up the table, Emily?" Dr. Blackstone asked.

She led them over to a section of wall centered down from the kitchen door. "Does this look like a good spot?"

Gabriella smiled. "I think it's perfect."

Dr. Blackstone set the table in place and attached the shelf, then said he needed to see a patient at the hospital.

"Thank you for your help," Emily called after him.

He waved and walked out the door.

"He's very nice," Emily said, turning to Gabriella.

"Yes, he is," she agreed.

"Do you like him?" Emily blurted out.

Gabriella stared at her for a moment. "Do you like Jonathan?" she countered.

It was Emily's turn to stare, then they both laughed.

"Shall we become confidantes?" Gabriella whispered mischievously.

"Yes!" Emily agreed, "I'll make us some tea."

"Okay, I'll go first," Gabriella said later, sitting at a parlor table and stirring rich cream into her mug of tea. "I do like Dr. Blackstone...Matthew...and I believe he likes me, but he has lost a wife he loved, and that makes him skittish. Death is such a crushing blow."

"So, what will you do?" Emily asked.

"I'll do nothing but be happy with the way things are at the moment, and I'll be kind to him. I won't try to force anything. If I don't like the way things progress, I can remove myself."

"Wouldn't that be painful?"

"Yes, but not as painful as being unloved. I've already been in that situation."

"Your first husband didn't love you?" Emily couldn't imagine someone not loving this lovely lady.

"He probably did somewhat," she replied, stirring her tea. "But he loved himself more. Self-centeredness is a beast to battle, Emily, and pretty soon you just protect yourself and quit trying."

"How do you know when someone is self-centered?" Emily asked, feeling frightened for a reason she couldn't name.

"You see the signs, but I was young and ignored them. I would run away if I saw those traits in Matthew."

"I think I know the signs, but I'd like to hear your version."

"Self-centered people are usually controlling; every angle is to get what they want. They aren't protective of your feelings, maybe not even aware of your feelings." She stared out the window for a moment, then looked back at Emily. "And the very most hurtful thing is when they *are* aware of your feelings, *but don't care.*"

Emily nodded, not saying anything for a moment. What Gabriella had just described sounded a lot like her parents. Her mom at least. Her dad always made sure she had the things she needed, and she made herself be grateful for that, but the reality was that alcohol was her parents' focus, and not her.

She turned her thoughts to Jonathan's character. He was none of those things.

"My parents were like that, but Jonathan isn't," Emily replied after thinking it through.

"Now, tell me your feelings for Jonathan."

"Well,' Emily began, "I'm the skittish one in the relationship. When I think about a commitment, my stomach starts to hurt."

"It sounds like your homelife was quite stressful."

"It was. I learned to take care of myself, which is good and bad. The good is that, well...I can take care of myself. The bad is, I have a whole lot of trouble letting people help me."

"You accepted my help!"

"That's because I'd just had a lecture from Jonathan on letting people help me," she laughed. "What I really want to do is ask you how much I owe for the furniture you brought over, and if there is something I can do to help you. My mind won't quit thinking about it!"

They both laughed.

"Well, I'm glad you let me help for now. To answer your question though, the furniture is extra that I have stored in the tea shop attic, so you may borrow it until you don't need it anymore, and I don't want a cent from you."

"Then let me offer this: if you ever need my help in your shop, please let me know."

"Agreed!" Gabriella smiled, rising to her feet. "Now shall we get to work making a lovely display out of those items in the box?"

They were both excited to see what had come, and it felt like Christmas morning as they began pulling the beautiful kitchen items out of the box. After checking the packing list for the suggested retail price of everything, they began labeling. Gabriella had brought small, stringed price tags, which they tied on each item.

Two hours later they stood back and studied the finished display. "What do you think?" Gabriella asked.

"I think you have a knack for knowing exactly how to arrange things," Emily said, looking at the flow of the displayed items, enhanced by the beautiful antique furniture. There was everything from fancy rolling pins, to fluted ceramic pie dishes, to multi-colored mixing bowls. There were even aprons that rivaled in brightness to her mama's, and Emily couldn't wait until she was strong enough to come downstairs and see it all.

The word spread fast about her new sales venture, and the village women came by in droves to look it over. Miss Rose stopped by and bought an antique bowl and pitcher set; Mrs. Green fell in love with the new aprons and bought two; Mrs. Kingery came in for donuts for the *Village Grocer*, saw the cast iron corn bread pan—shaped like an ear of corn—and bought it on the spot. Townspeople who had never been customers at the bakery came, and Emily finally asked one how they all knew about her new venture.

"There are flyers on nearly every telephone pole, and in every store and shop," the woman replied, looking puzzled. "Didn't you put them there?"

"I believe a friend did," she replied, thinking of Jonathan.

Chapter - 13

"Where do you want this, Emily?" Jonathan asked as he hauled Ike's expresso machine through the bakery door.

"Here behind the pastry case," she replied, scooting a cardboard box and a three-legged stool out of the way. "I've already set up a table to put it on."

"Do you know how to work it?" he asked, lifting it into place.

"No, but Ike is supposed to stop by and show me."

"Okay," he said, grinning as he leaned over and kissed her nose. "Cute freckles!"

Stricken, she touched her nose, and cried, "My freckles are back?" She had been so busy with the bakery, she barely had time to look in a mirror.

"Yep, they're back...and don't put make-up on them. It's you!"

"Freckles are me?" This was depressing.

"Yes, ma'am! Out there, sun-kissed, and rocking your face! And speaking of kissing..." he said, kissing her again.

"You actually like my freckles?" she asked, not quite believing him.

"Love 'em," he replied, giving her a quick hug. "But I need to get going, I'm running off some flyers announcing your coffee business. My dad is going to pay my little brothers to take them door to door."

"Thank you for helping me with all of this!" Emily was touched beyond measure, thinking of the dinners he had arranged, the garden he had planted, and all the emotional support he gave her. Now the flyers, both for her Country Store, as she had decided to call it, and for her specialty coffees.

"I'm trying to get you all set before I leave," he replied, drawing her close to him.

She nodded and didn't say a word, trying to manage the lump in her throat, absolutely dreading his leaving.

About then, Mr. Apple came through the bakery door pushing a small caged stroller.

Emily hurried over and gave him a hug. "What's this?" she asked, nodding at the stroller.

"Oh, Mrs. Apple thinks this blasted cat needs to go on walks," he replied, shaking his head, "so I ordered the stroller from a pet supply store."

"Oh!" she said, seeing a black paw bat at the zippered door.

"And Mrs. Apple insists that I walk him every day," he said gruffly, with a brief glance to see her reaction.

"Does Mr. Whiskers enjoy it?" she asked, as Jonathan strolled over, biting his lower lip. She could tell he was trying not to laugh.

He greeted Mr. Apple and gave Emily a quick hug. "I need to run some errands, see you later!"

"What can I get for you today?" Emily asked, as the door closed behind Jonathan.

"Mrs. Apple and I will take two eclairs, please!" he began, then cleared his throat, and looked a little embarrassed. "You don't happen to have any cookies for cats, do you? I hear that bakeries are starting to make pet treats, of all things!"

Bingo! she thought. *More upselling!*

"Well, I don't have any today," she replied, thinking quickly, "but you've given me a great idea! I'll have some here by next week!"

Mr. Apple's face actually lit up. "I'll be back in next week then!"

"Great!" she replied, handing him the bag of eclairs.

After he left, Emily grabbed her phone from the kitchen and began looking online for recipes for dog and cat cookies. She found a site that had not only the baking supplies, but also had cookie cutters shaped like dog bones, along with a fish shape for cats, and another shaped like a ball of yarn. She got the bakery credit card out of the cash drawer and placed the order, using the merchant number that Gabriella had left with her.

"Use it anytime you need to," the tea shop owner had urged.

Then she remembered, and quickly called Jonathan. When he answered, she said, "Don't run the flyers off yet. I have another pastry I'm going to be selling."

"What?"

"Dog and cat cookies!"

He laughed. "That'll work! You'll have every pet owner in town stopping in."

"Pet *parent*!" she said, correcting him.

"What?"

"They want to be called *pet parent* now."

There was silence on the other end.

"Jonathan?"

"I'll get the flyers out," he murmured.

Emily laughed and they hung up.

Two days later Emily popped into Gus's station where she found him napping in his swivel chair, with a ball cap over his face.

She tiptoed over. "Guess who got their learner's permit?" she whispered in his right ear, startling him.

"I betcha' Miss Em'ly did!" he said, sounding groggy.

She held out the permit and he leaned forward, squinting to bring it into focus. "Well, looky at you, little lady!" he grinned, showing even choppers. "Congratulations! We'll have you drivin' in no time!"

"I'm so excited," she gushed, wishing she weren't too old to do handsprings around his office.

"Yip Yap come over an' congratulate Em'ly!" Gus called, as his dog wandered in.

The dog sauntered over and Gus said, "Show him yer permit, Em'ly!"

Without hesitating, Emily held the piece of paper in front of the dog's eyes.

"Rice," Yip Yap yipped.

"He means *nice,*" Gus whispered, "but he has trouble pronouncin' his 'N's."

Emily nodded that she understood. "I'll keep it a secret," she whispered back, and they both laughed.

"So when do we commence with the drivin' lessons?" he asked, going over to the soda machine, and bringing two bottles of Orange Crush out of the chilled water.

"Are you free tomorrow?" she asked, accepting the soda from him.

"Tomorrow it is!" They clicked their soda bottles together in agreement. "I'll get Leapin' Lena all gassed up for you."

Emily, who was chugging a long drink of soda, almost spit it back out. "Oh, we can use Miss Mattie's Mazda," she said quickly, feeling soda dribble down her chin.

"Nah, I'm old school. You need to drive somethin' with a clutch and learn to shift."

"Why?" Emily asked, using the bottom of her shirt to wipe her chin.

"Always learn the most you can, Em'ly," he said, emphasizing each word with his soda bottle. "And don't restrict yer'self. *Knowledge is power,* as the sayin' goes. Who knows," he said, taking another drink, "you might wanna' drive a tractor someday, or a sports car in the Indy 500!"

"You're right, I just might," she laughed, as Jonathan's dream of a farm sprang to mind.

Ike was refilling Glen Kingery's coffee mug at *Good Eats* when they heard a truck backfire. They both turned and looked out the big plate glass window and saw Gus's Leapin' Lena lurching up First Street. The engine would roar, and the truck would leap forward, then die. It repeated the maneuver all the way up the street with an occasional backfire.

"What in thunderation is Gus doin'?" Mr. Kingery asked, wheeling around on the stool.

"He's given' Em'ly her drivin' lessons," Ike replied, going over to the window for a closer look.

Mr. Kingery shook his head. "Well, thanks for the warnin'. I'll stay off the streets for the next coupla' days."

They heard the backfire again a couple of minutes later and saw the pick-up coming back in the opposite direction, with a clear view of a determined Emily clutching the steering wheel, in what appeared to be a death grip. The truck leaped twice, then shot ahead.

"Don't know why he's teachin' the girl to drive with a clutch," Ike groused. "It complicates things tryin' to co-ordinate the shifter with pushin' in on the clutch."

"I'll say one thing," Mr. Kingery said, raising his mug in a salute, "that girl has a lotta' guts."

A few days later, Emily asked Jonathan, "Can you give me a couple of driving lessons in my mama's car? That's what I'm going to be taking my driver's test in, and I'm not used to driving it."

"Don't want to test in the Leapin' Lena, huh?" he laughed.

"I hope I never in my life have to drive that thing again," she said, meaning it. "But I am glad I can drive with a stick shift now."

"I'd be happy to help, but you can only drive with someone over twenty-one when you have a learner's permit. Do you want to wait until I'm old enough?" Jonathan asked with a grin.

"Ugh, who could I ask?" she wondered out loud.

"There's lots of people who would help. Just ask them."

"Okay," she replied, thinking of Mrs. Green, or Mrs. Kingery. "Then would you be able to drive me to Clayton to take my driving test later?

"Love to! We'll make a day of it since I'll be leaving soon."

Emily just nodded as her throat constricted, not trusting herself to speak.

When word got out that *Cooke's Bakery* was selling pet cookies, there was a line out the door, with Mr. Apple leading it. As Emily added up the sales, she realized what a huge profit maker the pet cookies were going to be. "Blessy," she said, walking back into the kitchen, "let's do two more batches of the dog cookies, we're almost sold out!"

"Never thought I'd be bakin' dog food," Blessy groused, as she lifted down a large bowl from a top shelf. "Does your Mama know you're makin' food for dogs and cats in her bakery?" Blessy was not happy.

Emily looked at her. "Blessy, remember, the bakery is in trouble, and we have to do whatever it takes to make a profit. No, Mama doesn't know yet, but I'll tell her at the end of the week and show her the profit sheet."

"Well, I guess sellin' dog cookies is better than nailin' up a *Goin' Out of Business* sign," Blessy sighed, shaking her head.

"Exactly," Emily replied, giving the loyal worker a quick hug, "We gotta' go with the flow, Blessy!"

The bell over the bakery door jingled, and the familiar tap, tap, tap, of Miss Violet's high heels was heard as Emily and Blessy were taking the cookies out of the oven. Then Emily heard a yip, and knew that Miss Violet's nutty bulldog, Mitzi, was with her. She looked up at Blessy, hoping she would go wait on them.

"Don't be lookin' at me," Blessy said, shaking her head, and meaning it. "That woman 'bout drives me nuts with that crazy dog of hers…"

"Hello, Miss Violet," Emily said, as she came out from the kitchen, noting that both Miss Violet and Mitzi were dressed in matching fuchsia skirts. Miss Violet wore a fuchsia turban, while Mitzi sported a fuchsia bow over her left ear and strained against a glittery fuchsia leash.

"Em-i-ly," Miss Violet trilled in her best English accent, as she tried to control Mitzi, "I hear that you have desserts for pets now!"

"Yes, Miss Violet, we have pet cookies," she replied, skirting around Mitzi, who snapped at her. Mitzi lunged, causing Emily to nearly spring over the counter to get out of the way of her sharp little teeth.

"Don't be naughty, Mitzi," Miss Violet cooed, reaching down and tapping the dog lightly on the head, which caused her fuchsia bow to fall off. The dog snatched it off the floor, and began to crunch it between misshapen teeth, chewing vigorously.

Emily stood there blinking as Miss Violet swooped the dog up and attempted to retrieve the bow, tugging this way and that, but Mitzi wouldn't let go. The bow stuck halfway out of her jutted jaw.

"Offer her a dog cookie, and maybe she'll release it," Emily said, holding out a Snickerpoodle, trying not to laugh.

Mitzi lunged for the cookie, and the sodden bow plopped to the floor. Emily watched as the dog devoured the Snickerpoodle, chewing rapidly with her jutted jaw, wondering how she chewed without biting her own nose.

Miss Violet stepped in for a closer look at the cookies. "What a lovely assortment," she trilled, looking over the attractively displayed pet treats. On a three-tiered rack to the left were the dog cookies labeled: Mutt

Macaroon; Snickerpoodle; Barkbar. On the right were the cookies for cats: Cupcat; Purrbar; Meow Munch.

"I must have a mixed dozen of the cookies on the left," Miss Violet trilled, picking Mitzi up. "You love them don't you, Poopsie," she said, rubbing noses with the dog.

Emily kept her eyes averted to the nose rubbing as she filled a small red box decorated with dog silhouettes and handed it to Miss Violet.

"What charming boxes," Miss Violet trilled, showing it to Mitzi, who attempted to knock it out of her hand. "I'll spread the word of your culinary canine treats!"

"Thank you," Emily said, meaning it. "And don't forget the felines' treats!"

Miss Violet studied her for a second. "I wish you the very best in your courageous business venture!" Her voice had lost its trill, and the overdressed woman looked at her sincerely, with what appeared to be *empathy*.

Touched beyond measure, Emily thanked her again, and even reached out to pat Mitzi's head. She was rewarded with her left index finger being bitten before she could recoil.

Emily felt her stomach cinch into a knot as Jonathan drove Miss Mattie's Mazda down the mountain to Clayton, where she had an eleven o'clock appointment to take her behind-the-wheel driver's test.

"Why are you so quiet?" he asked.

"Nerves!" she sighed, looking at him. "Will you stay in the car with me while I test?"

"They won't let me, or I would," he replied, "but you'll do fine." He reached over and took her hand. "I have a surprise afterward!"

"Yay, I love surprises!" she said, rubbing her belly with the other hand, trying to calm it.

Jonathan pulled up into the designated spot at the Motor Vehicles office right at eleven, where a man with a clipboard stood waiting for her. They got out of the car, then Jonathan hugged her and went inside to wait.

The man, who introduced himself as Mr. Earl, got in on the passenger side. Emily breathed a prayer and got in behind the wheel.

"Just pull out of the driveway and go left," Mr. Earl instructed.

She backed out slowly, concentrating hard, fervently hoping she didn't throw up.

Forty minutes later, Emily wheeled back into the parking lot, where Mr. Earl signed a piece of paper, and said, "Congratulations!"

She went inside and stood in line to have her picture taken, waving to Jonathan who sat reading a sports magazine. He stood up and joined her in line.

"Congratulations," he said. "What did you score?"

"Ninety-Four," she replied, looking quite happy about it. "What did you score when you took your driver test?"

"Don't ask," he replied laughing. "I was nervous, and it took me three times to parallel park. I barely passed."

As they walked out of the building a half hour later, Emily's temporary license in hand, Jonathan asked, "Do you want to drive?"

"Yes!" she replied happily, going over to the driver's side. "Where are we going anyway?"

"I'll give you directions as we go."

Ten minutes later they pulled up in front of a beautiful terraced restaurant.

"Wow, fancy!" Emily said, peering through the windshield at the impressive building that seemed to be completely made of glass. A valet opened her door, and she handed him the keys. Jonathan came around and offered his arm, still being unusually quiet.

The maître d' lead them to a secluded area with a garden setting and a small waterfall, and handed them menus after they were seated. Emily opened her menu, but noticed that Jonathan wasn't looking at his, and he seemed nervous.

"I'll have the crab salad," she said, looking up at him. She did a double take because he had a small box sitting in front of him.

"What's that?" she asked, finding it difficult to breathe.

He looked at her and reached for her hand. His was clammy.

"Emily, I'm going to be leaving soon, and I want something between us settled."

She gulped and thought of leaping over the waterfall and running away.

The waiter came over and brought sparkling water in small goblets, and when he left Jonathan looked at her. "I bought you this," he said, opening the small box.

She stared down at a lovely necklace of two entwined hearts made of delicate silver.

"I love you," he said, simply, sliding the box towards her. "I've always loved you.

He loved her! Jonathan loved her! Emily didn't know what to say and just sat in stunned silence, her heart a jackhammer, as she stared at the necklace.

"If this isn't what you want, or you don't feel the same about me, then just push the box back," he said, not taking his eyes off of her. "I don't want to avoid the subject anymore; I only want to go forward."

She picked up the box, and something in her shifted.

She said nothing for a moment as the jackhammer quieted. For no reason that she could explain, her fears were gradually replaced with a deep peace. He was her friend, her companion, her confidante, her protector. And now something more, and he was asking her to join him in it, to take a chance.

She lifted the necklace from its box. "Would you help me put it on?"

The ringing phone was incessant. Her mind was so tired she couldn't think of what it was. Was she dreaming? She became aware enough to try and make sense of it. Probably Blessy needing something in the bakery, she thought, prying her eyes open and looking at the clock -2:47 a.m. it read. Her heart began to thunder. "The hospital!" she said in her stupor, forgetting that her mama was in the next room, and not at the hospital anymore.

"Hello!" she said, barely above a whisper.

"I'm so scared," came a voice over the phone.

"Kelly Ann?"

"The baby's comin'," she wailed.

"Are you sure?" Emily was fully awake now.

"Pains seven minutes apart," she sobbed. "I jus' remembered that I never asked if you'd come to the birthin' center with me."

"Of course I will! "Where's your grandpa?"

"Sleepin'."

"Ok, I'll be over in just a bit. Why don't you wake your grandpa up? I'll get ready and tell Mama, then be right there.

"Should I call Gilbert? He wanted me to call him."

"Do you want him with you? It's all what you want now."

"He makes me feel safe," Kelly Ann sniffed.

"Then call him, silly. I'm going to hang up and get dressed. I'll be there as soon as I can."

"How will you git' here? It's dark."

"Mama's Mazda. I got my driver's license yesterday."

"I'm so scared," she repeated.

"You're going to do fine. I'll be there just as soon as I can."

She quickly dressed, wrote a note for Blessy and asked her to call Clara, and take care of the bakery all day, then went in to wake her mama and tell her where she was going.

"How far apart are her pains?" her mama asked, sleepily.

"Seven minutes. There's oatmeal in the refrigerator for your breakfast, and cold chicken for your lunch. I don't know how long I'll be gone, but I will call you every hour with an update." *And to check on you,* she thought to herself.

"I'm comin' too, Sugar" Miss Mattie said, throwing back the covers. "I promised Kelly Ann I would be there."

"That was before you got sick, Mama," Emily said, putting the covers back over her. "She knows you can't come now. Your job will be to stay here and pray for her to have an easy delivery. I'll tell her that's what you're doing."

Miss Mattie lay back on the pillow. "I guess I don't have any choice, do I?"

"No ma'am! But she needs your prayers, she's really scared."

"Ok, Sugar, and don't forget to keep me updated. Tell Kelly Ann I'm prayin'."

When Emily got to Kelly Ann's home, she saw that Ike was already helping her into his pick-up.

"Pains comin' five minutes apart," Ike shouted over to her, as he climbed into the driver's seat, looking pale.

She saw more headlights pull up, and Gilbert hopped out of the passenger side of Pastor Alex's black 4Runner, hurried over to where Kelly

Ann was sitting in the pick-up and hopped in the back. Ike pulled out, and Emily started to follow, but Pastor Alex waved for her to stop.

"I'm going back to get Penelope. We'll be there a little later," he said, and with a wave, got back into the 4Runner.

Emily was surprised at the atmosphere created by the birth of this child. Excitement! She gunned the Mazda and hurried towards the birthing center, checking the clock on the dashboard: 4:47 a.m. She decided to call Blessy when she stopped, and should she call Jonathan? And why not? He surely wouldn't want to miss the birthing party! Maybe she should stop at the bakery for donuts for everyone!

She sat in the parking lot and called Jonathan's number.

"Hello," he squawked, sounding like a muffled rooster. He cleared his voice, and tried again, "Hello."

"The baby's coming," she fairly shouted.

"Emily?"

Yes, it's me and Kelly Ann's baby is coming!"

"How far apart are her pains?" he asked, groggily.

"I think five minutes," she replied, disappointed at his lack of enthusiasm.

"Okay, it'll take a while yet," he mumbled sleepily, having been through the births of his younger brothers. "Where're you?"

"At the birthing center, don't you want to come too?"

"It's her first baby, and first babies take a little longer..." he said, his voice tapering off. Then she heard snores.

"What in the world," she said, looking at the phone. Disappointed, she gave up, threw the phone into her backpack, and hurried into the birthing center.

When she arrived, she saw Ike sitting in the waiting room. "Where's Gilbert?" she asked, sitting down beside him.

"Kelly Ann wanted him to come back to the labor room for a while," he said, yawning. "I was surely glad. Not sure I can do this birthin' thing!" Another yawn. "In my day, the men stayed o-u-t," he said, meaning it.

"How do I get into the labor room?" she asked.

"Just register at that desk over yonder."

"Do you want me to come out later and give you a turn?" she asked, knowing that only two people were allowed to be with the laboring mother.

"Nah, I'll jus' take a little snooze right here," he murmured, looking as though he might drop to the floor and nap under the magazine rack. "Jus' update me ever' now and then."

Men and their sleep! she thought, shaking her head, hurrying over to the registration desk. She was glad she'd skipped the donuts for everyone.

When she got to Kelly Ann's room, there was a trapped animal look in her friend's eyes. She hurried over to her side and took her hand. Gilbert, on the other side of the bed, held her other hand.

"You look a little nervous," Emily said, as Kelly Ann leaned forward to hug her.

"Scared outta' my mind," she replied, falling back on her pillows.

"Because you're in pain?"

"No! Because I'm gonna' be a mama today, an' I don't know if I can do it."

"Kelly Ann..." Gilbert said softly.

She turned towards him.

"You can do it; I'm gonna' be right here to help you, and so's your grandpa and Em'ly. A whole village is gonna' be here for you."

She nodded, but the fear didn't leave her eyes.

When Emily went out to report on the mother-to-be's progress, which was pretty slow going, she saw Jonathan sitting next to Ike, freshly showered. Pastor Alex and Penelope were on a nearby loveseat, and Iris Head in a straight-back chair, wearing some get-up of red, white, and blue, dotted with white stars. When Emily approached her, she resisted the desire to salute.

"How did you know Kelly Ann was in labor?" she asked the realtor.

"We ladies have a texting group for important events like this," she said, appearing excited. "All the ladies who came to Kelly Ann's shower are on it. Penelope messaged that the baby is coming, so here I am!"

"I'll let Kelly Ann know you're out here," Emily said, giving her a quick hug.

"I'll probably come and go," the realtor said. "I show a house at ten this morning."

Emily nodded and went over to Ike, to let him know Kelly Ann was doing fine. "It will be a while before the baby comes, if you need to go and open your café," she told him. "I can keep you posted."

"Naw, I'm not leavin'," he said. "Its' the least I can do to sit here while she'd goin' through all that. Gus just phoned, and he has a cold, so he's stayin' clear of us."

"What about your café?"

"I called and told Millie we're closed today. She's puttin' up the sign I made for the door, that the baby is comin'.'"

"I'm glad," Emily said, hugging him.

She sat down for a minute by Jonathan.

"Did you hang up on me this morning?" he asked, truly puzzled.

"No…You snored in my ear while I was talking to you!"

Ike guffawed, then hee-hawed. Emily shook her head, and said, "Aren't you guys even excited?"

"We're excited!" Jonathan said. "We just do our excitement different than you ladies."

"Yeah," Ike said, "We talk about stuff we know about while we're waitin'. Birthin' babies is for you ladies to talk about. But we're happy about it!"

She gave up and headed back to be with Kelly Ann.

The labor progressed rapidly. Emily went out every half hour to give a report to people, mostly ladies on the texting chain who came and went. She texted her mama at the same time.

Penelope, Mrs. Green, Millie, and other village ladies chatted excitedly about babies and the event going on in the labor room. Pastor Alex, Ike, and Jonathan sat watching the morning news on an overhead TV.

Every time she came out there were different people in the waiting room. Some came for an hour, some for longer to give Ike support. Once when she came out the men were in a lively discussion of fishing lures, of all things, appearing to be much more excited about that than a baby. Emily still didn't get it.

About 2:00 pm the pains got down to business, and soon they were wheeling Kelly Ann off to the delivery room. Emily and Gilbert joined Ike and Jonathan in the waiting room. All the others had left. Gilbert paced, and Emily could see his lips moving and knew he was praying.

Forty minutes later, the nurse came out and said to Gilbert, "You can see your new baby now. She's a beauty!"

"Would I be able to come, too?" Emily asked.

"Me too," Ike said, standing up.

"That's up to the daddy," she said, looking at Gilbert, assuming he was the baby's father.

Ike looked at him, and started to say something, but without missing a beat, Gilbert said, "Sure, they can all come."

When they got to the room, there was Kelly Ann holding a pink bundle, with brown hair peeping out the top. She looked radiant, and a glow had replaced the fear in her eyes.

They gathered around her bed, and she pulled back the blanket so they could see the child's face.

"Beautiful," Ike murmured, then turned and wiped his eyes.

Gilbert went over and laid a hand on the child's head, caressing softly.

Jonathan stood with Emily on the other side of the bed. "What's her name?" Emily whispered, touching the child's soft hand.

"Mia," Kelly Ann replied, looking at all of them. "It means, *mine.* She's mine, and I never knew I could love someone this much."

"It's beautiful," Emily replied, stroking the infant's hair.

"Her middle name is Christa," Kelly Ann continued, "you know, after Jesus. I want Him to help me raise her."

Emily looked at Gilbert and smiled, and there was nothing more to be said.

Chapter - 14

When Emily's alarm went off at 4:30 am, she shut it off, knowing the time had come that she'd been dreading. In six hours, she would be waving goodbye to Jonathan as he headed back to England.

She would make some coffee for her mama before leaving, and have a cup herself since she had very little sleep. She touched her necklace, feeling the two intertwined hearts; she hadn't taken it off for even a moment since Jonathan had fastened it around her neck. She swung her legs over the edge of the bed, and just sat there, needing a bright spot to look forward to, because Jonathan leaving was hovering like a dark cloud. She remembered that he'd be home at Christmas: four months away. That helped somewhat. She remembered the way he looked at her when he had given her the necklace; ok, that rocked her world! He loved her! She still couldn't quite grasp all that it meant. It seemed like a dream meant for someone else, not her.

Going into the kitchen, she saw her mama making the coffee. "What are you doing up this early?" she asked, hurrying over to finish the job.

"I knew this would be a hard day for you, Sugar," her mama said, "I'm feeling stronger now, and I want to start doing things for my girl."

Emily put her arms around her. "Just take care of yourself and get better. That's the thing you can do for me."

"I want to be useful," she replied, looking at her. "I can't just sit around anymore."

"Okay," she said, nodding that she understood. "When I get home from the airport, maybe we can figure things out then." She also knew that she hadn't told her mama they were selling pet pastries now. She wasn't looking forward to that little conversation.

"It's a deal," her mama said, hugging her. "Who is runnin' the bakery today? Blessy?"

"No, she's just going to do the baking, then Mrs. Charles is coming in at eight."

"She doesn't want to go to the airport with her son?"

"She thought Jonathan would like alone time with me, so they are all saying goodbye to him from home. They invited me over for breakfast, too."

"She must really like you, Sugar. A lot of mamas wouldn't make that offer."

"And I like her too!" Emily chirped happily. "And her son!"

All the lights were blazing when she pulled up in front of the Charles' two-story home forty minutes later. Mr. Charles answered the door, and the aroma of bacon and pancakes floated in from the kitchen.

"Yum," she said, sniffing. "Something smells good!"

"This way for breakfast," he said, with a sweeping bow.

Jonathan came down the stairs about then carrying a large suitcase and a backpack. He sat them down and hugged her.

Please don't let me cry, she whispered to herself as they headed to the kitchen.

The family sat around the table making every effort to sound upbeat and cheerful, as they passed around platters of pancakes, scrambled eggs, and bacon. Emily found herself touching her necklace often, feeling the sense of comfort it brought her.

"How come you keep touchin' your necklace?" Jonathan's younger five-year-old, Jacob, asked.

She felt her face flush, and said, "It's a gift from a special friend."

Jonathan stood up to get more scrambled eggs, and said, "No, it's a gift from her *boyfriend*."

Emily looked around the table, feeling her face heat up; all eyes were on her. *I can do this*, she thought, taking a deep breath. "This beautiful necklace that brings tears to my eyes and comfort to my heart is from Jonathan."

She saw Jonathan grin.

"Ugh! Why'd he give you a mushy thing like that?" eight-year-old Cameron asked, holding his nose, and pretending to gag.

"Because he loves me," Emily replied, letting the chips fall where they may. Looking around the table at the astonished faces, she asked, "Would someone pass me more syrup please?"

After a moment, Mr. Charles spoke up. "Well on that note, we have a surprise that we want to share."

Everyone at the table looked at him, except for Mrs. Charles who smiled knowingly.

"Since Jonathan won't be coming home for Christmas this year..."

He got no further before Emily interrupted, turning to Jonathan. "You're not coming home for Christmas?"

Jonathan sighed. "It was a last-minute decision, and I was going to tell you on the way to the airport. I didn't know my Dad was going to announce it now."

"I'm sorry Emily," Mr. Charles said, "I didn't realize that you weren't aware of that." He smiled. "But listen to this. We're all going to England at Christmas and we'd like you to go, too."

Emily sat there stunned, feeling like she'd been smacked in the head with a sledgehammer. Jonathan wasn't coming home for Christmas, and she'd just been invited to travel to England. She sat there silent, as everyone talked excitedly about the trip, the house they'd rent, and being in another country at Christmas.

Jonathan noticed, and leaned over to whisper, "Don't looked so shocked, we'll talk about it on the way to the airport."

She nodded and tried to finish her breakfast.

Jonathan reached for Emily's hand as they drove down the mountain towards the airport in Roanoke. "It was a last-minute decision to stay in England at Christmas," he told her. "Otherwise, I would have told you. As the time got closer to leave, I kept trying to figure out how to finish school sooner. I don't want to be in England anymore, and I hate leaving you."

She nodded, and he continued. "Taking a winter class is the only way I can do it. I'll also have to take one summer class. But when I come back in July, I won't leave anymore."

Emily didn't say anything, and he asked. "Are you mad?"

"Not mad, just surprised."

"Why are you being so quiet then?"

"I think my feelings were hurt that you didn't tell me. But I understand now."

"You don't seem very excited about going. "She looked up at him. "Jonathan, I can't afford a ticket to England!"

He laughed. "Well, that's where Aunt Mary comes in. She's donating her thousands of air miles to the family, and there's plenty for you."

"Oh!" Emily replied, feeling the stirrings of excitement. "What about my Mama? I don't want her alone at Christmas."

"I already talked to her to see if it was okay for you to go. She's planning on going to her sister's in Mississippi." He turned and looked at her. "Would you rather go with her to Mississippi at Christmas?"

"You're kidding, right? I'll go with her next year!"

He laughed. "Miss Mattie said you'll have to get permission from your social worker to go, so do that right away because you'll also need a passport, and those can take a while."

She grinned. "I think I'm feeling that excitement now!"

Emily stood at the huge bay window watching Jonathan's plane until it disappeared into the morning sky, feeling like part of her was flying away, too. "Bright spots, where are you bright spots?" she whispered for the second time that morning, her heart plummeting.

"Books!" she said out loud, as she drove back to Mountain Grove. She'd go to the library and find a story to get lost in. But when did she have time to read anymore?

The baby! She'd stop by Ike's house and hold Mia. That new life brought her joy.

She texted Kelly Ann when she stopped for gas to see if it was okay to come over.

Yes come over, came the reply. *Don't knock, just come on in when you get here. And don't mind the house.* Followed by a frowny emoji.

"Hello!" Emily called out, as she walked through the front door of Ike's home.

"Come on in!" Kelly Ann said, cuddling Mia in a rocker as she nursed her.

Emily noticed the room looked like a catalog display of every piece of baby furniture imaginable, with nearby stacks of small clothes and diapers, and a laundry basket overflowing with small clothes to be folded.

"Have a seat," her friend smiled, pointing to an easy chair near the wicker basket of laundry. "We'll be finished in a minute an' you kin hold her," she whispered, all but glowing with happiness.

"Take your time," Emily said, as she sat down. "I'll fold these for you."

"Thank you," Kelly Ann said. "There's lots to do with a baby. Gilbert will be here in a while. He usually cleans ever' thing for me."

Gilbert cleans for you? she thought but didn't say anything. "How's it going being a mom?" she asked, as she folded a small pink pajama bottom.

"I love her so much," Kelly Ann whispered. "I don't even mind her gettin' me up in the middle of the night, I just love holdin' her and starin' at her little face."

"You look really happy," Emily said, loving the smell of the tiny pajamas.

"I *am* really happy," she said, putting the baby up to her shoulder, and patting her back. "Did Gilbert tell you his news?"

"What news?" she asked, as she began matching up tiny socks.

"He's goin' to go to that theology school in Clayton and become some sorta' pastor!"

Emily looked up to see if she was kidding.

She wasn't kidding.

Emily opened her mouth to say something but couldn't think of one word to say.

Kelly Ann laughed. "I was surprised too!"

Gilbert came through the door about then, and took a look at the astonishment on Emily's face, and said, "Is somethin' goin' on?"

"I jus' told her about you goin' to theological school!" Kelly Ann replied, smiling up at him as he walked over to her.

"Were you surprised, Em'ly?" he asked, reaching down and kissing Kelly Ann.

"When did all this happen?" Emily whispered.

"The school?" Or me kissin' Kelly Ann?".

"Both!"

"Well, as you know, I've loved Kelly Ann a long time," he said, scooping the baby up in his arms and kissing her forehead. He started to hand

Mia back to Kelly Ann, but she said, "No, give her to Em'ly. She wants to hold her."

"And as you know," he continued, "I love God, and I just wanna' go into some sorta' ministry." He placed Mia gently into Emily's arms. "But I don't have it all figured out yet."

"Amazing!" Emily said, giving the child her own kiss.

"Me, or the baby?" he laughed.

"Both!" she said, kissing Mia's soft cheek again.

As soon as Emily opened the door at home, she smelled something mouth-watering. "Yum, who brought us dinner tonight?" she asked, walking into the kitchen.

"Miz' Kingery brought this fine pot roast," her mama said, happily, "and I was jus' makin' us a nice gravy to go with it!"

Emily's breath caught; gravy was something her mama should definitely *not* be eating. She tried to think of what to say. "That'll be yummy this once, Mama, but we have to be careful of your diet." She could feel the atmosphere change as her mama's excitement dwindled.

"Okay, Sugar, thanks for remindin' me," she said, attempting a brave front. Emily noted that her face was crestfallen and not at all brave.

Emily tried keeping up a cheerful chatter as they ate, but it wasn't working. Her mama loved good homemade food, and nourished others with dishes from her kitchen and bakery. She noted that her mama took no gravy, and they both fell silent and finished their meal.

Emily cleared the dishes after dinner, knowing it was time for the talk she had been putting off.

"Mama, I've made a few changes to the bakery to bring in more money," she began.

"What kinda' changes, Sugar?" her mama asked, vigorously scrubbing the dinner dishes.

Clearing her throat, she said, "I've tried to stay with a bakery theme and put in a beautiful display of kitchenware. Gabriella helped me pick out everything, then she came over and helped me with the arrangement."

"Did she tell you to call her by her first name?" her mama asked, meaning business.

Emily laughed. "I think you could be in a coma, Mama, and you'd wake up just long enough to make sure I was using my manners."

"That's right, Sugar," a grin broke out on her face. "Good manners are very important."

"To answer your question, Gabriella told me to call her by her first name, and I think I told you that before you got sick," she answered, and returned to the subject at hand. "I've put in a coffee machine for different flavors and types of coffee." She dreaded the next part. "And...people have asked me to bake cookies for their pets!"

Her mama turned slowly and looked at her with eyes nearly bugging out of her head. "You're makin' *dog food* in my bakery kitchen?"

"No...I mean yes, cookies for dogs and cats." she croaked, as she unfolded her profit sheet. "Look at how much money it's brought in. I never would've have dreamed it could earn so much, would you?" She found herself rambling as her mama stared at her, not even looking at the profit sheet. "Mama?"

"You're makin' and sellin' dog food in my bakery," she said flatly, "that's what I'm lookin' at."

Emily sighed. Time to come clean. "Mama, there's no choice. I saw your records and the bakery is, or was, in trouble. You know that. I just did what I needed to do to save it. I couldn't tell you everything or ask you first. The doctor said you shouldn't be involved at all. That also means that I need to take over and run it for you, Mama. You can't do it anymore; I don't want to lose you."

"Your school starts in two weeks; you can't be runnin' a bakery!"

"Sure I can! I told you I want to homeschool."

Emily was surprised to see relief in her mama's eyes. "Well, I don't know," her mama murmured. "I'm gonna' think long and hard about this."

"Would you like to go downstairs tomorrow and see it all?"

"Yes, I certainly would," she replied. "And now I'm tired of thinkin' about it. Why don't you dig out that sugar-free, fat-free, and I might add *taste-free*, ice cream that Miz' Kingery brought for our dessert, and let's watch a movie."

"It's a deal!" Emily laughed, hurrying to the freezer, feeling greatly relieved to have the talk out of the way.

Miss Mattie looked around her bakery for the first time in nearly two months. She walked over to the display of kitchenware and touched some of the items.

Emily stood back watching, finding that she was holding her breath. "What do you think, Mama?"

"I think you did a beautiful job," she replied, picking up a few of the pieces and looking them over. "Where did you get the money for all of this, may I ask?"

"It's on consignment," she replied, as her mama looked at the display of brightly colored aprons, one-by-one.

She decided to get it over with. "Come over here and look at the pet cookie display, Mama!"

Miss Mattie rolled her eyes but walked over.

She stood looking at it for a moment and said flatly, "You did a good job on the display."

"Anything else?"

"You'll jus' have to let me get used to sellin' dog food in my bakery," she replied gruffly, shaking her head.

Emily laughed. "It's not Purina, you know."

"I know, and I'm lettin' you make that decision. There's one thing I want though."

"What's that?"

"I want to bring my chair down so I can visit with my customers a couple of hours a day."

"And make sure they're minding their manners?"

"Maybe," she replied, with a side glance, and they both laughed.

"Okay, I'll get Gus and Mr. Kingery to bring down your easy chair again, but no working," Emily bossed, wagging her finger. "Now I need to ask you about something else. I've been keeping track, and very few customers come in after three o'clock. Would you be in favor of closing the bakery at three instead of five o'clock? It would save on wages and give me more time for schoolwork," she added, as a final pitch.

"You're the boss now, Sugar," she replied, "Just make sure you put up signs and give customers plenty of notice."

"I will," she replied, once again seeing relief in her mama's eyes.

"Thanks for helping me out with this," Emily said, as she and Miss Mattie rode down the mountain towards their appointment with Miss Tori, Emily's social worker.

"You're welcome, Sugar. I'm gonna' miss you at Christmas, but what a fine opportunity to visit another country!" her mama said, staring out the side window. She sighed, "I jus' love this mountain, don't you?"

"I do love it," Emily replied, as she rounded a hairpin curve. "And I love you for making sure I could live here with you."

"You're the sweet daughter I always wanted," she murmured, pointing out the window to a herd of deer peacefully grazing in a wooded meadow. She then yawned and put her head back on the seat for a little nap.

Forty-five minutes later, Emily wheeled into the parking garage of a five-story building, and she and her mama were soon seated across from Miss Tori.

"Glad to see you ladies," the pretty red head smiled. "What brings you to my office today?"

"I've been invited by a family in Mountain Grove to go to England with them this Christmas, and I need your permission, both to go, and to get a passport," Emily explained.

"You'll be traveling with adults?"

"Yes, Mr. and Mrs. Charles, and their kids."

Miss Tori wrote down their names and phone number, then sat twiddling her pen, mulling it over. "The trip sounds wonderful, Emily, but here's what concerns me," she finally said. "Have you heard of human trafficking?"

She nodded.

"It's a huge problem these days, and you are the prime age that these traffickers are looking for."

Miss Mattie sat bolt upright. "Is it dangerous for her to go?"

"It could be if she falls for any of their schemes," Miss Tori replied frankly.

Miss Mattie glanced at Emily, her eyes dark with worry, then asked the social worker, "How would she keep herself safe?"

"By always being with someone she is traveling with," Miss Tori replied. She turned to Emily. "You would have to promise me that you would never be out anywhere alone, Emily. Restrooms, restaurants, sightseeing, everything that has to do with traveling, would need to be done with others in your group for your safety. If anyone acts friendly towards you, or tries to help you, or asks you to help them, refuse to engage. I may be over stating all this, but I want you to understand the danger. It's happening too often, and once the traffickers have a girl, it's very difficult to find her and get her back. The traffickers and those helping them are not nice people.

"I didn't know it was such a problem," Emily murmured, wishing her mama hadn't heard all of that. "I know how to be careful though, and I've heard everything you said."

"I believe you have, too," Miss Tori replied. "If it were anyone less mature than you, I'd say no. But I believe you'll do fine, and I'll help you get that passport."

"Thank you." Emily was relieved. She noticed that her mama didn't share that relief.

"Are you sure I should even let her go?" Miss Mattie asked.

"I think she'll be fine," Miss Tori replied, "I just had to make sure she understood the danger of the traffickers."

The social worker turned to Emily and said, "I will send all the documents you need in the mail to you as soon as I talk to Mr. and Mrs. Charles. I'll have papers for them to sign, also, assuming temporary responsibility for you, along with the papers that Mrs. Cooke will need to sign, giving her permission for you to travel."

Emily sighed and thanked her, feeling relieved, and much like a pet on a leash.

Emily looked up and saw a young girl peering in through the glass door of the bakery. She appeared to be about ten, with unkept hair and a dirt smudge on her cheek. She saw Emily and slowly pushed the door open and stuck her head in. "Ya'all have donuts in here?" she asked, looking scared, and ready to run away.

"Yes! Come on in and show me which kind you like," Emily said, her heart going out to her.

The girl entered cautiously, barefoot and with the lean look of hunger, then walked over to the pastry case as though she were approaching something sacred.

"How much for th' chocolate," she asked, pointing to the smallest donut, and looking up hopefully.

Emily guessed that she didn't have much money. "Ten cents today. Are you new in town?"

"Yes'm. My daddy moved us here. He's runnin' from the law."

"Oh!" Emily replied, shocked. "Do you tell everybody that?"

"No ma'am, you seemed nice though."

"What's he running from the law for?"

"Drunk drivin'. He don't wanna' go to jail."

"I see," she replied, noting that the girl still appeared ready to turn and run. "What's your name?"

"Callie. What's yer's?"

"My name is Emily," she replied, reaching out and shaking the girl's small hand, "and I was just ready to take my break when you came in. Show me which donut you want and I'll have one too." Her mind sailed back to the time she'd come in after school, and Miss Mattie would say those very words to her, and the world would become right in this warm, safe haven.

"I ain't got no money," Callie confessed, looking down, ashamed.

"That's ok, it's my treat for first-time customers," Emily replied, setting out two small doily-lined plates.

Callie chose a large chocolate donut with sprinkles and stood looking at it hungrily as Emily chose a glazed donut for herself. "You like glazed donuts?" Emily asked.

"I like 'em all," she whispered.

Emily put a glazed donut next to the chocolate. "We'll celebrate since it's your first time here."

Callie didn't say anything, just stared hungrily.

"My Mama, Miss Mattie, always makes people say, *please and thank you*, or she won't let me serve them," Emily said softly.

"Oh, thank you, Em'ly," the young girl said, looking embarrassed.

"You're welcome, Callie. Why don't you go sit at one of those little tables, and I'll get us some hot chocolate to go with the donuts, then I want to hear all about your day."

Callie waited for her at the parlor table in front of the window, staring out at Emerson Park.

A younger me, Emily thought, as she brought the pastries over.

"Eat up," Emily said, "while I get our drinks." She poured the hot chocolate into two mugs, making sure to heap it high with whipped cream, grabbed a couple of spoons, and watched the girl's eyes light up as she brought it over.

"Here you go, Callie," Emily said, setting the mug and spoon down in front of her. She noticed that the girl had polished off one donut already and was starting on the other. "Do you live around here?" she asked, biting into her own donut.

"I live at the Sawmill in a trailer, and guess what?" the girl said, her eyes lighting up.

"You have purple grass, and pink trees..."

"No," she laughed. "Guess again."

Emily couldn't guess.

"All the other trailers are single-wide an' we got the only double-wide," she said, shifting in her seat with apparent pride.

"No kidding!" Emily laughed. "Do you have your own bedroom?"

"Yes'm, an' I put Elvis Presley posters up on ever' wall, and for my birthday I'm gonna' ask my mama for one of them lights that goes aroun' and makes light dots on the wall."

"Oh! A disco light," Emily said, spooning whipped cream into her mouth.

"Yes'm," she replied, her eyes growing bright.

"So, you're an Elvis fan, huh?"

Callie nodded.

Emily smiled, thinking back to another time. "My dad used to listen to Elvis when I rode in his pickup."

"He did?"

She nodded. "What's your favorite Elvis song?"

"Ummm....*Love Me,*" the young girl replied, licking whipped cream off the back of her spoon.

Emily held her spoon in front of her mouth, as though it were a microphone, and began to croon: *Treat me like a fool, treat me mean and cruel, but love me...*

Callie laughed and picked up her spoon, joining her: *Wring my faithful heart, Tear it all apart, but love me.*

They both howled with laughter, as Callie's eyes sparkled and danced.

"You have a really pretty voice, Callie!" Emily told her.

"I do?"

"Yes, ma'am, you do!" she said, standing up as a customer came in the door.

She went to wait on a man in a suit who wanted a blueberry muffin. He kept clearing his throat and rubbing a finger across his nose.

Emily thought he was weird and was glad when he left.

She came back to the table and sat down, smiling at Callie, who did a double take.

"You gotta' big blob of whipped cream on yer' nose Em'ly!" she said, bursting into laughter.

"What?!?" Emily said, wiping her nose with a napkin. "Was it on there while we were singing?"

"I dunno'," Callie laughed, "I was day dreamin' about Elvis!"

They agreed that Miss Mattie would sleep as late as she wanted, then come down to the bakery in the afternoon. Mr. Kingery and Gus had come over and carted her overstuffed chair down the stairs and set it near the parlor tables so she could visit with customers.

Emily saw the sparkle return to her mama's eyes as she sat and visited with various village people, and even tried a hand at her own up-selling at *The Country Store*. If a customer browsed the area, she would point out pieces which were her favorite, drawing them in. Emily once again saw the smile that rivaled a harvest moon when her mama sold a set of mixing bowls in shades of blue, and an antique wooden sign that read, *Be still and know that I am God.*

At Gabriella's suggestion, she had put a $95.00 price tag on a green tea kettle with a wooden handle, and a tourist from Redman, Texas had bought it on the spot after Miss Mattie pointed it out to her. Then a local schoolteacher, coming in for a dozen crème horns, browsed housewares, and fell in love with the large oval cast-iron cooking pot with a farm scene engraved on the lid, after her mama pointed out what a great piece it would be to roast her Thanksgiving turkey in.

"I am abso-LUTE-ly *thrilled* to have found this," the teacher said in her deep Southern twang, not even flinching at the $145.00 price tag. "I do believe it is the weight of a small Volkswagen, however, and I will send my husband over to fetch it home for me!"

Miss Mattie was watching as Emily rang up the sale, looking happy and content. They gave each other a thumbs up as the customer left.

Towards the end of the day, Callie peeped in the door.

"Come on in, Callie," Emily said.

She walked in, barefoot again, and laid a quarter on the counter. "Will this buy a chocolate donut?"

"Yes, it will Callie. But first I'd like to introduce you to my Mama," she said, nodding towards Miss Mattie who was relaxing in her easy chair reading the Mountain Grove Gazette. "Use your best manners and remember what I said about my Mama!"

Callie nodded.

They walked over to Miss Mattie's recliner, and Emily said, "I'd like to introduce you to Callie, Mama."

"How do you do, Callie! I'm Miss Mattie," she said, putting her hand out.

Callie shook her hand. "How'd ya' do," she replied, repeating the exact same greeting back, then looked up at Emily.

Emily nodded at her and smiled.

Callie talked to Miss Mattie as politely as she knew how.

At one point, Miss Mattie asked, "Do you enjoy going barefoot, Callie?"

"No ma'am, but my flip flops broke and I throwed them in a bush."

"I see," she murmured, looking up at Emily.

Emily nodded that she understood what her mama wanted, then said to Callie, "Are you ready for a donut?"

"Yes'm," she replied, then not knowing what to do, went over and solemnly shook Miss Mattie's hand again.

Miss Mattie chuckled, then drew the child to her for a hug.

"Sugar," she said, looking up at Emily, "would you help me upstairs after you get Callie her donut? I'm gettin' sleepy!"

On the way over to the pastry case, Callie whispered, "How come your Mama is brown and you'uns is white?"

"Because love doesn't care about color," Emily whispered back. "Plus, there's a story about it that I'll tell you some day."

"I love stories!"

"I thought you would!" Emily smiled, going behind the counter to get Callie her donut. "Do you want chocolate again?"

"Yes'm! Will you sit with me?"

"Sure! Right after I take my Mama upstairs."

Emily got Callie her donut, and said, "Watch the bakery for me, and if anyone comes in, tell them I'll be right back."

On the way up the stairs, her mama said, "That girl needs some shoes, Sugar. Do you have extra you can give her?"

Emily found a pair of pink flip flops with rubber flowers on the straps, and took them down to Callie. "Here's some extra flip-flops I found."

"Are you sure?" Callie asked, delighted as she put them on.

Emily laughed, "I'm sure! Looks like they fit perfectly!"

"I love 'em!" she whispered, and finished her donut sitting with her feet straight out so she could look at her new footwear.

Emily brought over a crème puff. "See if you like these!"

"Yum!" Callie said, biting into the pastry, as whipped crème squished out.

Emily handed her a napkin.

"You gotta' boyfriend?" Callie asked, between bites.

"Yes, but he's away at school right now."

"I'm gonna' git' me a boyfriend some day!"

"Oh really!" she replied, as something in her tightened. "What do you want your boyfriend to be like?"

"I hope he looks like Elvis!" she laughed, sticking her feet back out and having another look at her new flip-flops.

Emily laughed along. "Okay, he should look like Elvis, but how do you want him to treat you?"

Callie shrugged and took another bite of her crème puff.

Emily tried another approach. "When I say someone is a nice guy, what does that mean to you?"

"My daddy drinks and yells at my mom. He's the onliest guy I know."

"Will your boyfriend drink and yell at you?"

"I dunno!" she said, taking another bite of her pastry.

"Callie, look at me!"

The young girl stopped eating and looked up.

"You get to choose, and you can say no to anyone who drinks and yells. Understand?"

Callie stared off for a second. "That's a good idea," she shrugged, then changed the subject. "I gotta' cat."

Emily laughed. "What's your cat's name?"

"I call him Meow-Man," she grinned.

"I'll give you a cat cookie for Meow-Man when you leave," Emily smiled. She tried bringing the conversation back around. "What grade are you in?"

"I jus' started middle school," she replied, licking the icing off her fingers. "I like readin', but I hate the rest of homework. My trailer is too noisy, and I can't think a lick, so I usually don't even do it."

Emily thought a moment. "I'm homeschooling and I do my school work right after I close the bakery at 3:00. Want to come in on Tuesday and Thursday and do homework with me?"

"What about the other days? I have homework ever' night."

"When I close up here, I'll show you where the library is. That's where I used to read and do my homework."

"Hey, Mrs. Green," Emily said, as she and Callie walked up to the check-out desk. "This is my friend Callie, and she may be coming here to do schoolwork. Her home gets a little noisy sometimes."

"Welcome, Callie!" Mrs. Green said, her ears rising slightly as she smiled. She hurried around the check-out counter to give hugs.

"Do you live nearby?" the librarian asked, holding Callie at arm's length.

"Yes'm. We live at the Sawmill an' we got the only double-wide trailer in the park," Callie informed her.

"Wonderful!" Mrs. Green said, giving her a high-five. "Let me know if you ladies need help finding anything."

"You folks sure are a huggin' bunch," Callie whispered, as they headed for the fiction section of the library.

"Do you like hugs?"

"Um, sorta!"

They stood in the middle of the fiction section, and Emily swept her hand around it all, as though presenting something extraordinary. "Did you know that books can take you anywhere you want to go and teach you anything you want to learn?" she asked, pointing out the rows and rows of books to choose from.

"Maybe I oughta' try one," Callie said, pulling a book off the shelf, and thumbing through it.

"If you look at the back cover, it will tell you what the book is about."

Callie read it. "Yeah, I like this one."

"See those tables over there? You can do your homework there anytime you want to. The library stays open until seven o'clock."

"I like this place," Callie said, sniffing the air. "I want my house to smell this way someday."

Bingo! thought Emily. "Let's write that down, Callie! Remember, you get to plan out your own home."

Emily got a slip of paper and a pen off one of the tables and wrote it down.

Callie's House:

Smells like books and the library.

"I'll get you a small book called a journal to write other things you want in your house one day," Emily told her.

"You will? When?"

"Come in tomorrow after school," she replied.

Callie threw her arms around her, hugging her tightly.

Chapter - 15

Emily and Callie sat heads together at a parlor table in the bakery doing schoolwork. Out of the corner of her eye, Emily saw her young friend twiddling her pencil.

"Are you through with your schoolwork?"

"Do we havta' wait until schoolwork is done to have a donut?"

"Why? Are you hungry now?"

"Yes'm, I ain't had nothin' since breakfast."

Emily hesitated. "Callie, did you know that *ain't i*sn't a college word?"

"I'm too young ta' go ta' college, silly!" she laughed.

"I know but remember—you have to plan. So right now, you could stop using words that aren't college words."

"Is swearin' college words?"

"Do you swear?"

"Sometimes when Meow-Man gets in my way," she replied honestly.

"Hmmm! I think it would be a really good idea not to do that. Your words tell people about you and swear words don't show your best side. I'd stick with college words if I were you."

"I'll think about it," she sighed, then looked at her. "My mama an' daddy cuss like a monkey."

Emily wasn't sure what that meant, but said, "Well, what comes out of your mouth is your responsibility."

Callie wasn't going to let it go. "Most ever'one at the Sawmill cusses."

"Do you want to live at the Sawmill all your life?"

"No."

"Then you'll have to do things differently than the people who live there. You can start with using better words."

"What else," she said, showing a slight interest.

"Read and learn a lot; go to college. Then you can get a good job, or start your own business, and live anywhere you want.

"In Memphis, at Elvis' house?" she asked, brightly.

Emily laughed. "Sure! Or at Dollywood, with Dolly Parton!"

Callie threw her head back and laughed, then turning serious, said, "Wanna' know what my neighbor told me?"

"What?"

"Why even try, the gover'ment wants us poor," Callie said, in a mock falsetto voice. She looked at Emily. "It 'bout made my heart fall to my knees."

Emily laughed. "That sounds so hopeless it made my heart fall to my knees, too! But guess what? My parents were poor, and they drank, but I'm planning a better life."

"Yer' just like me?"

"Just like you! So don't listen to people who tell you you're stuck in the Sawmill, those are just excuses for not trying your best. And you know what?"

"What?"

"All excuses do is keep you at the Sawmill!"

Callie's stomach growled, and Emily looked at her, then they both laughed.

"Did you have any breakfast?"

"Some crackers is all."

"Don't they have a lunch program at school?"

"Yes'm, breakfast an' lunch! But my daddy says it's char'ty."

"It's not charity. The school knows kids can't concentrate if they're hungry. It's an investment."

"Okay," Callie said, meaning it. "That's what I'm tellin' my daddy then." She looked at Emily, her eyes sparkling. "They even have jello an' chocolate puddin'!"

"Yum," Emily said. "Be sure and eat the good stuff first though."

"That *is* the good stuff," Callie laughed, looking up at her like she wasn't too bright.

Emily sighed, deciding to talk about nutrition later, and closed her schoolbook. "I'm hungry too. Instead of a donut today, I'm buying you a hamburger at Ike's!"

"Who's Ike?"

"Have you seen the café on the corner called *Good Eats*?"

"I never ate in a cafe in my whole life," she replied, looking doubtful. "I'm kinda' scared."

"Do you know what I say when I'm scared?" Emily asked, putting an arm around her.

"What?"

"Do it scared until you're doing it brave." Emily looked at her. "Think you can do that?"

"I'll try," Callie sighed.

"Well, we'll have an adventure then! Pack up your books and come on!"

"I love adventures!" Callie yelped, slamming her history book shut, and shoving it into the worn Walmart grocery bag she carried her school-books in.

When they entered *Good Eats*, Callie looked around wide-eyed at the café, where two other customers sat. Ike was leaning on the counter with The Mountain Grove Gazette spread out in front of him; he looked up and gave them a nod.

The girls walked over. "Ike, I'd like you to meet my friend, Callie," Emily said. "Her parents moved here not long ago, and they live in the Sawmill area."

Ike gave her a knowing look, then said, "How ya' doin' Callie?"

Callie stuck out her hand and said, "Pleased to meetcha!" and looked up at Emily, who nodded in approval.

"Where'd you move from, Callie?" Ike asked, giving her small hand a firm shake.

"Georgia," she chirped, and to Emily's relief, didn't add that her dad was running from the law.

"You like it here in Virginia?"

"Yep. We got the only double-wide in the trailer park," Callie told him, her eyes lighting up.

"Real nice," he said, smiling as they fist bumped. "What are you girls up to t'day?"

"Callie has never eaten in a café, so we're having an adventure," Emily informed him. "We want burgers all the way!"

"Burgers all the way, it is!" he said, folding up the newspaper. As Emily walked past him, he said in a low voice, "Seems like you started your own *Pass It Along Club*!"

She grinned and followed Callie to a table.

Millie came over to take their order, and Emily introduced her.

"Nice to meetcha', Callie!" she said, giving her a quick squeeze, then added, "Ain't you the prettiest little thing!"

Callie looked at Emily wide-eyed, then told Millie, "*Ain't's* not a college word."

Millie stood there looking shocked, with her pen poised above the order pad.

Emily was horrified, and quickly said, "We're having burgers all the way, Millie, but we already told Ike."

Millie didn't say a word, just turned on her heel and left.

Emily whispered, "Callie, it's not polite to correct an adult's grammar."

Callie heaved a huge sigh, slouched down in the dinette chair, and stared up at the ceiling. "I can't 'member all this derned stuff."

Emily realized she'd overwhelmed the girl, and asked, "Do you like root beer floats?"

"Never had one 'afore," she replied in a monotone, keeping her eyes on the ceiling.

"It's root beer poured over ice cream."

She sat up immediately, and grinned. "That sounds so good I almost said a cuss word!"

"Don't say a cuss word," she laughed, "just run over and tell Millie we want two root bear floats and don't correct her English."

Miss Mattie was coming down to the bakery more often as she gained her strength. The customers coming in would go over and greet her, asking about her health, most giving her a long hug or a pat on the shoulder.

Emily watched as one of the elementary school teachers went over to her mama. "We've been worried about you, Miss Mattie," the young woman said, hugging her as though she were a long-lost friend.

With the opening of their pet cookies display, many customers now brought their pets into the bakery with them. When smaller dogs entered, Emily noticed that her mama would pat her leg, and make a kissing sound, coaxing the little animals to come over and sit on her lap. She would hold them, petting and speaking softly as their owners made bakery purchases.

One time when two miniature poodles came in and leaped into her lap, she began cooing, using baby talk as though twin babies were in her arms. Emily had to keep from laughing out loud, thinking her mama had come a long way from the person who was outraged about *dog food* being sold in her bakery.

"You seem like you're enjoying the pets that come in, Mama!' Emily said later, as Miss Mattie came over to the three-tiered display of dog cookies.

"Just bein' hospitable, Sugar!"

Emily watched her pick out two Snickerpoodles and two Barkbars and put them in her apron pocket before returning to her easy chair.

"Who are those for?" Emily asked, grinning.

"Free samples," her mama informed her. "Part of our upsellin'."

A thought occurred to her. "Mama, would you like to have a dog?"

"Well, I've been thinkin' about it," she replied, a smile as bright as the new moon lighting up her face, giving her a glow that Emily hadn't seen in weeks.

"What kind of dog have you been thinking about?"

"I don't know, Sugar. I like holdin' the little dogs in my lap, so one that's small. Not sure if we can afford it though."

"I'll check around," she replied, wanting nothing more than to make her mama happy.

After the bakery closed, Emily headed over to *Good Eats*, thinking someone there would know who sold small dogs.

She was just telling Mr. Kingery about her mama wanting a pet, when Ike spoke up. "There's an Italian guy out on Black Hawk Road who sells Yorkies. Name's Frank. I jus' talked to him over at the Grange Hall."

"Really!" she asked, growing excited. "Do you know his address?"

"Naw, jus' drive out there. You'll see a sign."

When Emily left the café, she headed straight for Miss Mattie's Mazda, sending her mama a text saying she'd be home in an hour.

She found Black Hawk Road and turned onto it, driving slowly as she looked for the sign spotting it about a quarter of a mile in. It read, *Bello Piccolo Yorkies* with a small drawing of Italy in the upper right-hand corner.

As the Mazda crunched down the long driveway, a dark-haired man came out, waved, and stood waiting as she drove up to the small home nestled in a stand of oak trees.

"Are you Frank?" she asked, getting out.

"I am," he said, taking a toothpick out of his pocket and putting it into his mouth. "How can I help you?"

She hadn't planned on what to say, so just blurted it out, "I'm looking for a small dog for my mama, Miss Mattie, who owns the bakery in town."

He nodded knowingly. "You're the girl that's come to live with her, right?"

"Yes, I'm Emily, but how'd you know?"

"Word gets around," he shrugged, shifting the toothpick to the other side of his mouth. "How's she feelin' these days?"

"Tired, so she stays upstairs a lot, but that's lonely. That's why I want to get her a dog."

"I got one Yorkie left," he said, with a wave of his hand, "I'll show her to you."

They went around to the back of the house where a pretty woman dressed in rolled up levis stood watering a small garden area.

"This is my wife, Hawley," Frank said, introducing them. "Hawley, this is Mattie's girl. She's lookin' for a dog to keep Mattie company."

"How sweet," his wife murmured, as she came over and hugged Emily. "How are things going with you and Miss Mattie?"

"Fine," Emily murmured, wondering if the whole county knew about her living arrangements.

"Well, the puppy is this way," Hawley said, looping her arm through Emily's as they went towards a long porch at the back of the house. "Are you hungry? Frank is bar-b-queing, and we have plenty if you'd like to stay for supper!"

"No," Emily laughed, "but thank you!"

"How about somethin' to drink then, darlin'? Thirsty?"

"No, I'm good!"

"Hmmm! What else could I offer you..." Hawley murmured as they stepped up on the porch.

"Hawley!" Frank said, coming up from behind. "I think she just wants to see the dog."

"Well, she's sweet... and I want to give her something," Hawley said, meaning it.

Emily looked over at Frank, who was grinning. "Hawley has a soft heart," he informed her. "She'd give away our house if I let her."

"Yes, I would," his wife replied, squeezing Emily's arm as they went over to a small dog bed in the sheltered area of the porch. "There she is," Hawley whispered.

Emily gasped as she stared at the tiny puppy, who peered back at her with soft brown eyes. She knelt down, and stroked the tiny head with two fingers, declaring, "I love her!"

"Pick her up, if you want to," Frank said.

Emily scooped the puppy up next to her face, where it licked her chin, then bit at her hair. "Hello, little dog," she murmured, as the excited puppy nestled into her neck, feeling right at home.

She looked up at Frank. "How much are you asking?" she asked, dreading the answer.

Frank rubbed the back of his neck. "We're goin' on vacation soon and I want to sell her fast, so I'll give you a deal."

Emily looked at him and waited.

He named the amount.

Frank's deal was still shockingly high.

She didn't know what to do. She desperately wanted this dog for her mama but couldn't afford the high price he asked. She put the tiny puppy back down in its small bed, and stood up. "I didn't realize dogs were so expensive, but thank you for your time." She nodded at them and started to leave.

"Frank..." Hawley said, softly.

Frank rubbed the back of his neck again and stared at Emily. "You know what?" he finally said, "Miss Mattie deserves this puppy. Why don't you tell me what you can afford."

Emily gulped, staring into Frank's dark eyes. "A hundred dollars," she murmured.

Frank took the toothpick out of his mouth, still staring at her.

Then she smiled and said, "And I'll give you fresh donuts from the bakery for a whole year!"

Frank threw his toothpick into a nearby trash container. "Make it scones for a year," he said, meaning it. "Hawley loves scones."

As they shook hands on the deal, it occurred to Emily that Hawley wasn't the only one with a soft heart.

Emily drove home after dark with the puppy sleeping in the back seat. She parked the car and tucked the tiny dog down in her jacket, deciding to surprise her mama.

When she walked up the stairs and opened the front door, her mama called out to her, "I was jus' gettin' ready to call you, Sugar! Our supper is just about ready!"

"I was picking up a surprise for you," Emily said, setting the dog down on the floor. It sniffed the air and followed the good aroma towards the kitchen.

"What kinda' surprise, Sugar," her mama said, walking into the living room. She looked down. "Oh, what in the world?" She reached down and scooped up the little dog, nuzzling it as it licked her chin. "What a cutey you are," her mama crooned happily, then stopped. "Sugar! How much?"

"I got a good deal!"

"How much?" she said, meaning it.

"One hundred smackers!"

"NO!"

"Yes! And a year's worth of scones!"

"NO!" was all her mama seemed able to say.

"We'll make up a batch that'll last a month, freeze them, and I'll drive them out there," she said, as she watched her mama cuddle the dog. "I told them delivery service was included!"

"Who are these people?"

"Frank and Hawley, out on Black Hawk Road. They said they know you!"

"I surely do know them! Nice folks!" she replied, nestling the tiny dog, unable to keep the smile off her face.

Later that evening, as they sat watching a movie, the puppy climbed up Emily's sleeve onto the back of the couch. She loved Emily's hair, and at every opportunity would grab a mouthful and pull.

"Ouch!" Emily said, handing her to Miss Mattie.

"You are just the tiniest thing," her mama crooned, planting two kisses on the top of the dog's head.

"What are you going to name her?"

"Well, I don't want to give her too long a name, she's so itsy," Miss Mattie said, nuzzling the dog as it burrowed into her neck.

"How about naming her *Itsy* then?"

Miss Mattie thought for a moment. "Perfect!" she finally said, sighing happily, as Itsy snored softly on her shoulder..

Blessy came hurrying out of the bakery kitchen, "Em'ly, could you run up to *Montoya's Produce* for me? We have orders for banana bread, and I plum forgot to order them!"

"Sure," Emily said, untying her apron. "You stay at the cash register, and I'll be right back."

When she got to the green grocers, she saw Mr. Apple in a deep discussion with Mr. Montoya, the owner of the produce market. She went over and grabbed two bunches of bananas, then walked over to the register where the two were talking. Mr. Whiskers lay in his stroller nearby taking a nap. He opened one eye when Emily came near, then closed it again.

"We'd have stayed in Florida longer, but we're more mountain peo-ple," Mr. Apple was explaining, as he paid for a head of romaine lettuce, a pineapple, and four Fuji apples. "But I think you'd like Florida. Nice and warm."

They both greeted Emily, then Mr. Apple gave her a brief hug before he rolled Mr. Whiskers away with his produce bag swinging from the stroller handle.

"It mus' be banana bread day at your bakery!" Mr. Montoya said, in his thick accent.

"You're right!" she replied, then asked, "I heard you talking to Mr. Apple. Are you thinking of moving to Florida?"

"Si," he replied. "Some place warmer when I retire. This cold ees' too hard on me, I have arthritis." He shrugged and smiled. "But not today, mi amiga! Maybe in two years, maybe three!"

"Will you sell your business, or will your son take over?"

"I think the whole family will go. We jus' started the discussion of it."

"Well, I'll be sad to see you go, but I understand," her heart weighted, as she gave him a hug. "I have to hurry these bananas back to the bakery, but I'll talk to you later," she said, and hurried off, hating that she was losing one of her village family members, even if it were *maybe two years, maybe three* years off.

Something about Mr. Montoya's move nagged her, but she was too busy to stop and process it as she hurried back to the bakery, where she opened the door to a line of customers. She flew behind the counter, handing Blessy the bag before she put on her apron of purple and yellow thunderbolts, and stepped behind the register.

People in line chatted, in no hurry, as they waited their turn.

A man she'd never seen before stepped up to the counter, and snapped, "I'm in a hurry. Give me two dozen chocolate chip cookies!"

The people in line grew quiet.

Emily looked at him evenly, slightly annoyed. "Maybe you are in a hurry, but here in our bakery you're still expected to use good manners. In fact, my Mama won't serve anyone who doesn't. Shall we start over?"

He glared at her, and the people in line shuffled uncomfortably.

Emily glared back, waiting.

He swore at her, and one of the men stepped out of line and walked up to him. "That's enough," he said quietly.

The man pounded on the counter with his fist, and stomped out the door, slamming it so hard the windows rattled.

The people in line murmured.

"Next!" Emily said brightly.

"You need a sign, tellin' people to use their manners, Em'ly," Bill Crocker from God Bless America Real Estate suggested.

"Good idea! What should it say?" she replied, speaking more calmly than she actually felt.

The people in line looked at each other.

Use your manners, or use the door! one customer squawked.

"With a silhouette of a foot kickin' someone's fanny out th' door!" another suggested helpfully, as the crowd snickered.

"Keep them coming while I take your orders," Emily laughed.

We speak manners here! croaked Mrs. Kingery, who came in craving chocolate fudge.

Good manners don't cost nothin'," offered a man in bib overalls, who was next in line and wanting a raspberry cheesecake.

Emily had an idea. "Write all your ideas down," she said, pulling out a long strip of cash register tape. We'll have a contest for the manners sign I need to have made up, and the one who wins gets a dozen donuts. In honor of Miss Mattie's good manners policy, we'll let her be the judge!" She set a small cardboard box on the counter, and tore the register tape into manageable pieces, setting it all out, along with three #2 pencils.

"Have at it!" she grinned and went back to filling their orders.

Chapter - 16

◄◆O◆►

"**I** might have me a bak'ry someday," Callie said, looking around, as they were doing schoolwork at the usual parlor table near the front window.

"That's a good plan," Emily said, taking a drink of the hot chocolate she'd made for them. "Did you write it in your journal?"

They had gone to the Walmart out on the highway where Callie had picked out her own journal—one with dancing poodles in pink tutus. Callie carried it with her everywhere, and Emily thought she'd never seen a journal fill up so quickly with everything the young girl wanted in her home one day. Emily had tried to explain it to her the same way Mrs. Apple had explained to her those many months ago, and apparently had done a good job, because Callie had shown her page after page of what she would allow in her home one day, and what kind of person she wanted to share that home with—and equally important—the kind of person she didn't want. And just like Emily, most of what she didn't want involved alcohol, or in Callie's case, alcohol and drugs.

"I'll write it in right now," Callie replied, pulling the journal out of her worn school bag, with the Walmart logo. Emily wished she'd bought her a new backpack while they were out, but had forgotten.

"I'm also startin' a grateful list and hangin' signs on my wall of what I'm thankful for," Callie informed her, as she penciled 'have a bakry' into her journal, under a page titled, "What I want someday."

"Where did you learn about a grateful list?" Emily asked.

"That TV doctor said ever'one should make one."

"You listen to the TV Doctor?" Emily asked, surprised, but pleased.

"You said you listened to him when you was my age, right?"

Emily nodded.

"An' you said I should copy the people I wanna' be like and do what they do—*foller' in their footsteps*, you said."

"Yes, I did say that..."

"Well, I wanna' be like you!"

Emily was stunned. *Who would want to be like her? Her life, her challenges, her situation! Who would EVER want to be like her?* She looked at Callie and smiled. *This young girl sitting right next to her, that's who!*

The word, *thrilled,* was an understatement.

"Next week is my birthday!" Callie announced out of the blue. "On October 8th!"

"No kidding! How do you celebrate your birthday?" she asked, already knowing the answer.

Callie shrugged and went back to her homework.

Emily backed up a little bit. "Who reminded you that it's your birthday, Callie? Your mom or dad?"

"No silly," she giggled. "My teacher tole' me. She wrote me and three other kids names on the blackboard 'cause it's their birthday in October, too! My mama and daddy probably don't know it's my birthday unless my teacher tole' 'em."

There were few times when Emily was at a loss for words, but this was one of them.

"Do you and your parents talk to each other?" she finally asked.

"And say what?"

"Things like, *How was your day? Are you hungry?* You know, like you and I talk."

"No," she shrugged. "I never hear their voice 'less they're yellin' at each other."

"Do you get lonely?"

"Naw, I talk to Miz Sanchez next door, Meow-Man, and Ole' Pete..."

"Who is Old Pete?"

"He lives down the road inna' single wide. His trailer stinks and he stinks, but he wants to talk to me, so I hold my nose an' talk a minute."

Warning lights went off in Emily's head.

"Does he invite you inside his trailer?"

"Yes'm, but it stinks and I ain't – aren't goin' in. Cept' he said his cat had kittens and I could come in an' play with them." She shrugged. "I might."

"No, Callie. Never go into a man's trailer alone. Never!" She nearly shouted the last word.

Callie looked up at her. "Are you mad at me?"

"No, you just scared me. Do you promise you'll never go in that trailer?"

"Okay, I promise," she murmured, puzzled.

"Some people aren't nice," Emily began. It was now or never, and she plunged into the subject of creeps who might not be nice.

"Yuck!" Callie said, holding her nose a few minutes later. "I ain't never taken' a chance on a creep."

"Smart girl," Emily said, with a sigh of relief.

"I fooled you!" Callie cackled. "I said *ain't*, and you didn't say nothin!'"

What?" Emily said, appearing shocked. "My "ain't alarm" didn't go off!"

"Fooled ya'," Callie laughed, and went back to her homework.

Emily checked the calendar on her phone and saw that October 8th was on a Sunday.

"Callie, do you want to come over on your birthday, and spend the day with me?"

Her face lit up. "Really! What are we gonna' do?"

Emily hadn't thought that far.

"Well," she began, making it up as she went, "we can go to church, then I'll take you to lunch at Ike's, then we'll go to a movie!" She held her breath, hoping it didn't sound too dull for a young girl.

Callie's eyes danced. "I never been to church, I never been to a movie!"

"Yay! We'll have a grand adventure then! Do you have a dress for church?"

Callie thought about it. "No, but I seen Miz Sanchez's daughter in a pretty dress once, and she said I could borrow it if I wanted to. It's beautiful, like a princess!"

"Perfect," Emily said, "'You'll be Princess Callie on your birthday!"

Callie's eyes danced, and she wriggled with excitement. "How 'bout a birthday cake?" she whispered." I saw it on TV to do a cake."

"Cake all the way, with ice cream! The bakery will make you one fit for a princess. What flavor?"

She shrugged. "The onliest thing is I don't like lemon."

"Vanilla, then, with a whipped cream frosting. Do you want a pudding filling?"

"That sounds so good, I'm nearly cussin'!"

"Don't cuss," Emily laughed. "Here's some other words to show your feelings...,happy, excited, over-the-moon!"

"Naw," the young girl said, her legs swinging happily. "It feels like I need ta' cuss my happiness."

Emily couldn't help laughing. "Well, thanks for restraining yourself," she said, adding a hug.

On Sunday morning, Miss Mattie waited with her downstairs in the bakery. She had told Callie to be there by 9:45, then they would all walk to church together. Miss Mattie spotted her first. "What in the world is that girl wearin'?" she asked, her eyes bugging out.

Emily turned to the window and watched as Callie crossed the street in a long, bright red, hooped dress, holding it up so it didn't drag in the street, looking much like Scarlett O'Hara in *Gone With the Wind*.

"It's a quinceanera dress," Emily murmured, remembering Callie telling her about the beautiful dress Mrs. Sanchez's daughter had worn to a special party. "And it looks like it's been used a few times."

"Well, she'll certainly be a showstopper in church," her mama laughed, as the young girl promenaded toward the bakery.

"We'll just be happy she's coming," Emily laughed along with her.

"Happy Birthday, Princess Callie!" Emily said, as she threw open the bakery door.

"I'm so excited," Callie exclaimed, trying to get the bottom of her hooped dress through the door.

"Here let me help." Emily picked up the hoop part and turned it at an angle, as Callie glided through the door.

"Happy birthday, Callie," Miss Mattie said, getting up from her parlor chair and going over to the girl. She attempted to hug her, but the hoop didn't allow for hugging. "Now don't you jus' look beautiful," she said, holding her at arm's length.

"Thank you, Miz Mattie. I like youin's hats!"

"Thank you!" Miss Mattie said, touching the wide brim of her deep purple hat, embellished with a crown of lavender flowers.

Emily had slipped on her blue, wide brimmed hat, with an arched feather, that Miss Mattie had bought her.

"I have this for you, Callie," she said, showing her a sequined crown she'd picked up at a party supply store near Walmart. "A birthday princess has to have a crown!"

"I love it!" Callie sang out, sitting down in a parlor chair while it was pinned into place.

"There!" said Emily looking her over. "Royalty goes to church!"

The crown was over-the-top with the quinceanera dress, but Callie was thrilled—and that's all Emily cared about.

"Let's get this party started," Emily said, swinging open the bakery door.

It was a good thing the church had double doors. As the ladies mounted the steps of the Mountain Grove Community Church, the ushers opened both doors wide as Callie sashayed through, with both men grinning from ear to ear, and one saying, "Wish we had trumpets to blow to herald this girl's entry!"

The procession flowed down the church aisle as heads turned.

Emily nodded to Mr. and Mrs. Green, and Mrs. Green blew a kiss; Miss Rose appeared shocked, while Miss Violet gave a nod of approval; Ike gave them a thumbs up; Kelly Ann and Gilbert raised their hands and gave a silent applause, and the rest of the congregation sat with mouths open.

Callie attempted to slide into a pew, but there was no way to do it without the hoop going sideways and sticking up in front of her face.

From two rows ahead, Penelope motioned to them, and called softly, "Come sit on the front row!"

The front pew worked out perfectly, and Callie sat happily, with the hoop in back of her, and her dress sticking straight out nearly touching the first step leading up to the stage. Anyone trying to pass would have tripped.

When Pastor Alex walked up to his podium, he glanced down where his wife usually sat, but instead saw two fine-hatted women, with a ballooning, hooped skirt between them. The young girl beneath the hooped skirt smiled up at him and pointed to her crown. *It's my birthday*, she mouthed, grinning like a Cheshire cat. He gave her two thumbs up.

A hush fell over the congregation as Pastor Alex began to speak. "I believe we have a very special guest with us today, and I hear it's her birthday!" he said, smiling down at Callie. "Emily, would you help your young friend up on stage?"

Slightly alarmed, Emily whispered, "Come on Callie! I think people want to sing the birthday song to you."

Unafraid, Callie hopped up, and Emily helped with her dress as she climbed the four stairs to where Pastor Alex stood waiting for her.

"I'm Pastor Alex," he said, leaning in and reaching across the wide dress to shake her hand.

"Pleased to meetcha, I'm Callie," she replied, vigorously shaking his hand.

"Are you new in town, Callie?

"Yessir, and we got the only double-wide at the Sawmill trailer park," she said proudly, turning slightly in case some of the audience couldn't see her pretty dress.

"Nice!" said the pastor, giving her a fist bump. "Does your daddy work at the Sawmill?

Emily cringed and thought about running to one of the tall church windows and leaping out.

"No sir," the girl replied, smoothing down her dress, "he's runnin' from the law."

There was absolute silence throughout the whole church, as Emily considered which window she might jump from.

Then a man in the third row started laughing; she heard Mrs. Green snort twice and start cackling, as did Mr. Charles, then the whole church nearly blew the roof off laughing. Astounded, Emily looked up at Pastor Alex who was hanging onto the podium as tears streamed down his face. "Oh Lord, my sides hurt," he howled, forgetting his microphone was still on.

Callie stood delighted, looking out over the roaring congregation, eating the laughter and attention up with a spoon. She grinned up at Emily, and said, "I really like this church!"

When the laughter died down, Pastor Alex wiped his eyes, and turned to the choir director, barely able to speak, "Time to sing to this girl on her special day."

The choir director, who had been howling in the corner, cleared his throat and started them, "Happy Birthday to you!"

The rest of the congregation joined in: "Happy Birthday to you!"

"Happy Birthday, dear Call-eeee!" They held the note, and Emily remembered the thrill of the very first time she heard people sing the birthday song with her name in it.

"Happy Birthday to you!" They all finished with great gusto.

Callie did a slight curtsy and clapped her hands. "Thank ya'll" she shouted.

Pastor Alex hugged Callie as best he could with the hoop between them, patted Emily on the back, and returned to his podium.

As Emily left the stage, she could've sworn she saw the pastor's stomach still jiggling with laughter.

Miss Mattie had arranged for Blessy to deliver Callie's birthday cake to *Good Eats*, and when they walked through the café door after church, there it sat in the middle of the room with pink balloons bobbing nearby.

The Sunday regulars had already gathered for breakfast, and broke into applause as Callie walked in.

Callie stood waving happily as they applauded, a look of absolute delight on her face. Emily led her over to see the beautiful cake done in pink fondant with small plastic princess figurines, posed on each layer wearing tiny dresses, much like the one Callie had on. *Happy Birthday, Callie!* had been written in glittery letters that twinkled under the overhead lights.

Callie clasped her hands as she took it all in. "A cake with my name on it," she whispered, then looked up at Miss Mattie. "Thank you, ma'am," she whispered.

"Stand by the cake and I'll take your picture," Emily said, bringing out her cell phone.

Callie put a hand on her hip, and posed by the cake, then said, "You come and be in the picture too, Em'ly!"

Emily handed her phone to Miss Mattie, who clicked off different poses of them laughing and being silly.

"Happy Birthday, little lady," Ike said, greeting Callie, as she attempted to sit down in the chrome dinette chair with her ballooning dress.

"Thank ya'all!" Callie said, trying another angle.

"I'll find ya a stool," Ike said, hurrying off.

After she was properly seated, Ike handed her a menu and said, "Choose anything you want, Callie! It'll be my birthday treat."

Callie couldn't believe all of the choices she had, as she looked the menu over. "I don't even know what some of this stuff is!" she said, laughing.

"Tell me what kind of food sounds good, and I'll help you choose," Emily said. "What kind of meat do you like?"

"I never had steak a'fore."

"Okay, steak it is!" Ike said.

"What do you want it with it?" Emily asked. "See here on the menu it gives you choices...there are potatoes, salad, corn on the cob, fried green tomatoes, red rice, grits..."

"Yes."

"Yes, what?"

"Yes, thank you?" Callie was confused.

"No," Emily laughed, "choose which of the foods I mentioned sound good."

"All of 'em do. I'm hungry."

Emily looked up at Ike, realizing that since there was no school today, Callie probably hadn't had any breakfast either.

"I'll find a servin' platter," Ike said, "if this girl wants ever'thing, she gets ever'thing!"

Callie did a fist bump with Ike as her stomach growled.

"I think I died an' went ta' Heaven," Callie said, after her first bite of steak.

"That good, huh?" laughed Miss Mattie.

"Yes'm," she sighed, as Emily showed her how to put butter on her baked potato.

"If you can't eat all of this, Ike will give you a box to take the rest home with you," Emily told her, watching her scoop bite after bite into her mouth, eating hungrily.

"And save a little room for birthday cake!" Miss Mattie reminded her.

The Sunday crowd had all finished their meals but sipped coffee while they waited for Callie to finish hers, knowing what an important day this was to her. When it was time for cake, Emily stood up and invited all the people in the café to come over and join in.

Miss Violet and Miss Rose hurried over, keeping their cloth napkins with them to wave in celebration during the birthday song. Mr. Kingery sauntered over with his mug of coffee, Iris Head walked over barefoot since her new high heels hurt her bunions, and five tables of people that Emily didn't even know all rose and joined them.

Miss Violet started them off, and for the second time in her life, Callie heard the birthday song with her name in it.

"This has been the most magic, fairy tale day I ever had," Callie said, as they left the movie theatre late that afternoon. She put her arms out, spinning in a slow circle, in front of the theatre. "I never want this day to get over," she said as patrons leaving the theatre stopped and stared at the young girl spinning in a dress looking much like a character in a Disney movie.

Emily grinned, "Come on Cinderella. I don't want you walking home in the dark!"

She turned to Emily, and said, "Thank you, yer' the best friend I ever had."

Touched beyond measure, Emily replied, "You're welcome, and Happy Birthday, Callie!" hugging her as close as the hooped skirt would allow. "It was fun, wasn't it?"

"Yes! I got to hear the birthday song with my name in it two times in one day," she said, talking excitedly as they walked along.

Callie stopped suddenly and spun around. "You know what?"

"What?"

"I'm the luckiest girl in the whole wide world!" shouted the young girl who was heading back to her double-wide trailer at the Sawmill.

Chapter - 17

Life at the bakery hummed on as usual. Gilbert had started seminary, but still came on Tuesdays to give Emily a day off. He'd bring his books and study between customers, and Emily would come in at the end of the day to put things away, and prepare for the next day. Since they had decided to close the bakery on Mondays, that gave her two free days to catch up on schoolwork, grocery shop, weed her vegetable garden, cook dinner for her mama, or whatever else needed to be done. If she needed more time off, there was always Blessy willing to work more hours, and glad for the extra money.

Emily watched the books like a hawk, and they were barely making it with the upselling of housewares, flavored coffee, and pet cookies, but at least they were making it.

Miss Mattie stayed upstairs more now that she had Itsy for company. "Are you sure you don't need my help downstairs," her mama always asked, while cuddling her dog.

"I don't need your help, Mama, but be sure you and Itsy go for your walk," she would remind daily. It hadn't occurred to her when she bought the dog, that it would be the perfect way to make sure her mama got the exercise the doctor had ordered. Emily never offered to walk Itsy or take her out for a potty break, ensuring that her mama went up and down those steps several times a day, and walked around the block a time or two.

At first her mama had wanted to know everything that was going on in the bakery, but gradually quit asking. "I think she's actually relieved that I took over," she told Blessy one day.

"Oh, I b'iieve that," the bakery's faithful worker replied. "She's done with this place. It's too much for her."

"Well, I'm glad I have you for a back-up, and I appreciate the baking lessons you've been giving me, too!"

"You are a kick," Blessy laughed. "Whoever heard of a person runnin' a bak'ry, and not knowin' how to bake?"

"You're lookin' at her," she laughed.

Emily tried to think of the future. She had this one more year of homeschooling and then she would challenge the high school graduation test, which she was sure she could pass. And then what? College, she supposed. But she wouldn't go to college unless she knew exactly what she wanted out of it. It was too expensive, and she wouldn't waste the money her grandmother had left her. She didn't understand kids going off to college when they hadn't a clue about what they wanted to do and were likely to change their minds five times.

Emily was taking some dog cookies out of the oven when the bell over the bakery door jangled, and she heard, "Yoo hoo, Em'ly!" followed by a baby's cry.

"Kelly Ann!" she said, hurrying out front.

She went straight to the stroller and scooped Mia up, then gave Kelly Ann a side hug. "I've been missing you two!"

"Why don't you come over then?" Kelly Ann chided. "I thought you left for Mars or somethin'."

"No, haven't been to Mars lately, just busy."

"An you look tired," her friend said. "You sit here with the baby. I'm fixin' us some tea, and if anybody comes in, I'm waitin' on 'em."

"Do you know how to use a cash register?"

"Don't you worry about nothin'" Kelly Ann said, heading for the tea kettle.

That's a no," laughed Emily to herself, but felt her mood brighten at the craziness of her friend.

"Now I need to talk to you about somethin'," Kelly Ann said a few minutes later, stirring her tea, "and if it puts any pressure on you, then jus' shove me out th' door!"

Emily laid Mia down in the stroller before taking a drink of her hot tea. "Go for it!"

"I'm havin' the baby dedicated at church in a couple of weeks, and she needs a godmother…"

"I'll do it," Emily said, not letting her finish.

"Thank you," Kelly Ann laughed, "but I didn't get to the serious part yet!"

"Oh, go ahead."

"I'm a single mom, and I'd like a back-up in case somethin' ever happened to me."

"What? You're only eighteen!"

"I don't mean dyin' of old age, silly! I'd jus' feel better havin' a back-up for Mia!"

"Okay, tell me what you need."

"I need you to be Mia's legal guardian!"

"Of course, I'll be her guardian!"

"Well, do you know what it means, Em'ly? Or doncha' need to think about it or somethin'?"

"No, I know exactly what it means—you want me to raise Mia if anything happens to you—and I'm honored to do it. I would want to do it. People would have to fight me if they tried to stop me from doing it. There. Are you convinced?"

Her friend laughed. "Well, you convinced me! Do you have time this week to go to a notary with me and sign papers?"

"Ugh! I just thought of something!"

"What?"

"I'm not eighteen for another year, and I can't enter a contract until then."

"Poop!" Kelly Ann murmured, having cleaned up her language since the baby was born.

"How about if Miss Mattie did it, and you could list me as the co-guardian, who at the age of eighteen becomes full guardian?"

"Would she do that?"

"Of course! And we'll take her out to lunch afterward. She loves going out to lunch."

They agreed on a date and time, clinked their tea mugs together, and laughed like six-year-olds.

"Yer' tiredness left, I can feel it's gone," Kelly Ann chirped.

"Just needed a good friend to laugh with, is all," Emily said, and they clinked their tea mugs together again.

How's my girl today? came a text from Jonathan just after Emily opened the bakery on a beautiful October morning, with fall fairly bursting in the air.

How was she? She decided to tell him. *Overwhelmed and tired today. Wish I had time to go to the river and just stare at the fall colors,* she dashed off, not giving it a second thought, or worrying how it would make him feel.

"If you ask me, I'll tell you," she murmured aloud, while wiping down the glass on the pastry case.

She waited for his answer with her phone tucked in an apron pocket. But he didn't answer.

Hello? she texted him again.

Still no answer.

Well, so much for baring my soul to him, she thought, straightening the display of new merchandise in her Country Store. It had become a small place of joy for her; she loved the new pretty teapots that had arrived yesterday, along with a sugar and creamer set shaped like Guernsey cows, and a tiny waffle maker that made heart-shaped waffles for those with a romantic inclination. It was all happy stuff.

Her first customer came in.

"Good morning," she greeted the older woman.

"It ain't good when you got arthritis," the woman squawked, looking over the pastries in the case. "Gimme' a dozen mixed cookies."

"Just point to the ones you want," Emily said, opening a white paper bag to put them in."

"Gimme a box, they git' broken in a bag," ordered the woman.

If her mama were downstairs, this woman wouldn't get a crumb without saying, *please*. But she wasn't her mama, and she was tired. The winning contest sign for manners, saying "Use your manners, or use the door!" was prominent, but obviously ignored. Her mama had been unable to choose just one winner for the slogan contest Emily held, so they had all the entries printed up, and rotated the signs each week. "They are all winners!" her mama had said, and insisted they give each entry a dozen donuts of their choice.

The woman picked out twelve different cookies, in twelve different flavors, changing her mind twice.

Emily felt a slight sweat break out on her forehead when the woman barked at her and changed her order again.

The customer left and a moment later the bell over the door jingled, and Mrs. Charles walked in carrying a small basket.

"Good morning," Emily greeted her.

"Good morning," Mrs. Charles said cheerfully, setting the basket on the counter and pushing it towards her. "For you!" she chirped.

"For me?"

"Yes, a picnic lunch! I'm taking over the bakery until two o'clock, while you go to the river!"

"Jonathan told you..." Emily felt embarrassed.

"Yes, he did, but I needed a reminder that you have a lot on your plate, and still need help! So here it is," she said, tapping the basket. "Go relax at the river and enjoy your lunch!"

"I don't know what to say!" Emily said, coming around the counter to hug her. "Thank you so much!"

"You're very welcome," she replied, hugging her back.

Emily picked up the picnic basket, then hesitated, "Do you mind checking on my Mama in an hour? I left her some lunch, but I still always check on her." She felt uncomfortable asking Mrs. Charles to do more.

"Of course! I'll set my watch to remind me!" she said, fiddling with her watch. "Don't forget to take your apron off!"

Emily glanced down at her purple apron with flying parrots and laughed. "Thanks for the reminder," she said, taking it off and tossing it on the counter.

"Enjoy yourself!" Mrs. Charles picked up the discarded apron and put it on.

Emily grinned. "You look great in flying parrots!"

Mrs. Charles laughed and did a small curtsy.

Emily inhaled the crisp autumn air as she closed the bakery door. She could smell wood smoke from the village's wood burning stoves, lit against the chill of the day. It felt wonderful to be free of all responsibility, and she resisted the sudden impulse to twirl around in circles as Callie had done on Sunday, with maybe a cartwheel thrown in.

Nearing the stands of maple and oak trees in the picnic grounds, she hoped to see fall colors, but it was still a little early. There was only the beginning tinge of color, which she would keep an eye on, because the leaves changed rapidly, and almost overnight went from brilliant flames of red, orange, and yellow to crunchy grey piles covering the ground like a drab carpet.

At the river, she tiptoed across the rocks to the flat-topped boulder she and Jonathan had always shared. It was tricky to climb, so she reached up and slid her small picnic basket onto the surface, then climbed up herself. The first thing she did was take out her phone and click pictures of her picnic basket and the rapidly flowing river, then sent them off to Jonathan, with the text saying, *thank you!*.

He sent back a text with hearts that filled the whole screen.

Amazing, she whispered, feeling awestruck as she took in the view around her: The powerful river coursed over rocks where eddies of water dipped and swirled; birch trees with golden leaves that fluttered down into the water, bobbing downstream, and always reminding her of tiny banana boats. Overhead, a bank of clouds, puffy and white and serene.

Amazing, she whispered again.

She sat without thinking, without figuring out, she just let these sights speak to her. The scene was so overpowering, so immense, so grand...and all under control. Her life was under control--watched over, and protected by the very One who made all this. She came to that truth, not because it was told to her, but because it was whispered to her soul, restoring her very being.

Emily sat doing her own schoolwork, waiting for Callie to show up. The bakery door flew open and in came Callie with a girl in dirty levis, a sweater that was a size too small, and unmatched shoes.

"Is it okay to bring a friend?" Callie asked, when she saw the look on Emily's face.

"Of course," Emily said, forcing herself to smile. There was no choice.

"This is Savanah," Callie said, introducing them. "She lives at the Sawmill too." She leaned in close and whispered, "In a single-wide!"

"How do you do, Savanah, I'm Emily," she said offering her hand.

Savanah just stared at it.

"Shake her hand," Callie said. "You don't get a donut if you have bad manners."

Savanah shook her hand and stood staring at her.

"Are you hungry Savanah?"

She nodded.

"Did you bring your homework?"

Savanah lifted a dirty, torn backpack as proof.

"Then we'll all have something to eat and do homework."

"I thought we got a donut *after* homework," Callie said, putting her hands on her hips.

"We usually do," Emily replied, giving her a warning look, "but today we'll celebrate Savanah doing her homework with us. Did you have lunch today, Savanah?"

Savanah shook her head, and Callie looked up with a knowing look.

They walked over to the pastry case, and Savanah stared at the mounds of delicacies as though she were viewing a king's treasure.

"What kind of pastry would you like?"

She pointed to a large crème puff drizzled with chocolate.

"Use your voice to tell me," Emily said, putting a hand on her shoulder.

"That 'un," the young girl whispered.

Callie chose the same pastry and they all settled in at one of the larger tables, since there wasn't room for three people, plus schoolbooks at a parlor table.

As they ate, Emily said, "Callie, tomorrow I want you to show Savanah where to go to sign up for school lunches."

She threw her head back. "Do I have to?"

Emily was shocked. "Don't you want to help her get nice lunches like you get? She gets hungry, too!"

"You do it," she barked, as she dug in her Walmart bag for her schoolbooks.

Emily didn't say anymore, just waited for Savanah to start on her homework, then said, "Come over here for a minute, Callie."

Taking her across the room near the cash register, Emily said, "I belong to a club I want you to join!"

"What is it?" she asked, her eyes lighting up. "Can I wear my dress?"

"No, you don't dress special for this club, you do it in your regular clothes every chance you get."

"What's it called?"

"The Pass It Along Club."

"Huh?'

"Have I helped you, Callie?"

"Uh-huh," she said looking back over her shoulder, wanting to finish her crème puff.

"I've been helped too, by lots of people, and I passed it along to you. Who are you going to pass it along to?"

"Sa-van-uh," she sighed, punctuating each syllable.

"And tomorrow when you bring your new friend, you'll have the papers for the lunch program with you, right?"

She slumped forward. "I'm so hungry I'm faintin'."

"Just give me your word, and we'll get back to homework and eating."

Callie stared at her for a second. "Okay, I'll do it," she replied in a squeaky Minnie Mouse voice, making Emily laugh.

The next day, as Emily studied, and waited for Callie and Savanah to show up, she looked up and saw *three* girls coming in the bakery door.

"I brought 'nother girl to join our club!" Callie said happily, setting a sheaf of papers on the table in front of Emily. "There's yer' dern' lunch papers."

"Thank you, but why so many?" Emily asked, as she stood up to greet the new girl.

"I don't wanna haveta' go into that school office again an' git more," she sighed, setting her Walmart bag on the table. "There'll be more girls comin' here who need to sign up for that lunch program. Girls at the Sawmill are hearin' 'bout you helpin' with homework, and handin' out donuts!"

"I see," Emily said, wondering how she could handle more.

She went over to the new girl and put out her hand. "I'm Emily, what's your name?"

The small girl shook her hand, and said, "Magnolia!"

"All her sisters got flower names," Callie announced. "Is it okay if they come, too?"

"Of course," Emily said, alarmed, but determined not to turn anyone away. "Just remember, they are coming to do homework," she added.

The girls finished their homework in record time, making Emily suspicious. "Are you girls sure you did all your homework?"

"I ain't got but one homework ta' do," replied Magnolia.

"*Ain't's* not a college word," Callie barked.

Callie's remark was rude, but it clarified something for Emily. This had to be more than just a homework-donuts session. "Girls!" she said, and three heads turned and looked at her. "We need to talk."

"A'fore we get dessert?" Callie asked, slightly irritated.

"No, and thanks for the reminder, Callie. Let's go over and choose a dessert."

As they sat happily eating their pastries, Emily said, "We need to have goals about why we're here."

"What's a goal?" Magnolia asked, squeezing her cream puff so the whipped cream shot into her mouth.

"It's something you want, something you're working for," Emily told her.

"My goal is some hot chocolate," Callie announced.

"One good way to get something, Callie, is with good manners. It makes you a more pleasant person to be around and people will be willing to help you reach those goals."

Callie stood up and curtsied. "I'd like some hot chocolate, please!" She took a bow and sat back down as they all laughed.

Emily chuckled as she headed over to make the chocolate. Callie was a smart girl, and danged if she didn't love that sassy kid!

"Okay girls, I'll have a plan next time you come in," Emily announced, as they drank their hot chocolate. "We're going to set goals, and the first one will be to learn good manners! I'll have a small book called a journal for each of you to write your goals and dreams in-- where you want to live and what you want your home to be like. Then we'll talk about ways to make that happen."

"I got a journal with dancing poodles on it," Callie informed the girls, as she spooned whipped cream into her mouth.

"Ohhhh!" the other two girls chorused. "We want that too!"

"I'll see what I can find," Emily promised. Then seeing that they were almost finished with their hot chocolate, said, "Does anyone have questions, or something they want to say?"

"I got somethin' I wanna' say," Callie said, standing up. She reached for her spoon, held it up to her mouth like a microphone and began to loudly croon, "Treat me like a fool, treat me mean and cruel, but love me..."

The other girls burst into gales of laughter, picked up their spoons, holding them at dramatic angles as they joined in singing, "Wring my faithful heart, tear it all apart, but love meeeeee!"

Emily laughed and applauded as they sang, thinking that Elvis must be very popular with families at the Sawmill.

Emily was infused with energy at the way things had gone today with Callie and the other girls. She sat down to work out a plan of all she wanted them to learn to help make them successful, but soon stopped.

How could she help with all that when her time was so limited? And what about boys? Boys at the Sawmill needed help to be successful, too! She thought of Gilbert—he was the poster boy of a great success story. When she met him, he was dirty and cold in an alleyway, running from an abusive father at the Sawmill, and now he was enrolled in college to be a pastor. A miracle on the scale of feeding the five thousand, or parting the Red Sea, as far as she was concerned.

She knew what to do but was frustrated by her lack of time to do it! Hadn't the townspeople done the very same for her? She sat drumming her fingers trying to figure it out.

Jonathan always had good ideas, maybe he could help her see her way through.

She texted him a quick summary of the day's events, and added, *I want to help the girls with goals and manners. I'd also like to start something for the boys at the Sawmill. Any ideas?*

Five minutes later, Jonathan sent back one word: *delegate*

Huh? she replied.

You're already too busy: bakery and country store, caring for Miss Mattie, finishing school. Your idea is great, but you don't have the time. You need other people to help you with it. Delegate!

That wasn't the answer she wanted! These were *her* girls! Frustrated, she set her phone down, not answering him back.

A few minutes later, she got another text from him: *Am I right?*

She wanted to fill up the screen with emojis sticking their tongue out but refrained. Why was he always so logical, and most of the time, right?

He tried another tactic and texted: *Assume I'm right for a few minutes. Who could help you?*

"Okay...." she murmured, relenting, and texted: *Miss violet, miss rose, with manners; mrs Green with homework; gilbert with anything I ask him to do.*

Bingo! he texted back. *Do it!*

Chapter - 18

Emily's main concern about introducing the girls to the Young Ladies Academy was she wasn't sure how they would be received. Miss Violet and Miss Rose tended to be haughty. Would they act superior to these girls, or look down on them? She'd have to see.

As she walked into Violet's House of Beauty she saw Charmagne at the wash bowl, rinsing red henna out of a client's hair.

"Hi ya' Em'ly," she greeted, blowing a small pink bubble with her ever-present bubble gum.

"Is Miss Violet or Miss Rose in?" Emily asked, watching as the hairdresser blew a larger bubble.

"The last charm school class jus' got out, so I'm sure they're back there somewhere," she nodded towards the back room.

"You mean the Young Ladies' Academy, don't you?" Emily laughed.

"Shoot! I keep fergettin' they changed the danged name!" Two bubbles in a row popped.

"Do they ever say anything about you chewing gum?" she asked, already laughing.

"They never see me doin' it!," she cackled, her eyes blinking rapidly under a thick layer of blue eye shadow. "They'd skin me alive and hang me out to dry!" Another bubble popped.

Yes they would! Emily thought as she went through the archway to the back part of the building in search of one of the sisters.

She found them snacking on saltines and Cheez Whiz in the back room. They greeted her, and Miss Rose said, "I do hope you've come to enroll in our next Academy session!".

Emily spotted a little Cheez Whiz on the corner of her mouth, and pointed, clearing her throat.

"Oh!" cried Miss Rose, mortified as she took a flowered hanky out of her pocket and dabbed the spot away.

"Actually, I've come to ask for your help with a group of girls," she told the sisters.

"Superb!" trilled Miss Violet, gathering up her long pink lame' skirt and sitting down. "Please be seated, Emily," she said, taking out her sequined cigarette holder, used for emphasis as she spoke. "Where do these girls hail from?"

Emily cleared her throat. "They hail from the trailer park at the Sawmill!"

"Oh dear!" Miss Rose uttered, clutching her chest, as she sat down.

Emily plowed on. "I want them to succeed, but they don't even know basic manners, and I was hoping you ladies would teach them."

"I see!" Miss Violet murmured; the cigarette holder forgotten for the moment.

"I fear their hygiene is amiss and bathing is not done on a regular basis," Miss Rose said, looking pale.

"Yes, that's something they would need to be taught, too," Emily replied, deciding not to sugar-coat anything.

"Might we assume they haven't been properly immunized?" Miss Rose croaked.

"Yes, you might assume that."

"Oh dear!"

Emily hoped Miss Rose didn't faint.

"We would be most honored to help these young ladies," Miss Violet trilled all of a sudden.

"Oh, Violet dear, we should talk it over!" her sister cried.

"There's nothing to talk over, Rose dear, if you don't want to participate, then you needn't," her sister said, with a flourish of the sequined cigarette holder. "You forget where we came from, Rose..."

Emily looked from one sister to the other, not quite believing what she'd just heard. "You ladies came from the Sawmill?"

"Yes, we came from the Sawmill," Miss Violet replied haughtily, with a slight English accent. "But we had a WONderful teacher who helped us! Isn't that right, Sister?" she said, with a steady look at Miss Rose. "We were determined to escape, and when we did, we determined to help other girls. That's why we have the Young Ladies Academy and encourage girls to attend; perhaps we even *pester* girls to attend," she said, staring at her.

"Yes, you do," Emily replied, thinking of her own session with them, and all that she had learned—even though she didn't appreciate it at the time. "And thank you for pestering me."

Miss Violet nodded to her like royalty bestowing grace on a commoner, and Emily understood everything, and knew the girls would be safe with her.

After the arrangements were made, and she was ready to leave, Miss Rose spoke up. "Emily, I don't wish for others to know where we came from."

Emily nodded that she understood, and said, "That's your story to tell, not mine, but from what I know about the townspeople, nobody would think less of you. They've been really kind to me, and my background is pretty rough with alcoholic parents. I didn't live at the Sawmill, but close to it."

Miss Rose nodded that she understood, and Emily left.

She found Mrs. Green at the back of the library helping someone find a Wolfgang Puck cookbook. "Be with you in a sec!" she whispered to Emily.

Emily meandered around, trying to visualize where young girls could sit and do homework without bothering others who were trying to read. The bakery was closed on Monday, and Gilbert watched it on Tuesday, so that was two days the girls needed a place to study. She knew they could study on their own, but they didn't. As a group, they had somehow formed a common goal, and they shared and supported each other's dreams. Each girl now thought it entirely possible to have the home they had described in their journals, along with details about who and what would be allowed in that home. The common thread about what would not be allowed was drugs and alcohol.

"College can be your plan to reach that goal for a home," Emily had explained to them.

"My parents said they's too poor to pay fer college," one girl said.

"Well, here's the good news," Emily had told them, "we live in a country where low income kids are given all kinds of help to go to college."

"Kinda like a leg up?" Magnolia asked, trying to understand.

"Exactly!" Emily said, "and sort of like our *Pass It Along Club*. When you get out of college, and get a good job, and pay taxes, that money will help the next person who wants to go to college."

"What do I need college for? I jus' wanna' bakery," Callie groused.

"You could go to a trade school and learn baking," Emily said, "but don't you think it would be fun to go to college? Live in a dorm, and be around kids your age, stuff like that?"

"Are you goin' to college?" she replied, eyeing her.

Emily tried to think of how to answer, because she knew she wouldn't go away to college.

"My situation is different than yours," she replied, and told them about how Miss Mattie had become her foster mother.

"Awwwwh, that's so sweet," the girls all chorused after she finished her story.

"Yes, it is sweet, and that's why I won't go away to college, but I'll still go. Miss Mattie needs me here"

"Well, where's that bakery school anyway?" Callie groused. "I don't wanna' leave you either."

That had been another challenge. The girls were afraid to leave Mountain Grove.

"Girls, it's fine to go to a nearby college," she had told them. "You're just starting to plan now, and you can change your mind as you go along. Just write your goals down because that's the first step to those beautiful houses you've told me you wanted! Just talking about it or daydreaming about it won't get you the house—it takes action!"

Mrs. Green hurried over to Emily, breaking into her daydreaming, and giving her a hug and a squeeze. "What can I help my friend with today?" she asked.

"This will take a minute; do you need to help check out that cookbook?"

"No," the librarian whispered, "that's Mrs. Barrett, a widow who spends lots of time here. She'll find other books and sit and read awhile. She used to be a teacher with people around her all day, and I think it's too lonesome at her house."

Emily nodded. "Okay, I have a problem I need you to help me solve!"

"Go for it," Mrs. Green said, looping her arm through Emily's as they made their way to a couple of easy chairs near the check-out desk.

She explained how she was helping the girls, and why, and where they were from, then said, "But I have to take Monday and Tuesday off to take Miss Mattie to her physical therapy and doctor appointments, shop, clean our apartment, and a whole bunch of other stuff."

"Where is some YOU time in all of that?" the librarian inquired.

"Jonathan told me to delegate, and that's what I'm trying to do," she said, wondering why tears sprang to her eyes.

She explained why she would like to keep the girls studying together, and at some point, help boys from the Sawmill in the same way. "They have so much to learn, she said, her lips trembling. "I'm trying to just teach them basic manners and good grammar. It's simple and gives them a chance in life. Otherwise, they'll pattern the things that got their families into the Sawmill to begin with."

"Come with me," Mrs. Green said. They went past the map section to a door that Mrs. Green unlocked. "It's the conference room, and it's yours," Mrs. Green said, showing her the room where she, Kelly Ann, and Gilbert had been in when they went to parenting classes. "But there's something I want you to do."

"What?" Emily asked, looking over the spacious room, and loving it. She noticed there was a long counter she could have donuts set on, and maybe she could get someone to donate bottled water. Her mind was spinning with the details of it.

"I want you to rest," Mrs. Green said. "You're on the verge of tears."

"But I have to find someone to monitor the girls."

"You're going to let me do that," she replied, meaning it. "I'll ask Mrs. Barrett to help."

"But..."

"The room is yours. Mission accomplished. Go home and rest. I'm having dinner sent over. You're not to clean or cook."

"I need to talk to Penelope about Sunday school for the girls."

"Home. Rest. Now." she ordered.

Emily opened her mouth to protest, but it all sounded too wonderful, so she just said, "Thank you."

"Dinner will be sent over at 6:00. Do you want Italian or Mexican?"

"Ike doesn't do those," she said.

"No, but there's two restaurants out on the highway that do. Which one sounds the best?"

"Italian!"

"See you at 6:00! Go home and play with your dog. No paperwork, no planning. You and your mama watch a corny movie."

"Done!" Emily said, happy and relieved for someone taking over.

Itsy ran towards Emily as soon as she opened the door. She scooped the dog up and went to find her mama.

She found her in her room, napping, and quietly shut the door, and went into the living room with Itsy and turned the TV on looking for that corny movie Mrs. Green had suggested.

Her mama came out a half hour later. "Well, don't tell me my girl is finally sittin' down and restin'!" she said, coming over and giving her a hug.

"Mrs. Green ordered me home and said we should watch corny movies together. She's sending up dinner from the Italian place out on the highway."

"I know the very place!" Miss Mattie said. "We're in for a treat!"

She sat down in her easy chair. "Now tell me all about your day!"

Emily told her, adding, "Tomorrow I'll go and talk to Penelope about getting the girls into Sunday School."

"What can I do to help with this wonderful project you're involved in?" her mama asked.

"Do?"

"Yes, I want to help."

"You can take care of Itsy."

"Sugar, my life has got to be more than sittin' upstairs and pettin' a dog. It was good to get rested up, but I'm recovered now and need purpose."

Emily was sure she was right, but too tired to think of things to give her mama purpose. "How about your purpose today is to watch a funny movie with me, and eat Italian food? I'm too tired to think of another thing."

Her mama stood up. I'll get us a couple of warm throws, and we'll binge watch the corniest movies we can find until our meals get here. How does that sound, Sugar?"

"Amazing!" she replied, hoping she didn't fall asleep in the middle of their binge watching.

The next morning, over breakfast, her mama brought the subject right back up. "How can I help with these girls, Sugar?"

"Do you have any ideas, Mama?"

"They're comin' to the bakery Wednesday through Friday, right?" Emily nodded.

"How many girls, so far?"

"Nine, but they will invite more."

"Then I will come down and help with their homework, if they need it. My next idea is to just be a mama to them. Sometimes that's all young girls want or need. I don't need a special job. How's that for an idea?"

"Perfect, but if you get too tired…"

"I know, Sugar. I know when to quit."

Emily was curious to see how all this would work out. It seemed simple enough.

After breakfast, Emily said, "Well, I'm off to talk to Penelope. I'll stop in and see if you need anything a little later, and you can phone me if you need something.

She sat across from Penelope drinking an Orange Crush.

"Of course you can bring girls to Sunday school," Penelope said, looking puzzled. "Why wouldn't you?"

"These girls are from the Sawmill, and I didn't know if the Sunday school teachers would be comfortable.

"I'll personally supervise, and help them out the first couple of Sundays," she replied. "Bring it on!"

Delegation done! Emily thought, heaving a sigh of relief.

The road might be bumpy for a while, but they'd get it running smoothly. The way it was set up, she'd only have the girls three days a week. Delegation worked, and she had her life back...somewhat. She would hand the boys over to Gilbert.

On Saturday Callie came in. "Can I still come by myself?" she asked. "Sorta' like teacher's pet?"

Emily laughed, and said, "Of course!" not mentioning that she actually was partial to her. "The bakery is too busy for me to sit and visit with you, but how about if you help me?"

"Do what?'

"My Country Store needs dusting, and a little rearranging. Can you do that, being careful not to break anything?"

"Can I wear an apron like you?"

Emily took her to the pegged wall in back where every shade of apron hung. "Pick one out, then come back out front," she said, hearing the bell over the front door jingle.

Callie came out front wearing a hot pink apron with sea turtles, a gift from a customer who had visited the Bahamas and knew of Miss Mattie's love for bright aprons.

Emily handed her a feather duster, telling her she could rearrange anything out of place.

"You want me to sell this stuff for ya?" Callie asked, looking it over.

"Go for it," Emily laughed.

When the next bakery customer came in, Callie lifted up a set of coffee mugs with wooded scenes, and said, "Is this fer' sale, Miss Em'ly? I love this 'un!" which drew the customer's attention.

"That is cute!" the woman said, going over to the display. She walked out fifteen minutes later with a dozen eclairs, the cups, and an expensive white soup tureen embossed with swans.

A man came in, and Callie held up a bar-b-que set with handles in the shape of farm animals. "Is this fer' sale, Miss Em'ly? I love this 'un!" she said, using the same line as before. She reminded Emily of a carnival barker she'd seen at the Apple Fair. All she needed was a straw hat and a cane!

The man stepped over for a closer look and bought, not only the bar-b-que set, but a colorful apron for his wife.

"Well, you're getting their attention," Emily said after the fourth sale, concerned about the honesty of Callie's approach. "Help me think of a way to get people to look over there without you pretending you want to buy something."

"Naw, let's keep doin' it my way, and I'll quit school and come and work for you," Callie offered, her apron dragging on the floor.

"Well, pretending something every time a customer walks in isn't the most honest thing in the world," Emily said, going over and retying her apron strings. "And second, I wonder how many laws I'd be breaking if I hired a ten-year-old girl, and had her drop out of school?"

"Tell 'em I'm twenty," Callie grinned, picking up her feather duster and hurrying back over to the Country Store, as the bell jingled, and two more people came through the door.

Yep, a carnival side-show could make a fortune off this girl, Emily thought as Callie sprang into action.

One customer ignored Callie, and the other took the bait, and stepped in for a closer look at a copper tea kettle. Five minutes later, Emily rang up the sale, giving side glances at a grinning Callie.

"Okay ladybug, no more pretending," Emily said, after the customer left. "Help me think of a way to honestly draw them back to the Country Store."

"But that was fun!" the young girl insisted, pushing out a lower lip.

"Help me think," Emily replied, meaning it.

"It makes you lots of mon-eeeeee," Callie sang, trying another approach.

Emily just looked at her. "Honesty is important. Help me think of another way to get their attention."

Callie threw back her head, and chanted in a monotone, "Give 'em free donuts when they buy somethin'; put up a fence so they have ta' walk by your stuff a'fore they can buy a donut; put a big sign outside with a whole buncha' balloons tied on it." She stopped and stared at Emily. "That's all my brain can think of."

Emily was impressed. "Know which idea I liked?"

"What one?"

"All of them!"

"Yay! Let's celebrate an' have a hamburger at Ike's?" she said, licking her lips.

"It's a deal!" Emily laughed. No doubt about it, this little schemer was good!

Emily's phone rang about eight o'clock that evening while she was watching a documentary with her mama. She answered quickly, thinking it was Jonathan.

"Emily?" said a familiar voice.

"Eva?"

"Yeah, it's me and I only have a minute."

"Where are you?" Emily asked, afraid she'd say Mountain Grove.

"I'm in a re-hab in Long Beach."

"Okay..." she replied slowly, wondering if that was true.

"One of the first steps they require in this program is that we apologize to the people we've hurt, and I know I hurt you. So, I'm sorry."

She didn't know what to say.

"Emily?"

"I don't know what to say."

"You don't have to say anything, if you don't want to. I just wanted you to know that I'm sorry."

"Where's Stan?" Emily asked, which seemed like a crazy question. But she still didn't believe her.

"I don't know. His grandma booted him out. He uses people. He used me."

Maybe she was telling the truth. "Why did you go into re-hab?"

"I was stealing from my work. They caught me, and I was arrested. The judge said I could go to jail or go to re-hab." She rattled it all off without sparing herself.

"Were you using drugs when I was there?"

"Yes, drugs and alcohol."

She had to ask. "Did you really want to see me, or were you just after the money our grandmother left me?"

"I was after your money."

"So, you were conning the whole time?"

"Yes. Wait a minute, no. I started feeling connected to you and didn't know what to do."

"So, you kept on conning?"

"I kept on drinking so I wouldn't care that I was conning. Drugs too. But I did care."

"What now?"

"I'm here for a year. It's a religious group; they say God can help me get off this stuff, but I can't even think past this phone call." She told her the name of the organization.

"When we hang up, I can text you their address, if you want to write. I can't make any more phone calls for a while."

Emily said good-bye and they hung up.

"Your sister?" her mama asked.

Emily nodded. "She said that she's in re-hab, and sorry for the way she treated me."

"How do you feel about all of that?"

"I don't trust her and wonder if she's conning."

Her mama looked at her. "But what if she's not?"

Her phone dinged with the text of her sister's address.

"I don't know. I have to think about it," she said, staring at the address.

"Sometimes people change!"

"Yes, and sometimes they don't," she replied, thinking of her parents. She hated that a spark of excitement flared at the thought of having a sober sister. She extinguished it, and said aloud, "We'll see how it goes."

Chapter – 19

Miss Mattie decided to start coming downstairs to help with the girls that very next week. Emily had already told them the story of how the bakery owner had become her foster mom, so those who hadn't met her mama were eager. As they waited for her to come downstairs from their home over the bakery, Magnolia said, "My nerves is excited; I bet she looks like a fairy godmother!"

"Well," Callie said, feeling proud that she'd already met her, "she's a strict fairy godmother, and youin's better use good manners or she'll boot you outta' here."

"No, she won't," chorused the other girls, looking over at Emily, questioning.

"Well, she does love good manners, but I don't think she'll boot you out if you slip up," Emily said, hoping that was true. "Just remember the manners that you and Miss Violet worked on last week. We're going to start using better English here, also. You need good English for college."

The girls moaned, and Callie stuck her finger in her mouth, making a loud gagging sound.

Emily looked at them. "I suppose you ladies already know that was rude..."

"Yeah, and Miz' Mattie woulda' kicked yer' little butts outta here for it!" Magnolia warned, as though she knew it for a fact.

The bell over the door jingled.

"It's her!" squealed Magnolia's sister, Azalea.

The girls sat up as straight as small soldiers, with hands folded, and mouths closed.

"Good morning, Mama," Emily said, rising and pulling out a chair for her. She had pushed the tables together so they could all sit in one place.

"Good mornin'," her mama said warmly. "Well, would you jus' look at all these sweet, pretty faces starin' at me!"

Grins emerged all around the table, with audible sighs of relief.

"Would you make the introductions, please Emily?" she intoned, sitting as pretty as a queen on her throne.

The girls shifted nervously.

"Girls, I'd like to introduce my Mama, Miss Mattie."

The girls nodded and gave small waves, unsure of what to do.

'We'll go around the table, and each of you can tell Miss Mattie your name," Emily instructed.

"Youin's already know my name," Callie blurted out, looking quite happy with that fact.

"Let's pretend that you're just meeting, Callie, and you start the introductions," Emily said.

Callie cleared her throat, happy to have the spotlight. "My name is Callie," she said, looking directly at Miss Mattie, "and it's very exquisite meetin' youin's!"

The other girls chorused, "What?!" looking confused.

Emily spoke up, "I see you've been learning more college words, Callie!"

"Yes,m!" she replied, appearing very pleased with herself.

"I'll go next," Emily said, "and the rest of you can copy what I say. "My name is Emily," she said, looking at her mama, who was trying not to laugh, "and it is very nice to meet you."

"Nice to meet you, Em'ly!" her mama replied, eyes twinkling.

"Azaelea, your turn."

"My names 'Zaelea," she mumbled, embarrassed and looking down. "Pleased to meetcha'!"

This is going to take some work, Emily realized, then said, "Savanah, your turn!"

Savanah strung it all out in one sentence, while picking at her fingernails. "Myname'sSavanahpleasedtomeetcha."

Emily looked up at her mama, wondering if she should insist they do it properly.

"This is so nice, sittin' here with you sweet girls," her mama said, soothing their nervousness with her mellow southern accent. "Sometimes practicin' can be hard. I think we should all have one of my world-class donuts, before we continue with the introductions."

"Yay," shouted the girls, breaking from whatever decorum that had held them.

"C'mon, ladies," Miss Mattie said, standing up and motioning them over to the pastry case. She put her arms around two of the girls as they walked over, and each girl began talking excitedly to her.

Later that day, Emily remarked, "I was surprised you let them get away with their terrible manners, Mama!"

"Well, Sugar, with these young ladies, bein' loved and accepted is more important than good manners. When a child knows you love them, they'll cooperate more with other things. Otherwise, it's just rules, and they'll balk most times."

Or stick their finger in their mouth and make gagging sounds, Emily thought.

She had a lot to learn.

"Sugar, November 7th is comin' up real quick,' Miss Mattie said, as she added more green peppers and mushrooms to their stir-fry dinner. "Any ideas on how you want to celebrate your birthday?"

Thoughts of a day to herself at the river sounded wonderful, but she didn't want to exclude her mama from her birthday. "Something simple sounds the best," she replied.

She kind of just wanted to leap over the day anyway. Would her parents even remember it was her seventeenth birthday?

"What are you frownin' about, Miss Em'ly?"

"I was wondering if my parents would remember my birthday," she replied, hating that she still viewed things from how her parents would react. She didn't know exactly how to break free from it though.

Her mama didn't say anything for a moment, then said, "I can see where you would wonder that. Birthdays are very personal."

"And parents should be happy that you were born."

"Yes."

"And they shouldn't abandon you, or at least make sure you're perfectly safe before they abandon you."

"Yes, they should."

Emily took a deep breath, surprised that she felt better. "I think I'd like to celebrate with the girls from Sawmill."

"Wonderful!" her mama said. "I'll take care of everything."

It was still dark on the morning of her birthday when her phone rang.

"Hello," she answered sleepily.

"Em'ly?"

"Dad?"

"Yeah, it's me. Happy Birthday!"

"Where are you?"

"In California for a while."

She found herself glad that he wasn't in Virginia.

"Where's Mom?"

"Sleepin'. Look, I can't talk long. I'm havin' trouble finding work and could use some of that money your grandma left you."

"What?" she said, thinking she'd heard wrong.

"We're broke, and need money," he said, flatly. "Your mom shoulda' got some of your grandma's money anyway. It ain't right. "

Well, Happy Birthday to me! she thought, but said nothing.

"Em'ly?"

"I don't have any money."

"No, but you're eighteen today, and can march yerself' down to that lawyer's office and claim it!"

"No, Dad," she sighed. "I'm seventeen today."

"Seventeen!" He swore. "Well can't you get your hands on some money in an emergency? We're about to get booted outta' this place."

He had only called her to get something. He didn't care if it was her birthday. He didn't care.

Something arose in her. "You know what dad? That's your emergency, not mine. So don't ask me to solve it for you. This is my birthday. You haven't called me since you left, you don't even know how old I am, and you're pressuring me to do something I have no intention of doing. Is there anything else?"

"You always was selfish," he shouted. "Your mom is sick and we can't even afford medicine for her."

"Yes, you can. Stop spending it on booze. If she's sick, put her on some sort of assistance program. You know all the answers, you just want the money."

"Yeah, well you're just selfish!" he screamed, repeating himself.

"I'm all done talking, Dad. If you ever want to talk to me because I'm your daughter, then call. Never call me for money again." She hung up the phone.

Emily waited for the guilt to smack her in the head, but it didn't come. She heard small footsteps clicking down the hall and into her room. Itsy jumped up on her bed and licked her chin.

"Thank you, Itsy," she said, reaching over and turning off her phone. Her dad was raging and she knew he would call back.

Emily drew the dog close to her as she lay there and shut her eyes, surprised that she didn't care and that she was simply done. "Happy

Birthday to me, Itsy," she whispered, and went back to sleep with the little dog nestled close to her.

When Emily awoke again, it was to the smell of bacon frying. She sat on the edge of the bed with Itsy, waiting for the emotions to slam into her. But guilt, shame, and sadness didn't slam into her, and she was fine.

"A miracle, Itsy!" she said, dancing the little dog around the room. "I'm fine!"

If she didn't get another thing for her birthday, she wouldn't care. This feeling was incredible! She carried the tiny dog out to the kitchen where her mama was preparing her birthday breakfast.

"Happy Birthday, Sugar!" her mama said, giving her a big hug. "Were you talkin' to yourself?"

"No, I was talking to Itsy!" Emily replied, and told her about the phone call from her dad, and what she had told him. "And I didn't feel the least bit guilty!" she said, still marveling over it.

"Well now, don't we just keep gettin' miracles," her mama, sighed, hugging her again. "We need us a victory dance!" She put her spatula down and turned off the stove; they both grabbed the white napkins off the breakfast table, waving them as they circled around the living room with Itsy.

"I'm free," Emily laughed, twirling her white napkin in the air as she danced around the living room.

"Happy Birthday to my girl," Miss Mattie said, dancing and flagging her napkin in the air. "She's free!"

Downstairs, the bakery help looked at each other.

"What in the world is all that thumpin'?" Blessy asked, looking up at the ceiling.

"Sounds like 'nother one of their victory dances," Clara replied, popping a plug of chewing tobacco into her cheek while Blessy was distracted.

At six o'clock sharp, five girls from the Sawmill, dressed to the hilt, came through the door of Cooke's Bakery carrying folded sheets of binder paper. Callie needed help getting her billowing quinceanera dress through the door, and the girls all stopped to help, clucking like mother hens as they tilted the hooped dress this way and that to get her into the bakery. They smoothed the dress down for her, then laughing and smiling, headed over to Emily.

"Happy Birthday!" Callie shouted, as she handed Emily her folded sheet of paper.

"Thank you!" Emily replied, "should I read this now?"

"No," her mama said, coming up behind her, "we'll have the girls read them to you in a while!"

Emily handed the paper back to Callie, as Miss Mattie instructed the others, "Girls, hang onto your papers. You can give them to Em'ly after you read it to her."

The girls looked at each other nervously, realizing that they were expected to read them aloud.

"Did you tell them to write these for me?" Emily whispered to her mama while the girls made their way over to the beautiful supper table Blessy had set up earlier.

"Yes, I did Sugar," she whispered back. "They wanted to give you somethin' and I told them showin' their appreciation was the nicest gift they could give you."

Emily went over and hugged each of the girls, commenting on their apparel, and loving the effort that had been made to dress up properly for her birthday celebration. Magnolia wore a ballooning prom dress with pink netting that must have dated back to the fifties, and she had clipped a red rose behind her ear. Emily peered closer, noticing that thorns were still attached to the rose stem. Azealia was outfitted in a red velvet lounging outfit that was way too long, so she had turned up the leg cuffs and pinned them into place with a row of large paper clips; Savanah came dressed in an aqua and black kimono-style bathrobe, which she had mistaken for an evening dress. It was held together with an ornate plastic silver belt, with half the silver peeling off.

After the greetings and the hugs, Miss Mattie said, "Ladies, please step over this way and fill your plates with my good lasagna, and there's also salad and fresh garlic bread. After you're all served, I will say the blessin'."

"What's lasagna?" Magnolia asked, standing still, afraid to try it.

"It's I-talian like spaghetti, 'cept it has fat noodles," Callie said, knowingly.

"That's right!" Emily said, "and it has cheese! You'll love it." She put an arm around Magnolia and scooted the reluctant girl forward.

The other girls, who hadn't eaten since lunch at school, were famished and hurried over, crowding in front of each other.

"Ladies! Please look out for one another and not jus' for yourselves," Miss Mattie instructed.

The girls looked sheepish, but each stood back and motioned for the other to go ahead.

"That's my girls!" Miss Mattie crooned, "And don't forget, we say a blessin' before anyone eats!"

After each plate was filled—and overfilled—the girls sat down and waited for prayer, each giving quick glances at their dinner plates, giggling as they gave exaggerated sniffs of the delicious aroma.

"Let's bow out heads, ladies, while I give thanks," Miss Mattie instructed, folding her hands and bowing her head. The girls watched what she did and did the same.

"Our great God," she began, and the girls grew quiet as a sweet presence filled the room, "how I thank you for this day that our Em'ly was born. Thank you for sendin' her to me, and to these girls, and for the great blessin' she is to all of us. Watch over her always, Lord, and guide her as she makes decisions for her future. Thank you for this food, and for lovin' us so much. In Jesus' name, Amen!"

"Whew!" Savannah chirped, "that prayer made me feel like God was sittin' in my lap." She wiped her eyes with the back of her hand. "That was really weird," she concluded, lifting a fork full of lasagna to her mouth.

"Yeah, that was weird," Magnolia piped in, with food in her mouth. "Are you a preacher or somethin' Miz' Mattie?"

"No ma'am, I'm not," she replied, "I jus' talk to Jesus, and He responds. That's what you sweet girls are feelin'"

"One of my Elvis songs made me feel that way one time," Callie said, biting off a large chunk of garlic bread.

"Which song was it?" the bakery owner asked.

"Somethin' about, *you'll never walk alone*," she mumbled, her mouth full. She swallowed. "That's the onliest part I can remember. I jus' remember the feelin' it gave me."

Emily waited for Callie to raise her fork like a microphone and belt out the Elvis song, but Callie just smiled at her and used the fork to spear a bite of salad.

Emily gave her a thumbs up.

"Okay ladies," Miss Mattie said, after the last bite of lasagna, the last piece of garlic bread, and the last lettuce leaf had been eaten, "let's clear our plates! It's time to read Em'ly the cards you made for her."

A nervousness settled over the girls as they picked up their plates and carted them back to the bakery kitchen, setting them in the stainless-steel sink.

"Youin's want me to wash these up?" Savannah asked, hoping to stay in the kitchen and avoid reading her paper out loud.

"No, we'll get to them later," Miss Mattie said, "but thank you."

An uncomfortable quietness settled over the girls as they sat back down at the table.

"Em'ly," Miss Mattie said, "for your birthday, these girls have written down what you mean to them, and why they are glad that you were born."

Emily nodded, as a knot formed in her throat. She didn't trust herself to speak.

"Would anyone like to go first?" Miss Mattie asked.

"Me!" piped up Callie, waving her hand in the air.

Miss Mattie nodded for her to go ahead.

She stood up and unfolded her piece of binder paper, which had dozens of flowers covering the outside, drawn with a set of colored pencils.

She cleared her voice dramatically and looked at Emily. "Youin's has been one of the best things to come into my life," she read from her paper. "I learnt how to decide what I wanted in my house someday—besides Elvis posters." She looked up, waiting for them to laugh, and was rewarded by howling laughter from the girls, and smiles from Miss Mattie and Emily.

When the laughter died down, she continued reading. "'Cause of you Em'ly, I know not to let drunks live in my house, and if some guy is mean to me, I'm breakin' up with him," she said, meaning it. "And I'll always be able to take care of myself and buy a pretty house, 'cause I'm goin' to college!" She looked up at Emily. "And that's what I learn't from you!" She curtsied and reached across the table and handed Emily her sheet of paper.

Emily stood up, and went around the table to hug her, loving this sassy girl.

"Who would like to go next?" Miss Mattie asked, after Emily was seated.

Magnolia raised her hand and stood up beside her chair. "Happy birthday, Em'ly," she read in a monotone. "I learnt that I ain't stuck, and I getta' decide what my future is."

"Don't say ain't," Callie blurted out, pointing a finger at her.

Miss Mattie interrupted, "For now, we are just going to speak from our hearts, and not worry about which words we use, Callie! Please continue, Magnolia."

Callie slouched down in her seat.

Magnolia stuck her tongue out at Callie, and continued her monotone dialogue, "I think youin's is pretty and I wanna look like you someday, 'cept for the freckles on yer' nose."

Emily burst out laughing. "If you get any freckles, Magnolia, I'll show you how to put make-up on them!"

"Yes'm, I'd 'preciate that," she said, and sat down.

Emily's stomach was jiggling with laughter as she went over and hugged her. "Thank you, Magnolia," she said, hoping the girl didn't notice her jiggling belly.

As Azalea stood up to read her birthday message, some of the paper clips holding the cuffs on her outfit caught on the chair and clattered to the floor. Her face turned bright red and she ducked her head. "Somebody else read mine, I'm too scared," she whispered.

"Do it scared 'til you're doin' it brave!" Callie barked at her. Quoting the very saying that Emily often quoted to her.

Miss Mattie shushed Callie and turned to Azalea, speaking softly. "It's alright, Azalea, jus' take your time and read your nice card."

Azalea's hands shook slightly as she read from the binder note, "Happy birthday, Em'ly. I think I want a bakery like youin's have some day, and you told me havin' my own business was good. I was glad you said that an' it made me happy. I don't feel like goin' to college, I jus' want a nice home to put my momma' in and sell cookies and cakes and donuts all day long."

"Thank you, Azalea, that sounds like a great plan," Emily said, hugging her.

Then Savannah stood up. "Happy Birthday," she read from her paper. "I like it that youin's is happy all the time. It makes me know I'm gonna' be okay."

"Hope," Callie barked. "That's the word you need for sayin' you're gonna' be okay."

"Yes," Savannah said, looking embarrassed. "Youin's make me hope."

Callie folded her arms and shook her head, looking slightly irritated with the girl.

"That's a beautiful thought, Savannah," Emily said, going over to hug her. "Thank you!"

"Who is ready for cake?" her mama asked, standing up and drawing attention away from the tension Callie had created with her barking tone.

"Me, me, me," chorused the group of girls, flagging their hands.

Miss Mattie went into the bakery kitchen and came back out a moment later carrying a beautifully decorated cake, lit with sparkling candles like tiny fireworks, and set it down in front of Emily. "Let's sing," she instructed the girls, leading right into the birthday song. "Happy Birthday to you!"

Most of the girls joined in, except for Azalea, who sat there looking confused.

Emily's heart went out to her. *How is it possible this girl has never heard the birthday song,* she wondered, smiling at her as she reached over and squeezed her hand, letting her know it was okay.

"Thank you for the wonderful party," Emily said later that evening, hugging her mama.

"You're welcome, Sugar," her mama said, hugging her back. "Wanna' tell me why there's a sad look in those pretty eyes of yours?"

She sighed. "I think Jonathan forgot my birthday," she replied, determined not to cry.

"Well, there's a big time difference between here and London, and the day isn't over with yet," her mama assured her, just as the phone in Emily's pocket rang.

"Hello!" she said, hurrying to her room.

"Happy Birthday!" Jonathan's deep voice rang out from across the ocean.

"Thank you," she said, her own voice ringing.

"Did you get my gift?"

"What gift?" she asked, as she sat down on the edge of her bed.

"Go look on your kitchen table," he instructed.

"I was just in the kitchen, there's nothing there!"

"Go look again."

She did as he asked and went down the hall where she saw her mama scurry into her bedroom and shut the door.

When she got to the kitchen, sure enough, there was a beautifully wrapped gift on the table.

"You plotted with my Mama," she laughed.

"I did!" he replied, sounding equally happy. "Put your phone on video so I can see your pretty face when you open it!"

She chuckled, as she brought up the camera on her phone, a little embarrassed about the thrill she still felt being called pretty. She grabbed a stack of cookbooks and set them on the table, then set her phone down and angled the screen towards the gift.

"Can you see me?" she asked, waving as she stepped over by the gift.

"I see the girl I love," he replied, giving her a small wave. "Open your gift!"

She tore the wrapping paper off the box and lifted the lid. Inside was a small table clock in the shape of Big Ben, and an envelope. She scooped up the clock, delighted with the miniature piece. "I love this," she said, holding it against her face. "Thank you!"

"You're welcome," he replied, his eyes dancing, "now open the envelope!"

Emily eagerly tore open the envelope, imagining a mushy card inside. She wasn't disappointed. The birthday card was glittery and heart-shaped, and she blushed at what he wrote. This guy was crazy about her!

"Thank you," she said, holding the card against her heart.

"You're welcome," he replied. "I'll take you out for a birthday dinner when you get here, too. Just the two of us! I have things figured out now and I want to tell you about it."

"What have you got figured out?" she asked.

He smiled. "I'll tell you when you get here!"

"But that's a month away!"

"I want to see your eyes in person when I tell you," Jonathan said, his own blueberry eyes sparkling with that look that turned her insides to mush.

They talked a few minutes more, as she stood holding her miniature clock.

When they hung up, she walked back down the hall, and heard Miss Mattie's door creak open. Her mama stepped into the hallway with her arms open. "Happy Birthday to my girl," she crooned, as Emily threw her arms around her.

"This is all like a dream," Emily laughed, hugging her tight.

Chapter - 20

Emily awoke the next morning finding that the excitement about a trip to London had been replaced with worry.

Who will handle the bakery? she fretted, tossing the bed covers back and sitting on the edge of her bed. Christmas was their biggest money maker of the year, especially with her Country Store, not to mention people buying special treats for their pets at Christmas time. She'd also thought about adding a few holiday pet items she'd seen thumbing through a catalog, thinking every dog and cat owner would want to see their pet in a Santa hat, or with reindeer antlers! Her joy seeped away like a pin-pricked balloon at the prospect of losing out on such a money-making opportunity.

"What's wrong with my girl now?" her mama asked, as she strolled out to the main living area.

Emily looked up and smiled. Her mama could read her like a book; she needed to be more careful with her thoughts and emotions, so she didn't worry her.

"Just thinking about who to hire while we are away at Christmas," she replied.

"From my experience," her mama offered, "business is very slow the day before Christmas. All the rolls and pies and cakes are bought, and people stay home makin' everything nice for their family."

"But you didn't have a Country Store before," Emily reminded her. "I was hoping they would stop in for last minute gifts!"

Her mama's brow furrowed in thought. "Here's what we'll do," she finally said, "I'll put up signs givin' customers plenty of warning that we'll be closed Christmas Eve. That'll make them plan ahead."

"Don't you leave the day before Christmas Eve though?"

"Yes, so we'll hire Blessy for three or four days. That won't break us, will it?"

"No, it won't," Emily said, feeling relieved. "Jonathan already arranged for his mom to help in the bakery, then Blessy can work a few days and it should all be covered until I get home."

"Now, all I want for my girl to do is relax and plan her trip," Miss Mattie said, wrapping warm brown arms around her. "You've been workin' real hard and getting away from it will be good for you."

"And good for you too, Mama," she said hugging her back. "I'm glad you'll be with your family."

"Now doesn't God jus' keep workin' things out for us," she sighed, holding Emily tight.

"He sure does," Emily replied, laying her head on her mama's soft shoulder, then quickly glancing up at the clock. "I need to get down to the bakery, I just remembered Blessy wanted to leave early today."

She hurried to her room and threw on clothes, mad at herself for forgetting that Blessy had a doctor's appointment and needed to leave by seven o'clock.

"You didn't have your breakfast," her mama called from the kitchen, as she rushed around.

"I'll eat something downstairs," Emily said, as she pulled on a warm sweater.

Her mama frowned but didn't say any more.

She flew down the stairs and into the bakery, where Blessy was boxing up some cookies for a customer, wearing a heavy coat with her handbag hanging on her shoulder, ready to run out the door as soon as Emily arrived.

"I'm so sorry, Blessy," Emily said, taking the cookie box out of her hand. "You run on and I'll finish up here."

"This is gonna' be a long day for you Em'ly!" Blessy said, her rich, mezzo voice sounding concerned.

"It's okay, you just go," Emily whispered, as the customer paid for the cookies.

Twenty minutes later, Emily looked up as the bell over the bakery door jingled and saw her mama march in with a platter covered with a white napkin.

"Mama! What are you doing down here?"

"I brought my girl some proper nourishment," she replied, setting the platter down.

Emily peeked under the napkin and saw scrambled eggs, bacon, hash-browns and toast, and her mouth began to water. "Mama," she began, intending to scold her for going out in the cold.

"Now don't get after me," her mama interrupted, "you have a long day in front of you and I intend to see that you're fed properly. It's no use me sittin' upstairs worrin' about you!"

"Thank you, Mama," Emily said, grateful for this person who cared so much about her.

"Now you sit right down and eat; if a customer comes in, I'm waitin' on them," she said, meaning it.

Emily did as she was told, gulping down the tasty food so she could get her mama back upstairs. Too many of the villagers were coming into the bakery these days sniffling with colds, coughing into their mittens, and blowing into handkerchiefs. The mountain's cold weather this time of year was no joke, and she wanted to keep her mama well for her Christmas trip to Mississippi.

Later in the day, she was glad for the fortifying breakfast. The day had been long, with a steady stream of customers. Just after three o'clock, she noticed school kids walking by bundled up in puffy jackets with warm hats, mittens, and scarves, and watched for the girls from the Sawmill, who would be going next door to Violet's House of Beauty. She spotted them across the street, walking huddled together against the cold, with chins tucked into thin jackets and sweaters. When they crossed the street in front of the bakery, she tapped on the window and waved at them, remembering the days when all she had was a thin jacket. They smiled and waved back, and Callie blew her a kiss. She laughed and blew one back, making a mental note to go out to the Goodwill on the highway when she closed the bakery, and find jackets for these girls. In some ways, she was happy to be relieved of the responsibility of them, but in other ways, she missed them like they were her own. She was glad to see that they had the routine down: two days at Violet's, and the rest of the school days they would go over to the library conference room which had been set up for them to do their homework, with Cooke's Bakery supplying the donuts for their afternoon snack.

Maybe she would take on more responsibility for them once she got back from England next month. But maybe not, too. She was at a point where she could finally breathe.

The bakery phone rang, and she hurried to answer it, singing out cheerfully, "Cooke's Bakery!"

"Em'ly?"

"Dad?" she gasped.

"Why'd you hang up on me a few days ago?" he barked.

She ignored his question. "What do you want?"

'Just lettin' you know we got us a lawyer, and we're goin' after some of your grandma's money. It ain't right she left everything to you!"

She felt like the wind had been knocked out of her. All she could think to say was, "If that's what you're going to do, then why are you telling me?"

"We're givin' you another chance to give us part of the money on your own," he shouted, growing angry.

"I already told you I don't have the money," she replied wearily, wanting nothing more than to get off the phone. "I'm done talking about it, so do whatever you're going to do."

"Oh, we will!" he snarled. "We got us a good lawyer, and he's told us to move back to Virginia while he gets us our money! And just remember this, Em'ly—we ain't given' up!"

Emily was at a loss for words, but it didn't matter because she heard a dial tone. He had hung up on her.

She stood there holding the receiver, numb with dread. The realization came slowly over her that this would never end. They would always be her parents: parents who were selfish, who would always drink, and who would never leave her alone. There was no escaping it.

She stood frozen to the spot, not knowing what to do or who to talk to about it. And what about Jonathan? If their future together continued, he'd be stuck with this mess, also.

"No," she whispered out loud.

The bell over the door jingled and she looked up to see Gus stroll in with a Santa hat and a big grin. "Hey, Miss Em'ly," he said, showing even white choppers.

"Hey, Gus," she said, an idea coming to her. "Gus, do you have time to watch the bakery for about an hour?"

"I surely do, little lady," he said, taking his place behind the counter. "It'll cost ya' a cinnamon roll though!"

"Help yourself," she smiled, grabbing her sweater.

"You'll need somethin' warmer than that sweater," he cautioned.

"I have a jacket back in the kitchen," she said, hoping she'd left it there.

When she walked back through the bakery in her warm jacket, Gus was already waiting on a customer. She waved and went out the door, turning left towards *Bloomin' Happy Nursery*.

"Hey, Mr. C," she called out as she went through the gate at the rear of the nursery.

Mr. Charles was restocking gardening books under a new, large green awning, and spun around when he heard her.

"Emily!" he said, his face lighting up as he hurried over and gave her a hug. "What brings you out on this cold day?"

"Do you have a minute to talk?" she asked, feeling her stomach tighten into a knot.

"Of course, let's sit under the awning; I have a warm stove going. Would you like me to get you some hot chocolate?"

"Not today, Gus is watching the bakery and I need to get back soon."

He set two canvas chairs near the small stove and motioned for her to sit down. He sat across from her and asked, "What would you like to talk about?"

"I don't know what to do…" she barely got the words out before tears started rolling down her cheeks.

"Uh-oh," Mr. Charles said, tearing off a paper towel sheet from a nearby roll and handing it to her. "Did you and Jonathan have a fight?"

She shook her head no, willing herself to stop crying.

"It's okay," he said, patting her shoulder. "I'm going to run in and grab you a warm drink. I'll be right back."

She composed herself while he was gone and thanked him a few minutes later when he handed her a cup of hot chocolate.

"Feel like you can talk now?" he asked, sitting back down.

Emily nodded, took a deep breath, and rattled it off all at once. "My dad has called me twice; he needs money. He thought I had turned eighteen on my birthday and inherited my grandmother's money. When I told him I was only seventeen this birthday, he tried to pressure me into going after the money anyway." She sipped the hot chocolate, embarrassed about her dad, not even wanting to tell the rest.

"There's more to the story?" Mr. Charles asked.

Emily nodded. "He has a lawyer who is going to go after the money and has recommended my parents move back to the state while he gets it."

"I see, is it a large sum?"

"I have no idea," she replied. "All my grandmother told me was that it was for my college. But I'm not that worried about the money, I wanted to talk to you about something else."

A customer came through the gate and Mr. Charles went to wait on him, leaving her to drink the hot chocolate.

"So, what is troubling you Emily?" Mr. Charles asked, as he sat back down in the canvas chair.

"The future," she sighed, her lips trembling.

"The future?"

She nodded, bringing her emotions under control. "It occurred to me after my dad's second phone call that this isn't going to end. He'll probably always be popping into my life; not because he loves me, but because he wants something from me. There is no peace when he and my mom are around, just chaos. When Jonathan gave me this," she said, pulling out her heart necklace, "I don't think he considered that. I don't think either of us did. So, to be fair to Jonathan, I think I should give this necklace back when I see him. He comes from a nice family, but he would be inheriting a crazy one if we ever got married."

Mr. Charles stared at her a moment, then said, "Have you told Jonathan any of this?"

"No, because he's taking finals, and if he thinks I'm upset, he'll hop on a plane and come here. I'll talk to him when we go to England. But I need to talk to someone now, and I thought of you. You and your family would be affected by it all, too."

"How often do you hear from your parents now?" he asked.

"I've heard twice from my dad since they left me. I haven't talked to my mom. Both calls were because my dad wanted the money. But now that they are getting a lawyer, I'll probably hear a lot."

"Any chance he'll move back to Mountain Grove?"

"He talked about moving back to the state; I just don't know if he'd move here," she sighed, overwhelmed at that prospect.

"Emily," he said, leaning back in his chair, "I think you're too worried. Just see what they do. As far as my family being involved, don't worry about that. It probably won't be a problem; but if it is I'll handle it."

"What if they hound me or come into the bakery?" she sighed, voicing her worst fear.

"What would you do?"

"I don't know," she shrugged. "I guess I would need help."

"Yes," he agreed, "you'd need help."

"Are you talking about a restraining order?"

"If there is no other way to keep them from making your life miserable, then yes, I'm talking about a restraining order."

"But these are my parents, I couldn't do that."

"I would agree with you if they were loving parents who were honestly trying to have a good relationship with you. Are they?"

"No."

"Do you have any power to turn them into those kinds of parents?"

"No," she said, thinking this conversation was extremely depressing. "I just keep hoping that's what they'll be."

"I understand, but today, this year, they aren't those kind of parents and you have to deal with the way things are, and not the way you want them to be."

Emily stared at him. "I've heard that so many times from the TV Doctor. Its' just really hard."

"I know," he replied, leaning back in his chair. "The good news is that you get to respond any way you want to their decisions. You are a free agent too, and you're not stuck. So, see what they do, and then respond. And please feel free to come and talk to me anytime."

"Okay, thank you, Mr. C," she said, standing to her feet. "I'll lay it all out in front of Jonathan. He gets to choose too."

"Fair enough," he said, standing and hugging her goodbye.

As she walked back to the bakery, she touched her heart necklace. "I'm still going to offer to give it back to him," she murmured.

When Emily returned to the bakery, Gus was boxing up a banana cream pie. He laid a twenty-dollar bill on the counter. "Buyin' this for Carlotta," he said, referring to Mr. Montoya's widowed sister. He got a huge grin on his face. "She's bringin' me tamales tonight!"

"You're going to miss those tamales when she moves to Florida!" Emily said, giving him a side glance, as she handed him his change.

He stared at her. "What in th' world are you talkin' about?"

"The whole Montoya family is moving to Florida in a year or two. Mr. Montoya is selling his produce market and farmland. I heard him tell Mr. Apple when I was in there the other day. Didn't Carlotta tell you?"

"No, but I haven't seen her for a few days," he said, looking pale. He hesitated, then said, "She can't do that!"

"Sure she can," Emily grinned, "unless you marry her!"

"What?! I ain't the marryin' kind! You know that!"

"Well," she shrugged, "become the marrying kind!"

"Tell ya' what!" he snorted. "Some people need to tend to their own business, like YOU, Miss Nosy!"

"She'd cook for you every night, and scare Cousin Alice off!" Emily laughed, not backing off in the slightest.

Gus tugged his ball cap on, picked up his boxed banana cream pie, and stomped towards the door. "As I said," he called over his shoulder, "some people need to tend to their own business. This is the snoopiest town I ever been in!"

"It's the *only* town you've ever been in," Emily laughed, trying to stop a belly laugh, as she hurried past him. "Let me get the door for you!"

She opened the door while humming the Wedding March.

"Shoot! Git me outta' here," he said, hurrying past her.

"Dum, dum, de, dum!" she chanted as he exited the door.

Gus mumbled something she couldn't exactly hear, as he hurried away.

"The bakery sells wedding cakes!" she shouted after him, jiggling with laughter, and feeling much better than she had all day.

Later, upstairs while she was looking through the Mountain Grove Gazette, it occurred to Emily that they hadn't made plans for Itsy in December.

"Mama! What shall we do with Itsy while we're gone?"

"I already arranged for Miz' Kingery to take her," her mama replied, coming in drying her hands on a dish towel. "She said they'd love to have her."

"That's good!" Emily replied, relieved that the problem had been taken care of. She turned the page on the newspaper and yelled, "What?!?!".

"What is it, Sugar?" her mama asked, hurrying over.

"Look!" Emily said, laughing as she held up a picture of Dr. Matthew Blackstone and Gabriella Brookfield.

"Are they engaged?" Miss Mattie gasped.

"They are engaged!" she laughed. "My plan worked!"

"Oh, you little scamp!" her mama said, taking the newspaper out of her hand, and reading the article. "They're marryin' in the spring!"

"Wonder if they'll ask me to be flower girl," she laughed.

Her mama shook her head and grinned. "I don't know 'bout you, Em'ly!"

"Next, I'm working on Gus and Carlotta," Emily announced.

"You know that Gus says he'll never marry!"

"We'll see!" Emily replied, and they both laughed.

Emily tiptoed into the small room at Creekside Villa, being quiet in case Mrs. Tupper was napping.

She was met by a smiling Mrs. Tupper, who'd just had her white hair permed for Christmas, and sat looking pretty in a lavender bed jacket.

"Merry Christmas!" Emily said, going over and kissing her soft, mottled cheek. She laid a small gift on the afghan that covered her.

"Is this for me?" the older woman warbled, as she picked up the package.

"Yes! I won't be here at Christmas, and I wanted to bring you a gift."

"Oh," she murmured, setting the gift back down. "Where are you going?"

"Jonathan's family is going to England for Christmas, and he invited me too. I'll be spending Christmas with them."

"I see," the frail woman replied, looking slightly puzzled. "Will you be marrying while you're there?"

Emily laughed. "No, I'm only seventeen, remember?"

"Well, it has been a long time since I've seen you."

"No," Emily replied, "I was here about eight days ago! Maybe it's hard to remember because you fell asleep so fast."

"Is this for me?" Mrs. Tupper asked, picking up the gift, as though she hadn't asked just two minutes before.

Fear clutched Emily's heart. "It's your Christmas gift," she whispered, reaching out and taking her hand. "Are you having trouble remembering?"

"No. Would you mind getting me a glass of water?"

Emily put the gift on the side cart near the bed and got up and poured a glass of water.

"Would you like ice in it?" Emily asked, holding the glass out to her.

"No thank you, I'm not thirsty," she warbled, laying back on her pillows and closing her eyes.

Emily didn't know what to do. "Would you like to open your gift before I leave?" she asked, picking up the gift and holding it out to her.

"Oh! Is this for me?" Mrs. Tupper asked for the third time, as she held out a shaky hand.

"It's your Christmas gift," Emily replied, blinking back tears. "I'll help you open it."

The nurse came in and smiled at them both. "Do you need anything Mrs. Tupper?" she asked.

"No, I'm perfectly fine, and my Oliver will be here soon!" She turned to Emily. "I was a war bride, you know."

"Yes, I know," Emily replied, looking at the nurse, questioning.

"Mild stroke," the nurse whispered before leaving.

Chapter - 21

"**S**ugar, the Apples have invited us for Thanksgivin'!"

"Fun!" Emily replied, still getting a kick out of the last name of her rosy cheeked, round friends who greatly resembled two apples.

"They said to bring Itsy, too—to play with Mr. Whiskers," she informed her, looking very pleased with the idea.

"Mr. Whiskers isn't very friendly, Mama..." she started to say.

"It'll be fun!" her mama interrupted.

Oh sure, lots of fun, Emily thought, thinking of the way Mr. Whiskers always batted at her. That cat would knock Itsy across the room. Her mama looked so pleased by everything that she didn't want to put a damper on it, so said, "Well, let's take Itsy's carrier in case she gets tired, she can snooze in a familiar place."

"Good idea," Miss Mattie grinned, not suspecting the real motive.

Emily got a text from Mrs. Apple asking for Kelly Ann's phone number so she could invite her and Gilbert for Thanksgiving, also.

I realy wanT to get to kno themm, Mrs. Apple's text concluded.

"Well at least she's a little better at texting," Emily laughed, as she messaged the phone number to her.

Thanksgiving Day turned out to be the coldest day of the year. Emily pushed the thermostat up in their living quarters over the bakery, to make sure her mama didn't get chilled.

"Would you just look at that ice hangin' from trees in the park," Miss Mattie mused, standing at their upstairs bay window, where she had a clear view of Emerson Park across the street. "It looks like a winter wonderland out there."

"Wow!" Emily said, walking over to the window. "It's beautiful!"

"Another blessin'!" her mama murmured, slipping an arm around her.

"Do you see all things as a blessing, Mama?"

"No, I don't," she replied, turning and looking at her. "But I can sure ask the Lord to turn it into one."

"How about my parents. Can He turn them into a blessing?"

"That's a huge ball of tangled up fishin' line to bless," she fretted. "But one of the blessin's in that situation is what you learned from it. Just look at you helpin' those sweet girls from the Sawmill with what you learned! The other blessin' is that I got a wonderful daughter that I always wanted! Someone to call me Mama!"

"And I got the Mama I always wanted," Emily chuckled, hugging her.

"Now aren't we both jus' the most blessed people you ever heard of? Your parents can choose to be blessed, too. For now though, I don't believe they're choosin' that; they're fightin' tooth an' nail for money."

"Money first on their chart, daughter second!" Emily chirped. "Or maybe daughter not even on the chart..."

"Backwards and upside down, if you ask me!" her mama said, hugging her again. "You are the true treasure." She kissed her forehead, "Now come help me in the kitchen. I'm makin' my ambrosia and yeast rolls for our Thanksgivin' dinner."

"I'm going down and warm up the car for you, Mama," Emily said that afternoon, as they put aluminum foil over the freshly baked rolls and covered the ambrosia for the trip over to the Apple's home.

"Watch the steps for ice," her mama warned, as she put the food in a carrier.

Emily put on her warm jacket and grabbed the broom out of the closet, "I'll sweep the steps to make sure there's no ice."

"There's a box of rock salt in the pantry, take that," Miss Mattie laughed. "You can't jus' sweep ice, silly California girl!"

After she made sure the steps were safe for her mama to walk down, Emily got the car keys, and warmed up the car.

She came back upstairs shivering. "Put on your warmest coat, and hat, it's freezing out there," Emily instructed, rifling through the closet for a sweater to wear under her jacket. She put Itsy in her small carrier with a thick blanket over the top, hoping to trap in warmth for the tiny dog.

It was precarious driving up the icy hill to the Apple's, and twice she felt the tires spin.

"Jus' slow down a little, Sugar," her mama instructed, clutching the arm rest.

Emily was concerned the car would slide backwards down the hill if she went slower, but did as Miss Mattie told her, and they managed to crawl up the hill, veering sideways only once.

As they pulled up to the house, Gilbert and Kelly Ann pulled in behind them.

"Well, they timed that jus' right," Miss Mattie said, noting the arrival. "Where is Ike? Wasn't he invited?"

"Yes, he was invited but he's having Thanksgiving with Gus and Yip Yap," she explained. "Kelly Ann is here at the same time because I texted her when we left. She was nervous about meeting with the Apples again and wanted us here at the same time."

"I'm sure there is nothing to be nervous about."

"Tell that to Kelly Ann," Emily said, opening the car door to get out. "She's nervous about everything."

Emily went around to get Itsy and help her mama up the walk, saying, "I'll come back for the food."

"Brrrr!" Kelly Ann said, shivering as she walked up to them. "It's colder then a frog's butt out here!"

Emily rang the doorbell, and both Mr. and Mrs. Apple came to the door. There was hugging and introductions as Gilbert stood holding Mia in a baby seat, and Emily stood holding Itsy in her carrier. She set the dog down in the entry hall and ran back to the car for the food.

When she came back in the house, everyone was in the living room, and she saw that the dog carrier had been moved there also. Mr. Whiskers was investigating it, hissing twice and batting at the cage.

"Mr. Whiskers, quit that," Mr. Apple ordered, picking the cat up and putting him in a carrier in the hallway.

"Put the cat carrier near the little dog, Herbert," Mrs. Apple suggested. "Let them get used to each other."

He did as she suggested and came back in as they were lifting Mia out of her car seat.

"Oh my!" gushed Mrs. Apple, "She is absolutely beautiful. May I hold her?"

Mr. Apple came over as she took the baby. "You're right, Helena, she is an exquisite child."

They both walked over to the couch and sat down, totally enamored with the baby and forgetting their other guests.

Emily looked at Kelly Ann and Gilbert, who actually looked quite pleased at the attention Mia was getting, grinning foolishly and following the couple into the living room.

Everyone stood there awkwardly as the Apples clucked and cooed over Mia. They all looked at each other stifling laughs.

Finally, Miss Mattie said, "Where should I set my ambrosia, Mrs. Apple?"

"Oh," the woman replied, peering at her over her large glasses, "Emily will show you the kitchen." And she went back to cuddling the baby, as Mr. Apple took the child's hand in his, marveling over how small it was.

Miss Mattie, Emily, Kelly Ann and Gilbert all went into the kitchen and set the food down.

"I think the Apples are in love with Mia," Emily whispered, and they all laughed.

"What should we do now?" Kelly Ann asked.

"We better go back to the living room and get Mia, or all the food will get cold," she said, seeing the beautiful dinner that Mrs. Apple had already laid out. She noticed there was a pot of something bubbling on the stove.

"I'll tell her about the stuff on the stove, and you grab Mia," Emily laughed, as they went back into the living room.

The Apples didn't even look up as they all trooped back in.

"Mrs. Apple, something is bubbling on your stove!" Emily informed her.

"Let me take Mia while to go see about it," Gilbert said, gently picking up the child.

Mrs. Apple bustled off, her wedged shoes squeaking slightly as she hurried away.

With the baby removed, Mr. Apple resumed his duties as host. "Let's all go into the kitchen for eggnog," he chirped, ushering them towards the kitchen.

Emily and Kelly Ann grinned at each other. "They are crazy about your baby!" Emily whispered, as they walked.

"I know, an' I love it," Kelly Ann whispered back.

Emily stopped to check on Itsy, and found her asleep. Mr. Whiskers, who was asleep in his small cat carrier nearby opened one eye, then closed it, disinterested in what was going on around him.

The meal was fun and festive, with lots of stories, as Mr. and Mrs. Apple took turns holding Mia, so Kelly Ann could eat.

"Please give me the recipe for this delicious turkey dressin'," Miss Mattie said, taking a large second helping. Emily noticed that she didn't make eye contact as she ladled a large helping of turkey gravy over--not only the dressing—but also the buttery mashed potatoes.

"Oh well," Emily thought, deciding maybe holidays wouldn't hurt for her mama to indulge a little. She could only imagine what rich, Southern food might be served when she went to see her family in Mississippi at Christmas.

Mia began to fuss about halfway through the meal. Kelly Ann stood up and reached for the child saying, "She's gettin' hungry, where could I nurse her?"

Mrs. Apple kissed the child on the forehead before handing her over, and whispered, "Grandma loves you!" then stopped and stared at Kelly Ann, realizing she had been presumptuous.

"It's alright," Kelly Ann assured her, "she kin' call you Granma. She doesn't have one."

"Well now," Mrs. Apple said, eyes sparkling as she turned to her husband, "I'm a grandma!"

"Then I must be a grandpa!" he said, looking just as pleased.

Kelly Ann looked a little flustered. "You kin' be Papa! My grandpa, Ike, has already claimed the other name."

"Papa, it is," he said, thumping the table as he stood up. "I better check on that blasted cat."

"Herbert, dear, why don't we leave Mr. Whiskers where he's at until after dessert," his wife blurted out.

"Well, some of our guests haven't met him yet!"

"I'm sure they don't mind waiting until after dessert."

"I wanted them to see how that cat licks whipped cream off a spoon."

Emily clamped a hand over her mouth, while Mrs. Apple rolled her eyes, and appeared at a loss for words. When Kelly Ann slipped out of the room to go nurse Mia, she was stifling a laugh.

Miss Mattie stood up, "Let me help you with the dessert!" she said brightly, breaking through the awkwardness.

As the two women fussed with dessert plates, Mr. Apple went to retrieve Mr. Whiskers. He came back to the kitchen with the cat sitting on his shoulder boxing his left ear and appeared thoroughly charmed by the antic.

Miss Mattie served Mr. Apple his pumpkin pie, piled high with whipped cream. Each of the guests kept glancing at him waiting to see what would happen with the cat.

They didn't have long to wait as Mr. Whiskers pounced on the piece of pie and began lapping the whipped cream.

"Herbert!" screeched Mrs. Apple.

"Well, that was unexpected!" he said, pulling the cat off the table. His pie had paw prints in it, and he set it on the floor, along with the cat, who began to lap eagerly at the whipped cream.

"Herbert..." Mrs. Apple protested weakly.

"Oh Helena, its Thanksgiving, and a piece of pie won't hurt him!" He chuckled as the cat gobbled up the pie. "Would you mind getting me another piece?"

Mrs. Apple just sat there glaring at him, and Emily offered, "Let me get it!"

"This pie is absolutely delicious, you'll have to give me the recipe," Miss Mattie said, hoping to break the tension. "Absolutely delicious, and the crust is just perfect," she prattled on, as Emily served Mr. Apple another piece of pie.

"Wonderful pie, Helena," Mr. Apple said, chewing happily, and oblivious to the tension he had created, which made everyone break out in laughter. Even Mrs. Apple laughed, much to the relief of her guests.

A few days later, Emily was working in the bakery when the bell over the door jingled, and she looked up to see Logger walk in, and her stomach clenched.

The last time she saw him was when he was dating Kelly Ann, and she'd been tricked into going to a movie with a creepy friend of his. She and Kelly Ann had wound up running away from the two.

She glared, knowing that there was probably going to be trouble, as there always was when Logger was around.

"Hey," he said, looking nervous.

Emily didn't speak, and just nodded, waiting to see what he wanted.

"I was wonderin' if you know how I kin' get ahold of Gilbert," he said, rubbing the back of his neck, as he glanced around.

"What do want with Gilbert?" she asked, thinking the worst.

He sighed, and glanced away, as though he were considering whether to tell her or not. "I jus' need to talk to him," he replied, staring at her.

She suddenly felt emboldened. "Are you mad at him, or is this friendly?"

"I'm sick a' my life," he said irritably. "Sick a' goin' nowhere, and sick a' the Sawmill, an' I know Gilbert got hisself out, an' I wanted to talk to him about it."

No way, she thought to herself. Was Logger drunk?

"Are you drunk?" she blurted out.

He glared at her. "I ain't drunk or high. I already told you, I jus' want a different life."

Were those tears in his eyes? Her heart shifted, and she found herself saying, "Give me your phone number and I'll tell Gilbert you want to talk to him."

She handed him a pencil and paper and he scribbled down a number. He handed it to her and said, "An' I'm sorry for being such a jerk to you."

She nodded, shocked at his apology.

"Okay," she replied, "I'll let Gilbert know that you want to talk to him."

Kelly Ann came bursting through the bakery door with Mia a day later, looking very angry. She saw that Emily was waiting on a customer, so went over and sat at a table.

Emily handed the boxed cookies to the customer, then went over to where Kelly Ann sat with the baby.

"Hey, what's going on?" Emily asked, getting right to the point.

"Gilbert is helpin' that creep, Logger!" she sputtered.

"You don't want him to?"

"Logger is a mean, pot-head creep," Kelly Ann said, meaning it.

"Did you talk to him?"

KellyAnn glared at Emily. "I'm not talkin' to him! No way!"

"He told me he's tired of living the way he was living," Emily replied, leaning over and giving Mia a kiss.

"And you believed him?" Kelly Ann asked, incredulously.

"Not at first, but the more he talked, I did."

"Well, I told Gilbert not to bring him around Mia, I'm not takin' any chances."

"That's fair," Emily said. "We don't have to automatically believe him. He has a little proving to do after the way he's acted."

"Yeah, I'm wonderin' if it's just a con job."

"It could be," Emily said, repeating herself, "but it's okay to wait and see."

"All right," Kelly Ann said, calming down. "Gilbert is all in with helpin' him, and it made me mad. I jus' wanted to talk to you about it."

"Want a donut to calm your nerves?"

Kelly Ann smiled. "Chocolate oughta' do it."

Emily picked up Mia, "Help yourself while I hold this sweet baby."

She nuzzled the baby's small head as Kelly Ann went to get her donut, feeling like she would burst with love for this little girl.

"She's so sweet; I just love her," she said, as Kelly Ann came back over, chewing happily.

Kelly Ann took a hefty bite. "I'm glad. I want lotsa' people to love her."

"What will she call me?"

Kelly Ann quit chewing. "I dunno', what do you want her to call you?"

"Hmmm," she replied, "Auntie Em sounds like a character from *Wizard of Oz*, and Aunt Emily is a mouthful. So, I'll think about it."

"Whatever you chose is fine with me," Kelly Ann said, stuffing the remaining donut in her mouth. "Want me to take her?"

"No, I love holding her," Emily replied, glancing out the bakery's picture window and seeing Gilbert and Logger crossing Emerson Park, going towards the church. "Looks like Gilbert is taking Logger to meet Pastor Alex."

Kelly Ann turned, looked out the window and sighed. "Guess I better get used to it. He wants ever'body to know about God."

"Well, that's a good thing, isn't it?"

"Yep, it's Logger that bothers me."

"If you marry Gilbert, there will be a lot of people like Logger he'll be talking to."

"Yeah, but not ones I was dumb enough to date," she replied, and they both burst out laughing.

Kelly Ann got up, poured some tea, and asked, "So when do you fly outta' here to see that cute boyfriend of yers'?"

"In a couple of weeks," Emily replied.

"You don't sound too excited about it!"

"I was until my dad called."

"What's yer dad got to do with it?"

She told Kelly Ann the story of her dad's plan to sue for part of the inheritance she would get from her grandmother on her eighteenth birthday.

"That's horrible!" she yelped, then looked at Emily, "but what's that gotta' do with you flyin' to London?"

"It made me realize that my family isn't going away and will probably always mean trouble. I want to make sure Jonathan knows what he's getting into, and offer to give my necklace back," Emily told her, barely getting the last sentence out before choking up.

"What?" Kelly Ann bellowed. "He already knows 'bout yer family."

"He doesn't know what they're up to now!"

"Well, if you ask me, yer' makin' too big a deal outta' this with him. If he loves you, he loves you…and he's no dummy! He probably already knows what might happen with yer' family."

"Well, I want to make sure."

"Then make sure, you goofy girl," she replied, taking Mia from her. "All Jonathan's going to do is hug you tighter."

Emily shrugged, tired of thinking and worrying about it. As the time got closer to seeing Jonathan, she worried more; but she would be absolutely honest with him, even if he wanted his necklace back.

On the Sunday before Emily was leaving for England, Miss Mattie said, "Let's celebrate our trips and splurge on breakfast at Ike's after church! This is the last Sunday we'll be together for a while, Sugar!"

"Sounds great," Emily said, as she put on the beautiful, fawn colored Sunday hat with the arched feather, that had caused Jonathan to turn and stare at her in church those many months ago. It still warmed her heart to think of the look in his eyes.

They arrived at church before the service started, and Emily noticed a row of young girls from the Sawmill seated next to Miss Rose and Miss Violet, including Callie who turned and waved like crazy. All the girls had found church hats to wear, and when Emily went over to greet them, she told them how beautiful they looked.

"We found a buncha' our hats at th' Goodwill!" Callie informed her, adjusting hers, which was a red sun hat. "And we decided to trade hats ever' Sunday."

Miss Rose put a finger to her lips, so she would talk lower.

"Good plan," Emily whispered, hugging her. She missed this girl. She spoke to each girl and commented on how nice they looked, and chuckled over Magnolia's hat, which was a dated pea-green color, with sequined netting.

"I'll be gone for a couple of weeks," she whispered to the girls, "but when I get back, please come and see me in the bakery. Donuts for everyone."

The girls did quiet fist pumps, then glanced at Miss Rose, who had been instructing them on good manners.

Miss Rose nodded her approval.

Emily gave Miss Rose and Miss Violet quick hugs, and as she went in search of her mama, Mr. and Mrs. Charles waved and she went over and hugged them.

"Excited about our trip?" Mr. Charles asked.

"Very excited. I can't wait to see Jonathan," she said, not bringing up her actual fears.

"Well, we know Jonathan is excited too!" Mrs. Charles informed her. "Let's get together soon and hammer out all the trip plans."

She was surprised to see Logger, Gilbert, and Kelly Ann sitting on the left side of the church together. They waved and she noticed that Kelly Ann sat happily holding Mia, not appearing to be at all distressed about Logger sitting down the pew from her. She was puzzled but would have to wait until she got back from her trip to ask Kelly Ann about it.

They found a seat in the pew behind Penelope, who stood and hugged them both. "I hear you're leaving us for a while," Penelope whispered to Emily.

"I am," Emily replied, suddenly extremely happy about it all.

"Have fun!" the pastor's wife whispered, hugging her again, as the choir began to sing, and Pastor Alex came and stood behind his pulpit. He noticed Emily standing with his wife, and gave her a thumbs up, as everyone stood singing.

After church she and her mama walked down the hill to *Good Eats*, and waved at Ike as they walked in the door. Emily looked around the café, full this morning with the people she loved. Montana and Mr. Kingery waved from their stools at the counter, Iris Head nodded and smiled, sitting at a table with her real estate listings spread in front of her; Mr. and Mrs. Green, seated at their favorite rear booth, waved with huge grins on their faces. Dr. Blackstone and Gabriella smiled at her from the booth next to them.

As they sat down at a table in the center of the room, Mr. Kingery turned on his stool, took a noisy slurp of coffee, and said, "I hear someone's gonna' be travelin' soon!"

"Yes, in about a week!" Emily replied, as others in the café looked up and listened.

"Where are you going?" Montana asked.

"To London for Christmas!" she replied happily.

"Aha!" Iris replied, looking up from her listings. "I hear there is a handsome gentleman going to college there!"

Emily blushed as those in the café chuckled. "His family is going and invited me to go with them."

"Well, bon voyage," Mr. Kingery said, raising his coffee mug in a salute. "Don't ferget' us now that yer' a world traveler!"

For some reason, that made tears spring to Emily's eyes. "I could never forget any of you," she replied, "you're my family!"

Mr. Kingery cleared his throat. "I see," he replied, obviously moved. "And yer' my family, too Em'ly," he replied quietly.

"And mine," Montana said, raising his coffee cup.

"And mine," Iris Head said quietly.

"And mine," Mrs. Green called from the back booth, as Mr. Green echoed her sentiments.

"You're my girl, too," Millie said gruffly, standing nearby with her order pad ready.

"We all love you, and wish you a wonderful trip, Emily," Gabriella said demurely, raising her teacup, as Dr. Blackstone raised his.

"Bon voy-a-gee, and don't forgit' to write!" Ike said, poking his head over the kitchen swinging doors, as everyone laughed.

Chapter - 22

The day of the trip to England finally arrived and Emily double-checked her suitcase, making sure she had remembered everything. Her mama had left two days earlier for her family in Mississippi, and Emily was surprised at how abandoned their home seemed with her gone.

"I miss you, Mama," she whispered as she went from room to room shutting off lights, and unplugging small appliances in the kitchen.

She got a text from Mr. Charles saying they would be over to pick her up for the trip to the airport in twenty minutes. She folded up a blanket of Itsy's, missing her too, but glad that the dog was housed safely with Mrs. Kingery, the grocer's wife.

They'd all agreed that they wouldn't carry Christmas gifts on the plane, and in all actuality, the trip would be their gift to each other, except for the little boys, Jacob and Cameron, who would receive gifts that were shopped for after they arrived in England.

The text came and Emily picked up her suitcase, and the box of pastries she had packed for the trip, knowing that little boys loved special treats. She'd also tucked small games, a coloring book and crayons in an oversized handbag to help keep them entertained during the long flight.

She locked the door behind her just as the Charles family pulled up in their Ford Explorer, then began to bump the suitcase down the stairs. Ed, Jonathan's older brother, jumped out of the car to help her.

"Ed!" she said, happily. "I didn't know you'd be able to come too!"

"I took some time off from my work, and there's no college classes for a couple of weeks, so here I am!" he replied, looking very happy about it.

"Yay," she said, knowing that Jonathan would love seeing his older brother.

She greeted Mr. and Mrs. Charles as she climbed into the back seat. Cameron and Jacob, the two younger boys, were buckled into their seats in the third row of the SUV.

"What's in that box?" Cameron, the eight-year-old asked, leaning forward as far as his seat belt would allow, sniffing dramatically.

"Some treats for our trip," Emily replied, as Mr. Charles headed down First Street towards the highway.

"Isn't this a trip in the car right now?" he asked.

Emily laughed. "Yes, but I should have said our *airplane* trip. I think you just had breakfast, didn't you?"

"Yup," replied the boy, "but smelling donuts makes me hungry again."

"They're for the airplane ride, Buddy," Ed told his brother, settling the matter.

Emily felt a thump on the back seat as Cameron kicked it in frustration.

"Hey!" Ed scolded his brother. "No more of that!"

"Sorry," the little boy murmured.

Two hours later found them boarding the jetliner, then searching for seat numbers as they walked through the cabin of the plane. Emily saw them first: six seats, three on each side of the aisle. "Would you like me to sit here with Cameron and Jacob?" she asked pointing to the seats on the left.

"They can be a handful," Mrs. Charles whispered.

"That's okay, I came prepared," Emily whispered back, ushering the little boys into the seats.

"Can I have a donut now?" Cameron asked, first thing.

"We'll have them soon," she replied, making sure their seat belts were fastened.

Mr. and Mrs. Charles and Ed sat down in the row across from them. Mrs. Charles put her head back on the seat as soon as the plane began to taxi, and by the time it was in the air, she was asleep.

"Thanks for watching the little guys," Mr. Charles whispered across the aisle. "My wife hasn't rested much in the last two days, getting everything ready for the trip. And she's been so excited, she hasn't slept well."

"Looks like she catching up now," Emily smiled, then felt a tap on her shoulder.

"Donut," whispered Cameron.

Mr. Charles nodded that it was okay for them to have one, and she let them pick one out of the box, then handed it over to Mr. Charles and Ed, who each took one.

Emily kept the boys busy with games, stories, and snacks for the next two hours before she felt her own eyelids growing heavy. Mrs. Charles wasn't the only one who had been too excited to sleep.

"Do you know what time it is boys?" she whispered, as Cameron and Jacob looked up at her with two sets of blueberry-colored eyes.

"Time to get off this dumb plane?" Jacob asked, yawning.

"Not yet," she whispered. "It's rest time, so that the time goes by quicker."

"I'm not sleepy," he replied, sleepily.

"Just rest your eyes for ten minutes then," she said, watching his eyes droop. She reached under the seats and retrieved blankets for them all, and covered the two little boys who were already asleep.

Mr. Charles gave her a thumbs up before folding his arms and nodding off himself.

Hours later, as their plane taxied into London's Heathrow Airport, Mr. Charles said, "I just got a text from Jonathan and it seems the Abernathy's want us to come for breakfast before we settle in at our rental house. Is everyone okay with that?"

"Breakfast sounds wonderful," Mrs. Charles yawned, stretching her arms.

"Who're the Abernathy's?" Ed asked, also stretching.

"Jonathan's host family," his dad replied."Our rental house is not too far from them."

"I'm game," Ed said, "How about you Emily?"

She nodded, and it was all settled. She couldn't wait to see Jonathan, and her mouth watered thinking of the breakfast later; the airline dinner a few hours ago had left a lot to be desired.

When the airplane came to a standstill, Emily helped the little boys gather their things.

"If you can help Mrs. Charles ride herd on the boys," Mr. Charles told her, "Ed and I will get all of your things off the plane."

"It's a deal," she said, remembering Miss Tori's warning about traffickers at airports and elsewhere.

"I'm tired," complained Jacob, when she tried to get him to follow his parents.

"I think you're being a really brave five-year-old!" Emily told him.

"Don't forget, I'm almost six," he reminded her, using both hands to hold up six fingers.

"Wow!" she said, acting surprised. "When we get to our rental house, you and Cameron can tell me your birthdays so I can be sure and write them in my calendar."

"Don't forget to get us presents!" he reminded her.

"Of course!" she said, hanging onto them as they followed the rest of the family off the plane.

She kept turning this way and that looking for Jonathan.

"Did Jonathan say where he'd meet us?" she finally asked Mr. Charles, as they hurried along.

"He'll meet us downstairs in front of a Starbucks. We still need to go through customs," he replied.

The airport was crowded and she tried holding the boys' hands as they hurried on.

"We're too big to hold your hand," Jacob said, shirking away from her.

"Well, is it okay if I hold onto your shirts so I don't get lost?"

"You can hold our arms like my mom does to my dad. That's all!" Both boys stuck their elbows out so she could grab hold.

"Thank you both, I feel safer now," she said, as they walked quickly to keep up with the rest of the Charles family.

Emily was standing at the luggage carousel when she felt arms around her, causing her to jump with fright.

"Hey," came a familiar voice.

She turned and threw her arms around Jonathan. "I thought you were meeting us in front of Starbucks!" she said, holding him tight.

"I couldn't wait to see you," he laughed, kissing her. "Welcome to England."

The family gathered around Jonathan and he greeted them all.

"I saw you kissing Emily!" Cameron cackled when Jonathan hugged him.

"Hey, no peeking when I'm kissing my girl," Jonathan said, causing both of the boys to giggle.

"Yuck, kissing!" Jacob said, making a face.

"I'll see if you still feel that way in about ten years," Jonathan replied, ruffling his hair.

Mr. Charles picked up two of the suitcases. "I just got a message that our van is out front."

Ed and Jonathan grabbed the rest of the baggage, and Mrs. Charles pulled a large suitcase on wheels. Emily took hold of the boys' arms as they hurried through the terminal, wishing they could walk a little slower and look closer at the beautiful Christmas decorations that seemed to fill every corner.

The sun was bright and reflected off the snow in the yard when they pulled up in front of the two-story brownstone of the Abernathy's.

"I wish I'd had time to freshen up," Mrs. Charles said, peering into the rearview mirror and patting her hair.

"You look fine!" Mr. Charles told her as he got out, checking his own reflection in a side mirror.

They all got out, smoothing down clothing that had wrinkled during the flight.

"Are you nervous?" Jonathan asked Emily, as they went up the walk.

"Should I be?"

"Nope," he said, opening the front door. He stood back letting the rest of his family go ahead of him. They walked into a living room where Emily saw a large Christmas tree, a huge fireplace with a roaring fire, and an elderly couple sitting near the hearth, smiling up at her. She looked again, noticing that only the man was smiling at her.

"Well now," the older gentleman said, rising to his feet wearing an odd-looking red jacket with black lapels. "Who have we got here?"

Jonathan made the introductions, starting with his parents.

When he introduced Emily, she hurried forward and shook the older man's hand, liking him immediately. "Nice to meet you!" she smiled, at the same time smelling a delicious aroma coming from somewhere in the house.

"Lovely, to meet you," he said, in a beautiful English accent. "Please do come over and meet my wife, then I'll get us all some refreshments. Maizie, our cook, will have breakfast ready soon."

She was led over to the older woman. "Speak loudly," he instructed, "she's a mite deaf."

"I'm Emily!" she shouted much too loudly, as she reached for the woman's hand. She heard Jonathan chuckle behind her.

"Hello, Emily," the woman said, an edge to her voice as she barely brushed her hand. "Jonathan has told us so much about you. Do have a seat."

Emily felt a coldness from her that she didn't quite understand, as she sat in a nearby loveseat while Jonathan introduced the rest of his family.

Mr. Abernathy greeted each family member warmly, and after all were seated, left the room saying, "Excuse me while I go fetch tea for us all."

He soon returned with a wheeled trolley carrying a teapot, cups, and a sugar and creamer set, then poured hot tea for everyone, looking very much like an English butler.

The two younger boys watched in silence as the teacups were passed around, and finally Cameron said, "Hey, where's ours?"

A grin spread across Mr. Abernathy's face. "Thought I forgot, did you?" Reaching into the pockets of his red jacket he brought out two juice boxes, and handed one to each boy.

"Thank you," both boys said, looking a little disappointed that they weren't offered tea.

As they all talked and sipped tea, the front door was thrown open and a pretty girl about Emily's age hurried in.

"Hello everyone," she sang out, "I hurried right over from school to meet Johnny's family."

Johnny? Emily thought, as the men stood up to greet her.

Jonathan made the introductions. "This is the Abernathy's granddaughter, Julia."

Emily noticed that Julia's eyes actually lit up when she looked at Jonathan, then she quickly turned to Emily, "And you must be the girl Johnny has told us about," she remarked, in her lovely English accent, as she warmly shook Emily's hand. "He didn't mention your beautiful red hair!"

"Nice to meet you," Emily murmured, wondering why Jonathan had never mentioned this girl.

Jonathan introduced the rest of his family to Julia, who then turned to her grandparents.

"Grandfather, you look adorable in that smoking jacket." Julia hurried over to give him a kiss. She then went over to her grandmother, who looked up at Julia like she was topping on a dessert.

"Julia, dear!" her grandmother murmured, embracing her warmly.

The one thing Emily knew instantly was that Julia liked Jonathan. She could see it in her eyes and she could feel it. The grandmother knew it too, and it explained her coolness towards Emily. She unconsciously reached over and took Jonathan's arm, at the same time touching her necklace.

About then a plumpish woman in a gray dress came out, and announced, "Breakfast is ready, and the table is all laid out."

"Thank you, Maizie," Mr. Abernathy said, standing up and smiling at his granddaughter. "It looks like you arrived just in time for breakfast!"

"Well, are you sure there's enough, Grandfather?"

"There's always room at the table for you, dear." Mrs. Abernathy rose from her chair, and looped her arm through her granddaughter's.

They all went into the dining room where Jonathan and Emily took a seat next to each other at the large table. Emily watched as Julia hurried to sit across from Jonathan, the two boys were seated between their parents, and Ed sat down next to Julia. After they were all seated, Mrs. Abernathy sat down next to her husband.

"Shall we say grace?" Mr. Abernathy asked, bowing his head.

After the *Amen*, they began to pass the platters around. "We asked Maizie to cook up a proper English breakfast!" Mr. Abernathy announced, looking very pleased.

"It looks delicious," Mr. Charles remarked, scooping fried eggs from a large platter onto his plate. "And I believe there's enough here to feed the British Army!"

"We don't want anyone leaving our table hungry," Mrs. Abernathy smiled, cutting into her sausages.

"And Johnny is a big eater," Julia said, giving him her best smile.

Emily noticed that Mrs. Charles kept staring at Julia, then at her, and realized she also was aware of Julia's feelings for Jonathan.

Emily was ravenous, and took a little of each dish which included eggs, bacon, sausage, and fried potatoes, as any other American breakfast would have, but also saw that there were platters of fried tomatoes, fried mushrooms, and a bowl of beans. She began to scoop a little of each onto her plate, and when a bowl of food that was black and disc-like was passed to her, she took some of that too, her plate becoming full.

"You must be very hungry!" Mrs. Abernathy remarked, staring at the amount of food she'd taken.

"Starving," Emily replied, digging into the eggs and potatoes. "Yum, I love it," she announced to the group.

"Emily's little, but she eats like a dockhand!" Jonathan chuckled.

All heads turned to see how Emily would take this comparison and found her laughing along with Jonathan.

Emily took a large forkful of the round, black food. As she chewed down on the odd texture, Mr. Abernathy appeared delighted and said, "Ah, brave Emily! You've tried our blood sausage!"

Emily stopped chewing, and her stomach actually lurched. "It's blood?" she muttered, the half-chewed food in her cheek.

"Oh, indeed," he replied cheerfully, forking a huge piece of the blood sausage into his own mouth.

She looked at Jonathan, not knowing what to do.

"You better swallow it," he laughed. "You look like a chipmunk!"

And that's exactly what she did, gulping down the half-eaten lump of food, which caught in her throat and caused her to go into a coughing frenzy, barking like a seal.

She covered her mouth with a napkin as those around the table stared wide-eyed, watching Jonathan pound her on the back until a final cough caused the sausage to fly into the napkin.

She took a deep breath when the coughing frenzy was over, and looked up to see Julia staring wide-eyed. Then both she and her grandmother gave Emily a smile that was slightly superior.

Oh no, you didn't just give me that smile, Emily thought.

"Well, that was nothing," she announced, staring directly at Julia. "Jonathan held a puke bag open for me once while I vomited my guts out on a public bus!"

Both Julia and her grandmother drew back in horror as Mr. Abernathy burst into gales of laughter.

"Oh my, you are delightful, Emily." He chuckled as he speared a piece of potato. "Refreshingly honest!"

"Thank you," she replied, then looked directly at Julia again. "And we forgot and left the puke bag on the bus when we got off. Jonathan has been with me through a lot."

Julia glared at her, understanding perfectly.

"Please pass the beans," Emily chirped, looking up at a grinning Mrs. Charles, who blinked her amusement. Emily blinked back.

An hour later, they were all back in the van and heading for the rental house. They pulled up in front of a cottage looking home, and Mrs. Charles said, "I love it!" She hopped right out, then opened the rear door. "Come on Emily, let's go look while the men park and bring our things in."

"It looks like a home out of one of my English novels," Emily said, delighted as they went up the flower-lined walk. "It just needs a thatched roof!"

"I agree." Mrs. Charles unlocked the large, wooden door and they went into a living room from a different time era.

"Amazing!" Mrs. Charles exclaimed as she turned a slow circle. "They even furnished it from a different time period."

Emily wasn't sure she cared for the oversized, ornate furniture, but she didn't say so because Mrs. Charles was so thrilled with it.

"All we need is a Christmas tree to make it magical," Mrs. Charles announced, as they headed into an arched hallway. "And the owner said we could use the Christmas decorations from a shed out back."

There were three bedrooms: the largest had two sets of bunkbeds lining the walls. "Perfect for the boys," Mrs. Charles murmured, heading to the next room.

The master bedroom held a massive canopied bed. "Oh lovely," Mrs. Charles murmured. "We'll feel like royalty."

The word, *gaudy,* sprang to Emily's mind as she peered into the overly decorated room.

The third bedroom was quite small with a step-down leading to a cozy looking narrow bed.

"Oh Emily," Mrs. Charles said, "I hope you don't mind this tiny room!"

"I actually love it!" Emily sat on the bed and gave it a bounce. "It's simple and cozy, and I love that snow-covered tree just outside the window. It feels like I belong here."

For no reason that she could explain, Mrs. Charles came over and hugged her.

After they were all settled in and the little boys were put down for a nap, Mrs. Charles said, "I think I'm going to take a nap, too!" and hurried off to try out her canopied bed.

Emily just wanted her talk with Jonathan to be over with, so she whispered to him, "Can we go somewhere private? I need to tell you about some things?"

"Sounds serious," he said.

Emily just nodded.

They went to get their jackets, and when they came back out, Mr. Charles said, "We're going shopping for a Christmas tree when everyone gets up from their nap. Are either of you interested in coming along?"

"No thanks," Jonathan answered, "I think we're going for coffee."

"Alone time, huh?" Mr. Charles was grinning.

"Yes, and I want to show Emily around London," Jonathan replied, as they headed out the door.

He grabbed Emily's mittened hand as they walked down the street, both bundled in jackets and scarves. "There's a great little place about two blocks from here where we can talk."

The coffee shop was a rather bohemian style with posters of rock bands on the walls. Instead of tables, there were couches and coffee tables. It reminded Emily of a giant living room.

"You find us a seat while I get our coffee," Jonathan said. "What kind do you want?"

"Surprise me!" Emily looked around the room for a secluded place to talk.

There was a tall bookcase in the center of the room and behind it she found a small couch and coffee table, which was loaded with different sugars, creamers, spoons and napkins.

"Here's your surprise coffee," Jonathan said, a few minutes later, looking pleased as he handed her the over-sized mug. "You have to guess what's in it."

She took a drink and sputtered. "Snake venom!" she laughed, then took another sip. "It kind of grows on you though!"

"You're close,"he laughed as he sat down next to her. "It's called Dragon's Breath! It's supposed to set your mouth on fire!"

"Here's to Dragon's Breath." They clinked their mugs together.

"All right, what are we here to talk about?" Jonathan asked.

"Us!"

"Okay, so what about us?"

"I heard from my dad again, and in a couple of months he's suing for part of the money that my grandmother left me," Emily said, stringing the bad news out in one sentence to get it over with.

"Well," he shrugged, "that's rotten, but what does it have to do with us?"

"They will never leave me alone..." she said, choking up.

"Hey..." Jonathan slid over and put an arm around her. "Are you okay?"

Emily shook her head, as tears coursed down. "My parents will always be popping into my life, not because they love me, but because they want something," she wept. "I don't want that for you."

"Hmmm...don't I get a say in it?" he asked, getting napkins from the dispenser on the coffee table and handing them to her.

"You have a nice family, and you should marry someone with a nice family."

"Wow," he chuckled, "Have you already picked her out?"

"Julia likes you," she sniffed. "And she has a nice family."

She felt his stomach start to jiggle.

"So, after you marry me off to Julia, what then?"

"I can feel you laughing," she said, muffled by the napkin.

"Well, what if I don't want to marry Julia, and I want to marry you someday?" Jonathan said, trying to control his laughter.

"You should think more about it," she said, peeking over the napkin. "I should give your necklace back until you think about it."

"Leave your necklace right where it is." He pulled her close to him. "I already knew about your family when I gave it to you."

"You didn't know they might move back near me!"

"I don't care, they can move wherever they want to. We'll work it out together."

"We will?"

"Of course! Isn't that what couples do when they love each other?"

"I don't know," she sniffed, "I've never lived with a couple who love each other."

He laughed, which made her laugh.

"We'll take marriage classes someday then, in case we're missing something," he said, handing her more napkins. "So quit worrying."

Emily nodded.

Jonathan kissed her, and said, "And please don't try to marry me off to Julia."

"It's a deal," she said, sounding rather nasally after her cry.

She finished her coffee, "Now tell me what plans you've been thinking about these past few weeks."

He sat forward in his seat, and she could tell he was excited. "I want to somehow get a farm in Mountain Grove and make my living that way," he said, looking very happy.

"Really? What kind of farm?" she asked, loving the way his blue eyes were sparkling.

"I'm not sure. I love soil and making things grow, but I don't have it all worked out yet because there's too many unknowns. I just know it's what I want to do. When I come home this summer, I'm signing up for Ag classes to finish out my college in whatever nearby school offers me the best in the field." He looked at her. "No pun intended."

She laughed. "You've probably already heard that Mr. Montoya is selling his farm in a year or so, right?"

"I didn't hear. Why would he do that?"

She shrugged. "He wants to move to Florida. That's all I heard when I was in his store. You should talk to him if you're interested."

"Hmmm, I'll talk to him, but it's probably too expensive for me to start with. That's a big chunk of real estate he's got with all the land, out buildings, and apple orchards."

Emily shrugged. "Well, it won't cost anything to talk to him."

"Okay, I'll call him later." Finishing his drink he asked, "Ready to go look around London?"

As they headed out into the London cold, Emily looped her arm through Jonathan's and remarked, "I can tell you're still thinking about that farm!"

"Yeah, I'm always thinking about it," he laughed, then pulled her close to him. "The only thing I think about more is you."

When Jonathan and Emily got back to the house after their walk, the home was filled with the scent of pine from the enormous tree the Charles family was decorating. Emily and Jonathan hung their jackets and scarves on a nearby rack and stood watching the family work together. Mrs. Charles held a large box of ornaments and handed them one by one to the younger boys who hung them in clusters on lower branches. Mr. Charles took care of decorating the higher branches, while Ed sat in an easy chair watching, as Christmas carols played softly in the background.

Harmony! Emily thought. She'd write that word down in her journal later. It's what she wanted in her own home someday, and here it was.

Mr. Charles noticed Emily and Jonathan watching and motioned them over. "Want to come and join us?" he asked, grinning.

Jonathan looked at Emily, questioning.

"I'd love to," she replied, taking Jonathan's hand and hurrying over.

Sharon Armstrong resides in Northern California with her husband, Chuck, and a large extended family.

Her love of children and teen-agers is the primary reason for writing *Emily's House.* She served on a hotline, counseling young women for over ten years.

Much of their story is Emily's story.

You can reach her at:

SharonArmstrongAuthor@gmail.com

Facebook: SharonArmstrongAuthor

Instagram: sharonarmstrongauthor

Webpage: SharonArmstrongAuthor.com

www.ingramcontent.com/pod-product-compliance
Lightning Source LLC
Chambersburg PA
CBHW052027220726
48293CB00015B/429